KT-394-895

'Although this novel covers a very uncomfortable topic, I found the author covered it well and sensitively ... I really felt for and rooted for the main characters'

'This book was brilliant ... The plot was extremely well thought out and the characters all came beautifully to life'

'I really love Michael Malone's writing, his books are very much character led which adds a lot of depth to his stories, you really care about what happens to them ... I would highly recommend this book'

'The first book I've read by this author, but it captivated me so much that I want to read more'

'A new author for me and one I will definitely read again. What a great book. I couldn't put it down. It's a psychological / crime / courtroom drama with a bit of romance thrown in ... Well written and enough twists and turns to keep you guessing'

PRAISE FOR MICHAEL J. MALONE

'A beautifully written tale, original, engrossing and scary ... a dark joy' *The Times*

'A complex and multilayered story – perfect for a wintry night' *Sunday Express*

'Vivid, visceral and compulsive' Ian Rankin

'A terrific read ... I read it in one sitting' Martina Cole

'A deeply satisfying read' *Sunday Times*

'A fine, page-turning thriller' *Daily Mail*

'Malone is the master of twists, turns and the unexpected, with the skill to keep things grounded. So much so, that the reader can picture themselves in the very circumstances described. Superb storytelling from a master of his craft' *Herald Scotland*

'Beautiful, lyrical prose takes the reader through a perfectly constructed, often harrowing tale' Denzil Meyrick

'With each turn of the page, a more shocking detail is revealed and some of the people John thought might help him are not who they seem ... The domestic noir tale is one that many families will be able to relate to ... There is barely enough time to catch your breath' *Scotsman*

'Challenging and emotional ... enthrals as it corkscrews to a shocking, yet ultimately rewarding end' LoveReading

'Malone's latest is an unsettling, multi-layered and expertly paced domestic noir drama that delves into one family's dark secrets, shame and lies' *CultureFly*

'Malone is a poet, there are wonderful lyrical passages here and very skilful storytelling. Some issues are not spoken about enough, Malone raises a couple of those issues and sensitively but realistically addresses them' *New Books Magazine*

'Engrossing, hard-hitting – even shocking – with a light poetic frosting. Another superb read!' Douglas Skelton

'A dark and unnerving psychological thriller that draws you deep into the lives of the characters and refuses to let go. This is a brilliantly written book; I could not put it down' Caroline Mitchell

'A chilling tale of the unexpected that journeys right into the dark heart of domesticity' Marnie Riches

'It's a tough high-wire act, balancing believability with surprise, but the author pulls it off with aplomb. Excellent stuff' Doug Johnstone, *The Big Issue*

'Bristling with unease, this is domestic noir at its very darkest, twisting the marriage thriller into a new and troubling shape' Eva Dolan

'A deeply personal thriller that will keep the reader turning those pages, with twists and turns designed to keep the heart pumping' Russel D. McLean

'A tightly wound page-turner with real emotional punch' Rod Reynolds

'A story that I won't forget in a hurry. Malone is a massive talent' Luca Veste

'A disturbing and realistic portrayal of domestic noir with a twist ... a shocking yet compelling read' Mel Sherratt

'Malone perfectly balances storytelling with a brutal commentary on a dysfunctional relationship' Sarah Ward

ABOUT THE AUTHOR

Michael Malone is a prize-winning poet and author who was born and brought up in the heart of Burns' country. He has published over 200 poems in literary magazines throughout the UK, including *New Writing Scotland, Poetry Scotland* and *Markings. Blood Tears*, his bestselling debut novel, won the Pitlochry Prize from the Scottish Association of Writers. His psychological thriller, *A Suitable Lie*, was a number-one bestseller, and the critically acclaimed *House of Spines, After He Died* and *In the Absence of Miracles* soon followed suit. A former Regional Sales Manager (Faber & Faber) he has also worked as an IFA and a bookseller. Michael lives in Ayr. Follow him on Twitter @michaelJmalone1.

A SONG OF ISOLATION

MICHAEL J. MALONE

ORENDA
BOOKS

Orenda Books
16 Carson Road
West Dulwich
London SE21 8HU
www.orendabooks.co.uk

First published in the UK in 2020 by Orenda Books
Copyright © Michael J. Malone, 2020

Michael J. Malone has asserted his moral right to be identified as the author of
this work in accordance with the Copyright, Designs and Patents Act, 1988.

All Rights Reserved. No part of this publication may be reproduced in any form
or by any means without the written permission of the publishers.

*This is a work of fiction. Names, characters, places and incidents are either products of
the author's imagination or are used fictitiously. Any resemblance to actual events,
locales or persons, living or dead, is entirely coincidental.*

A catalogue record for this book is available from the British Library.

ISBN 978-1-913193-36-2
eISBN 978-1-913193-37-9

Typeset in Garamond by typesetter.org.uk

Printed and bound by CPI Group (UK) Ltd, Croydon CR0 4YY

For sales and distribution, please contact *info@orendabooks.co.uk* or visit
www.orendabooks.co.uk.

Prologue

London, 2010

She sat in the back of the parked taxi, hand tight on the handle of the door, and looked around, scanning the street for strangers.

'You okay, Miss Hart,' the driver asked.

'I'm...' It always took her by surprise when people recognised her. She'd only been in three movies so far, two as a background character and one as the main character's best friend. '...Fine. I'm fine, thanks.' She met his gaze in the rear-view mirror. His expression was open, growing concern in the strip of face she could see as he read her lack of movement.

She felt her pulse thrum in her throat and forced a long, slow breath, hearing the quiver of it in the shell of the car. It's fine. Everything will be fine. Leaning forward in her seat, she looked around herself again, cursing the poor light.

Then she thought of that morning, just a week ago, waking up and finding a small photo beside her on the pillow. A photograph of her own sleeping face, with just enough of her shoulders showing above the bedclothes to see the blue pyjama top she was wearing at that very moment.

She'd screamed, jumped out of bed and checked every window, every door, every cupboard. Looked under her bed, checked the shower, looked behind every door again. Then she called the police.

'We'll send someone round as soon as we can,' the person said.

'Just like you did the other nine times I called.' She couldn't keep the sarcasm from her voice, and had hung up. There had been other strange happenings: letters in the post every day for a month, each one saying if she didn't return his love he'd kill himself; panties missing from her washing line; small love hearts drawn in the corners of her windows with spray paint.

This was the first time she'd been back here since the photo mysteriously settled on her pillow.

'Anything I can do?' the driver asked. He hadn't talked too much during the journey from the studios. Only to ask about the movie she was working on. And to say he'd read in a movie magazine that they thought this new one was going to be her breakout role. 'Fancy being in a movie with Tom Hardy,' he added. 'My missus proper fancies him.'

He'd taken her low-key response as a cue not to ask anything more.

'Can I book you in for noon tomorrow, please?' she asked. She was due on set with Tom at 2.00 pm. That would give her time to get through make-up and wardrobe, and have a quick read through the scene.

'Noon tomorrow.' The driver took his phone from its holder on the dashboard and scrolled onto another page. 'That's fine, I'm available.'

'And … can you wait until I'm inside before driving off?' She almost asked him to go into the house and check it for her, but she hated appearing so weak.

'Course, mate,' the driver replied, his eyes crinkling in a manner he probably thought reassuring, but it just looked creepy when all she could see was the back of his head and his eyes in a strip of mirror. 'I always do for my ladies.'

'Thanks,' Amelie said. Then she read the price on the meter, found a note in her handbag and handed it to him. 'Keep the change.'

She braced herself, and opened the door. Staying at Lisa's had been a welcome retreat, but she couldn't continue to impose on her friend, and she couldn't let this freak, whoever he was, run her life.

On the pavement, she scanned the house. The creep of the ivy over the large sandstone blocks, handsome bay windows either side of the oak door, the lion-head brass knocker. It looked exactly the same as when she'd left. Just as it was the first time she'd seen it and fell in love and couldn't not take over the rental. But that simple image had tarnished what had once been her haven.

Like most of the homes in this part of London the house was set back from the street by a small front garden. Six paces and she was up her garden path and at the door. As she walked she rummaged in her bag for her keys.

With a start she realised they weren't in the little zipped compartment in the side wall of the bag. Nor in the middle section. She pushed aside her purse, her diary, her phone, fingers scrabbling for the tell-tale solid metal. Where were they?

She became aware of movement in her peripheral vision. To her right. Coming up from behind the still-waiting taxi.

Jesus. Where were her keys? She remembered checking on them when she'd left Lisa's that afternoon.

A cough. Her head whipped round. A man. Head bowed, wearing a flat cap, walking slowly.

Mouth dry, she dug furiously through her bag. Where were they? How many times had she told herself to get a smaller bag?

She tried the zipped compartment again. There they were. She exhaled in relief. How had she missed them?

Key now in hand, she thrust it into the lock, but before she opened the door she turned. The man was at the top of her path. The streetlight just above cast him in a jaundiced glow.

He grunted. 'Evening, sweetheart.'

'Oh, hi, Mr Denby.' She almost sagged with relief against the door. It was only the old man from three doors down.

'Told ya,' he chuckled, 'it's Larry.'

'Course it is. Larry,' she said and worked a smile into her expression.

'Lovely evening.' And with a tip of his hat he continued on his way.

Waiting for a moment till her heart slowed, Amelie turned the key in the lock, opened the door and stepped inside. Before she shut it, she waved at the driver. He returned the gesture and drove off.

Inside, back against the door, she listened as the car moved away, then she strained to hear if there was any other noise in the house.

Silence.

The familiar sounds of the area registered. A dog barked from somewhere behind her. A door slammed next door. A car, then another, drove past. Someone, a child, called out to a friend as they ran past. Life, moving on, completely unmindful of her troubles.

She put the chain on and clutched the keys in her fist, one pointing out from between two fingers like a makeshift knuckle-duster. A stunt guy on her last movie had shown her this little trick when weird things first started to happen in her life. She suspected it wouldn't cause much damage, but she felt reassured by it. If anyone came at her she'd aim for the eyes. Make as much of a mess as she could before running to safety.

Keeping her footfall as light as she could she made her way down the long hall, past the dining-room door and through into the kitchen. The back door was locked, just as she left it, and all of the windows were closed.

Retracing her steps, she went back down the hall and edged into the living room. All the seats were vacant, the windows shut.

But the curtains were open. Meaning if he was out there he could see everything.

On her hands and knees, she crawled over the carpet to the large bay windows, and eventually, with a lot of tugging and some heavy breathing she managed to close them. Then she made her way onto the sofa, where she collapsed.

What are you doing, she asked herself?

Who crawls along their living-room floor to shut their curtains?

She looked down at her hands, they were shaking. Wine would help; she could almost hear Lisa's voice. And smiled. And felt that smile loosen the muscles in her neck, in her back, all the way down to her feet.

She was safe. There was no need to worry.

A noise.

A creak as someone moved above her head.

In her bedroom.

Without thought, barely breathing, she made her way towards the door as silently as she could. From the creak of the old floorboards she could tell whoever was up there was also on the move.

At the living-room door she paused. Thought about her phone. Would she have time to call? No, her best plan was to get the hell out of this house.

Now.

Folding herself into a crouch she stuck her head beyond the doorway and looked up. There, as if inhabiting the shadows at the top of the stairs, stood a man.

Cursing her decision to put the chain on she charged at the door. The man thundered down the stairs. Fumbling with the chain, she managed to release it. Hand on the snib lock, she turned.

The door was open. Just.

He was right behind her.

He slammed her into the door and it closed.

She tried to scream, but a hand clasped over her mouth. There was some sort of cloth in his hand. With a sweet, chemical scent. She felt the weight of him crush her against the door. His hardness at her hip. Hot breath, and beard bristles scratching her ear as he whispered:

'Do as I say and you'll get out of this alive.'

Chapter 1

Lanarkshire, Scotland, 2015

There was a knock at the door.

Loud and firm.

'You going to get that?' Amelie looked at her boyfriend, beside her on the sofa, thought about the bottle of champagne she'd found hidden at the back of the cupboard under the sink, and was relieved there might be some sort of a distraction.

Was he really going to do it? Now? Today?

Shit.

How was she going to respond?

She shifted in her seat, and, plucking a cushion from the pile at her side, placed it over her tummy.

'Wish you'd stop that,' said Dave. It may have been her imagination responding to the champagne sighting, but he seemed a little on edge. 'You're not fat.'

'And you're still not going to the door,' she replied with an inner grimace. She hated it when he did that. Read her movements and got them spot on. 'Anyway, it's nearly dinner time. Why are you snacking?' she asked, looking at the giant packet of crisps beside him on the sofa. Another giveaway, she thought. He always ate when he was nervous.

'Starving,' he said. 'Doing the garden's hungry work.' Then he laughed, leaned forward and snuffled at her neck.

Despite herself she laughed, but then pushed him away. Then felt guilty for doing so. She'd been doing a lot of that lately. Feeling guilty. About how she was treating him.

'You okay?' he asked, his tone all honest concern as he leaned back into his cushion.

'Door?' she repeated,

'It's probably someone trying to sell us something. Ignore it ... they'll go away,' Dave said, brushing crisp crumbs from his jeans.

'It's Good Friday and nearly dinner time. Who's going to be selling stuff at this hour?'

'Someone who's desperate.' He sat back in his seat and regarded her. 'You okay, honey? Something bothering you?'

She crossed her arms, thinking she wasn't ready to unburden herself in case she said something she would later regret. When they'd met she was Amelie Hart, movie star. One-hit wonder, to be precise. Against all the odds, and after a few flops, her fourth movie had hit the public consciousness and the great unwashed couldn't get enough of her.

Her dream came true.

Except the dream came with a whole lot of baggage she couldn't deal with. Most of which Dave knew nothing about, and that was why he couldn't understand why she was always reluctant to answer the door.

It sounded again. Amelie turned away from it and pulled her knees up to her chest as if that might form some kind of protection.

'Jesus, they're not for giving up, are they?' Dave looked over his shoulder in the direction of the front of the house. He got to his feet as if it was a huge effort. 'I'll get it then, will I?'

'Please?'

Whoever it was, Amelie hoped it was something important. Something big enough to distract Dave from asking a question she wasn't sure how to answer.

Chapter 2

Dave walked to the door, checking the little box was still in his pocket, aware he was possibly about to make a huge mistake, but unable to step aside from the path he had decided upon.

A marriage proposal would do it, right? Clarify Amelie's mind as to what she wanted. He couldn't bear the thought of life without her, and he was all but certain she only needed a nudge to settle things in her own mind once and for all. And he needed to risk that nudge because the uncertainty was driving him mad.

To be fair, he was lucky to have her.

The Amelie Hart shared a home with him. They'd met in the north of Scotland, up by Loch Morlich. He'd been there on holiday on his own. Nearing the end of a week he'd devoted to learning about forestry in an estate nearby. It was a job he'd long wanted to do, but Dad insisted he go to university and get the required qualification to join the family accountancy firm. It hadn't stopped his longing to be in among the other, more important to the planet, green stuff, so he'd jumped at the chance he was offered while attending a stuffy champagne reception for some equally stuffy law firm. One of the partners had just invested in an estate 'up there' – he'd waved his hand lazily, struggling to remember the name of the place, as if the entirety of the Highlands of Scotland hung in the air just above his head. Dave perked up at the mention of it and said he'd always wanted to work on the land, and it was arranged. A week's work experience. He remembered the feeling of elation, and the lawyer's look of incredulity.

Amelie had been walking between one of the lodges on the estate and the local shop, at a time when she had disappeared from public view. Romantic cliché alert, they would always say as they recounted this to new acquaintances: she'd dropped one of her gloves, he raced after her to return the errant item.

Their eyes met.

And hearts collided.

It helped that he had no idea who she was. Most of his time was spent at work, and what free time he did have he was countering the effects of sitting hunched over a computer by training down at the local rugby club, so the world of film and TV celebrity completely passed him by.

Must have been all that fresh air. Why else would he have taken one look at this amazing woman and asked her if she wanted to go and see – the first thing he thought of – the local reindeer herd? Amazingly, she said yes, and the rest was history.

But the most recent part of that history was worrying. There were too many times when he entered a room and she'd hurriedly finish the conversation she was having on her phone. A phone that was more than ever stuck to the side of her head. The way she covered up whenever she came out of the shower, whereas nudity had never bothered her before. Then there were the long silences, when the air between them had always been filled with words and laughter.

He'd asked her if she needed to get back into that world.

'It's not all glamour, you know,' she'd said as she tucked a strand of flaxen hair behind a perfect ear. Dave could watch her all day, just doing simple things like that. He'd joke with her; it was because she was half French – full breeds just don't have that exoticism he'd say. There *was* an effortless grace to her that ordinary humans lacked; there was a good reason the camera loved her.

'It's beyond boring. And stressful. Worrying whether people will like your hair, your dress or even the bloody shade of lipstick you're wearing. It's exhausting.' No, she went on to say, her charity work and her yoga were where her life was at, for the foreseeable.

Exhausting it may have been, but Dave knew Amelie well enough to see that whatever she had in her life at this point, no matter how much she protested, wasn't enough for her.

And worryingly, he was no longer sure that he was enough for her anymore.

The letterbox creaked open and a voice boomed, 'Mr Robbins. It's the police. Will you please open up?'

Chapter 3

Amelie's phone rang. She watched Dave's back as he walked towards the front door. Read the tension in it as he moved away. He deserved more than this from her. He deserved a woman who would be every bit as kind, gentle and considerate as he was.

She pushed a breath through her pursed lips and heard a note of frustration in that small expulsion of air.

The screen on her phone displayed a name. Lisa. The one friend who remained from her time in the limelight. She'd played her best friend in Amelie's first movie, and happily their on-screen chemistry had been real. The only thing about that movie that actually worked, she remembered ruefully. From the moment they met they'd sensed the other was on the exact same wavelength. Now, though, they rarely got together, as Lisa's career had rocketed, meaning she had her own team of paparazzi who followed her about, but the two women spent hours on the phone. It seemed that Lisa's function, other than to listen to her complaints, was to alert her to any news stories that were about to break about her.

Even four years after walking away from it all, the press, and by extension the public, were still fascinated about why she had abandoned the opportunity to live the life that most people wanted. Lisa had lots of media contacts so she was happy to alert Amelie that a fresh batch of paps might be beating their way to her door. 'Get the wide-brimmed hat and the large sunglasses out, darling,' she'd say. 'The vultures are about to come calling.'

Looking at the screen for a moment, Amelie cancelled the call. She couldn't even be bothered speaking to her best friend.

'Have you told him yet?' Lisa had demanded, the last time they spoke.

'Oh, Leece,' she replied, and sank back into the sofa.

'Don't *oh Leece* me, Amelie. You need to put the poor schmuck out of his misery.'

'But I don't know if I want to dump him. I'm not even sure he's the problem.'

'What *is* the problem?'

'I don't know.'

'I'm calling bullshit on that, honey. You know.' Lisa's tone weighted the word *know* with a burden of importance. 'You just don't want to face up to it.'

'But what if I'm wrong and I lose out on one of the best things that has happened to me?'

'What's meant to be, is meant to be.' Lisa had a strange relationship with the notion of fate. When it suited her, something was *meant to be*. When it was an inconvenient notion, she railed against it. She was as capricious as the weather on a mountain top, and Amelie loved her for it. Life was never dull with Lisa wittering in her ear. 'He came along at the right time, honey. That's how life works. Just when you needed something – *someone* – solid in your life, he appeared. Now you're going through another transition and you need to face up to that. If he's still there at the other side, great. If not, he'll hopefully find someone as amazing as you.'

Amelie snorted, mentally retreating from the compliment. 'Me? Amazing? I'm a witch.'

'You're being too harsh on yourself, babes. Relationships change. People move on. We *have* to move on, or it just gets too...'

'What about you and Pretty Boy?' Amelie interrupted. She'd already had enough of talking about herself. Pretty Boy was what she called Lisa's latest lover. He was a hot young actor, famous for taking his shirt off in TV period dramas, and for not having too much between the ears.

'Oh, I dumped his scrawny ass,' Lisa cackled. 'Haven't you been keeping up to date with the goss?' She paused. 'Sorry, I forgot you have no access to the wider world in that little haven of yours.'

Don't you even have satellite TV? Lisa had asked her, incredulous, when she first moved in.

Her haven was an estate in the Lanarkshire countryside. It offered them the best of both worlds. A manageable daily commute for Dave into Glasgow, and for Amelie, spirit-reviving time in the heart of nature. The family who had owned it for generations had hit on hard times and sold the whole lot to a development company. The big house had been converted into luxury flats, and the stable block renovated into a row of quaint mews cottages. She owned the largest, end cottage and fell in love with it the moment she stepped inside.

It even came with its own cat, a tortoiseshell named George. The previous owners had tried a number of times to take him to their new place, but each time they'd carted him off in the back of their car to their new home five miles away, he'd turned up a week or so later, licking a paw as if to say, *Well, that was a bit of a walk.*

Never was a cat person, or so she thought, but George managed to worm his way into her heart – that purr of content as he lay on her lap became part of the music of the cottage, and the last time the previous owners turned up to collect him again, she suggested, hoping she didn't sound too desperate, that he stay with her.

Said cat padded into the room. Sat in the middle of the floor. Curled his tail around his feet and stared at her.

'Needing fed, George? she asked him. He opened his mouth and let out a long, low noise. Amelie had counted a 'vocabulary' of about ten different sounds that George used to communicate. She hadn't managed to work out which noise equated to which need, as he seemed to change them at his own whim.

She heard a rumble from the front door. Two different male voices. A long silence and then a high-pitched, in-panic Dave as he shouted, 'Amelie?'

Chapter 4

Dave made out two tall figures through the small marbled-glass insert on the front door. They looked as if they were in uniform and they were both wearing hats. The police?

His first worry was for his father. He was in his early sixties, still spent long hours at the office, and had a large paunch and a ruddy complexion thanks to a career of liquid lunches. He was a heart attack in waiting as far as Dave was concerned, so with a charge of worry in his stomach, he reached for the door and pulled it open.

There were two policemen and one policewoman. Behind them like a squat reminder of officialdom was their police car. None of the officers was smiling.

It takes three cops to tell me that Dad's ill? Or dead? Dave became aware of a tremble in his thighs and steeled himself. He thought of his mother. She was the most fragile being he'd ever met. Shit, how must his mum be feeling? He had to go to her.

'Mr Robbins? Mr David Robbins?'

'Yes, that's me. Can I help you?' His voice was a squeak. He cleared his throat. 'Is my dad okay?' His mind was racing away from him. He should ask them all in. They were working on a public holiday, poor bastards, he should at least offer them a coffee. Then he dismissed the thought as silly, processed the correct movements to place a smile on his face, while bracing himself against the side edge of the door.

'We've received a complaint from your neighbours, Mr Robbins, that you touched their daughter, Damaris, inappropriately.'

'Wait. Damaris? Next door? Me?'

The policeman on the right stepped forward. Metal glinting in his hands. Handcuffs. Dave felt his face flush. Watched as the cop continued his movement: hand on his shoulder, pulling him round and out of the doorway onto the path. He felt his arms being held behind his back and the pinch of steel on his wrists as his arms were secured in position.

Later on as he reflected over events he'd hear himself shouting for Amelie. Think it was pathetic, but wondered what else he could have done.

'We are placing you under arrest, Mr Robbins,' the policeman continued, his tone polite. Might have been remarking that this was nice weather for an April Easter, for all the threat in his voice. But there was a threat, thought Dave as his stomach grew heavy. His vision narrowed. Pressure on his sphincter. And he was aware of all of this as if from a distance.

The policeman was still talking. His voice coming to him through a fog of confusion. Under the something-something act he was being taken to the local police station for questioning.

A neighbour from the stables opposite opened her door, stepped outside, took one look at the tableau in front of her and, face white, went back inside.

'It's all a mistake,' he shouted at her. Mrs Wallace. She was a nice old dear. With a bad heart, she was fond of saying. She wouldn't be able to handle all this excitement.

He was guided over to the police car. The back door on the near side was pulled open. Pressure on his head. He ducked and sat inside. Almost before he had his feet positioned in the footwell, the door was slammed shut.

Amelie was at the door of the cottage, her face pale and long. She shouted. Her voice reached his ears as if through a time delay.

'Dave? Dave? What the hell's going on?'

She approached the car and knocked on the window. Her face loomed before him, her expression twisted with fear and worry. *Lawyer*, she was saying. *I'll get you a lawyer*.

'S'okay,' he shouted, determined to display a stoic front. He could handle this. Everything would be okay. Except it wasn't. They claimed he'd touched her inappropriately. What did that even mean? What did Damaris say to her mother that made her phone the police?

Mentally, he ran through the encounter that afternoon. It was just like many other occasions in the garden. The girl was bored. There were no other kids on the estate to play with. He'd given her the time of day loads of times. She would circle him on her bike, judging if he would be up for some fun. Then he'd feel sorry for her, giving in and giving her half an hour of his time. Throwing a ball, or playing with a hula hoop, willing to look like an idiot for a few seconds to win the prize of her laughter.

Today was a little different from the usual. He had work to do and he had his tools around him on the lawn. And he did warn her she might fall off.

As if at some silent signal two of the police officers and Amelie disappeared inside the cottage, leaving Dave alone in the car. He looked around and saw his neighbours around the little square, one by one, look out of their window or front door, and take in the sight of him in the backseat of a police car.

'It's all been a mistake. A huge mistake,' he shouted. But no one could hear him, and they all ducked their heads and retreated back into their houses. He imagined them all pinking a little at the shame he'd brought into their little enclave. It was just not the done thing to be seen in the back of a police car. Whatever would we have next? People shooting up heroin?

'Shit,' Dave whispered, feeling fear claw at his gut. He studied the door handles, but with his hands behind his back they were unreachable. In any case, the central locking was sure to be activated and the doors could only be opened from the outside.

The car was facing the exit, so he tried to twist round in order to look back at number six – the Browns' door. He'd maybe catch their eye, get them over to the car and ask them to tell the police that it was all a big mistake. Sure, he maybe manhandled Damaris to keep her safe – he could remember picking her up, one hand under each oxter – but he'd never do anything dodgy.

There was no one there.

If he could just speak to Roger and Claire. Clear this misunderstanding up.

As if by magic, Roger appeared and marched towards the police car. His red face and clenched fists were not a good sign. He pushed the cop who was by the car so hard he fell onto his back, then he wrenched the door open and dived in.

'This is a terrible misunderstanding, Rodge,' Dave shouted.

'Don't fucking, Rodge me, you evil prick. When I'm done with you...' The rest of what he was saying was lost in a snarl as Roger began to punch at Dave. The confined space meant he couldn't get much purchase on his swings, but he still managed to connect a couple of times, once on the bottom lip, before the cop got back to his feet and pulled Roger away.

The door slammed shut and Dave was alone once again. Head bowed, ignoring the physical pain. But what did that matter, really? That would fade – but Roger's fury...? The man truly and deeply believed that Dave had harmed his little girl.

'But it's not true,' he shouted. 'It's all a mistake.'

A horrible mistake. The police would come to see it. The Browns would come to see it, and he'd be allowed back inside and everyone could get on with their lives as if it never happened.

Chapter 5

'Name, please?' one of the police officers asked her, as they stood in an awkward clump of human flesh in her narrow hallway.

'Amelie Hart,' she said, feeling that was all a bit unnecessary. Judging by the way he was staring at her he knew exactly who she was, and couldn't wait to phone all his mates later to say whose house he'd been in.

Then she felt a stab of resentment. Her hard-won sanctuary was lost, thanks to that stupid little girl – she'd heard that much from the exchange at her door. But with a cringe of guilt she forced that down. How could she be so selfish? This was about Dave and how his life was going to be affected, because not for a second did she believe the allegation.

'May we come in?' the policeman said.

'You *are* in,' she replied, crossing her arms.

It's like that is it? the man's expression read.

'We've had a complaint of sexual contact between a man named Dave Robbins and a child under the age of thirteen. We'll expect you down the station...'

At that Amelie almost detected a smile. This was clearly the most exciting thing that had happened to this guy in years. His eyes roamed over the cottage, and then over her.

The policewoman took over, sending her colleague a look of admonishment. 'We'd like you to come down and give a state-ment, please, Miss Hart. In the meantime what can you tell us about this afternoon's events?'

'Nothing, really. I'm mystified as to what's supposed to have happened.'

'Were you in the house this afternoon?' the policewoman asked, undeterred by Amelie's brevity.

'I had yoga class this lunchtime, stopped off at Tesco for some shopping and was home from about two pm onwards.'

'And what did you do from two till now?'

'Sat on the sofa and read. One of Maggie O'Farrell's ... What's going to happen here?'

Bloody hell.

How could a normal day turn into a nightmare so quickly?

'What exactly is Dave supposed to have done?' she demanded, looking at each of the officers. 'And are three of you really required? By all means come through...' she said, and moved into the open-plan living and dining space, thinking, *Let them see how modestly we live.*

A large sofa sat in the space in front of the patio doors. It had red, plump, velvety cushions, was a little worn, but looked much loved. She sat in the middle of that, legs crossed, arms wide resting along the back of the settee, hoping she was presenting an image of a strong, capable woman. One who would never allow herself to be caught up in something as tawdry as a child-molestation claim.

The novel she had been reading was on the long, low coffee table in front of her.

'Can you tell us, as far as you know, what Mr Robbins was doing this afternoon?' The older male officer was back in charge, the tilt of his chin telling her he wasn't impressed by her theatrics. *Oh, but you are*, she thought, as she uncrossed and crossed her legs, from left over right to right over left. Since a very young age she'd been aware of the power her unusual beauty conferred on her, and however shallow it might be, she was prepared to use it to her advantage if the need arose.

'Dave loves his little patch of garden. He was out there most of the afternoon, taking advantage of the dry weather...' She smiled at each of the officers in turn. *This is how much I feel I have to worry about this nonsense charge*, she was telling them. 'I heard Damaris singing at one point as she went past the doors and further into the garden. She popped her head in first. Said hi, and then went off to annoy ... sorry, find Dave.'

'That suggests habit?' The female's tone made this a question. Amelie noticed a small notebook in her hand. Pen scratching over the page.

Amelie paused before answering. Could she be hinting at some kind of grooming practice? Didn't paedophiles do that? They thought Dave was a paedophile? Jesus. She had been about to say that Damaris's parents ignored her and she practically brought herself up, but she edited that. 'There are no other kids on the estate.' Shrug. And she knew there was an elegance to that movement that could captivate. After all she'd seen herself do it on the big screen. 'Now and again she pops in, asks me a lot of questions about being in the movies...' See, it wasn't just Dave. 'Then goes off to find him. Most times he fobs her off. What does a grown man have in common with a little girl, after all? But occasionally he feels bad and gives her a moment or two.'

'And today?' the female asked.

'I heard and saw nothing until Dave came back in complaining that Damaris was extra annoying. He said she caught her bike on the flex of the lawn mower, fell off and hurt herself.'

'You saw and heard nothing more?'

Amelie gestured towards the novel on her coffee table.

'Mind if we take a look in the back garden?' the male cop asked.

'Please. Be my guest.' Amelie shot a look over her shoulder. 'The door's open.'

Before he made for the door, his head cocked as if he'd heard something that concerned him and instead he went back the way he'd come in.

As he moved away Amelie looked at the only cop now in the room. 'PC...?'

'Talbot.'

'PC Talbot, don't tell me you're taking this claim seriously?' asked Amelie.

Talbot's brow furrowed. 'We take all claims seriously, Miss Hart.'

'Of course you do,' Amelie agreed, allowing her features to soften. 'People who suffer from this kind of thing have to feel safe enough to come forward. I can't imagine...' She shuddered. 'But Dave. He's one of the good guys.'

'If that's the case then you've nothing to worry about.'

'We both know miscarriages of justice happen, don't we?' And she cringed as she thought of how the media would spin this. *Hollywood star hiding out with paedo*. Then the talking heads would get involved. Opinions as rancid as their so-called person- alities, wearing hair extensions and Botox stares as they demand, *how could she not know*? And then they'd wonder if she was ac- tually involved in some way. Before they knew it they'd be painted as the twenty-first-century version of Brady and Hindley.

Jesus.

You can jump off that bridge when you come to it, Amelie, she told herself. First, she needed to make sure Dave was okay.

'We'll need access to Mr Robbins' laptop, please,' PC Talbot said.

'Sorry?' Amelie was so lost in her doomsday scenario – media darling to media demon – she didn't catch what the constable said.

'Often we find that perpetrators of such crimes have a multi- tude of illegal images on their personal technology...' Oh, laptop, thought Amelie. 'I'm sure a quick look by our people will cross off that particular box.'

Amelie hugged herself, dipped her head. Dave was in real trouble here. 'He has an office at the top of the stairs. Two laptops. A company one and a personal one. His iPhone will probably be up there as well, on the charger. Don't know why he bothers, barely uses the thing.'

'Is it okay if I...?' The officer looked back towards the stairs.

'We have nothing ... Dave has nothing to hide.' A bitter smile.

'Please. Do what you need to do.' As soon as the words were out of her mouth, she wondered if this was the right thing to do. Didn't they need a warrant or something?

PC Talbot gave her a polite little bow and left the room, just as the cop who'd gone out the front returned.

'Mr Brown has been ordered to stay indoors until we have taken Mr Robbins from the premises.'

She jumped to her feet. 'Why, what happened?'

'It's all under control now, Miss Hart.'

'Dave was in your custody. If he's been hurt because of your mistreatment I will sue your arse.' Roger was fat and lazy, could barely fit through his own front door, but he would have enough heft to cause some damage.

The policeman was unfazed. He held up a hand. 'Mr Robbins is fine.'

It occurred to her the policeman didn't much care if he was or not.

Then the thought hit that, given a supposedly vulnerable child was living right next door, Dave wouldn't be allowed back until this had all been settled.

Perhaps, not even then.

Chapter 6

Dave had no idea how long it took to get from his home to the police station. Could have been the twenty minutes it should have taken, or it could have been ten days for all the sense his brain was making of things.

Surreal didn't cover it.

This kind of thing happened to other people. Thieves and murderers and actual real paedophiles, not guys like him. The closest he'd ever come to being arrested prior to this moment was while taking a leak up a town-centre lane in Blackpool during a stag weekend. The cop who'd seen him was right at the end of his shift. Gave him a bit of a dressing down and mumbled something along the lines of *bugger that paperwork*, and let him go.

Once they arrived at the station, he was taken into a room to be 'booked in'. It had to be the custody sergeant who did it, and he was currently doing something else and then he was having his tea, so get comfortable, buddy, he was told, this could take a while.

The bucket seat made his backside ache after about half an hour, other than that he barely registered a thing. He was in shock and completely unable to process anything with any degree of sense.

They thought he molested a child.

Him.

A molester of children?

Didn't they know how ridiculous that was? He was good with kids. Enjoyed their honesty and energy. He even volunteered in a befriending project recently. One of those where young men from chaotic backgrounds are given a positive role model. Lee was the young fella he'd been put in touch with. His father had died two years previously in a car accident, and his mother couldn't cope with the combination of Lee, his five siblings and her dependency on alcohol. He'd thrown a rugby ball about with Lee a couple of times, gone to the cinema and eaten a couple of illicit burgers at McDonalds.

Shit.

Lee. What would he think? Another adult male had let him down.

No. This is all a mistake. Any minute now a camera crew would come marching in and say this was all part of some documentary. A documentary about what, he wasn't sure. How to mess up someone's life? Because that was what was going to happen to him.

Life ruined.

At least he was employed by family. Surely his own father would believe him? They might lose a few clients, but most of them had been with them for decades, and you don't change accountants just for the sake of it.

He became aware of someone in the space and he summoned the wherewithal to look around. It was like a waiting area that had been designed by someone with only one colour in their pallet. Grey walls, grey linoleum on the floor and grey chairs. The lights on the ceiling had bars in front of them. Who'd try and steal them?

He wondered what he should do and say. Don't they ask for a lawyer in the movies? Why didn't they have him in a cell or something? How was he supposed to act in this situation?

'What's this guy's story then?' another officer asked.

'Molesting a wee lassie.'

'Oh, shit. Right.'

The man gave him a hard look. Scrutiny that was like a scouring of his soul. With the wrong word and a cursory examination, he had been found wanting in the worst way possible.

More people came and went. And more scrutiny. He was beginning to read the signs. Clenched fists, hard eyes and thin lips. Say it and it was so. Guilty until proven innocent. Be accused of something like this and everyone looked like they wanted to punch the last blood cell out of him.

Time passed in a slow torment of worry before his name was read out, like a klaxon into a heavy silence.

'Mr Robbins, if you would come this way?' The skin on the guy's scalp refracted the light almost like a disco ball, and he looked like he had half of one at his midriff, under his white shirt. Shoulders that had seen a few rugby scrums no doubt, so he was not to be messed with.

It was strange how his assessment of people had changed so quickly. Rather than assessing people for a potential pleasant social experience, he was instantly measuring them up as a source of risk.

He was guided through to a small room, which was every bit as grey as the space he'd just left.

'I'm the custody officer,' the man said in a bass that reverberated almost to Dave's toes. 'You are now being processed. Do you understand?'

Dave nodded.

'Please speak.'

He coughed. 'Yes.'

'Your rights, while you are in my custody are...'

Shit, thought Dave, this was as real as it gets. The man continued speaking, Dave doing his best to listen, but only able to concentrate on the odd word. Noises about free legal advice, medical help if he was feeling ill. Something about regular breaks for the toilet and food was written on a card.

The police officer, with a matter-of-fact expression, pushed his great mitts into blue gloves. 'Now I need to search you. Please stand.' At this, Dave's chest began to thrum so hard he had no idea how he had the energy to get to his feet. 'Arms out, please.'

Every part of him was touched. Every part. Almost enough for the man to make an educated guess as to whether or not he was circumcised. The swabs were taken from his hands and arms, inside his mouth and then his prints were taken, just before he was asked to stand in front of a camera.

There was a loud knock on the door, it was pushed open and a man in a suit walked in. A black pinstripe. His face was lean, his dark hair streaked with grey and his eyes scanned the room like a laser.

'Mr Robbins, my name is Joseph Bain.' He stood feet shoulder-width apart, briefcase hanging in one hand. 'Do you require legal representation?'

Dave nodded.

'Please speak.'

'I think I do.' Dave looked from the policeman to the lawyer, neither giving anything away. 'I do,' Dave asserted. 'Not sure I can afford you though,' he said and gave Bain the once over. Saw a suit worth hundreds of pounds.

'My fee has been taken care of, Mr Robbins,' said Bain. Then he looked at the custody officer. 'May I have a word with my client in private, please?' His tone brooked no dissent. Not that he would get any, Dave was sure. This was a man who was clearly all about the theatre, and Dave was strangely reassured by it.

The officer left the room. Bain took a seat, across the table from him where the policeman had been. Looked at Dave. 'Bloody hell, that was close. I was three gins into a supper party when the call came.' He glanced around. 'I'm a solicitor advocate, would you believe? Don't normally do house calls.' He sucked in some air. 'Good news or bad news?'

'Wait a moment. How can I afford you?'

'Your father pulled in a favour.' His eyes narrowed. 'Few people in Glasgow don't know who Peter Robbins is.'

'I know Dad is well connected but...'

'Let's keep the conversation to pertinent matters, Dave. May I call you Dave?'

Dave nodded. 'But how did Dad get to hear about it?'

'Your lady friend, Miss Hart, called him.'

Shit. Dave wanted to be the one to do that. His father was big on 'avoiding avoidance'. All through his childhood the mantra was: a man squares his shoulders and faces life's problems. *Never forget that and you will do well, my son.*

Dad was big on advice, and problems were like numbers in a spreadsheet, to be analysed and dealt with. Emotion at a remove. He'd seen his father cry exactly once in his life. When his own father died. Other than that he misted up when athletes were awarded gold medals at the Olympics and then he'd walk/run away from the TV as if he'd just been caught with a urine stain on the front of his trousers.

'So, good news or bad news?' Bain repeated.

'What I don't feel like is drama, so just tell me, for fuckssake.'

Bain's smile was genuine for the first time since they'd met. 'Good. A backbone. You'll need it for what you are about to go through.' He placed his briefcase on the table. 'Good news: the evidence I've seen so far is weak. The bad news is that Roger Brown's uncle is a senior-ranked police officer, with a lot of pull.'

Dave had forgotten this. And then recalled the local gossip that Claire and Roger's family ties to both sides of the law had created a lot of tension in their lives. He searched his memory for a possible uncle who might have come visiting. Remembered a man of whom Damaris appeared to be fond. Heard her singing 'Uncle Jack' from the garden. Then, he caught an image in his mind of them strolling side by side. The low rumble of the man's voice as he pointed out which were flowers and which were weeds.

'And,' continued Bain, 'Great Uncle, Chief Superintendent Brown is baying for blood.'

Chapter 7

As soon as the police left with Dave, Amelie ran to the parking bay at the side of the cottage and jumped in her car.

Driving into town she realised with a start that she wasn't quite sure where the police station was. Near the library perhaps? Should be quite central, she reasoned and aimed for the road that sliced through the heart of East Kilbride.

An approaching driver flashed his lights at her and as she drew close, she could see an old man. He was waving at her. What the hell was his problem? Then she realised all the parked cars either side of the street were facing in the one direction, towards her.

She was driving the wrong way down a one way. Idiot.

Feeling her face heat with embarrassment, she held a hand up in apology. Then she stopped the car, stuck it in reverse and manoeuvred to the end of the street. She parked. Held a hand to her forehead and realised she was trembling.

Emotion demanded a release and she started to cry. Great heaving sobs.

Get a grip, she told herself. This wasn't about her. Dave. Poor man. What must he be going through?

She heard a knock at her window, turned, and saw the man who'd been waving her down. On automatic pilot she located the window switch and opened it a little.

'You okay, hen?' the man asked in a tremulous voice. Nothing to do with his emotion, more to do with his great age, she thought as she looked at the deep wrinkles around his rheumy eyes.

She nodded. Sniffed. 'I'm fine, thanks.' Even managed a bit of a smile.

He reached a hand through the window and patted her shoulder, his concern for her a reminder that there were decent people about. 'A large whisky,' he said. 'Always works for me.' And with a sad, but supportive smile, he straightened his back with a little groan and ambled off.

Her phone sounded an alert. She fished it out of her pocket and read her manager's name. Had he heard about this already? Bernard Mosley had come into her life just at the right time. Camp as a fortnight in Butlins, was how he described himself. He loved nothing more than a fresh orange and champagne for breakfast, was rarely seen without a cravat and fob watch. He found her her first role and took the place of the father who'd run out on her and her family and returned to his native France when she was around eleven years old.

About the same age as Damaris Brown.

She stuffed the phone back in her pocket with the thought; not now, Bernard.

Amelie forced a deep breath. Right. Where was she? She stepped out of the car and straining her neck, looked down the street. A part of a sign caught her view; blue background and white lettering, edging out from beyond a building further down. *ICE* she read.

When she started walking towards it she realised she was still wearing her slippers, a shapeless brown cardigan over a baggy T-shirt and black leggings.

She reached the glass double door of the police station, pushed it open and walked into a reception area. Facing her was a desk area. On the wall behind it a plethora of community-service posters. Drug abuse and suicide helplines. Something about how the local police were there for you.

Right.

Pulling her cardigan tight around her, she moved closer to the desk and noticed a buzzer. She pressed it and a few seconds later, a door opened and a female entered. Pretty, middle-aged, ample-bosomed, matronly type.

Of course the woman recognised her. Her look said, *oh dear, you look a mess*, but that quickly passed and she switched into polite and professional mode. 'How can I help you?'

'My ... friend has just been brought in.' Part of her mind paused and wondered why she'd left the 'boy' out of that statement. 'And I was wondering who I should speak to about what was going on.'

'Name, please?'

'Amelie Hart.'

'No, your friend's name, Miss Hart. I know who you are. Of course I do.' The woman's eyes brightened and she looked like she was about to go into full-on fan mode, but she stiffened her stance as if she had just reminded herself of their situation.

'Dave. Sorry, David Robbins.'

'You just have a seat over there, Miss Hart,' she pointed to an area behind Amelie, 'and I'll go check.'

Amelie turned and saw a row of four plastic chairs in front of a panel of wood-coloured Formica. Tall plastic ficus plants had been placed at either end of the row, probably in an effort to make the place appear friendlier.

She sat down, crossed her legs and, leaning forward, became aware of the weight of her mobile phone in her cardigan pocket. Before she left the house she'd made a couple of phone calls. Lisa made her regret the call to her. She screeched and went into full drama-queen mode. Said 'ohmygod' at least a dozen times on the one breath.

Then she phoned Dave's father and got a response at the other end of the drama spectrum. When she'd told him what had happened, there was a long silence.

'Mr Robbins,' she asked. 'Are you still there?' They'd met only a handful of times. Christmas and birthdays, and never had the chance to build any sort of relationship, so the man was effectively a stranger.

'Sorry.' He roused himself. 'Ah ... I ... does he have access to a lawyer?'

'My lawyer was going to be my next call. She's an entertainment lawyer, but I'm sure she'll have a few contacts in the criminal side of things.'

'This far into a bank holiday, that's a bit of an ask.' He paused. 'Leave that with me. I'll be able to draw in a favour.'

His measured delivery and pragmatic approach had a temporary calming effect on Amelie, and she wondered if he was always that controlled.

'How is he?' Peter Robbins asked.

'Not sure,' Amelie replied. 'They whipped him away without me getting a chance to talk to him.'

'What can you tell me about what happened?'

Amelie relayed as much as she knew. 'It's a steaming pile of horse shit,' she added. 'No way Dave would touch that little girl.'

'Quite.'

'Miss Hart?' A female voice interrupted her musings.

She looked up. 'Yes?' It was the woman from earlier, and she was wearing a quite different expression now. Gone was the warm tone and in its place, raw judgement. *What kind of person are you who would associate with a man like that?*

'We can't tell you much at the moment. Best if you go home and phone in on Tuesday.'

'Tuesday?' But this was Friday. *That may be a perfectly reasonable explanation to you, lady,* thought Amelie, *but it means nothing to me.* 'Tuesday?' she asked again. Then realised: Bank Holiday weekend, pretty much everything ground to a halt.

Back home, with mounting trepidation, she had to turn on every light in the house, checked every door and window, and closed every curtain before she could relax. Then, on the sofa, with a large glass of wine in her hand, she noted how badly she was shaking.

And with a strong sense of dismay realised she'd just performed a home-entry checklist she hadn't run through for years, not since life with Dave had banished most of her fears about life with a stalker.

Next morning, Amelie came to on the sofa, still wearing the same cardigan and leggings, eyes nipping with lack of sleep. This had been her tactic of adapting to life after *that night*. Sleeping on the sofa, dressed, ready to run for the door should someone be in her house. Again, something she hadn't done since setting up home with Dave.

There was a timid tapping against glass, so quiet that she thought she might be imagining things. It sounded again. And again. Was it a bird? A bird wouldn't be that persistent. She sat up, rubbed at her eyes and looked over at the patio doors that led out into the garden. The curtains were shut so she couldn't see what, or who, it was.

With a groan that protested her aching muscles and joints, she got to her feet, walked round the sofa, and pulled back one side of the ceiling-to-floor curtains.

Damaris was standing on the other side of the glass, in her My Little Pony pyjamas, hands clasped in front of her, eyes large with confusion, looking a lot younger than her eleven years.

'Where's your mum?' Amelie shouted through the glass.

Damaris screwed her eyes almost shut as if that might help her hearing, and cocked her head to the side just like a pup keen to understand might do.

'You shouldn't be here,' Amelie said when she pulled the door open.

'Mum and Dad are still sleeping,' the little girl said. 'I saw Dave in the police car.' She stood completely still as if movement was forbidden to her. 'Will he want to play today?'

Amelie got down onto her knees so that she was at eye level with the girl. A number of replies coursed through her mind in a blink. She felt a confusing mix of emotions. Wanted to call her a stupid little girl, demand she tell her exactly what she told her mother, tell her to piss off. Instead she did none of that. She saw nothing but a large-eyed, scared little girl and with a charge of guilt for her previous thoughts, she wanted nothing more in that moment than to pull her into a hug and reassure her that everything would be okay. Instead, she let her arms hang by her sides, hands as useless as rocks.

'Oh, Damaris,' she said with muscle-draining sadness. None of this was her doing, her parents were completely to blame. 'I really don't know if Dave will be okay. Thing is the police think he hurt you yesterday. Did Dave hurt you?'

The girl just stared at her while chewing on a thumbnail, as if answering that question was completely beyond her. It occurred to Amelie that Damaris was every bit as lost as she was.

Amelie got to her feet, put a hand on each of the girl's shoulders, turned her to face her own garden, and, keeping her tone as gentle as she could, said, 'Off you go before Mum and Dad notice you're missing.'

Amelie knew, and thought that any right-minded person would agree, that it had to be easier for victims of such crimes to be able to come forward and seek the help they needed. Somewhere out there, likely within a short distance of where she was standing, there was a girl, or a boy, who needed the abuse to stop, needed to be protected; needed to be listened to. But as sure as night follows day, it wasn't Damaris Brown.

Chapter 8

After Damaris left, Amelie phoned Dave's father and asked for the lawyer's details. Then she phoned the lawyer, introduced herself and was impressed by how unimpressed he appeared to be that she was *the* Amelie Hart. She listened to what he had to say, and no sooner had she ended the call, than there was a knock at the door.

She swore out loud and marched through to see who it was. When she opened the door she was almost bowled over by a close-to-tears Lisa.

'Darling, how the hell are you?' Lisa asked. Then she stepped back, recovered her equilibrium with remarkable ease, looked her up and down and said, 'Jesus, you look like shit.'

Lisa was her usual impeccable self. Hair a black sheen, make-up artfully applied, and wearing an outfit that probably cost more than most people earn in a month. Then Amelie noticed her luggage: two large suitcases and a massive handbag arranged around her like a pack of at-heel dogs.

'How long are you here for?' Amelie asked.

'Aren't you going to ask me in? Quick, before the neighbours dive out and take a selfie.' She bent down and picked up one case.

Despite herself, Amelie felt a lift from Lisa's energy.

Her friend bustled past her, as she did so, throwing over her shoulder, 'Get the rest of my luggage in, will you?'

Thinking she should be miffed at her friend's assumption that she was there to lift for her, Amelie nevertheless did as she was asked, and arranged the cases in the hallway at the bottom of the stairs. Then she went into the living room. No Lisa. She found her in the kitchen staring at the coffee machine as if the instructions for use were printed in the air in front of it.

'Not that I'm not happy to see you, Lisa, but what are you doing here?'

'My BFF needs me.' She turned to face Amelie, hands out to the sides.

They hugged and Amelie fought desperately to keep her emotions in check. She stepped back from Lisa, cleared her throat and asked, 'Coffee?'

'I could murder my Granny for a coffee.'

'And then you'd get your trust fund sooner.' Amelie joined in with their usual banter, wondering where that energy had just come from.

'You know me so well.' Lisa's half-smile acknowledged Amelie's effort.

Moments later, warm mug in hand, Lisa looked Amelie up and down again. Made a sad face as if she was on the verge of grief because Amelie had let herself go so badly. 'You've been wearing those clothes for days, haven't you?'

Amelie laughed, and when the sound hit her ears was amazed that she was still capable of such a response. 'You are incorrigible.' Then the emotion that had been building since Lisa appeared at the door breached through her defences and she started to cry.

'Oh, honey...' Lisa sat her mug on the work surface, stepped closer to her friend and pulled her into a hug. Amelie felt the arms around her, rested her head on Lisa's shoulder and allowed the emotion to take over.

Minutes later, Lisa stepped back, reached over with a thumb and wiped a tear from Amelie's face. 'Puffy eyes are not a good look on you, babes.'

'Shut it,' Amelie said and sniffed. Wiped at her face with the heel of her hand and then crossed her arms. 'This is all so unfair. I can't stop thinking about Dave in that awful police station.' She paused. 'You know, you rarely give them much of a thought, do you? The police. Aware that they're there. Grateful. But when you become the focus...' She shuddered. 'Officialdom can be quite scary.'

Lisa took her hand. 'C'mon through for a comfy seat. My feet are killing me.'

Amelie looked at her feet. Raised an eyebrow at the toe-pinching shape of Lisa's shoes. 'Serves you right.'

Lisa breezed past her and made her way into the living room. 'I could walk for miles in these babies, and look fabulous doing it.' She reached the sofa. Sat. Pushed off each shoe with a groan. 'But my pinkie toes wouldn't thank me later.'

Amelie sat beside her, kicked off her slippers and pulled her feet to her side. When she'd first seen Lisa at the door, she didn't think she could handle another living being around her, but now she was almost pathetically grateful for the company.

'What's the latest then?' Lisa asked, the rim of her mug poised before her mouth. Amelie told her everything that she knew. Lisa listened intently, taking everything in and then when Amelie stopped she said, 'Follow the money.'

'What do you mean?'

'Is there any chance that Dave is secretly a paedophile?'

'Don't be ridiculous.' Amelie assessed her knee-jerk response. Was there a chance this was true? She couldn't meet Lisa's eyes.

'Lots of people have been fooled by loved ones, you know,' Lisa said as if she read Amelie's failure to look at her.

'Yeah, but Dave? Doesn't have a bad bone in his body.'

'Mmm.' Lisa cocked her head to the side. 'Not sure I'm completely buying that. *Everyone* has a skeleton in their closet, but if, as you say, he's to be completely believed, then you need to follow the money.'

Amelie shook her head. 'Nope, still not getting you.'

'A little girl that age is not going to report that sort of intimate contact from a man unless it actually happened, or without some sort of direction.'

'No...'

What Lisa was getting at dawned on her. She fought down the impulse to doubt the man she'd been living with for over three years.

'I'm going with an extreme overreaction on the part of Damaris's mum and dad,' Amelie continued. 'Those two next door are never going to win Parent of the Year, but to allege something like that in order to make money?'

'Jesus, you've practically been living in a cave, Amelie. People, given the chance, are vile. Have you forgotten that already? Mummy and Daddy will be praying for a conviction so they can sell their story to the highest bidder.'

Amelie shook her head. 'I'm not buying that.'

Lisa tapped the side of her nose. 'Trust me. What other possible motivation could there be?'

'They really believe Dave hurt their child?'

'And Dave just happens to be living with one of the most popular media darlings since, well, Princess Di.'

'Princess Di, my backside,' Amelie said as she allowed the rest of what Lisa said to settle in her mind. 'You really think so?'

'I really, really think so.'

They made a pact to have a news blackout. No TV and phones switched off, in case the media had got hold of the story already, and Saturday passed in an aimless mix of chat, wine, tears and long silences. On Easter Sunday, Amelie made the dinner Dave had planned for her. Turkey and all the Christmas trimmings, to be followed by trifle she announced with a smile.

'Really?' asked Lisa, screwing her face up when Amelie placed it on the table in front of her.

'We never have proper Christmas dinners at Christmas, for some reason, so Dave joked that we should do it at Easter.' Shrug. 'Kinda makes sense to us.'

'Kinda does,' said Lisa with a smile. 'And it's cute.' She watched Amelie as she took her seat at the table. 'And this is the guy you wanted to dump?'

Amelie shivered, reached for her cutlery and whispered, 'God, I'm such a bitch.'

'Don't be hard on yourself, babes. You weren't to know this bomb was going to drop.' She reached across and grabbed Amelie's right hand.

'And now if I do dump him he'll think it's because of all of this.'

Lisa pursed her lips. Exhaled. 'And the delights keep coming.' She forked a piece of white meat into her mouth, chewed and swallowed. 'Still, you serve up a delicious slice of turkey.'

On the Monday, when Lisa eventually got out of bed, she came into the living room and found Amelie laid out on the sofa, following another sleepless night.

'You been here all night?' she asked, sitting on the edge of one of the cushions.

'Better if I'm restless here rather than in the next room to you. At least one of us gets a good sleep.'

'You're a proper saint, babes.' Lisa rubbed at her eyes. 'Now get your scrawny arse through to the kitchen and make me some scrambled eggs.'

Amelie pushed herself into a sitting position. 'I would if I had any eggs.'

'Croissants?'

Amelie snorted.

'Toast.'

'Nope.'

'A girl's got to eat, Amelie. What have you got?'

'Turkey leftovers.'

'Not going there again until I'm surrounded by snow and jingling bells.'

'Sorry, Lisa. I need to go into town for some stuff. Not sure I can face it. What if everyone knows? They'll all be looking at me and judging.'

'Then, babes, you put your slap on and stare them down. How dare they judge you?' She jumped to her feet, her expression suggesting she'd just hit upon a cunning plan. 'I'm getting stir crazy.' She rubbed her hands together. 'I have a plan and it involves you having an actual wash and change. Then I'll disguise you and we'll hit the town.'

'Disguise? No,' Amelie said and crossed her arms.

Lisa leaned down, took hold of her right forearm and, with surprising speed and strength, pulled Amelie to her feet.

'C'mon,' Lisa said. 'If you're going to be miserable, at least look magnificent while you're doing it.'

Ninety minutes later, they were both standing in front of the full-length mirror in Amelie's bedroom, neither of them recognisable.

'What the hell, Lisa?'

'Don't tell me you never go out in public in disguise?'

'Dark glasses and a big hat are my go-to.'

'But don't you look bloody amazing?'

Lisa had dressed herself down and Amelie up. Amelie's famous blonde hair was underneath an auburn wig cut in a chin-length bob, and thick eye make-up on the upper lid only completely changed the shape of her eyes. Lisa on the other hand was wearing a long blonde wig and the lightest make-up she could apply.

'I like the natural look on you, Lisa. You should do it more often.'

Lisa made a dismissive sound and put a hand on her hip as if she was on the end of the catwalk. 'See how much I love you, that I put myself through this?'

'Shut up. You look amazing.' Amelie studied them both in the mirror and it occurred to her that this might be the way to go about in public from now on. Not even her mother would know her.

After a whistle-stop tour of the supermarket, which involved buying mostly eggs, bread products, wine and cheese – and avoiding the newspaper stand – they loaded the backseat of the car and Amelie made as if to drive back to the house.

'I've an idea,' she said as she put the key in the ignition. 'I can't face going back to the house just now. There's a lovely wee place over on the Braehead Road that Dave and I went to once for lunch. I've heard they do an amazing all-day breakfast.'

'You will eat something?' Lisa's eyes were piercing.

Amelie nodded, feeling the lie diminish the energy of her response as her head moved.

The car park at The Hungry Monk was half empty, so, emboldened by her success at the supermarket, Amelie was on her way to being almost relaxed when she made her way to the front door of the white two-storey building with a roof that sloped at a surprisingly steep angle. Half-barrels filled with daffodils that had lost their heads stood sentry at either side of the door.

Inside, the room was just as she remembered. White walls, dark beams, low ceilings. A long oak-topped bar lining the far side of the pub, and beyond that a wall covered in blackboards looked as if the owner had raided an old school after it had been shut down.

They'd been here several times over the years they'd lived in the region. The first time was a folk night, and her celebrity status had caused quite a stir. It seemed that everyone turned to stare at her. Then they'd look at Dave for a moment as if searching for some sort of recognition. Finding none, they'd gone back to staring at her.

One couple sailed over on a wave of craft beer and gin, smiles too large in that way of the pleasantly pissed.

'Oh my God, you're her, aren't you?' the woman said. And Amelie thought now that she was up close that she was way too old to be fawning over a celeb. The woman then turned to Dave. 'Are you anyone?'

Amelie almost left there and then, but sensing her movement, Dave grabbed her wrist. Held her. Sent her a signal with his eyes. This is fine. We're fine.

'I'm a film director,' Dave said. 'You seen the new *Alien* movies? That's me.'

The lie was so outrageous but so casually delivered that Amelie relaxed as if she'd been given a shot of something.

Now, no one turned and looked when they walked in. They were just two women out for lunch. Not a whisper of fame and its glamour in the vicinity. A good sign, thought Amelie, and then gave herself a row. She needed to stop looking for omens. This wasn't the sixteenth century.

Lisa made for a table near the corner, in front of a small window. Amelie followed, but then with a start realised the couple she had to walk past to get there lived in an apartment in the big house on her estate. She struggled to remember their names, but they were usually friendly enough, always gave her a wave if they came across her when she was out walking. She stiffened as she passed them, but they gave no signal that they'd seen through her disguise.

With a grateful sigh she took a seat beside Lisa.

'What?' her friend asked.

'Jesus, you miss nothing.'

Smug grin. 'My brother always said I should work for the CID. Anyway...' She planted both hands on the small surface of the dark wooden table between them. 'Feed me.'

'The menu is on the blackboard behind the bar.'

Lisa looked across. Spotted the young, slim-waisted man. She watched him for a moment. 'He's barely looked at me and he can't take his filthy eyes off you.' She harrumphed. 'Now you see why I don't much go out *au natural*.'

'I thought we were here *not* to be noticed?'

'There's being noticed and there's being noticed, babes.' Smile. 'What do you fancy eating?'

Amelie ordered scrambled eggs with smoked salmon and when it arrived was genuinely surprised at finding she had an appetite. She even managed to eat some of the extra toast that Lisa ordered.

She washed it all down with a second cup of black coffee, trying to force down her guilt at being so well looked-after while Dave was in a cell.

'Stop it,' Lisa said while dabbing at the side of her mouth.

'What?'

'I could read your expression. You've done nothing wrong. There's no need for you to feel guilty.'

Just then a woman walked in the front door. Her long black hair was pulled back in a ponytail, she was wearing a navy cable-knit jumper and a pair of tan jodhpurs. Her face split in a smile when she spotted the couple beside Amelie. She was so lean Amelie could almost see the individual muscles in her face work as her lips were pulled away to display her expensive veneers.

'Honey,' the woman cried and made her way over to Amelie's neighbours, giving them both a hug. 'This was a champion idea. Have people cook breakfast after the night before.'

'It was a fun night, eh?' her female friend said. 'Although that last cocktail was definitely one too many.' Her name, Amelie suddenly remembered, was Helen. Her husband was Drew.

Pony-tailed woman sat, spine rigid as if she was holding in something incredibly exciting. 'And did you happen to see the news this morning?' Her anticipation at delivering something of shock value was palpable

Amelie felt Lisa's hand on her knee.

'What?' Helen sat forward.

'Your neighbour who was in that shit movie?'

'It wasn't shit, I loved it,' said Helen.'

'It was dreadful,' said Drew, looking from his wife to the other woman. 'Well, Mags, don't keep us waiting. What about her?'

'Her boyfriend's a paedophile.'

Amelie noticed that she was so excited at passing this on that she was sitting on her hands. 'The bitch is actually *thrilled* about this,' she hissed at Lisa.

'Don't say anything,' Lisa whispered in reply. 'I want to hear.'

'Her boyfriend's a what?' asked Helen.

'He's been locked up for molesting the little girl who lives next door to them.'

'What? There's been a trial and everything?' asked Drew.

'No, silly,' answered Mags. 'This just happened on Friday. The police were called. He was locked up. He goes in front of the Procurator Fiscal tomorrow.'

'Bloody hell,' said Helen.

'Poor guy,' said Drew. And Amelie felt a little heartened.

His wife punched his arm. 'He molested a child. How can you say, poor guy?'

'Typical bloody man,' said Mags. 'You'll believe the accused first.'

'How long's he been living there, and he suddenly turned paedo? I ain't buying it,' Drew said while rubbing his arm, otherwise fine that his wife was so willing to strike him. 'He played cricket last summer with the lads at the village fete. He was a decent sort. There were loads of kids there that day and he never as much as gave them a look.'

'Call yourself a Scotsman? You and your bloody cricket,' said Helen. 'And they're much more subtle than that. He's hardly likely to go full on grooming mode when every parent in the village is in attendance.'

'I never liked him,' said Mags, relieving her hands from their trap under the bones of her thighs and crossing her arms. 'Gave me the willies.'

'Oh my God,' Amelie said quietly. 'Would you listen to her? I can't believe these people.'

Lisa shushed her. 'Just a little more, babes. We need to get a feel for what people are going to be saying.' Lisa managed to speak while barely moving her mouth.

'He did help me out of a spot one year when my accountant took ill just before a big tax deadline,' said Helen with a face of apology, as if sorry that she wasn't fully supporting Mags' narrative.

'Cunning bastard,' replied Mags. 'That's what they do, innit? Play all respectable and helpful to your face, while behind your back they're totally fiddling with your kids.'

'Why are you suddenly defending him, Drew?' Helen now demanded of her husband. 'I remember you after that cricket match, you said he was a wrong 'un.'

'He couldn't catch the ball, is what I meant. Not that he was some sort of deviant.' His expression was full of disbelief.

'Tried too hard for my liking,' said Helen. 'All that smiling and not charging for doing my accounts. Nobody's that nice, really.'

You're certainly not, you witch, thought Amelie. *And there's your reward for your kindness, Dave.*

'I just met him once,' said Mags. She chewed on the inside of her mouth as if trying to come up with the right words to match her thoughts. 'It was like he'd learned to be nice out of a book, you know?'

'Exactly,' said Helen. 'Totally dodgy.'

'Oh for God's sake,' Amelie said loudly and got to her feet. She stepped closer and looked down at the surprised faces staring back up at her. 'Idiots. Pitchforks at the ready. Let's go and storm the local nick, eh?'

Chapter 9

Tuesday morning announced itself with the small shutter at head height on Dave's cell door being slid open.

'Tea or coffee?' the policeman on the other side asked him.

'Tea, please,' Dave answered as he slid his legs to the side and sat up. He groaned, feeling the weight of fatigue in his eyes, his mind, his limbs. Had he slept? He tried to re-collect if there were any moments in the night when he wasn't acutely aware of his surroundings and what he'd been accused of.

'And would sir like marmalade on his toast this fine morning?'

He paused before he replied to this one. The 'toast' he'd received each morning had yet to defrost properly, and the butter had been a solid clump in the middle of the bread.

The policeman made a sharp buzzer noise. 'Eeee. Too late. Just butter it is.'

It didn't much matter in any case. Dave had no appetite and had only eaten the food he'd been served since he was locked up in an attempt to keep his wits about him. Each mouthful had the taste and texture of card, and his jaw muscles ached as if he had been working his way through thick board. Still, he recognised that he needed nourishment and having something in his stomach would help his brain process events.

That was the theory. In reality, he ate, sipped, slept and shit on some kind of automatic process. The only thing that felt real was the solid surface of the bunk in his cell, the coarse blanket under his chin when he pulled it there in an attempt to sleep, and the apparent restraint from a succession of turnkey police officers. They were all far too professional to be explicit in their wish to see him come to harm, but it was apparent in every pair of eyes that moved in his direction.

He rubbed at his face and heard the rasp of bristle. Boy, did he need a shave. He'd never been one of those guys who looked good with designer stubble. It made him look like he was a breath away from stealing someone's wallet.

Now, after an interminable weekend of long minutes and excoriating thoughts it seemed that officialdom was moving. He was on the wheel and there was no way he was getting off. After he'd made a stab at eating his 'breakfast' his shoe-laces and belt were returned to him, signalling he'd be making his way into the court for his hearing.

'Not guilty,' he said, practising for the moment when he'd be asked how he intended to plead. Again and again he said the two words. Under his breath. Out loud. With a defiant tone. An apologetic tone. A tone of fuck you and fuck that pair of stupid bastards masquerading as parents who lived next door.

The hearing, like everything else that had occurred since his nightmare began came at him through a surreal fog. He found it difficult to believe that this was happening to him, and was terrified by the process. The whole system was set up to intimidate and he felt the weight of the centuries of that process like a pressing on his brain; an ache in his lungs.

Breathing was difficult.

Clear thought impossible.

Mum and Dad were there, sitting beside Amelie. Dad, unreadable as always. Mum looked older, as if the simple process of walking through the door and taking a seat had added twenty years to her life. Dave tried to signal to them that he could deal with all of this. But he couldn't raise enough energy to press past the fear and worry.

Chapter 10

Peter Robbins looked at the young man in the dock flanked by policemen. Saw himself in the oval of his face. The hook of his nose. But he had his mother's eyes and they cast a benevolent air. Normally. Today his son was strained beyond measure. His skin grey, eyes shadowed, mouth a tight line of trepidation and disbelief.

His wife gripped his forearm. He turned to her, with the aim of offering a smile of encouragement. A smile that would say this would all be over soon – they'd see their son was incapable of this kind of thing. But his message failed. Norma was looking straight ahead, eyes fixed on Dave, every line and curve of her frayed with worry.

The magistrate said something. Norma whispered out the side of her mouth. 'What's that? What does that mean?'

'Ssshh,' he answered, more harshly than he intended. He'd been so intent on studying the two most important people in his world that he missed what the judge had said.

That morning, sitting outside in the car, he'd been amazed that he'd managed to arrive at the court in one piece. Couldn't remember most of the journey. How did you process this? Where was the context? In a movie? Some sordid drama on TV?

Staring straight ahead in the passenger seat, Norma had said, 'No smoke without fire.'

'What?' Peter demanded, ready to be outraged. How could his wife, Dave's mother of all people …

'That's what people will be saying. No smoke without fire. I could see Jenny Johnson next door at her curtains, watching us leave.' She gave a little hiccough of a sob, and reined it in as if she'd promised herself there would be no crying.

'We don't care what those idiots say, dear. The Johnsons can go to hell.'

'They're nice people really,' Norma said. Her default state of politeness asserting itself. 'But they can be pretty small-minded. Remember that time the McKee's eldest boy came home with an arm full of tattoos? You'd have thought he'd signed a pact with the devil the way they carried on.' Then she had fallen into silence, eyes fixed on the building ahead of her as if she was lost in a sulk of memory.

Peter felt guilty on hearing the news of Dave's arrest because his first thought hadn't been about Dave, it had been a stab of worry at how the news would affect Norma. Dave's twin sister died hours after her birth, and Norma focused all of her grief, all of her energy, into making Dave's life as safe and easy as it could possibly be.

They'd named the dead child Sarah, after Norma's mother. Then worried that might send the wrong signal, but by the time that had occurred to Norma the registration had been completed, the child's remains were buried and nothing was going to change. Granny was just going to have to live with having a dead infant in her name.

Of course, Granny Sandison had loved the idea; she was a generous soul, if not a little fey, and was convinced baby Sarah would be waiting for her at the pearly gates just as soon as she turned up.

One dead and one living child presented its own kind of waking nightmare. Celebrate one child too much and Norma worried you gave less to the other. So there followed three decades of his wife living a half-life. Her spirit wilted, a weakness dragged on her heart and soul, and she'd gone from never even having as much as a cold to falling prey to all kinds of illnesses. She'd live part of each day in melancholy and the other part as if fully engaged in Dave's development. They'd come to see those regular occasions when she was close to a faint while still functioning, as 'Mum's episodes', and did everything they could to help until they passed. If this all didn't turn out well, Peter worried what it would do to his wife's sanity.

Now, in the court, he reached across and held the hand that gripped on to his forearm, praying that the heat from his skin would transfer strength and positivity.

Everything would turn out fine, he told himself.

Of course it would.

Dave was no child molester. As a boy he'd brought home countless injured birds and small mammals. Looking after his mother demonstrated an empathy that almost made the boy shine. At this thought Peter gave himself a mental ticking-off. Of course he was no saint. He got into scrapes just like any other kid, and there was that assault charge around his twenty-first, but there was a softness in him he hadn't observed in many other lads. Norma often said it was the soul of his dead sister. He'd got the best of the masculine and the feminine.

Whatever it was, his son was no paedophile.

They'd spent the Easter weekend trying to make sense of it all.

'Ever since he took up with that Amelie woman he's been a different boy,' Norma had said earlier, before they left the car. They had paused in the act of leaving the safety of the vehicle, each taking a moment before the world crashed back into their lives. Norma had played with the fastener of her handbag, which was resting on her lap like a comforter. 'Nothing good comes from falling in love with an older woman.'

Peter had almost corrected her. There were only six years between them, as far as he could remember. And David was a man, not a boy. But that was how she'd always see him.

'And you,' she aimed at Peter. 'You encouraged him. Caught up in all that glamour. Can't see past a pretty face, Peter.'

'What are you talking about? So, she's a good-looking woman. Does that make her Satan?'

'No, but he's been a little bit weird since he moved in with her.' She crossed her arms and he was reminded of how slight she was. A draught from a passing lorry would be enough to push her over.

'When you say weird, you mean he has less time for us. That's inevitable, Norma. The lad has his own life to live.'

'Weird, I tell you. Weird. Who runs away from a career like that?' she asked. 'Other people would give their left arm for a life like that.'

Norma folded in on herself. Everything seemed so big, and it all reeked of power and formality. Wood panels everywhere. Grand crests. Coats of armour, whatever. All of it made her feel that if she spoke into the heavy space the only sound from her throat would be the squeak of a mouse.

The Fiscal sat, shoulders back, her expression chipped from ice, and Norma couldn't help but feel Dave was being judged and found wanting even before the facts of the case had been aired.

He's a good boy, she wanted to shout. Never harmed a soul in his life. Good to his mum. Or he was until he met that woman.

She stole a look to the side and looked at Amelie. All glossy hair and cheekbones. And easily the most striking woman in the room.

Norma felt a pang of guilt. She was better than that. Aiming insults at the woman. She was suffering too, judging by the slump of her features. Besides, surely the court would look at this wonderful example of womanhood and be certain that if her son could win the heart of a woman like that, there was no way he was a pervert.

The judge was speaking but Norma was so distressed by the strain showing on her son's face she couldn't take in what was being said. *Help him*, she wanted to shout at the Fiscal. Couldn't she look at him and see the innocence blazing out of him?

That need for her to constantly protect Dave almost ended her marriage. Right up until Dave was a preteen he often – almost nightly if she was being honest – climbed into her and Peter's bed. She would never have the heart to refuse him and was often unable to sleep with their son spread out like he was attempting a snow angel. With a low groan of dissatisfaction Peter would pad through to Dave's bed.

'You're suffocating him,' was Peter's almost daily accusation. She'd simply tut and turn away, determined to protect her son. She'd lost one child; she'd do everything in her power to make sure she didn't lose another.

Dave eventually strained at the maternal leash. His satisfaction with the situation changed to teenage frustration and his chant became 'Stop mothering me, Mother' before he'd run outside to play football or go skateboarding with his mates. And then she'd wait by the window, arms crossed, jaw tight – delighting in his ability to make friends with other children while her heart was sparking with fear at the possibility of harm.

The first time he'd been in her care and out of her sight brought her first panic attack: chest pains and difficulty breathing and she was sure she was suffering from heart failure. It was only when Dave reappeared with a massive smile on his face – he'd climbed a tree apparently – that her breathing eased.

Throughout her life since, the attacks had been an almost weekly occurrence. Peter had pushed her in the direction of the doctors and when faced with her intractability even went so far as to threaten to throw her over his shoulder and carry her there. She convinced him she'd been on her own, selling him a story that the doctor said her fainting episodes were the symptom of delayed grief and they would surely pass in their own time. Which they didn't. They were as much a part of her life as Dave was, and she didn't want to lose them. If that was her only tangible link to Sarah she would gladly pay that price. Self-aware enough to know that this was flawed thinking, nonetheless she persisted with it, and each time the tingling started in her fingertips and the heavy clouds of dread gathered, a small part of her mind welcomed it like an old and trusted friend.

Norma took a deep breath and felt a chill at the tightness in her chest and her thundering heart. An attack was gathering there and then. She tightened her jaw against it. Not now. *Not* now. Not *now*.

Please let her see her son to safety first.

Chapter 11

After the decision, Joseph Bain drew Amelie, Norma and Peter into an anteroom.

'Please, sit,' he said to them. 'You must have questions.' Barely noticing her surroundings, Amelie edged round a large oak table that covered over most of the floor space and found a seat before the weakness in her thighs robbed her of the ability to stand.

'Questions?' Peter drew up to his full five feet six and thrust his face into Bain's. 'You're right we have bloody questions. What the hell just happened in there? I thought this was all a formality?'

'Peter, please sit,' said Norma. 'The man is trying to help us.' Her quiet authority cut through Peter's anger and he slumped red-faced into a chair.

Amelie sat staring into nothing, hand over her mouth, trying to come to terms with the magistrate's findings.

'He's being held in custody on remand?' demanded Peter. 'For what? Removing a little girl from his workspace in case she got hurt? The world's gone fucking...'

'That kind of language doesn't suit you, Peter,' said Norma, but the admonishment felt to Amelie like it came from Norma falling into habit in her time of stress, rather than a need for propriety.

'Oh, by all means pick on my use of language while our son goes to prison.' Peter wasn't in the mood to be aware of nuance.

Amelie roused herself from the murk and tangle of her thoughts. 'Guys, Dave needs us to stick together right now.' Without waiting for a reaction from either of them she turned to the lawyer. 'What exactly does that mean and how long is it likely to last?'

'The average term of custody on remand is about ten weeks or so,' replied Bain with an apologetic cast to his face.

'Ten weeks?' the three of them asked at the same time.

'That's the average, so it could be longer? And why didn't the Fiscal go for bail?' Peter asked.

Bain was clearly biting back his instant reply. Peter had badgered him about this as they walked along the long corridor straight after the hearing.

'Because the girl lives right next door and because the Fiscal was swayed by the family's argument of possible grooming.'

Grooming, thought Amelie. How utterly ridiculous. She heard again the gasp she made in court when this point was made. This could have been going on under their noses for a long time, they argued. The little girl looked on her neighbour fondly. Dave had wormed his way into a position of trust. The implication between their stream of words: *This is all kinds of wrong. What grown man spends all that time with a little girl*? One who notices her parents pay little attention, Amelie wanted to shout out into that almost sacred space where one had to be invited to speak.

'Are they being extra careful because this is the family of a senior cop?' she asked.

Bain made a face, as if to say you might well have a point there, but said, 'The police will not be able to influence anyone unduly.'

Peter snorted. 'My arse. You can bet your well-tailored suit –' he looked Bain up and down ' – your wardrobe of well-tailored suits that the police relative of this girl will have been jabbing a finger between the ribs of every lawyer he could find.'

'That's as maybe,' said Bain. 'But we have to deal with what we know. Speculation doesn't help.'

Peter exhaled as if he'd been holding his breath in from the moment he'd entered the court building. He sat. Gathered himself, and it looked to Amelie that he did so at some cost.

'What now?' He looked up from the table and stared at the lawyer.

'I press for a trial date and we prepare as best we can.'

Everyone in the room fell silent as they tried to process their new reality. Amelie had the image of Dave being led from the court by two policemen, his hands behind his back and his face heavy with disbelief. She leaned forward on to her arms and started to cry.

After a few moments, she managed to gather her wits, leaned back into her seat and accepted the white cotton handkerchief that Bain was holding out to her. Dave's mother and father stood apart in awkward silence, as if her obvious upset had robbed them of the ability to act in the same way.

There was a burst of noise from outside the building, and Amelie's mind realised that there had been a hum of chatter and movement sounding beyond the large windows since they'd entered the room.

The lower half of the windows held smoked glass, so she approached them and stood on a chair to peer over the clear glass in the top half of the window. And almost instantly recoiled; stumbling back off the chair to stand on the floor.

'What is it?' asked Norma. She held a hand to her heart, frightened by her reaction.

'The press are out in force.'

'Shit,' said Peter.

'This is big news, sadly,' said Bain. 'Child abuse with a celebrity connection and...' He tailed off as if there was nothing more to add, while all three of them stared at Amelie.

She was grateful when Peter spoke.

'*Alleged* child abuse,' Peter corrected the lawyer.

'Bastards,' said Amelie. Then she acknowledged she had been lucky to have avoided them so far. In only that brief glimpse she'd seen a sizable press pack: a number of journalists whose usual patch was the entertainment pages, a fair number she'd never seen before and even a couple of TV crews. One of them had a logo for a news channel from the US on their camera.

Her phone had been switched off in her handbag. She pulled it out and switched it on. Within seconds her screen was alive with alerts. Most of them for texts from Lisa and Bernard. She felt guilty about ignoring Bernard. He'd tried to get a hold of her numerous times over the last couple of days; she had no idea why she was so reluctant to talk to him. He was part of that world, a world she'd walked away from, a world that would now be sharpening its collective claws, preparing to tear into her and her reputation.

That was unfair. Bernard had only ever been supportive of her. Why would he change now? Still. She couldn't quite face him yet, so she turned off her phone again and dropped it into her handbag. Then she looked at Bain.

'When do I get a chance to speak to Dave?'

Chapter 12

'Hey,' said Amelie. They were in a small room in the prison, with about half a dozen tables, each with a pair of chairs facing each other. At the door stood a couple of guards. One male, one female. Both of them looked like they had a lifestyle evenly balanced between lugging huge weights at the gym and eating all the pies they could get their hands on. They both stared at her as she walked in. Clocked who she was immediately, and from time to time she could feel their eyes on her.

Amelie had chosen her outfit with care that morning. She wanted to look rich, successful and make the most of her looks. It was vapid, she knew, but she wanted the people around Dave to get a shot of her glamour, and prayed that this would give him some sort of cachet in the world he now found himself in.

When she left the house, and it was too late to change, a contrary voice muttered in her mind that it might have the opposite effect: make people jealous and end up with Dave getting a kicking.

'Hey,' replied Dave. His forearms were resting on the table, hands clenched, his knuckles almost white against the pink of his skin.

'You doing okay?' As soon as the question was out of her mouth she wanted to reel it back in, but Dave appeared to accept it with as much grace as he could muster, and with a twitch of his lips; a vague attempt at a smile, as if the signal to do so got lost on its way from his brain.

'Been a lot better,' he said in a low voice, and Amelie could read the change in him. He was already a smaller, greyer, haunted version of himself.

'They'll laugh it out of court. You'll be a free man in a matter of days.' She injected energy into her voice. A performance worthy of at least a shortlisting for an Emmy.

Dave coughed. Shifted in his seat. Scratched at the side of his face. 'Yeah.'

Amelie read the defeat in his voice, his posture. She leaned across, grabbed at his hand. 'Everybody knows this is rubbish. Nobody thinks for a second you abused Damaris. Nobody.'

He looked up from the table. Eyes beseeching. 'You know I would never harm a child. You believe me, don't you?' He looked like a lost and bewildered little boy.

'Jesus.' She gripped his hand tighter. 'Of course I do. You're the kindest, most gentle man I've ever met.' She met his stare and held it. She would not be the one to release first. He had to believe her. Be bolstered by her certainty in him.

'That's what I'm struggling with most,' he said, and his eyes fell to the table top. He removed his hand from her grip and scratched at something only he could see on the surface of the table. 'That people look at me and think there's truth in this nonsense. Can't they see I'd never do anything like this?' He remained leaning forward, back hunched, and crossed his arms.

'Well, if they can't see it they're worse than idiots.'

'How's Mum?'

Amelie considered how she might answer this. The woman she saw during the hearing and afterwards was close to snapping. This was clearly too much for her to handle, but if she told David the truth he would feel even worse.

'Your father is being a big help to her.'

'He is?'

She nodded.

'Of course he is. To me he was always like, boys don't cry. Be strong. Take it on the chin. He never accepted any sign of weakness from me. But Mum, he was a big softie with her.'

Amelie studied Dave as he spoke, read a wealth of story in his eyes. Some good, but mostly what she read was a series of struggles; Dave had spent his life trying to live up to the version of manhood his father expected.

'I don't want Mum to see me in here. I can't let her.'

'Dave, honey, you can't not see your mum. It would kill her.'

'I can't...' He looked away, but not before Amelie saw a tear brimming over the lower lid of his right eye. 'She can't see me ... in this place.' Then his eyebrows raised as if a thought had entered his mind. 'Shit. Lee. I was supposed to take him to that new Marvel movie.' He looked at her. 'Can you get in touch and cancel?'

'Sure,' she said, part of her mind thinking he'd have to be living in a cave not to have noticed what was going on, the other part amazed that Lee had entered Dave's head during all of this.

'Dave. About your mum,' she began to plead.

'No.'

'Dave, please. You can't do that to her.'

'No,' he shouted and slammed the palm of his left hand down on the table top. The male guard took a step forward.

'Any trouble over there?'

Dave ignored him.

Amelie looked over and gave him her five-star smile. 'Everything's fine,' she said and the guard puffed up under her gaze. Shoulders back. Chest out. Until his female colleague shoved an elbow in his ribs and mouthed, *Get a grip.*

'And while we're at it, you don't need to bother coming to visit either,' Dave said as he leaned back in his seat, crossed his arms and looked off to the right.

'What?' Her heart beat heavy. 'Don't do this, Dave. Don't shut us all out.' She stared at him and saw a film forming over his eyes. Stern and uncompromising. An invisible shell. Already he was preparing for the worst. He was trying to protect himself by closing off everyone who might care. 'We'll fight this. We'll prove there was no way you did anything to harm this girl,' Amelie continued.

This girl. Already she was removing Damaris from any position of sympathy in her heart. Dehumanising her so it would be easy, despite promising herself not to, while knowing the poor soul was as much a victim as Dave was.

'You were going to dump me anyway. We both know that.' He studied her face, both expecting and dismissing her denial. 'Might as well save us both a lot of heartache.'

'Dave, please...' She injected as much honesty as she could muster into her words, tone, posture. *Believe me.* She sat with the words in her mind and heart. Wore them like a cloak of certainty. 'Yes, I was going through some stuff. But that was more about me than it was about you. Three years of hiding out, away from the public eye...'

'Well, that's all changed.' He looked away from her. 'You can go and get your old job back now.'

'Stop it,' Amelie said. 'Stop it. I care about you and I will not abandon you.'

'You care about me,' Dave said, and fell back into his defeated slump. He raised an eyebrow, curved his mouth into a loose, weak smile, and Amelie barely recognised the person he now was. 'Notice how you didn't say you loved me.'

Chapter 13

As Dave walked away from Amelie he felt his heart close down, and his legs heavy as if he was dragging chains. What was he doing? Was he insane? Amelie was one of the best things in his life; why was he shutting himself off from her?

Get real, a voice said. *She's only with you out of guilt. Your relationship wouldn't have lasted the bank holiday weekend. If you'd still been at home you'd be online looking for a new house right now.*

Dave felt a heavy finger prod his shoulder. 'Get a move on. We don't have all day,' said the female guard.

'Did I hear right?' the male guard said. 'Did you just tell Amelie Hart to do one? You must be a frickin' paedo. I'd give my left nut to shack up with her.'

'Then you'd have an empty sack, Smith,' said his colleague.

Smith chuckled before answering, 'Shut it, Leggatt.'

Dave paused at a set of bars as they were unlocked from the other side. Stepped through and heard them close. The lock turned with a loud jangle of keys and he was back in E Hall.

He was in *prison*. No matter how often he thought those words, he'd never get used to it. He felt himself shrink and stuffed his hands in his pockets. Then, aware this might signal 'weakling' he pulled his shoulders back and pushed his chin forward.

Perhaps he could fake it. Ignore the fact that every cell in his body was sparking with fearful energy and pretend he was adapting to the situation. He could adopt the posture of someone who was already part of the furniture.

Except he was nowhere close to that.

He felt the tip of one of the guard's boots hit his left heel and became aware that he had slowed down again.

'Keep walking, Robbins,' said Smith, not bothering to hide his irritation.

They were almost back at his cell and Dave could hear men in the cells along the corridor stir as they heard movement.

'Hey, I need my medicine,' one guy shouted. His voice a needy challenge.

'This guy spent the whole night wanking. Can't you guys do something about it? He's disgusting.'

'Did my son call yet?'

The voices were all gruff in their attempt to demonstrate a harsh version of masculinity that Dave hadn't much encountered in his life. Sure, he'd come across a few macho arseholes now and again, but it had never been so concentrated. It felt like that was the go-to mindset to help guys survive in this place.

He squirmed at the thought he was about to be back in his narrow cell, dreading the noise of the door closing behind him and the loud clunk of the key in the lock. With a start he remembered what Bain his lawyer had told him about the different treatment that remand prisoners should receive. Technically, he was still an innocent man and therefore should not be treated the same as those who had been judged guilty. One of those benefits was to have reduced time in their cell, and he should therefore take advantage of any educational or arts programmes available to him.

Before they'd come for him to take him to the visitors' hall he'd filled in a request form for a short course on creative writing. That would get him out of his cell and hopefully out of his own head.

Smith opened his cell door, and before he could close it again Dave ducked in, found the form on the small table where he'd left the piece of paper, turned and handed it to him.

'What's this?' asked Smith.

Dave coughed. 'It's a request to attend...' He heard the weakness in his voice and despised himself for it. As he finished his explanation he fought to add the attitude he'd heard from the other men in the cells around him; '...a writing course.'

'Really?' said Smith, his eyebrows raised in a silent *fuck you*.

'Yeah.' Dave coughed again and swore that would be the last time he'd be so weak. 'My lawyer tells me as a remand prisoner I get access to…'

'But as a paedo you get access to nothing.' Smith's expression was hard and unyielding. He took the paper, tore it up into shreds and threw it back into Dave's face. 'Pick that up, Robbins. We don't stand for untidy cells.' Then, with a satisfied grin, he slammed the door shut.

And he was on his own. Bare walls. A metallic bunk bed. A tiny cubicle with a toilet in it. And God knows how many hours before his door was even opened again.

He fell on to the thin mattress, turned on his side, pulled his knees up to his chest and let the tears flow. His mind's eye was full of the image of Amelie's face when he told her not to come back for another visit. It was the hardest thing he'd ever had to do. Of course he wanted her to come and see him. The knowledge that there was someone out there who believed him innocent was incredibly powerful, but he couldn't bear for her to see him in this place. He couldn't bear to see *her* in this place. It was like an assault on his senses. Like getting a glimpse of a Michelangelo painting after spending days looking only at the work produced by a chimp given a butter knife and a colour palette of two.

He'd almost buckled when she'd leaned across and held his hand. The soft warmth of her hand and the trust it implied was too much. He couldn't afford to consider for even a moment the comfort he might find there. That was where insanity lay, he was sure. If he was to get through this he had to accept what had happened, deal with it and not look for relief anywhere.

Of course he'd heard stories of how badly sex offenders, and in particular those who had abused children, were treated. And given the high-profile nature of his case there would be a queue of men intent on violence, looking to carve a name for themselves, quite literally, on his flesh.

He wasn't a complete stranger to violence; in his preteens he had a bit of a temper on him. He'd lash out with little provocation. And this went on until the school called in his parents. He'd never forget the shame on his father's face when the headmaster asked them if there were any issues at home.

'Would you call it an issue when you find your father shagging the neighbour's wife?' Dave wanted to ask.

He'd managed to cool it until later in secondary school, when he became the target of some bullies. To deflect this he occasionally tried to act the big man – which often resulted in a fat lip and bruised pride.

And he walked home daily through an area of town where the youth wore their disadvantage with a scowl, brand-name clothing, and permanently grazed knuckles. He negotiated that by ignoring any challenge, and whenever it looked like the threat might turn physical he took comfort knowing he was one of the fastest runners in his year and would easily get away from most threats.

In his time at university he was aware that his mop of blonde hair, bookish aspect and willowy frame would make him a target on nights out for any pissed-up loser who wanted to demonstrate they had the attitude to be anything but, so he joined the local rugby club and in doing so gained twenty pounds of muscle and a group of zealously loyal young men who took shit from nobody.

But here, he was acutely aware he was on his own, and a target. He'd have to find another way to negotiate the violence many men used to validate themselves and the mess of their lives. Or somehow tap into that fury he'd felt as a kid when his father betrayed him and his mother. But for now he'd press his knees against his chest, stare at the wall and try to ignore the feeling of helplessness that was growing in his bones.

'So, you're Amelie Hart's boyfriend?' a guy had asked him that morning as he'd queued for his breakfast, letting him know that without doubt the word had gotten out in to the prison population. Already he was learning how important gossip was in a place like this. When there was little to do and all day to do it, the details of other people's stories could gain the allure of gold dust. 'What's it like shagging a movie star?'

'Fuck off.' He'd turned to face the guy down. Show no weakness. This was an older man, sharp-featured, white hair, and facial skin loosened by too many cigarettes and deep-fried burgers.

A guard moved across to them before the situation could escalate. 'Everything okay here?' he asked. With an effort, Dave took control of himself.

'Everything alright?' The guard's repeated question indicated he wanted a verbal response.

'Aye, boss,' the other man said. 'Was just curious, like.'

'And I don't want to talk about a past relationship with a fucking deviant,' said Dave in a calm and reasonable tone.

'Oi.' The older man bristled.

'Back to your cell, Mr Robbins.' The guard stood between them, his frame so large Dave couldn't see past him to the other guy.

Without another word, Dave took his instructions and moved back to his cell. Once inside he sat his breakfast tray on the small table that was bolted on to one of the walls and lay on his bed. He wasn't hungry, and besides, if he drew out the moment of eating he could perhaps alleviate his boredom later on.

The older man's voice sounded in his mind now, and he clenched everything against the disgust that bubbled through his veins. He wouldn't be the only man on this site wondering about that very thing. It was unbearable. And you could bet your last penny the old pervert would be back in his own cell, beating off to the thought of doing unspeakable things to the woman he loved.

Chapter 14

Damaris was in her bed, listening to her parents arguing in the next room. When her mother tucked her in, she'd surprised herself by asking her to leave the big light on.

Her parents' voices grew louder, but unable to hear what they were saying and desperate to know, she edged out of bed, pressed her head against the door and listened.

'Can't believe that evil bastard hurt my little girl. What kind of father am I that I would let that happen?'

'You're a good dad. A great dad.'

'If I was, my little girl wouldn't...'

'Don't do this to yourself, honey.'

Damaris heard a smashing sound. A whelp of pain and then sobbing. She'd never heard her father cry before, and she stuffed her thumb into her mouth in a desperate attempt to stop her joining him. This was all her fault. Her toes curled into the carpet as if trying to hold on to a more solid world.

After a troubled night's sleep she made her way down for breakfast, but only once she heard some movement from the kitchen. When she got there her mother turned to her from the stove and smiled.

'Just making your favourite breakfast, honey. Waffles and ice cream.'

'Really? When we aren't even on holiday?' Damaris scrambled up onto a high stool at the breakfast bar.

'Mummy's going to look after you much better, honey. I'm going to be the best mummy ever.' She stopped speaking and, hunched over, started to cry.

Damaris jumped off her seat and ran to her mother. Holding her round the waist she said, 'Please don't cry, Mummy. Please don't cry.'

Her mother stopped crying and gave a weak smile. 'I'd hoped you wouldn't see me like this. I need to be strong for my little girl after what she's been through.' She started crying again.

'But Mum...'

'I was standing at the window. I could see up the garden to where you and Dave were. Why I didn't shout you in...?' She wiped at her face.

'But Dave's my friend. He would never hurt me.'

'He's not your friend, darling. Friends don't hurt each other like that.'

Just then her father appeared in the doorway.

'Everybody okay?' he asked.

There was something unsaid in his eyes, an uncertainty. Damaris looked from him to her mother and read a silent answer in her gaze. Her father then gave a little nod of confirmation. What had just happened, Damaris wondered? Grown-ups were so confusing.

'D and I are just about to have some waffles.' Her mother sounded like she was forcing some fun into her voice.

'Well, that's ... a nice surprise,' Rodger said as he moved closer. He came over to Damaris and kissed the top of her head. 'How's my little princess this morning? Sleep alright?'

'Yes,' Damaris lied. She might be confused with what was going on but she knew this was not a moment to tell the truth about her restless night. And the dreams.

In one she had boobs. Actual boobs. And Dave next door kept staring at them. In another he was sitting on top of her while her parents watched and she couldn't breathe. And she woke up, almost terrified to go back to sleep again, ever.

After they'd all eaten her mother reached across the table and patted her hand.

'How was that, darling?'

Damaris nodded. 'Great, Mum, thanks.'

'And don't worry.' Claire teared up again. 'We'll get through this, as a family.'

'But, Mummy...'

'That's your memory protecting you, Damaris. It's like when the light goes out when you close the door of your en-suite upstairs. It's still there but you can't see it for now.'

Damaris understood about the room being out of her vision, but how that applied to her memories of Dave she wasn't sure.

'Honey, when something bad happens,' her father joined in, 'sometimes our mind protects us. Shuts that thing down, you know?'

'Uh-huh...' Damaris replied as she remembered her strange dreams. Perhaps if her mind was protecting her from something horrible she should let it.

Chapter 15

There were paparazzi in the prison car park. More as she drove through the village. And a scrum of them, elbowing their way in front of each other, waiting outside the long drive up to the big house. She was almost tempted to try and mow them down, but settled for driving past as if they didn't exist.

What a bunch of vultures. A whiff of human misery and there they were with their long lenses and desperate expressions: worried they might not get *that shot* before their competitors. During the good days she'd been on speaking terms with a few of them. She didn't want to encourage their worst excesses, but courtesy cost nothing, and giving a little of her time, on her terms, meant she was mostly left alone.

Now, even through the windscreen of her car she could sense a change in them. Judgement. No more smiles for Amelie Hart, darling of the media. Instead as they thrust their cameras forward they held a little of themselves back.

They were thinking she must have known. How could she not have? But they wouldn't know innocence if it lay in a manger surrounded by cattle and fairy lights. Everyone was guilty of something to them. It just took some digging and some flashlights to find out what it was, and if there was collateral damage then so be it.

As she negotiated the long, slow bend that brought the grand house into view a picture of Dave presented itself in her mind. The tension in his bearing. The white of his face. His words, 'Notice how you didn't say you loved me.'

She heard those words again with a lurch in her gut and a souring in her mouth. Did she love him?

Would they ever recover from this? He'd always doubt the

reason she stayed, if she did. So would she. She searched her mind and heart for the truth of her feelings for him, but came up numb. Nothing. There was too much noise to work it out.

She parked in front of her house, and pulled on the hand brake, wondering how she had managed to negotiate her car into the correct position successfully. Almost dreading going into the house on her own, she simultaneously craved the silence it offered. She could close the door on Dave's office and the mess the police had left there. Pretend that part of it never happened. Forget that the police had worked their way through her sanctuary, looking for evidence of horrible crimes.

Gathering her handbag to her, she climbed out of the car. Turning to face her front door she became aware that there were people near. To her right, a blonde woman wearing a navy suit, carrying an oversized handbag, her expression calculated to portray a mix of *won't take no for an answer* and *I'm sorry to trouble you*. Then she became aware of movement to her left. Damaris and her mother had just walked out of their door.

The journalist, for that was what Amelie assumed she was, inhaled sharply.

Amelie saw the little girl was desperate to speak to her, but she ignored the plea in her eyes. She just didn't have the energy to accommodate both her and Damaris's needs in that moment. Instead she focused on the girl's mother.

'You should be ashamed of yourself. What mother does this to their daughter?'

'What kind of woman lives with a freak?' Damaris's mother asked, her face in a twist of loathing.

'Miss Hart, what are you implying?' The journalist strode forward, sharp with the query.

'Go away,' Amelie told her. 'You're trespassing.' Then she unlocked her door, stepped inside and banged it shut behind her. There she fell into a slump at the foot of the stairs and gave in to her tears.

The letter box squeaked open and something dropped inside. A card fluttered onto the mat. Then a voice. 'We want to tell your story, Amelie. Give me a bell when you're ready.'

Amelie ignored her. In any case, what did that mean – tell her story? She probably meant what was it like shacking up with someone for years to find out they were a paedophile? The minute she tried to protest Dave's innocence the woman would likely yawn and turn off the voice recorder on her iPhone.

Her handbag began to vibrate. She stuck her hand in and pulled out her mobile. Bernard. Shit. She'd been ignoring him for weeks now; she should really talk to him.

'Hello, my sweet Amelie,' he said after she answered, his voice thick with sympathy.

She sagged a little with relief when she heard him, and felt a warming affection at his usual, overly dramatic greeting. It had always been one of the interesting things about him. Rumour was that he came from an upper-middle-class family and his mother had links to the aristocracy. A career had been laid out for him with Coutts, the bank to the royal family, but he'd eschewed that for acting. When that hadn't gone the way he wanted, he realised all of the networking skills he'd learned at private school could be put to good use as an agent. Whenever she'd asked him about the truth of this he'd wave his hand, make a dismissive sound and change the subject.

'How are you, dear?'

What could she say? 'Bloody awful.'

'I know.' Bernard sighed with the weight of his concern for her. A sound so heavy it was almost like he was suddenly asthmatic. 'And...' He paused.

'What?'

'I have been trying to get a hold of you for an age, Amelie.' A gentle admonishment. And she read something in his tone. This wasn't about Dave. *Whatever you need to say, just say it*, she thought. Although if Bernard was anything but supportive she didn't know how she would cope. He was always the one she could turn to. 'I can't say this over the phone. We simply must meet up,' he said.

Her stomach roiled. What the hell could he want to tell her?

'I've got half of the world's paparazzi on my doorstep, Bernard. Not a good time to leave the house. Just spit it out.'

A moment's pause. 'I can't. This must be said face to face.'

'Bernard, I won't be offended that this conversation happened over the phone. I can't leave here at the moment. Just tell me, please.'

There was a moment's pause before he replied. 'Did you catch a whiff of that story in the press recently about a bunch of celebrities who needed to stump up a lot of cash for a huge investment that went belly up?'

Amelie sat on the lower step feeling a note of relief. It was only about money.

'I've been distracted.' Pause. 'Go on...'

'Your liability in it is massive, my dear.' He took a deep breath and Amelie could hear a quaver in it. 'You're down to your last hundred and fifty grand.'

Amelie let that settle in her mind. 'All my...? How could...? How did that even happen?'

'Something about an unlimited liability for losses. And this thing lost big.'

'But...' Amelie was confused. Her face had been *everywhere* at one point. How could that not have made her a lot of money, and how could most of that money now be gone?

She had no memory of any of her money being in such an investment. To be fair, she left most of the financials to Bernard, despite living with an accountant – perhaps *because* she lived with an accountant, who over the years had continually told her she needed to take more notice. But who has the inclination, really?

Dave had said to her numerous times that he was concerned about how many people out there were truly financially illiterate, and she'd simply held a hand up to the issue. Now she was beginning to regret that attitude.

She had an image of her moving out of the home she'd come to love so much. Sure, outside, even in the courtyard, the world was now a nasty place, but here, with the doors, windows and curtains shut it was her little haven. Looking around the hall and through into the living room, she noted the little knick-knacks she'd carefully placed here and there. Her home was lovely. No way was she losing it. She felt her throat tighten and her eyes sting, and fought to tamp it down. She would not cry. She would *not* cry.

'There's nothing that can be done, I'm afraid. It's all legally binding. Don't pay? You get sued and the courts *will* find against you. Probably best to just bite that bullet.' He paused. 'Sorry, Amelie. With everything else you're going through ... But it was simply unavoidable. I had to tell you.'

'What are my options?' she asked, hearing the tremble in her voice. Could the shit get any deeper?

'Well, unless you want to go back to being poor, you need to get back to work.'

'What, like, acting?'

'No, in your local supermarket stacking shelves.' He tutted. 'Of course I mean acting, silly.'

'Will anyone have me? Are people still interested?'

'I get at least a couple of scripts for you every month, my darling.'

'You do?' Amelie was astonished, and felt an ember of hope flare in her mind. Some good news for a change. It was nice to be wanted. Even though she hadn't wanted to be wanted. And she shook her head at her own crazed logic. 'Why didn't you tell me?'

'You told me not to, remember?' He spoke the next sentence in a terrible impression of her accent. '"I don't want to know, Bernard. The movie world is over for me."'

'Yeah. Right. I remember that moment.' They were in the bar

at the Groucho Club in Soho, sipping G&Ts, studiously ignoring all the other famous faces in the room. The place was symptomatic of Amelie's confusion over her celebrity. She loved the feel of the place and how it didn't matter to anyone inside who she was, while at the same time despising the reason for its existence.

Bernard had been silenced, at first, by her statement. Then increasingly frustrated that she could feel so. 'But this is the big dream, dear. Do you realise how many people would give their right arm to be in your position?'

'Let them donate a limb then. I've had enough,' she'd said and felt the conviction of that statement in her bones.

Now there was a way back? Could she face all that again? Then with a spark of insight she realised the life had never really left her. She just had all of the attention without any of the work.

'How long would a hundred and fifty grand last me?' she asked, steeling herself.

'At the rate you spend? Three years? Four, max. If you get cheaper lodgings you could perhaps stretch that out to five or six.'

No way was she being forced out of her home, even if those arseholes still lived next door. She made herself ask the question. The answer might provide the motivation to get up off her backside and do something. 'Then what?'

'What skills do you have?'

'I worked in a call centre that one time,' she replied, half joking and praying it would never ever come to that.

'And as I remember you got fired for calling your boss a C-U-N...'

'Yeah, forget that.' She shuddered at the memory. 'What a horrible job that was.'

Amelie paused and thought of the other jobs she had over the years. Because of her chaotic childhood, thanks to her father, she hadn't bothered with education beyond secondary school. Then, after he died, she thought about moving to France to see what that kind of life might offer and make an attempt to acknowledge her roots. At least the weather would be better, but instead she moved down south to stay with a friend of her mother's and attained her degree in life on the streets of London. Her first job was on a market stall selling women's products. 'Trim your lady garden with one of these, sweetheart,' she remembers shouting at a scandalised matronly type, while wielding a pink pack of five razors. She graduated to working in pubs and clubs, and doing the odd piece of modelling. Which prompted her next question:

'Any modelling jobs out there?'

'There are. But they depend on you being Amelie Hart, movie star.'

Could she really do all that again? She loved getting into a role, and always felt like she was born to pretend that she was someone else, but it came with so much baggage. Baggage that she never really left behind, she heard a small voice in her mind say. *You're getting the rough without the smooth. Why not just dive back in?*

'Would anyone really want me?' she asked.

'Course they would, you're *the* Amelie Hart.'

Amelie read the pause before the response. There was something he wasn't saying.

'But...'

'You would have to distance yourself from Dave.'

'What?'

'According to Lisa you were going to give him the heave-ho anyway...' he said in a wheedling tone.

She cringed at the thought that she might even consider this, and ignored the fact that Bernard's comment meant her two friends were talking behind her back. 'Nope. I can't do it,' she said. 'You can't imagine what he's going through right now. I'm not going to make it even worse.'

'You want to get your life back on track, my dear? You're going to have to go Judas.'

Chapter 16

There was nothing to differentiate one day from the next. Wake up from a series of dreams that felt like one long terrifying chase, and stand emptying your bladder while wondering if the horrors of the night could be any worse than the unrelenting shame of each day.

When your door was unlocked, shuffle down to the end of the row of cells where breakfast was served. Cornflakes and semi-skimmed milk. Weetabix on a good day. Take the tray back to your cell. Close the door. Eat. Take as long as you can to clean the plate and plastic cutlery in your tiny sink. Lie back on your bed. Wait. Lunchtime. The same process: collect food, bring it back to the cell to eat it. Wait for the cell door to be opened up again for one hour of exercise, which consists of walking round a high-walled courtyard open to the skies. Apply once more to be allowed to use the gym. Then back to the cell to wait for dinner. And then the last wait of the day, for lights out.

When collecting his food, or going for his daily constitutional around the yard he never engaged with anyone else. He was in the sex-offender unit. Meaning all of the men around him, apart from the guards, were either rapists or child molesters. And they all made him feel sour to the depths of his stomach. He felt tainted just by being in their presence and often caught himself examining the faces of the guards, looking for hints of the strain that this must have on them.

Of course, being the 'celeb' inmate, many of them tried to get a conversation going with him. He rebutted all of them with a gruff 'fuck off'.

'Think you're special or something?' One young lad faced up to him, shoulders back, chin up, arms out.

Dave put his face close to the young man and laughed. Loudly, and for a good long minute. Then he turned and walked away.

'Boss.' He approached a guard standing just beyond the feeding station. 'I sent in a request to have a meeting with the governor.'

'The governor, is it?' It was the guard's turn to laugh.

'Aye, three times. And I haven't heard back.'

'You should send in a complaint to the I Don't Give a Shit Dot Com website.'

There was a resolution in the other man's face. He would give nothing away in this transaction. As far as he was concerned Dave was worse than scum.

Dave bit down on his lower lip in an effort to tamp down on his rising anger, and mumbling, 'Fuck you very much,' he returned to his cell.

That evening, Dave had a chance to use one of the public phones situated at the end of the hall. There were three of them, the one in the middle was missing a canopy and a receiver, making Dave wonder if some guy had gone crazy during a call home and battered one item with the other.

'When's the phone gaunnae get fixed?' someone shouted from the middle of the queue. Ironic laughter rang round the hall.

Eventually his turn came and he picked up a phone. He dialled, praying he'd got the number correct.

'Bain,' the man said.

'Dave Robbins here.'

'I know, Dave, they tell us ... Never mind. How can I help you? Am I not due a visit with you anyway, next week?'

'This can't wait.'

'How can I help?' The man was all business.

'I need to be in the general population. Failing that I need a word with the governor.'

'I'll see what I can do about the second request, Dave, but the first one would be suicide.'

'Don't care.' Dave hunched over the mouthpiece. 'I can't spend another day in among these...' He was aware his voice was coming out in a strangled whisper.

'I see.' Bain's voice softened with sympathy. 'I really don't think the remand hall, which is where they might put you, is an option. You would be in very real danger there. Perhaps,' he said as if thinking aloud, 'we can see about getting you a cell in the segregation wing.'

Dave didn't warm to the idea but nonetheless felt his legs all but sink with relief at the thought. 'That would be great, thank you.'

'Promising nothing. The Prison Service has been handling dangerous men for a long time and everything they do has a purpose. They won't just try to please us on a whim. I have to give them a good reason. Have you received any threats recently?'

Dave considered the febrile atmosphere every time he left his cell. The looks, the comments, the fists tight and poised as if to strike.

'Just the usual shite.'

Bain sighed. 'Leave it with me. In the meantime do nothing that's going to piss anyone off. Head down, understand?'

If you keyed the words 'civil servant' into your Google Images search, Dave was sure it would come up with a picture of the man in whose office he sat.

'I can't agree to every meeting that inmates request.' Callan McClymont, the governor of HMP Blackhill Prison, fixed the right cuff of his white shirt, which was jutting out from under the sleeve of his dark-blue suit. 'We're running at almost forty percent overcapacity at the moment so that would be lunacy.' He offered a smile that was all business. 'Having said that, you are...' he paused, as he thought of a suitable word; '...an interesting case, David. We've had a lot of high-profile people in my time as governor of this prison, but I don't think anyone has had the gossip machine churning out there ... or in here, for that matter ... to this degree. So I thought it best I make my acquaintance.' He sat back in his chair, head cocked to the left, and studied Dave for a long moment. 'I understand you want to be moved in to the general population?'

'Yes, please...' Dave wondered what the correct appellation might be, 'sir.'

'Why?'

'I'm a remand prisoner, sir, in with convicted sex offenders, sir.' Dave heard himself speak as if in the abstract. Too many sirs. And a hint of aggression. He needed to rein it in or he would get nowhere with this guy. 'Sorry,' he added. 'I don't know the correct way to behave in this place. With anyone.' He coughed to hide his discomfort and hated himself for that moment of weakness. 'Convicted sex offenders who are obsessed with me and my girlfriend. I can't wait to get out of my cell and then when I am, all I meet is these horrible men who're ... virtually pleasuring themselves in front of me at the thought of what they'd like to do with the woman I...' He stopped, aware that the man in front of him was wearing an expression that was as blank as an unplugged TV screen.

'Yours is a unique case, David. And we are in a difficult situation. There's a target on you, so remand would be dangerous. There's no room in the segregation unit, so the sex offenders' unit it is, I'm afraid. We've done the best we could do for you: given you a cell on your own.'

Dave examined that last sentence for irony.

'Are you aware of our listener programme?' McClymont asked.

'No,' said Dave while thinking about going back to that cell in among those other men. He couldn't help but give an involuntary shudder.

'These are trusted prisoners who perform a valuable service in the prison. We all need someone to talk to, yes? And these listeners, as the word suggests, provide a willing ear. I suggest you avail yourself of this service as soon as possible.' He stood up. Fixed an already neat line by tucking his shirt into the waistband of his trousers. 'This really is a volatile place, David. Part of my job is to keep a lid on that as much as possible, and if I were to put you in the hall with the other prisoners on remand everything would kick off. No matter how much you think you'd prefer it, your life would be at real risk.'

Chapter 17

Each day blended in to the last, and each morning Amelie woke up feeling the weight of Dave's incarceration and wondering if she was able to throw him to the wolves to save herself. Her only real breaks from the fever her life had now become were her moments of dreamless sleep, and long telephone conversations with Lisa.

Twice a week she made the trek to the prison, each time to be told that Dave didn't want to see her. After a couple of weeks a guard had taken pity on her and let her sit just out of sight of the reception area for half an hour before she went outside to face the photographers who seemed determined to chart her every movement.

The first few times she'd driven across the city to the prison it was like she was leading a cavalcade, but then the photographers realised where she was going and settled for a photo of her leaving her house and another leaving the prison. At each place they thrust their lenses in her face, looking to capture that one expression that would reveal the toll all of this was taking on her so they could sell it to the highest bidder. And she was determined, time after time, that they were getting nothing.

Zen, she told herself, she was Zen.

Most days, despite her best intentions, she opened the social-media apps on her phone to see what was happening in the world. And then, despite herself, she had a quick peek at her messages and mentions.

'Die, PaedoBitch' was one of the less cruel ones of late.

A meme that consisted of a still from one of her earlier movies, showing her as a young mum holding her daughter, with a speech bubble that read 'Just warming her up for the boyfriend' was trending.

'If you ever have kids, hope another paedo fucks them' had over a thousand likes.

With a shudder she closed down her phone and threw it on to the sofa beside her.

Although it was difficult Amelie recognised the importance of trying to look beyond all of this and to think about what might come next. Her cash wouldn't last forever so she would need to start working again. Could she do another movie?

The day after her last conversation with Bernard, three scripts had arrived. Four the day after. They had been coming in sporadically ever since, but she had let them pile up.

Bernard had clearly been working his contacts, and every now and again he would phone her to check she'd received the latest proposal.

'They're not going to wait around forever, love,' he'd chided. 'You might not like it but your name has cachet ... for the moment.' His pause was calculated to remind her what the personal cost to her must be. 'Anything in there that you fancy?'

'Not really.'

'You haven't looked at any of them, have you?'

She said nothing.

'I have other actors on my books who would die for these kind of roles.'

'Pass them on, then.'

'Don't be a child,' he scolded and in her mind she saw that expression he favoured for his more unruly clients. Then his tone softened. 'We've had some interview requests ... BBC, ITV, CNN...' He paused and she sensed he was about to unleash his ace. 'Oprah.'

Despite herself, she felt her chest lighten at the prospect. She damped it down. 'Piss off.'

'Her people got in touch this morning. They're offering to fly you out to her ranch where she'll spend a couple of days talking to you, finding out how tough it is...'

'...Living with a paedo.'

'Living in a world that has an intense need to know what it's like to be you. She's a powerful and compassionate woman, Amelie, who just wants to know the truth.'

'Truth, my arse.'

'Who knows more than her what it's like to live with the trashy media detailing her every move? She sees you as the twenty-first-century Lady Di...'

'I'm not royalty and I'm not—'

'You're a beautiful woman who was being used as a shield.'

Amelie heard the pitch Oprah's researchers would have used and recoiled.

'For pity's sake, Bernard, that's shit and you know it. I wasn't a shield. Dave never harmed anyone in his life.' She paused and allowed the thought to enter her head. Teasing it out a little, she saw herself on a cushioned seat under a tree. Oprah leaning towards her, tapping her on the arm in a 'it's just us girls' gesture. She shook her head hard. 'It would be trial by public opinion before this even gets to court.'

'That's what's happening anyway, honey.'

Of course it was.

'And what's the verdict so far?'

'You don't want to know.'

'Oh, someone's on the other line,' she lied. 'Got to go.' She ended the call and threw her mobile onto the sofa beside her.

When was this ever going to end? She could feel the emotion bubbling up, but she refused to give in to it. She was done crying. She was done being the world's worst bitch.

She pulled one of the large cushions over, pressed her face into it and started to scream. Once she was out of breath and her throat was hoarse she could hear Lisa's voice in her head.

Better?

Not even close.

She reached for the TV remote and switched it on in an

attempt to distract herself. The screen flashed into life, and there she saw a male and female host sitting at one end of a large table. Her name was mentioned.

What the...?

Part of her mind searched for context, another screamed at her to press the red button, while the rubbernecker part of her psyche held everything still. She needed to know.

The camera panned to a young woman at the other end of the table. Blonde hair cut in a short bob that was as even and straight as her teeth. The woman was wearing a black turtleneck sweater with a large, silver, peace-sign pendant over her chest.

Amelie was aware of her mouth dropping open. She didn't need to read the tag at the bottom of the screen to recognise Vanessa Court, a young actress she'd shared one scene with in her big movie, *The Story So Far*.

'Tell us about your time working with Amelie Hart,' the male host asked. 'Were you friends?'

'Initially, we really hit it off, like, massively,' Vanessa breathed. Then the screen cut to an Instagram post of the two of them, big smiles, heads together, the sun a halo behind their heads, and with the hashtag #besties. 'But it soon, like...' Vanessa paused and adopted an expression that was designed to read, *I'm trying to be kind here*. 'She wouldn't talk to me on set ... wouldn't return my calls.'

'Because you were a bloody egotistical nut job,' Amelie screamed at the set. She finally got her thumb to work and she turned the TV off.

Her phone rang. It was Lisa.

'I hope you're not watching Breakfast TV?'

'I caught about a minute of it,' Amelie answered.

'What in the actual hell is going on with her?' Lisa said. 'Besties? And a black turtleneck? When did you ever see Vanessa wear anything that didn't show off her tits? Anyone who knows her will see what she's wearing and know she's lying through her shiny little veneers.'

Amelia couldn't help herself. She turned the TV back on.

It opened with a moment from the movie. It was from their one scene together. Sharing a hug. The camera cut to Vanessa's face, which was arranged in a hopeful expression. Then it moved to Amelie's face. She, in contrast, looked like she couldn't wait to get away from this woman.

'Oh, for crying out loud,' Amelie shouted, aware how that might present to the viewing audience. 'That was the character in a bloody movie.'

'Have you turned it back on?' Lisa demanded in her ear.

'When Miss Hart turned her back on the movie industry, the whole world thought she had gone mad. She was on the brink of amazing things. A follow-up that was going to earn millions. More and more lucrative deals with fashion and perfume brands … Did she talk her retirement over with you?' the female host asked.

Amelie recalled a short conversation with Vanessa while they were both at a charity awards dinner. It was the last thing Amelie wanted to do but it was for breast-cancer awareness. Her mother had died from the disease so she felt she had to attend.

'I told her she was nuts,' Vanessa replied to the interviewer.

Which was true. She had.

'Her mother had just died a few months earlier after a long battle with breast cancer,' Vanessa continued. 'And I told her that to make such a massive decision during, like, such a difficult time might turn out to be a mistake.'

Up to that point Amelie had told none of her acting colleagues about her mother's illness. Why she had confided in this conniving bitch in the ladies at the awards ceremony, was beyond her. The wine, it could only have been the wine.

Vanessa's interviewers looked sympathetic to this for just a moment, but then, as if he realised this wasn't the agenda, the male host asked, 'Did you ever meet David Robbins, the paedophile?'

'Alleged paedophile,' the female host corrected; an eloquently raised right eyebrow suggested she believed it was only time before the allegation turned into a conviction.

'Just once at another charity affair. I didn't like him.' Vanessa made a face.

'As far as I could see you were thrusting your boobs into his face every time he came near you,' Amelie shouted.

'Turn it off,' Lisa said.

'Apologies to our viewers.' The camera focused on the TV hosts. The man was speaking, one hand pressed to his left ear as if listening to a message from the team in the background. 'This is a live case, and we have to cut that conversation off there.'

His expression was apologetic, but his colleague was wearing a smile of pleasure. They'd got something on live television that people would be talking about for weeks.

Chapter 18

As soon as Damaris got in from school she ran all the way up to her bedroom, slammed the door shut behind her and fell onto her bed.

Ever since ... whatever happened, happened, all the teachers at her school had been acting weird. It was a relief to get away from their assessing eyes.

'Everything fine there, Damaris?'

'Anything we can get you, Damaris?'

'Anytime you need to talk, Damaris, come and see me, eh?' That was the head, in one sentence effectively tripling the number of words she'd spoken to Damaris all the time she'd been at the school.

After Dave moved out – she couldn't even say the words 'went to jail' in her head – her mum had kept her off school for a couple of weeks. But then Damaris had begged to be allowed to go back. At first it was cool, to be left at home to do what she wanted: watching movies all day, eating her favourite snacks at every meal. But, surprisingly, that grew boring and she wanted to be back with her friends, talking about the latest celebs, gossiping about the other girls – you know, normal life.

'Honey...' A knock at her bedroom door.

'What, Dad?'

'Can I come in?' he asked as he opened the door.

'Already are,' Damaris mumbled and lay back on her bed, head on the pillow, hands clasped over her stomach.

She watched as her father padded across the carpet and sat on the bed beside her.

'How was school today?' he asked.

'Fine.'

'Speak to any of the girls? What did you get up to?'

'Nothing.'

'What did you learn?'

'Nothing.'

'You were all day in school and you learned nothing? What subjects was the teacher covering?'

Damaris assessed her father, his hands clasped before him, the way he tilted his head in her direction. Why was he being so awkward with her? Why was everyone so awkward with her?

'Just the usual boring stuff.'

'Like what?'

'Nothing really.'

Her father rested a hand on her forearm. She felt the weight of it, solid and reassuring, and she wanted nothing more than to jump up off the bed and into his arms for a good long hug. That's what she always used to do, but now it felt different. As if it might not be welcome. As if there was something wrong with her now.

Since...

'You know you can talk to me,' her dad said, his face long. He needed a shave. And to take off his tie and unfasten that top button that way he always did when he came back from work.

'And you can talk to me, Dad.'

At that he managed a chuckle, and gripped her arm a little tighter. Gave it a shoogle. But his smile was a weak, sad thing. A clown in half make-up.

'Are we going to be okay, Dad?' A remembered conversation jumped into her head, from where she couldn't remember. 'We're not going to lose our house, are we?'

'Whatever makes you ask that, D? Of course we're not going to lose our house.' He twisted in his seating position so that he was fully facing her. 'Where on earth did you get that idea from?'

Something told Damaris to make something up, and fast; she didn't want him to know she'd been eavesdropping.

'One of the boys at school. His dad ... and something ... and anyway, he lost his house and had to move in with his granddad.'

'Oh man, can you imagine moving in with your grandfather?'

Damaris loved her granddad and thought this was a strange thing to say, but sensing this was not a time to debate the issue she just smiled.

Dad turned away for a moment as if there was something he wanted to say but wasn't quite sure how to.

'I just wanted to make sure you were ... alright,' he managed eventually.

Damaris loved it when Dad used to lie on the bed beside her, both of them on their backs, staring at the ceiling, the weight of him at her side making her roll towards him slightly. Occasionally during their aimless chat he'd nudge her foot with the side of his leg, or he'd push at her gently with an elbow, then they'd turn to each other and share a smile.

More than anything she wanted that to happen.

That was normal, but it felt like her life would never get back to normal ever again.

Chapter 19

The small TV in his cell was on pretty much twenty-four hours a day. It was the only way he could hope to dim the sounds in his head. Even then he could watch several hours of shit daytime television and lose track of who was getting what trinket at auction, how many letters there were in the word 'countdown', and who preferred home or away for their future living.

He'd tried, and failed, to meditate; and you could only do so many press-ups and sit-ups, so despite the many ways he attempted to distract himself, his mind ran on a loop: How could this happen to him? How could Damaris accuse him of this? Why would *anyone* believe it?

He had wondered about throwing himself down the stairs on the way to rec, but thought he'd probably only break an arm or something. Then he'd tried to choke on a piece of fish at dinner, fantasising as he did so about all the people who would queue up to apologise at his funeral for not believing in him. Of course it failed. How could you force yourself to choke? All he ended up doing was bringing up his dinner and giving himself a sore throat.

And he hated himself for succumbing to suicidal ideation. He was better than that. He would see this out and show himself to be the man of character he believed he was.

Thoughts of Amelie were bittersweet. They had such a good time together and he had so many good memories, but while he still loved her he was clear-sighted enough to notice her moods and read that their relationship had soured.

In the weeks leading up to the incident he had wasted a lot of energy trying to convince himself that everything would turn out okay. That all Amelie needed to do to return to a sense of herself was go back to work.

'You didn't end your career on your own terms,' he had argued.

'What do you mean?' Her words were clipped with a defensive tone.

'Sorry, sweetheart, I don't mean to—'

'What do you mean?'

'It was your dream, yeah?'

A nod as she crossed her arms.

'The non-stop online abuse, the letters from that freak, all the catty comments from TV hosts, and your mum dying...' As Dave recounted the words he also remembered the trepidation he was feeling at the time. Amelie wouldn't want to hear this, but he felt he had to say what was on his mind. 'That was a pretty potent combination of events, and it all kind of got jumbled in your head.'

'Oh, give me peace.' She lay back on the sofa. Examined her nails. 'Those letters were awful, to be fair.' A shadow cut the light in her eyes, her skin paled to the colour of putty and it made Dave wonder if there was more to this than she was telling him. What else had happened to her?

The letters arrived every day for months. At least ten pages, hand written in purple ink, on A4 lined paper, all of them detailing what sex acts the writer would like to do to her.

'He must have spent all day, every day writing them.'

Amelie shuddered.

'And then your mum died.'

'Don't, Dave,' she warned.

'Can't you see? You have this massive sense of disconnection or something...' *And it feels like I'm bearing the brunt of it*, he wanted to add.

'I do not.'

'And it comes from that big stew of horribleness.'

'Sounds like our school meals.' Amelie tried to laugh it off.

'I think you should think about going back to work.'

She'd looked at him for a long moment, shook her head and stood up. 'I could murder a coffee. Want something?'

Conversation over.

Twelve o'clock. Lunch. His stomach rumbled and he groaned at the thought that he was already being conditioned to jail time. His cell door opened, but he waited for a moment before going out, bracing himself against the thought of being back among his fellow prisoners. Or *beasts* as the rest of the prison population termed them.

His stomach rumbled again, and thinking, *Let's get this over with*, he stood up, stepped out, and made for the pantry at the end of the section.

As he passed one cell door he noticed the inhabitant was standing at the doorway as if frozen. The man was hunched over at the waist, fingertips trailing the floor like a life-size puppet waiting to be reanimated.

Unsure what to do, Dave paused. Instinctively he reached out and touched the man on the shoulder, then realising what he had just done he retrieved his hand, wiped it on the side of his trousers and asked, 'Need a hand?'

Nothing.

He heard a scuff of feet behind him and then a chuckle. 'He's wasted, mate. Totally on the spice.' Dave turned to see another prisoner, his face filled with glee at the thought of this other guy's predicament. 'He'll be fucking ruined, mate, once he comes aff it.' He chuckled again. 'What a roaster.' And continued down the corridor to be served his lunch.

The callousness of the other man's attitude set Dave back. Better get used to it, he thought. Then he thrust his hands deep into his pockets, as if he was pushing down his urge to help a fellow human being ever again, and made his way down to the pantry.

Waiting in the queue there, he felt someone come close. Too close. The moist heat of their breath on his neck. The man spoke, his voice calculated so that no one else would hear. 'Saw your missus on telly this morning. Fucking beautiful, by the way. Did she know you were a beast?'

Dave stepped back, standing on the other man's foot. Hard. And was rewarded with a grunt of pain. According to the gossip this guy was a serial rapist, with at least six victims.

'Ya big prick. Ah'll fuckin' have you.' The man was on one knee, face turned up to Dave, expression in a snarl as he nursed his sore foot.

'Everything alright there, Mark?' A guard moved closer.

'Aye, boss,' Mark replied as he got to his feet. He shot Dave a look that promised retribution. Dave stared him down, everything clenched, and it was all he could do not to launch himself at the man and give him the kicking of his life.

'What about you, Dave? Cos I don't want to have to remove TVs from anybody's cells...'

'Hunky dory, boss,' replied Dave, forcing himself to relax. 'This guy was just asking how to join my girlfriend's fan club.' He spoke just loudly enough for everyone around him to hear. 'Think he got the message.' Then he gathered his food from the passman and ignoring a tremble of adrenaline in his hands, he walked back to his cell.

The attention from his fellow inmates was ramping up. He'd better brace himself, because the next time it would surely involve much more than harsh words.

Chapter 20

Damaris ran up to her attic bedroom, jumped on her bed and leaned over the far end to pluck out the notebook she kept hidden under the mattress there. She loved the thing, not because it was a genuine movie star who bought it for her last birthday, but because it was covered in dark-blue leather, the pages were lined and the paper had a nice heavy feel to it when you turned them; and it smelled gorgeous.

She held it to her nose to confirm that was still the case and breathed in.

So nice.

Then she found the pen that came with it – dark blue to match, with a tiny, pink voile tutu on the end – and thought about everything she needed to write down about that night's sleepover.

All the girls were coming – Vanda, Louise, Helen, Simone, and Jo – and she was so excited. It was so great that something nice was happening. In careful script she wrote down each girl's full name on a separate line and then beside their name what she knew were their favourite snacks.

Because you couldn't have a sleepover without snacks.

That was the law, right?

Vanda and Jo loved Haribo. Simone loved chocolate. Well, everybody loved chocolate. And everybody loved cheese and onion Pringles.

Pringles, chocolate, and Pepsi. Surely Dad could remember that much when he went out later for the shopping. It was a bit of a family joke that whenever he went to the supermarket he would forget something, even when it was written down for him. Three items would surely be okay. Four, with added Haribo. Everything was better with added Haribo.

Food taken care of, Damaris tucked her notebook back in its place and headed over to the stack of DVDs at the side of her TV, where she ran a finger down the spines, wondering which ones to place at the top, and would therefore be more likely to be chosen. Which really wasn't much of a decision. It had been a while since she'd watched any of the *Twilight* movies, and surely everyone would want to get back in to the Bella, Edward and Jacob mood?

Next, she opened the blanket box at the end of her bed and pulled out two quilts and a sleeping bag. One of the girls – when they eventually went to sleep that was – could share the bed with her and the other three could pick from the other bedding and camp out on the floor.

That morning, before he'd gone out to work, her dad had a word with her about her friends coming over. It had never happened before and they usually ended up at Helen or Simone's houses, and every time Damaris had pleaded with her parents for her to take a turn they'd refused.

Dad needs his sleep, was the usual response, *and doesn't want an army of girls on the floor above him giggling and gossiping into the next morning.*

But it was Dad who said yes. Damaris wasn't dumb, she knew why he'd caved this time. Still, if he wanted to make it up to her for what had happened with Dave – whatever that was; she still didn't have it worked out in her mind – she was more than happy to take advantage of the distraction.

'Midnight,' Dad said. 'The TV goes off at midnight and you all go to sleep, right?'

Damaris nodded her reply and smiled full beam while thinking, yeah, right, last time at Simone's house they'd still been talking when the sun came up, and feeling quite pleased with themselves that they'd been grown up enough to last the full night.

She heard her mother's tread on the carpet outside her bedroom. The door opened.

'D,' her mum said from the open doorway, and Damaris heard

an *uh-oh* in her head. Mum only ever used that short version of her name when something was wrong. 'D, honey, I've just had a call from Vanda's mum.' She waggled her left hand with the phone still in it, by way of evidence. 'Vanda and Louise can't come tonight. They've got this sickness thing that's going around.'

Damaris felt her chest constrict with disappointment.

'Helen's mum phoned just before that to say they had surprise visitors arriving from America so she wouldn't be here...' Her mother's face slumped with commiseration. 'I'm so sorry, honey...'

Her phone rang. She looked at the screen and mumbled, 'Don't recognise this number.' She answered. 'Hello?'

Damaris could hear someone – a female someone – on the other end, but not what they were saying. Judging by how her mother's face tightened it wasn't good. Then her mother mouthed the words, 'Jo's mum.' And judging by her expression this was another cancellation.

Damaris felt her bottom lip tremble. She sucked it in behind her top teeth. She refused to allow herself to cry.

Her mum closed the connection on her phone and looked as if she was about to throw the thing away. 'I think you've worked out who that was.' Her eyes narrowed with irritation.

Damaris nodded.

'At least Jo's mum had the decency not to try and make up some kind of crappy excuse.'

Damaris sat down on her bed and thought about tearing the page she'd just written out of her notebook and scoring through the names and treats with her heaviest pen.

The bed gave a little as her mother sat down beside her.

'Don't you worry about those little tramps,' her mother said while putting an arm over her shoulder. 'All you need is me, and we girls will have a lovely night together.' Her voice grew lighter and her smile brighter and Damaris read that it was coming at a cost. 'We can do our nails, catch up on all the gossip, eat lots of cake ... and we can watch *Twilight* as many times as you want, okay?'

Damaris knew this was an empty promise. Her mother would watch five minutes of the movie, moaning about how unrealistic the whole thing was the entire time, and then leave the room saying she was just going to fill up her glass, only returning when she heard the movie theme tune coming in at the end.

Nonetheless, playing the role she was given, Damaris did her very best to swallow her disappointment and gave her mother her best smile.

'Yeah, Mum, that will be fab.'

Her mother patted her hand and then got to her feet. She crossed her arms.

'You've been so brave, honey, after everything...' She wiped a tear from the corner of her eye. 'And as for those little brats, wait till I see—'

'Please, Mum, don't say anything,' Damaris said. School was bad enough these days with everyone staring at her as if she had some strange disease.

'Don't worry, honey. I'll say nothing. And anyway it's the mothers' faults,' she said as she walked out of the room. Her mobile rang. She answered.

'Hey, honey.'

Damaris guessed it was her father and that he'd forgotten what he was to buy at the supermarket.

'Don't bother,' her mother said as she continued out onto the landing. 'It's off.'

Damaris got to her feet and silently followed.

'I've been getting phone calls all bloody afternoon. One after another they've dropped out,' her mother continued.

Mum listened, nodding her head as Dad spoke.

'I know, honey. Next time I see them I'll be giving them a piece of my mind.' Every word was clipped with anger. 'You'd think it was bloody catching.'

When her mother had gone, Damaris brought her notebook back out from its resting place and scored out all her writing, noticing that as her teardrops fell onto the paper they were doing as much damage to her friends' names as the ink.

Chapter 21

Amelie was in the car and almost at the shopping centre before she wondered if it might be better if she was in disguise. For a moment she considered taking the next motorway exit and going home to change.

'To hell with it,' she said out loud. People could take her as she was. Which was probably a mistake given the recent interview on television.

Lisa did her very best to mitigate the damage, speaking to every journalist she could find, but the damage was done, and as far as Amelie could see every media outlet on the planet was showing, over and over again, the moment when Vanessa Court said she felt uncomfortable around Dave.

Which, ironically was true. He was a good man who'd never harm a child, but that was not the way the world saw him now, of course. She gripped the steering wheel. If she ever came across that woman again she'd find it difficult to keep her hands to herself.

She heard the sound of a slap in her imagination, felt sudden heat in the palm of her hand and sat for a moment in satisfaction. A car horn sounded behind her. She looked in her mirror to see an angry driver behind her, gesticulating.

Distracted by her imagined moment of revenge she'd taken her foot off the accelerator. Feeling her face warm up, she waved an apology at the guy and re-engaged her driving brain.

At Waitrose she found a space and parked. Before she climbed out of the car she scanned the space around her for possible danger. Another bad habit she thought she'd lost. Few cars, a few people here and there. Most of them elderly as far as she could tell.

Good. She breathed out her relief. It should be safe.

Inside, she collected a basket and quickly went around the usual food stands, gathering her usual items. No one bothered her, but she did notice a couple of double-takes.

As she approached the line of tills she judged which one had the fewest people queueing and moved in that direction. Out of the side of her vision she saw a couple heading towards her. Thinking they were heading to the same queue, she slowed her pace to allow them in before her and turned her face to them in anticipation of accepting their thanks.

They were both white-haired, slim, well dressed and walking with a purpose that was almost military.

'You should be ashamed of yourself,' the man said.

'Bitch,' the woman said. And spat in her face.

Chapter 22

Dave was walking from E Hall to the communications hub and the library. For the first section of the walk, as always, he was acutely aware of the industrial nature of this part of the criminal justice system. Concrete walkways, leading past a group of massive, warehouse-like buildings, the sandstone, laid by the Victorians, stained to a sullen brown by more than a hundred years of city pollution. As he walked he noted the lines of small, barred windows and dark-slated roofs topped by rows of tall chimneys. Beyond them the sky was painted a uniform grey, like a giant sheet of aluminium, as if nature had provided a roof to the complex, ensuring nothing within could ever reach the outside.

The gloom of his thoughts brought his attention back down to the ground, and he looked at the potted plants dotted about everywhere. Red and yellow blooms hung from walls and squatted in large pots at the side of the path, like garish paint on the face of an overworked prostitute.

His walk then took him through a space in the wall into a newer part of the prison compound and open air for about thirty strides before he reached the building that housed the library.

Those few minutes were a welcome break for Dave, regardless of the weather. Through the cold and wet of the spring, and the warm and wet of the summer, it was the only way he could tell the passing of the seasons – he'd been brought here in early April and it was now well into August.

Waiting for a guard to unlock the door and usher him into the library he thought about his recent chat with Graeme Corden, one of the listeners recommended by the governor.

Graeme entered his cell with a broad smile. His head was as

bare as his chin, and he looked like he regularly managed to wangle extra time in the gym.

'Awright, mate,' he said.

Dave was on his bed, cross-legged, back against the other wall, wondering how this was going to work.

'We can chat, or I can just sit here quietly and keep you company for a wee while...' Graeme said.

Dave crossed his arms.

'How long you been in now, mate?' Graeme asked.

'Twenty weeks, four days and nine hours.'

'But who's counting, eh?' Graeme laughed. 'You're on remand, aye? Any word on your court date?'

'My lawyer's due in at the end of the week. I'm hoping he's got news on that score. What about you? How long have you done?'

'Four years, eight months, four days and nine hours.' Graeme cocked his head to the side. 'Actually I haven't done a proper count, but it is four years and eight months. I just added the rest in to match what you said.'

'Much longer to go?'

'Four months.'

Dave assessed the other man, wondering what he was in for.

'Rape,' Graeme said. 'It's what we're all wonderin', eh? What the other guy's in for, so I just tell folk.' There was a weight to his words, a shadow behind his eyes, and a contrite line to his mouth as he spoke. He was stating a fact he was deeply ashamed of. 'Not making excuses, like, but I was an angry young guy. So fucking angry. Both parents were on the smack. In and out of the jail all my life. I got into a right bad place and hurt somebody that deserved so much more from me.'

Dave said nothing, simply allowing the silence that followed Graeme's words to unfold.

'What made you ask to join the listener programme?' Dave asked eventually.

'Gets you out of your cell, eh?' Graeme replied, but Dave could see he was holding back.

'I'm thinking there's more to it than that,' he said.

Graeme uncrossed his arms and put his hands in his pockets. He looked up from the ground and into Dave's eyes. 'I'll never be able to make it up to that lassie. She'll be hurt by what I done for the rest of her life, but maybe I can help other people, you know?'

Dave heard the truth in the other man's words, but he also read the tactic. If he opened up, it might encourage Dave to do the same.

'How about you, mate?' Graeme asked. 'I'm supposed to be doing the listenin', no' the talkin'.' Graeme leaned forward from his perch. 'How are you doin'? How are you gettin' through your days?'

'Books help.' Dave inclined his head to the novel that sat just inches from Graeme.

He picked it up. '*Theory of War*,' he read, 'by Joan Brady. What's this aboot?' He pressed a thumb against the side of the book, flicking through it and the sound of unspooling paper filled the cell. 'The pages are going yellow, must be an old book.'

'Came out in the nineties. The author's grandfather was sold as a slave in America after the Civil War. But he was white.'

'That happened?'

'Apparently.'

'Wow. Every day's a school day. What made you pick this one up?'

'Dunno.' Dave gave a little shrug. 'The slavery thing, maybe? Remind myself there are folk worse off than me.'

'I hear you, mate.'

Silence.

'How are you, mate, really?'

Dave thought about the anger held tight in his gut. His bewilderment at the system, the police, the court, his fellow prisoners, Damaris's parents, Damaris, himself for giving her any attention at all. He felt a sense of complete and utter helplessness weigh down his stomach, work into his chest, drying the air in his lungs, stifling the muscles of his throat. He coughed, preparing to speak, hoping that his voice wouldn't be croaked, and cloaked in emotion.

'Putting one foot in front of the other, mate. Just putting one foot in front of the other.'

As day slumped into night, and noise around the prison block heaved almost to a halt, Dave lay on his bunk, turned to face the wall and pulled his knees up into the foetal position. Like most nights Damaris's little face popped into his mind as if it had taken up residence behind his eyelids.

How could people think he would hurt her?

And again, like most nights, he ran through his experiences with the opposite sex, wondering what he could learn. Where he could have been better. There was Sandra McGregor in the third year at school, her breasts already like pillows, attracting attention and bullying comments from all the boys, and a few of the girls. Page Three McGregor was her nickname. Face a furious red, she'd simply stare at the ground when cruel comments were hurled at her and walk past as quickly as she could. In the few, rare, quiet moments he had with her she showed she had a quick mind, an abundancy of wit and a ready smile, and yet he'd joined in when the name calling started, a realisation that now had his face burn. Whatever happened to her? Last he'd spoken to her she was going to study to be a doctor. He hoped she'd made it and that men were less concerned with how she filled her tops than how she used her knowledge.

And Carole Carver, a girl he occasionally slept with after a few beers at the rugby club. He didn't call in between shags to see how she was, but then he'd turn on the charm when he was pissed after a night out with the boys. Whatever happened to her? Had she found a partner who treated her with respect? How did she now view her time with him?

Then there was Amelie. Was he always his best self with her? He thought about those last few months and how, sensing her retreat from him, he'd tried to build his own emotional moat as protection, but encroached upon her space now and again to test where he was with her.

The couple of times he cajoled his way past her 'no' until she relented with a sigh and a reluctant 'okay'. His face heated with shame at the memory of the perfunctory couplings that followed; his forehead burrowed into the pillow at her shoulder until that last, hurried, quivering breath.

Jesus. He felt shame bubble in his veins until it lay over his mind and heart and soul like a tombstone slab.

He was better than that.

He was a good guy, wasn't he?

Chapter 23

Damaris knew this was serious. Both Mum and Dad were at the table, either side of her, both of them had their hands clasped in front of them and both of them were showing their worried faces.

'Is Dave going to be okay?' she asked.

'Of course he is,' said Mum.

'Don't worry about him,' snapped Dad. Damaris caught the warning look her mum sent to him. In response he breathed out, squeezed his eyes shut and rubbed at his head. 'Sorry, wee love,' he said as he leaned towards her. 'Let's go through this one more time.'

'Daaaad.' As she said this part of her mind was assessing her father. He'd changed since all this happened. His face looked grey and his clothes were hanging on him now. Grown-ups lost weight when they were worried about stuff, didn't they? She didn't want her dad to worry.

'Just once more,' Mum said. 'You're giving evidence next week. And this guy has to go to jail for what he did to you.'

Damaris leaned back in her chair and crossed her arms. She just wanted to go up to her room and make plans for school going back next week. Holidays were boring when you were stuck at home all day and your parents worked and none of your friends were allowed to come and play with you.

She liked all the stuff that came with her parents working: the two, sometimes three holidays a year; Dad's sports car was sweet; and her friend Jo said living in this place must cost a bomb. But sometimes it would be nice if they had more time for her.

Maybe once this lawyers' meeting she had next week was over then her friends would be allowed to come over. Maybe when they were all back at school it would be back to the way it was before.

'So, remind me what happens at this thing next week?' Dad asked her mum. Damaris knew he knew. She also knew this was really for her benefit.

'We'll both be there, honey,' Mum said in that slow and deliberate tone that she used sometimes. When she spoke like that it really annoyed Damaris. She wasn't five years old. 'Two people will ask questions about what happened that day, the day the police came for Dave. And any other days he might have been...' she paused while she searched for the right word; '...tricky with you.' Her smile at this point was supposed to be reassuring, Damaris thought, but it came across as if Mum was trying to pretend her stomach wasn't sore.

'You were saying ... two people?' Dad pressed her along.

'And we'll both be there...'

Damaris chewed at the nail of her left thumb.

'And there will be someone, a commissioner or something, like a judge kind of person who'll be overseeing things.'

'And there will be a camera there so people in the court can see and hear it all,' Dad finished.

That was the bit Damaris wasn't looking forward to. A camera. That would be weird.

'Once you start talking you'll completely forget it's there,' said Dad as if he'd read her mind.

'And we'll both be there,' said Mum again, and Damaris wondered whose benefit that was for: Damaris or herself.

'If you just run over one more time what happened that day, for us, pet.'

'Daa-aad,' Damaris protested. 'I've gone over it, like, a million times.'

'Then this will be a million and one.'

'No, I'm not doing it,' she shouted. 'And you can't make me.' She ran out of the room.

'Let her go,' she heard Dad say. 'The wee soul needs a break.'

She ran up to her room, dived onto her bed and covered her

head with a pillow. This was all so horrible. Going through all this stuff. Where Dave had touched her. Knowing this was important to her parents and trying to remember everything was so hard. Every time they brought it up she just wanted to sleep.

Sometime later, there was a knock on her door.

'C'mon, D, darling,' her mum said. 'We'll go over it one more time and that'll do okay?' She paused. 'Please?'

Back down in the living room Damaris ran through the events of the day as she now remembered them.

'Where did he touch you?' Mum asked. Dad shrunk a little as she did so.

Damaris pointed to her lap.

'When they ask you about that, can you hold yourself as if you need a pee?'

'Mum, I'm not a baby.'

'I know that, sweetie. A visual will help them understand better, okay?'

'Okay.'

'And don't say it like that either,' Dad said.

'Like what?'

'Like you're fed up.'

'Yeah,' said Mum. 'You have to say it like you mean it.'

'And remember the Haribos,' Dad said. 'That Dave said next time he'll have a giant bag of Haribos for you.'

'I'm worried there's too much to remember, honey.'

'That's a strong detail,' Dad replied over the top of her head.

'And if you feel like crying don't hold it in, honey,' Mum said to her.

Damaris looked from one parent to the next, imagined a room that might be like a classroom, with her parents either side of her, three other grown-ups in the room and a camera pointed at her. She didn't think she'd have any problems crying.

There was a knock at the door. Her mother went to answer it, but not before she patted Damaris on the back of the hand.

A voice sounded from the door when her mother opened it. Deep and loud and full of swagger.

'Awright, sis. Long time no see.' It was her uncle Cammy. Dad's least favourite relative from her mum's side of the family. They all pretended they got on fine, but Damaris could see her parents becoming tense whenever he came around.

'To what do we owe this pleasure?'

'You gaunnae let me in, sis? Or do I have to stand here and let all your neighbours know your business?'

Damaris heard the creak as the door opened more widely, and then the heavy footsteps of her uncle as he moved up the hall. He entered the kitchen and, arms wide, gave Damaris a huge smile.

'How's my favourite niece?' he boomed.

'I'm your only niece, Uncle Cammy,' Damaris said before walking across the room and into the offered hug. She couldn't help but be cheered a little by Cammy's big personality. He was never serious and always had something tucked away in a pocket for her.

She stepped back and assessed the large bag he was carrying in his left hand.

Cammy laughed. 'Didnae take you long to spot that.' He handed it to her. 'A little something for my wee doll. I know it was just out at the pictures a few weeks ago, but I managed to get you a cheeky copy.'

Damaris pulled out the bigger box first, and saw it was a pair of white Converse trainers with pink piping. 'Wow, the girls are going to be *so* jealous.'

'See anything else in the bag you fancy?' Cammy asked.

She plucked out a DVD and let out a little cheer when she saw the actors on the cover. 'Excellent. Divergent. Thank you, Uncle Cammy.' She held up the small case, and then looked at her mum. 'Can I watch it now, please, Mum?'

'Have you done all your homework?' her mother asked, while wearing that smile Damaris had come to know over the last few months. The one that was tinged with relief that her daughter was happy.

As she turned to run up the stairs to her bedroom, Cammy reined her in.

'Here, don't be putting that on just yet. I want to watch it with you.'

'Since when were you into watching kids' movies,' Roger asked.

'I'm more into hanging out with my favourite niece,' Cammy replied as he sent Damaris a wink.

'Only niece, Uncle Cammy,' Damaris repeated.

'Whatever,' he replied and made a face. 'Away upstairs and set it up. I'll be there in a minute.'

She climbed the stairs, but paused when she heard her uncle's voice again. He was speaking in that low, quiet way the adults did when they didn't want her to hear what they were saying. Which had been happening a lot lately.

'This is nice,' Damaris heard her mother say. 'Really nice. But please don't...' The pause suggested that her mother was struggling with what she wanted to say. Damaris heard the back door slam. Her father must have gone outside.

'Spit it out,' Cammy said.

'...Spoil her. Don't spoil her.' It was clear to Damaris even from where she was perched that this wasn't what her mother *really* wanted to say.

There was a long pause before Cammy replied.

'She's changed,' he said. 'Used to be when I saw her she was skipping all over the place. A right wee ray of sunshine.'

Damaris felt bad at that. When her uncle came upstairs to sit with her she'd try and be a little happier. If she could. It was so tiring trying to act all okay when all she wanted to do was curl up into a ball.

'If I ever get my hands on that prick,' Cammy said. 'It's the trial next week, eh?'

'What if he gets off with it?' her mum asked.

'Don't worry,' Cammy replied. 'I've got a boy in his block primed to make sure he pays. One way or another.'

Chapter 24

'What will it be?' asked the man standing behind Dave with a small pair of very sharp scissors.

Their eyes met in the mirror. Dave assessed the other man's cropped scalp, yellowed teeth and full sleeve of tattoos, and wondered if this man should ever be allowed near such a sharp implement. 'Court case start the morra, aye?'

'In a couple of days' time,' Dave answered, feeling the roil in his stomach in reaction to another reminder that his day in court was approaching. 'How did you guess?'

The barber grinned. 'Haven't saw ye afore, likes. And your hair' – he lifted up a strand from the top of Dave's head in a way that suggested competence – 'hasnae been done in a good while.' He then looked down at Dave's beard. 'Want a wee trim there as well, mate?'

Dave nodded and looked either side of him at the other prisoners sitting in front of mirrors, one to each side, both of them in the throes of a good chat with their barber.

'People are always surprised when they first come in here. As if they forget that guys still need to look after their appearance even when they're in jail. I'm Tony, by the way.'

'Dave.'

'So, Dave,' Tony said as he cocked his head to the side while he assessed the state of Dave's hair. 'Just a tidy-up, or something wi' a bit of style?'

Before he answered Dave looked to the guy at his right whose head had been shaved up to a line about two inches above his ear and from there round his head, but his barber had left the top section of his hair in longer layers.

'I need to look presentable for the jury,' Dave answered. 'A sensible short back and sides, and just a wee beard trim, thanks.'

'Captain Sensible it is,' Tony replied, and set to cutting Dave's hair with practised ease while maintaining a dialogue about what he'd heard was happening in the world outside. After a few minutes of this he stopped speaking and simply concentrated on his job, as if he'd read the occasional grunt from Dave as a sign that this guy wasn't interested in his chat.

That left Dave to concentrate on what was filling his mind.

The trial.

His mum and dad would be there. As would Amelie. And he hoped beyond hope that they'd all be rewarded with those two little words: not guilty. The alternative just didn't bear thinking about: Dave Robbins a convicted paedophile. Even setting those two words against his name was enough to set off his gag reflex. He closed his eyes against the impulse to be sick.

'You awright, mate?' Tony asked as he held his scissors away from Dave's head. 'You look like you're going to keel over.'

'I'm fine,' Dave managed. 'Just need a drink of water.'

'Nae bother,' Tony said. He stepped over to the sink, plucked a plastic cup from a small tower of them and filled it from the tap. 'Here ye go,' he said as he offered it to Dave.

He sipped. Said, 'Thanks.'

Tony looked at him for a long moment in the mirror before he next spoke. 'I've been at this a long time. And it's never as bad as you think it's going to be, mate.'

Dave took a long, tremulous breath and nodded. 'Aye,' he said, thinking the other man's kind thought needed to be acknowledged, while at the same time wishing he would shut up and let him sink into the terror of his thoughts.

Once Tony finished, he stepped back and said, 'There ye go, mate.' Then he removed the sheet from around Dave's neck, brushed away any shorn hair and then held up a mirror at various angles so Dave could see the back of his head.

Dave went through the motions of nodding and mouthing 'Aye, cool' at each new vista of his head the foot-high mirror offered, but he was really seeing nothing.

Tony gripped Dave's right shoulder in an attempt at reassurance, while Dave stared at himself. He could see the haircut and newly trimmed beard was a massive improvement on the man who sat down in the chair twenty minutes or so earlier, but he struggled to get past the shadows gathering around his eyes. This was the face of a man strung so tight it was a wonder his heart could cope with the strain.

Leaving the chair, Dave barely had the presence of mind to thank Tony for his services. This act of preparation for court made it all so much more real. He was just glad that it was his lawyer bringing in his suit later, rather than his father. If he was the one to show up there was no telling what his response might be.

But you're innocent, he told himself and lifted his head up as he walked back to his block alongside a few of his 'neighbours', who'd also been for a haircut.

A breeze cooled his face. A spot of rain sparked on his forehead. He pulled in a long breath. *You did nothing. This is all a sham. The judge will throw it out of court. The jury will see that Damaris is being coached. And you'll be a free man.* Free to go back to work. Free to find out whatever life might have in store for him next.

A life without Amelie, for sure. A new home somewhere. And stares from people who saw the smoke, greedily imagined the fire and were sure he was guilty. The stain would never be washed from him, but still, that kind of attention would be better than being dubbed up in here for years.

The guard opened the block door and stepped aside while they all trooped in.

'Just in time for dinner, guys,' he said. 'And it's your favourite. Shepherd's pie.' A few of the men responded to his good cheer. Dave just let the words flow over him and trudged down the corridor to the middle of the hall, where the passmen were doling out the food. He wasn't sure he could stomach anything but he knew he would need all the strength he could muster and would therefore need to eat something.

Standing in the queue, lost in his doomsday ruminations Dave became aware of movement at his side. Movement that was too fast. He turned towards it. Saw a mug coming towards him. Above it the face of a man who'd served him food every day since he'd arrived.

His mind struggled to make sense of the action, but his body was way ahead. Automatically, his arm lifted and he ducked his head behind it, but not before pain burst across his skin. An agonising flare of heat.

He fell to his knees. What the hell was happening?

Boiling water?

Acid?

He heard a scream. Realised it was coming from his mouth, but couldn't stop. Oh my God, the pain. The scorch of it.

A scuffle as guards jumped on his assailant.

'Get some water. Quick,' he heard someone else shout as he fell forward.

Yes, water, he thought. *Please.* The side of his face, and neck and forearm felt like they were on fire.

And felt as if the pain would never stop.

Chapter 25

The woman seated on the sofa in her living room was a bit fat. And her teeth were wonky, but she seemed nice. Mum was all over her when she came in. Need some tea? Want a biscuit? Is it too hot, should I open a window? Is the light in your face, should I close the blinds? Want a cushion?

Godsake, Mum, you're embarrassing, Damaris thought. But the woman handled it all with a quiet authority.

'I'm fine, thank you,' she said. 'A glass of water would be lovely.' When her mum left the room to get the water the woman turned to Damaris.

'Just to remind you, my name's Shona. And I'm here because the court has appointed me to help you process what's been happening to you, okay?' Damaris realised she'd only asked for the water to get her mum out of the room.

There was a human-to-human note in her little introduction that Damaris appreciated. If one more grown-up did that fake too-nice voice when they were talking to her she was going to scream.

Then Shona said some other stuff that Damaris zoned out at, struggling to keep her eyes open. This talking stuff was so *exhausting*. Especially talking about the stuff with Dave.

'Can you just go through the events of that day with me, please, Damaris?'

Damaris opened her mouth to speak, but before she could say anything Shona continued. ' ...I understand you've gone over it before with the police, but they might have missed something. And they're only looking for evidence. My intention is quite different. I want to help you. Do you understand?'

Damaris nodded. She thought she did. She certainly wanted to.

Then she quietly went through the events, as refined by her mum and dad, but before she finished, Mum returned with the water. She placed it on the low table in front of Shona, the woman thanked her and then asked, 'Could we possibly have one for Damaris as well, please? Talking is thirsty work.'

Claire looked at Damaris to check if this was necessary, but Damaris didn't meet her eyes; instead she looked down at Shona's glass. Usually, Mum was the queen of everything, and it felt strangely pleasing that this woman was having her run about doing things.

'And this wasn't the first time this had happened?' Shona asked when Damaris finished.

Damaris heard her mother return to the room and looked up at her before answering. Claire sent her a small nod and Damaris said, 'Yes.' This really was all very confusing. After talking all of this over with her mum and dad over and over again, whenever she went into her thoughts it wasn't quite what she expected. She held a hand to her mouth to suppress a yawn.

'And Dave showed you his penis, didn't he?' Shona asked.

The word no longer had that little frisson of shock for Damaris. She'd heard it used so often recently. Of course, with her friends she didn't use that word. It felt too posh when she was speaking with them. Especially when one of the girls brought up some, what she called 'dick pics' on her phone. Her big sister got them, apparently, and shared them with her. They'd all cooed over it, and laughed, like, a lot. And some of the girls acted like they'd like to see one for real, in the flesh, but Damaris knew that was all fake cos when she looked at it on that phone it just looked gross. Of course she'd seen her dad naked – being nude wasn't a big thing in her house; but the thought that her dad's body might also behave in this way made her unable to meet his eye for a few days.

'You need to answer the question, honey,' Claire said.

Damaris nodded.

'Do you know what happens when a man gets an erection, Damaris?' Shona asked.

Damaris nodded, and felt her face heat a little.

'I understand this might be uncomfortable for you, Damaris, but there's no need to feel any shame or embarrassment. The shame belongs firmly with the abuser, okay?'

Damaris nodded again, and felt silly that all she could do was nod.

'And you know what happens when a man ejaculates?'

'Not sure she knows that word,' Mum interjected.

Course she knows, thought Damaris. She wasn't a baby. Well, in one of those pictures on her friend's phone there was some white stuff. Her friend called it 'jizz' and said that when the man rubbed himself that was the stuff that came out. The stuff that made babies. So when Shona used that posh word she was able to work it out.

'Uhuh,' Damaris said quietly, ducking her head, and looking over at her mother from under her fringe. This was all so cringey.

'Did Dave do that in front of you, Damaris?'

Damaris had another flash of that phone picture and in her imagination imposed Dave's face over it and it all suddenly seemed so real. And much too much. She started crying.

'Babe.' Her mother moved over to her, knelt before her and drew her into a hug. Over her shoulder, Claire spoke to the other woman. 'I think she's had enough now, don't you?'

'Let's just give her a moment,' Shona answered.

Damaris managed to bring her tears under control, and despite feeling so heavy she thought she'd be able to sleep for weeks she sent both women a small smile of reassurance. They both looked so sad. Even Shona, who had been all professional up until then.

'Mum tells me you haven't really been crying that much, Damaris. I want you to know it's okay to cry. It can be a powerful part of the healing process. A perfectly human response to an inhuman action, so whenever you need to cry just you go ahead.'

Chapter 26

To show a united front to the world's press Norma and Peter Robbins walked to the court with Amelie, flanked by Dave's lawyer.

From the car park to the stairs up into the court house they were followed by a large scrum of reporters, cameras flashing, questions being shouted at them.

'Are you still going to stand by your man, Miss Hart, if he's convicted?'

'What do you think are the chances of an acquittal?'

'Any words of support for the young girl your boyfriend abused, Miss Hart?'

It was all Dave's mother could do to stop herself from stepping between Amelie and the reporters, and screaming in their faces to leave them alone. How on earth did this poor woman put up with this? Only now was she getting an insight into what Amelie's life might have been like as a Hollywood star. As far as she was concerned all those fame-hungry idiots on those TV wannabe shows deserved all the nonsense they got.

But she knew that any reaction from her would be used against her and her son. An image of her face contorted in anger would play into their hands and be on every news outlet, demonstrating that she was undoubtedly as evil as her son. So, instead of screaming at them she settled for a scolding.

'I hope your mothers are proud of you,' she said as firmly as she could, and holding her handbag high over her chest like a shield she turned and walked towards the door.

One last question was hurled at them when she got to the top of the stairs:

'Are you aware that Dave Robbins was attacked a couple of days ago, Miss Hart? Mrs Robbins? Are you surprised he's still able to appear in court despite his injuries?'

'What?' Amelie looked from the reporter to Norma and Peter.

'We need to go inside, Amelie. Don't give them the time of day.'

Once they were through the door Amelie rounded on the lawyer.

'What was he talking about? Dave was attacked?'

'Sorry, dear.' Norma touched her lightly on the forearm, cringing a little that they hadn't made sure Amelie knew. 'We thought the police had been in touch.'

'About what?'

'Another prisoner threw scalding hot water over him,' Norma replied, her voice quivering. She held her arms out to the side to offer the succour to Amelie that she couldn't provide for her son. Then aware of what she was doing she stuffed her hands into her coat pockets.

'Oh my God,' Amelie exclaimed, hand to her mouth.

'Thankfully the idiot who did it didn't use enough sugar in it to make it more of a paste or Dave would be in a much worse state,' Bain said.

'What?' Amelie asked. 'Sugar? What was that about sugar?'

'It's an old prison thing. When you add sugar to boiling water it sticks to the skin, intensifying the damage.'

'Oh dear God.' Amelie looked like she was struggling to conceive of such cruelty. 'Is Dave okay?'

'Luckily, he managed to get his arm up and that took most of the damage, but he has burns to the side of his face and his neck. The doctors say there will be some scarring.' Bain gave them all a reassuring smile. 'But it could have been much, much worse.'

'Who would do such a thing?' Amelie demanded. 'Poor Dave. The pain and shock must have been horrific.'

'The authorities reckon the guy who did it was put up to it by someone else. He was a passman...'

'A what?' Amelie asked.

'A trusted prisoner. They get the plum jobs in prison. This guy worked in the pantry, reheating and serving up the food. This means he'll be punished and lose out on all that extra time out of his cell. Whoever got him to do it must have something over him, or offered him a lot of cash. Prisoners don't give up that kind of job lightly.'

'You think someone else put him up to this?' asked Dave's father.

'I'm sure of it.'

'Yeah, but aren't sex offenders a target for the other prisoners anyway?'

At this, Norma held a hand out to her husband to steady herself. Of course this was no secret, but hearing it out loud made it sink home.

'Yes,' Bain said. 'But a guy with all these privileges inside isn't going to risk all of that for the kudos of getting at a beast.'

Norma watched as Amelie slowly shook her head. This was almost too much to take in. And not for the first time she thought about this strange and dangerous world her kind and gentle son was being forced to navigate.

In court, after they had taken their seats, Norma looked at the young woman sitting beside her out of the corner of her eye. She watched her for signs that might suggest how she was bearing up. She knew Amelie had stayed in a city-centre hotel rather than go home and be next door to the people who had made such horrible accusations against Dave.

Despite not having her home comforts – and who sleeps well the first night in a strange bed? Norma wondered – Amelie looked as if she'd dropped down from Planet Beautiful to spend time with the ordinary people. Her hair tumbled over her shoulders, her face was bare of make-up, her clothes were plain, but clearly expensive, and yet she had an air of something other-worldly. Norma often teased her husband about how Amelie had the Robbins men under her thumb, but she had to admit that even she was affected by the younger woman's star quality.

At that moment Amelie turned and looked at her.

'How are you doing?' she asked quietly, and Norma felt the heat of her hand on the back of hers as she gave it a little squeeze.

Norma looked into Amelie's eyes and could see that she was suffering hugely. She placed her free hand on top of Amelie's. The last time she spoke with Dave he'd said they were entering a make-or-break period. Whatever that meant. He hadn't gone into detail. So she was aware that Amelie and her son had been going through a difficult time before ... all of this. She also knew that Dave crossed her off his visitors' list. Well, the whole world knew that. Still, whatever was going on between them, it was clear she still loved her son. Why else would she be here? A woman with her connections and money could be anywhere in the world.

'Thank you,' Norma whispered. 'It means a lot to me that you're here.' At this Amelie's eyes misted over, and for a moment it looked like she might lose a little of her obviously hard-won self-control. They'd never really got on, and in this moment Norma accepted responsibility for that, and felt huge regret. 'You are a good woman, Amelie Hart.'

Amelie sobbed a little and held a hand to her mouth. She closed her eyes and squeezed Norma's hand hard. 'Thank you,' she mouthed, and then wiped a tear from her cheek with the back of her hand.

The first witness called for the prosecution was Claire Brown, and as Norma watched Damaris's mother walk to the stand and sit to be sworn in she hoped that her antagonism towards the woman wasn't showing. Because as sure as eggs were eggs people were going to be watching her for a reaction. She held her hands tight in her lap and forced her face into an expression that would give nothing away. This woman with her hand on the Bible, and her long, carefully styled hair, light make-up and blouse buttoned to the neck was the architect of all of Dave's suffering, Norma was certain of it, and it was all she could do not to get to her feet and denounce the woman.

But she knew that they were on this train of justice and there was no way to get off it. She had to face up to this helplessness and pray that they all ended up in the right place, with Dave free and clear. At that thought she looked over to him, sitting at the side of the court, flanked by a pair of policemen.

As if he was aware of her attention he turned to face her. A faint, quick, smile sketched itself into his carefully compacted expression, and as it did so it pushed up the white dressings that had been attached to the burn wounds on the side of his face. This cost him a stab of pain, judging by the way his brow immediately furrowed.

Oh, son.

Norma felt tears sting her eyes. This was so unfair. This fine human being was being sacrificed on the altar of Claire Brown's get-rich-quick scheme. What sort of mother was she? What could her motive be? She'd chatted with Amelie over the phone the other day and shared her thoughts. Was her friend Lisa correct when she said it was all about money? If this was true, how could they prove it? How could they use it in Dave's defence? She looked at the broad, well-clothed back of Dave's lawyer. She'd have to have a word with him at some point and see if this was part of his strategy.

'And you saw your daughter Damaris up at the back of your neighbour's garden with Dave Robbins?' Mr Melville was asking. Earlier he'd been introduced as the advocate depute and looked uncompromising in his wig and black robes.

Pay attention, Norma told herself. She was missing so much, being so caught up in her worries.

'Yes,' Claire Brown answered.

'What were they doing?'

'From where I was sitting I couldn't be sure ... but now I know.' As she added this her face crumpled.

Oh, for God's sake, thought Norma. *Even I'm not convinced by that*. She turned to examine the fifteen men and women of the jury and tried to assess what they were thinking. A couple of the women in the front row were clearly affected by Claire Brown's apparent emotion.

Mr Melville continued to ask Claire about the time Damaris spent in Dave's company, and she managed to convey a sense of wrongness in her answers, without actually saying anything concrete. Norma hoped the jury recognised the lack of anything definitive in her testimony.

When it was Joseph Bain's turn to question Mrs Brown he slowly got to his feet.

'Mrs Brown, you say you saw your daughter in the garden with the defendant, Mr Robbins, yes?'

'Yes,' she said and crossed her arms as if setting up to defend herself against whatever this man might throw at her.

'Precisely what did you see, Mrs Brown?'

'I saw my daughter. And that man.' She threw a look of pure hate in Dave's direction.

'What were they doing?'

'Talking. Playing.' She managed to add a stress to the word 'playing' that suggested there was much more than that going on.

'Playing at what precisely?'

'Damaris has a frisbee. It's probably her favourite toy.'

'It's been a while since I had the occasion to throw a circular piece of plastic around. Please remind me what this game entails.'

'They stand a few feet apart and throw it to each other.'

'With what aim in mind, Mrs Brown?'

She looked at him as if he was mad. 'To catch it; what else?'

'Is Damaris good at this game?'

'I guess,' she answered. 'More often than not she manages to catch the thing, so I would say yes.' There was a little glimmer of mother's pride in the way she finished her reply. When those words, 'mother's pride', settled in her mind, Norma felt as if she was going to be sick. She reached out for Peter's hand and gave it a little squeeze.

'Did Damaris and Mr Robbins play with aforementioned frisbee regularly, Mrs Brown?'

'Every chance he got he was round ours playing with her.'

'Doesn't Mr Robbins' piece of the garden abut on yours?'

'Yes, but...'

'So it would hardly be, as you say, every chance he got. By all accounts Mr Robbins is a keen gardener. He has every right to be in his garden. Would I be right in saying that when Mr Robbins was in his garden, Damaris took every chance she could to have someone to play with?'

'That's not...'

'Have you ever played with Damaris and her frisbee, Mrs Brown?'

She paused as if wary she was about to enter a trap.

'Please answer the question, Mrs Brown.'

'Well, no, not really.'

'No, not really,' Bain repeated and looked over at the jury members. 'This favourite toy, this game that your daughter loved, you never, ever played with her.'

'No, but...' Her face twisted. 'What kind of grown man plays games with a small girl?'

'A kind man who sees a lonely, bored little girl and feels it might be a kindness to keep her company.'

'But...' Claire's face was bright red and she jumped to her feet.

'Please stay seated, Mrs Brown,' the judge said from her perch directly under the massive, gilded court symbol on the far wall.

Norma looked at the judge properly for the first time. Under her court wig she appeared to be sweltering, her face ruddy and glistening with sweat. Norma wondered if that might mean she might try to rush things along.

'Mrs Brown...' Bain continued as if he hadn't noticed her brief outburst. 'How many times did you see Damaris and the defendant in the garden?'

'Loads of times. Too many...'

'Too many times to count do you think?' And Norma thought how clever Bain was to head off that potentially tricky response and turn it into something benign. 'And on any one of these occasions did you ever see them do anything other than play with a frisbee?'

'Sometimes it was a football.' Claire scowled.

'Anything else?'

'There might have been a doll now and again.'

'And during these many games under your direct supervision, where were you directly supervising from, Mrs Brown?'

'My kitchen.'

'And it offers a good view of the garden?'

'Yes.'

'And what were you doing while Damaris and Dave Robbins were having a little bit of harmless fun?'

'Mr Bain,' the judge warned. 'Thin ice.'

'Apologies, your honour, let me rephrase.' He nodded in the direction of the judge. 'Mrs Brown, please tell the court what you were doing while Mr Robbins and your daughter were kicking a ball about in your garden.'

'Working.'

'What kind of work do you do, Mrs Brown?'

'I'm a book-keeper.'

'Are you aware that Mr Robbins works for his father, who has one of the most prestigious accountancy firms in the country?'

At this Norma looked to her husband. He was stock still, giving nothing away.

'Yes.'

'And did you once apply, and fail, to get a job there?' Bain looked meaningfully in the direction of the jury.

This was news to Norma. She gave her husband a nudge and then had a look over at Dave to check his reaction. From his expression it was news to him too.

'I know what you're trying to suggest. Very clever, but you're not going to trip me up.'

'Let me remind you, Mrs Brown, that you have sworn in front of this court to speak the truth and nothing but the truth. Do you intend to speak the truth, Mrs Brown?'

'Of course.'

'Well, in that case I wouldn't worry about being tripped up. Now back to your work. A book-keeper. One who failed to get a job in the accountancy firm owned by the accused's father. Does this failure' – each time he used the syllable 'fail' Bain managed to add a little emphasis – 'mean you harbour any malice towards the Robbins family?'

'My learned friend,' the depute advocate spoke from his seat. 'appears to be on a fishing expedition. Perhaps he should stick to trying to ascertain the facts of this case, your honour?'

'Agreed, Mr Walker,' the judge said. 'Mr Bain, I can see what you're up to. Please stop there.' She turned to the jury. 'You can disregard any mention of Mrs Brown's past job history.'

'Very well, your honour.' Bain gave her a solemn little nod, then undeterred faced the witness. 'Book-keeping is a job that is very particular and requires an eye for detail I imagine? Do you have many clients?'

'Mr Bain,' the judge warned.

'Please may I have your forbearance, your honour. This is pertinent, I assure you.'

The judge sat back in her seat and fixed Bain with a glare for a moment. Then, as if reading something in his expression that satisfied, she said, 'Carry on, but I'm on to you, sir.'

'Very well, your honour.' Another nod. 'Mrs Brown, you

perform book-keeping services for some local business people from what I can make out from your website, yes?'

'Yes.'

'And some family members?'

Claire's mouth hung open a little as if she suddenly knew where he was going with this line of questioning. She looked to the judge to see if she was going to get any help there.

'Please answer Mr Bain's question, Mrs Brown.'

'Yes,' she huffed.

'Including your brother, one Cameron Walker.'

'And what does your brother do, Mrs Brown?'

'He's a businessman.'

'What kind of business?'

'A bit of this and a bit of that.' It occurred to Norma that everyone in the court could see that Claire was squirming.

'A bit of this and a bit of that,' repeated Bain. 'Is it not true that he has served time at Her Majesty's pleasure for passing on stolen goods?'

'Yes.' Claire was staring straight ahead of her as if she couldn't wait for this to be over.

'And at his trial did you appear as his witness?'

'Yes.'

'And what was the outcome of that?'

Claire looked at the judge again, an appeal in her eyes.

'Please answer the question, Mrs Brown.'

'I was found guilty of perjury.'

'Not at that point, that came later as a consequence of the trial during which you perjured yourself, is that not correct, Mrs Brown? You provided an alibi for your brother that was a downright lie.'

'Your honour.' Melville got to his feet. 'Mrs Brown is not on trial here, and might I remind my learned friend that she has done her time for her crime and has since proven to be an upstanding citizen.'

'Goes to show previous character, your honour. I'm thinking of her attempts during her testimony with my learned colleague to characterise my client in a demeaning way. If the witness has previously been convicted for lying in court for a family member, she is more than capable of doing it again for her daughter.'

'I'll allow it for now, Mr Bain, but don't chance your luck with this witness.'

'Yes, Your Honour.'

He turned to Claire. 'How much time did you serve for perjury, Mrs Brown?'

'Ten months.'

'Now, if we could go back to your job, Mrs Brown. I assume it is one you can do from your laptop at your kitchen window?'

'I have a breakfast bar in my kitchen. I sit there and work and I can keep an eye along the open-plan lower floor, and out into the garden.' Claire sounded a little relieved the previous line of questioning was over.

'And during all those working sessions when you sat there at your laptop, with a view down the garden – too many times to mention,' he pretended to read his notes, 'is what I think you said. Did you ever see David Robbins do anything other than play harmlessly with your little girl?'

'No.'

'In all those times from your breakfast table in the kitchen, while you watched over your daughter, Mrs Brown, did you ever see David Robbins act in any way towards your daughter that was illegal, improper or immoral?'

'No,' she replied in a small voice.

'Thank you for your testimony, Mrs Brown. You may leave the stand.' Bain, Norma realised, was using his tone and inflections to tell the jury that he had Claire Brown's number, and with hope a light flare in her stomach she assessed the two rows of people who were sitting in judgement on the man she loved.

She saw nothing in their faces but a need for more answers.

Chapter 27

It was day two, and before they took their seats Joseph Bain had a quick word with Norma and Peter.

'I thought you should know that today we'll be hearing testimony from Damaris. She's in another room and we'll be able to watch through a live feed. Depending on how well she presents herself, this could be our trickiest day.'

'What do you mean?' asked Norma, while suspecting she knew the answer. A small girl talking about such things, about what a grown man allegedly did to her, would be difficult to hear.

'We can't risk the jury turning against us, which they will if she responds badly to me. I can't question her the way I would, say, an adult or even a teenager. I will have to be gentle with her then get her mother back on the stand and have another go at her.'

A couple of men wheeled a giant TV in front of the stand, rousing Norma from her thoughts. It came to life and a little girl appeared on the screen. She was sitting behind a table and from her posture it was clear she was sitting on her hands.

A woman was sitting to her right and she spoke first.

'Now remember, Damaris, we can stop anytime you feel uncomfortable, alright?'

Damaris bit her lip and assented with a nod.

Dear God, she looked so young, thought Norma. Poor wee soul. Then she checked herself. This *poor wee soul* had made some terrible accusations against her son.

'Now if you would just go through the events of Good Friday this year. You were on school holidays. It was a lovely, sunny day. Probably one of the first proper sunny days this spring after a long winter.' The woman paused. 'None of your friends were about so you went out into the garden...'

When the interview finished a court official paused the feed. The screen was frozen on an image of Damaris's face, her eyes looking up from under her fringe. Eyes that displayed a world of sadness. Not one person in the room could tear their gaze from her, and while the little girl's testimony filtered into everyone's minds, a hush as heavy as a shroud fell over the court.

Norma looked over to her son and saw his open mouth and a look of utter disbelief in his eyes. From there she looked at the faces of each of the jury members, and saw nothing but condemnation.

The girl had spoken with a quiet, chilling certainty and for a moment – just a moment – even Norma, a woman who was assured of her son's innocence, wondered about it.

'Where did that come from? She's lying through her wee teeth,' Norma hissed to Peter. Then she turned to assess the jury again. 'Oh no,' she said. 'They're buying it.'

The woman who'd spoken to Damaris indicated that she was finished, and Joseph Bain stood up to ask his questions.

A few minutes in and most of Bain's questions were aimed at seeking clarification around Damaris's answers, and despite his experience he was clearly finding it difficult to strike the right tone. A couple of times it looked like Damaris was going to start crying, so he stopped and suggested she take a sip of water.

'This must seem weird to you, Damaris. I can see you but you can't see me. I'm just a voice in the room, eh?'

At this Damaris gave a little smile.

'Now. You have a doll on your lap, Damaris, could you once again show the camera where Dave touched you?'

She held the doll up and placed her other hand over the junction of the toy's legs. And then withdrew it suddenly as if she had just been burned. An action that led Norma to question if this was any indication of the girl's state of mind. Retreating from a lie? Or would the jury see it as a reaction to a painful memory?

'You are absolutely sure about this?'

'Yes.'

'Damaris, do you know how serious it is to lie in a court of law?'

At this she said nothing but she pushed her bottom lip out and her eyes grew large.

'On your say-so someone who was a friend to you will lose everything. His home, his relationship, his job, his freedom. He'll spend years locked up in a small cell, so it's important that what you say is the absolute truth, do you understand?'

'Yes.' Her voice was just audible.

'Did your parents tell you what to say today?'

'No.'

'Did they tell you to lie?'

'No.'

'You have to tell me the truth, Damaris. Isn't everything you said about Dave a lie?'

At this Damaris crumpled forward in her seat, her little shoulders heaving. A woman appeared from the side – her mother, Claire – and she pulled her daughter into a hug.

'I think now is a good time to take a recess,' the judge said and the screen went blank.

An hour later they got word that Damaris was ready to resume.

'Thank you for coming back to us, Damaris,' Bain said. 'I know this isn't easy for you, but we need to get to the truth of the matter. Do you understand?'

Damaris's eyes were puffy. 'Yes.'

'Just to finish up, Damaris. You said earlier in your testimony that Dave was a friend. He played games with you in the garden when everyone else – your parents – were too busy to. Are you sure this story about where he touched you and him showing you his private parts is the story you want to tell everyone about your friend?'

Damaris crossed her arms and fixed the camera with a hard glare. At this Norma quailed. It looked like by repeating the question, but in a different way, Bain wasn't getting a different response, he was simply starting to annoy the girl.

'I thought he was a friend,' she replied with a hard pout, her eyes like little black buttons of hurt. 'But friends don't do bad things like that to each other, do they?'

Chapter 28

There followed a series of experts, who were there to back up the prosecution's case. First was the police doctor who treated Damaris after the incident. He was a small, lean man with a well-worn weary expression that suggested he'd seen every bad thing that people could do to each other. Melville asked him to point out, on a screen that was displaying the outline of a female child, where the girl's injuries were.

'Some bruising on the left arm, upper part on the inside. And here, some bruising on the upper inner thigh, right leg and...' he paused while a medical diagram of female genitalia appeared on the screen; '...and on the right side of the mons pubis and labia majora.' He pointed while he talked.

'Are these injuries consistent with sexual assault, Doctor?'

'Putting words in the doctor's mouth, M'lady,' Bain said.

'What might have caused these injuries, Doctor?'

'They may well have been sustained in a sexual attack.'

'Was there any indication of penetration?'

'None.'

'Thank you, Doctor.'

Bain stood up. 'Might these injuries have been sustained in any other way, Doctor?'

'It's possible,' he answered.

'Any examples?'

'If a girl was to come off a boy's bike, these kind of injuries would be likely, depending on speed and angle of fall.'

'Thank you.' Bain sat down.

Chapter 29

The next day it would be the defence team's turn to present their case, and Joseph Bain let Amelie know before she'd gone to her hotel the previous evening that she'd be first on the stand.

She spent the whole evening and night firstly worrying how she might appear to the jury; would they be looking for the movie star, or would they be able to see past the glamour and simply see a woman who was certain of her boyfriend's innocence? Then there were the questions she'd face from the prosecution. Would the advocate depute try to trip her up? Try to confuse her? Over and over she imagined herself on the stand and replying to his questions with a polite calm.

Not to forget that there was the trial by public opinion being hosted all over social media and across most of the TV and print news outlets. In that particular 'court' she was aware that she was on trial every bit as much as Dave was.

But the image that repeatedly pushed those worries from her mind was Damaris's angry little eyes and the question: *Friends don't do bad things like that to each other, do they?*

Could the unspeakable be true?

Could Dave have been grooming the little girl? Why else would she be so adamant? No, there must be another explanation. She refused to believe it. This was all a concoction from the parents to try and raise some money off the back of her fame. Dave would never behave like that. He was one of the good guys.

Wasn't he?

Certain that she'd only managed a minute's sleep she obeyed the alarm on her phone and got out of bed. A shower, followed by a black coffee, and then she faced herself in the bathroom mirror. With a grimace of acceptance she applied some concealer to the shadows under her eyes. Other than that, she thought as she stepped back from the mirror, she was going bare-faced. And if the talking heads on TV didn't like that they could take a long walk off a short pier.

When she looked at her phone she saw that she'd had several missed calls from Bernard and Lisa. Both had left messages wishing her luck. No one else in her life even bothered. All those friends she had when she was in that life had faded away as she refused to join in the celebrity merry-go-round, and when the case hit the news those numbers dropped to almost no one. It was as if everyone was distancing themselves from her until they were confident the allegations were found to be untrue.

So much for being innocent until proven otherwise.

There was more than the usual pack of reporters and news crews at the entrance to the court than on previous days. Of course, she thought, word would have gotten out that she'd be giving evidence.

Norma and Peter were waiting in the car park, and they walked to the front doors together. As they approached the crowd at the entrance, Norma took Amelie's hand and walked tight by her side, sending a very public signal of her support.

Too soon, Amelie's name was being called and she was walking towards the stand, where she was sworn in.

Bain asked her to recall the events of the day and in a calm, clear voice she did so. Once she had finished Bain asked:

'How would you characterise David Robbins' interactions with Damaris Brown?'

'She was a lonely wee girl. I could count the number of times I saw her playing in the garden with either of her parents on one hand. Dave was kind enough to give her the time of day when she was bored. That was it.'

'Did Dave ever instigate any of these games, to your knowledge?'

'No.'

'Do you think it strange that a grown man would play from time to time with a young girl?'

'Not in this situation, no. We're neighbours. Dave is out in the garden a lot. So's Damaris. Interaction in such a situation is what human beings do. Also, Dave is an only child and I think that in those moments Damaris was like a substitute for the little sister he never had. There is nothing more sinister in this whole thing than that.'

'Thank you, Miss Hart.' Bain sat down.

Melville got to his feet, 'You are a resident at 2 Mews Cottages, Bishop's House Estate, Thorntonhall?'

Amelie replied, and was pleased to hear that her voice was even. Before Melville asked his next question she shot a look at Dave. He was sitting as stiffly as she was. And his face was giving absolutely nothing away.

'You have been living there for how long?'

'Three years.'

'Next door to the victim?'

'Your honour.' Bain jumped to his feet.

'Apologies, your honour,' Melville said before the judge remonstrated with him. 'Alleged victim.'

'Yes, next door to Damaris and her parents.'

'According to the newspapers today you're thinking about moving.'

'Don't believe everything you read in the newspapers, Mr Melville,' Amelie replied, and several people in the court laughed out loud.

'The papers also say that you were about to dump your boyfriend, the defendant, David Robbins, before he was arrested. Is that true?'

'Your honour.' Bain got to his feet. 'Is my esteemed colleague going to regale us with gossip from the tabloids all morning?'

'Stick to ascertaining the facts, please, Mr Melville. There's enough of a circus outside the building. I don't want it to enter my court as well,' the judge said.

'Apologies, your honour.' Melville gave a stiff bow in her direction before turning to Amelie.

'In your testimony you talked about Damaris pestering David Robbins. Did you actually see Damaris pester Mr Robbins that day?'

'No, I—'

'So that would be hearsay, Miss Hart.'

'I witnessed it on plenty of other occasions. It happened almost on a weekly basis.'

'Quite,' Melville replied as if he didn't believe her. 'You are adamant that nothing untoward happened between Damaris and David Robbins in all the time since you moved into that house.'

'Absolutely. Dave is one of the good guys.' She could hear the doubt she had experienced through the night in her voice and worried she was being less than the adamant support Dave needed. So she coughed, then forced some energy into her voice and added, 'He would never hurt a fly.' Crossing her arms she tried to rein in her emotions.

'A good guy that you were about to throw out of your house.'

'That's enough, Mr Melville,' the judge said. 'Jury members, you will disregard that last remark.'

During recess Amelie had a strong coffee to try and recalibrate her nerves. Both Norma and Peter thanked her for her efforts, and as she smiled her appreciation of their thanks she wondered if it might all be in vain.

She plucked her phone from her pocket and switched it back on. More from habit and a need for temporary distraction. There were three missed calls from Lisa and a text:

I've got info that might help Dave. Call me asap. xxx

Chapter 30

Dave watched Amelie give her testimony, feeling hugely thankful for her support. Their gazes met for the briefest of moments while she was being questioned and he held a hand over his heart in thanks as she watched. Then he dropped his arm, worried that the jury might see and think it was some kind of signal. He was rewarded, however, by the flash of warmth in her eyes as she caught his gesture.

She could have been anywhere in the world, but despite the risk to her reputation she had stood by him, and for that he would be eternally grateful. But while he basked in the sight of her he knew that their relationship would never recover, regardless of how things might have been before Damaris's accusations. Whether he was found guilty or innocent, there was simply no way back for them, he was certain.

With a twist deep in his gut he realised he was due to give evidence next.

Bain previously told him he didn't need to do so. That there was no legal requirement for the defendant to speak at their trial. But he couldn't not speak. He had to assert his innocence in this place, before that great seal of justice carved in to the wall above the judge's seat.

Besides, he had only ever looked upon Damaris with the affection a big brother might have for a much younger sister. To claim anything else was absurd. And yet, Damaris's testimony to camera was so powerful. Where had that version of the little girl come from? Sure, she could be moody, but to be so angry as she was when she gave that last answer?

Friends don't do bad things to each other like that, do they?

If he hadn't been there in that garden himself, even he would be doubting his innocence.

All night as he lay in his cell her little face haunted him. What had been happening to her since he last saw her? How was she able to perform the lie so capably? It was as if Damaris had actually come to believe she'd been sexually assaulted by him.

Just before his name was called out by the court official, he saw Amelie standing over the desk where Bain had sat throughout the trial. Their heads were close together and there was an urgency about their communication. What was that all about?

On hearing his name, he stood, and with shaky legs and the feeling that he was walking to his certain doom he moved from the dock to the stand. The judge swore him in and he turned to face Bain.

'Please tell the court about the events of Friday the second of April this year.'

For what felt like the thousandth time, Dave recounted that day from the moment he left the house through the patio doors to attend to his garden, to the moment the police knocked on his door.

'At any time during the course of that afternoon did you behave inappropriately towards Damaris Brown?'

'No, absolutely not.'

'At any time since you've known Damaris Brown did you behave in an inappropriate manner?'

'No. Absolutely not.'

'How did you feel while you were watching Damaris give her testimony?'

'Shocked.'

'Why shocked, Mr Robbins?'

'Shocked that our perfectly innocent interactions had been twisted in her mind to such an extent. She must have been coached by someone. There's no way...' This wasn't happening. Couldn't be happening. Damaris was lying; couldn't they all see this? How could anyone look at him and see a paedophile?

'The defendant is speculating, your honour,' Melville shouted.

'Please stick to the facts, Mr Robbins,' the judge said.

'Sorry, your honour.' Dave ducked his head. Bit his lip.

He felt as if his emotions were about to burst out of him. Every part of his body was trembling. His breath was shallow, his fingertips were tingling. His vision was shrinking to a pinpoint.

Breathe, he told himself. Breathe.

He was aware that Melville was on his feet. 'Thank you for recounting the events of that day, Mr Robbins. It's very noble of you to step in and help out a lonely child when she had no one else to play with.'

'Nothing noble about it,' Dave replied, clenching both fists. 'Just being a good neighbour.'

'Good neighbours don't molest their neighbour's child, Mr Robbins.'

'What the hell?' Dave felt a hot surge of fury. 'You grandstanding prick...'

'Mr Robbins,' the judge shouted. 'We do not tolerate language like that in my court. And Mr Melville, you should know better. Mr Robbins hasn't been convicting of anything. Restrict yourself to questions. Less ... grandstanding, please.'

This last comment received some laughter from one or two people across the court.

And the laughter felt like a slight easing of tension. *Breathe*, he repeated in his head. *Slowly*. If he lost his temper again he knew he would be playing into Melville's hands.

'Won't happen again, your honour,' Melville said. 'Mr Robbins, your testimony is self-serving tosh, is it not?'

'No.'

'Designed to make you look good in this court.'

'No.'

'When in fact you've been grooming this little girl for months, haven't you?'

'No.'

'I put it to you that you are lying in this court, Mr Robbins, that you have, as we heard from Damaris Brown's lips, been grooming and molesting her for months if not years, haven't you?'

Chapter 31

Norma thought her heart would explode under the strain. How could that horrible man ask Dave those questions? It was all she could do not to rush over to him and give him a piece of her mind. Courtroom or not.

She felt Peter's hand on hers and she looked up at him. His face was showing the same strain she was feeling, and she wasn't sure if his gesture was an attempt to offer her support or a request to receive some from her.

'I have not,' Dave shouted at Melville, and although part of her was pleased Dave was so definite in his response, another part of her worried that he was playing in to the lawyer's hands.

'Asked and answered, your honour,' Bain interrupted, and as he did so Norma saw him send him a look of warning. 'Mr Melville is badgering my client. And indeed, grandstanding.'

'No more questions, your honour.' Melville sat back down.

Bain stood. 'Apologies for the bluster of my colleague, Mr Robbins. Perhaps my learned friend is hoping Miss Hart has brought a Hollywood agent with her and he's praying to be noticed for the next John Grisham movie.'

Everyone laughed. Norma could see the calculation in this comment. It lightened the mood in the room, lifting it from a place where the jury might have been envisioning him being dragged out of the court by the police.

The laughter died down, but not everyone had been amused.

'Get on with it, Mr Bain,' the judge said.

'Mr Robbins, please, once again for the court, did you groom or sexually molest Damaris Brown.'

'No, Mr Bain. She's a sweet little girl. A bit of a pest at times, but I would never, never harm her. Or any other child for that matter.'

'Thank you, Mr Robbins. You may return to your seat.' He looked down at his notes. 'The defence would like to recall Mrs Claire Brown to the stand.'

Norma looked to Peter to see if he knew what was going on. But he looked as surprised as she felt.

Melville stood up in protest. 'Your honour, is this badgering of my client really necessary?'

'I'll allow it,' she replied. 'This time.'

Claire Brown took her place, hands in front of her, head cocked slightly to the left as if to say, 'Really?'

'Thank you for your patience, Mrs Brown. I have just a few more questions for you.'

'Fine,' she replied, her guard up.

'A mother would do anything to protect her family, yes?'

'Of course.'

'A mother and father would do anything to *provide* for their family, yes?'

'Of course.'

'And desperate times call for desperate measures, don't they?'

'If you say so, Mr Bain.' Claire's face was white, her mouth a tight line of concern.

Bain gave a nod in the direction of a court official who was standing in front of some kind of flat contraption. All the screens in the court came to life.

'Under a production order, as you know, M'lady, we were able to access Mr and Mrs Brown's financial records.'

'Your honour, Mr and Mrs Brown are not under investigation for any wrong-doing,' Melville objected.

'My client has asserted his innocence time and time again,' Bain said. 'And if that is the case there has to be a reason behind these allegations. I'm confident I have evidence to demonstrate that Mr and Mrs Brown have serious financial difficulties and they—'

'This is ridiculous, your honour,' Melville said.

'Your objection has been noted, Mr Melville,' the judge said. 'Please continue, Mr Bain.'

Norma read a look that passed between Melville and Claire Brown, which made her think this was all part of their game. They knew this was coming and had prepared. But the need for the reassurance made Norma wonder if that meant this was something Claire was concerned about.

'As you look through Mr and Mrs Brown's financial affairs it is clear that they are in serious debt. Credit cards maxed out. Mortgage payments in arrears. Regular and large overdraft fees. No savings to speak of. Next, if the court would allow...' The court official fed a different document into the projector. 'Mrs Brown, please explain what we see here.'

'It's an email. Obviously.'

'To?'

She leaned forward a little, the better to see the screen nearest her. And paused.

'Yes?' Bain asked.

'To B.C. Francis and Co, Literary Agents.'

'From?'

'Me,' she replied in a quiet voice.

'You are looking for literary representation, Mrs Brown?'

'I was, yes.'

'What are you writing?'

'Nothing.'

'You haven't written anything but you are seeking a literary agent? Why?'

'I haven't written anything *yet.*'

'I see. How many literary agents did you contact?'

'Six.'

'Six literary agents and you haven't written anything. Yet. Surely it is in your plans then if you are going to go to the bother of researching literary agents and typing out an enquiry letter?'

'It is, yes. Nothing wrong with wanting to write a book is there?'

'Indeed,' Bain agreed in an almost conciliatory tone. 'Your email didn't go into much detail about said book, other than there would be a celebrity angle concerning the live-in boyfriend of Amelie Hart.' Bain stopped for a moment as he hitched up the waist of his trousers. A ploy, Norma was sure, to allow the ramifications of this to sink in each of the jury members' minds. 'Could you please read out the date of this email, Mrs Brown?'

Claire Brown mumbled something.

'Could you repeat that so everyone can hear, please?'

'The sixth of April, 2015.'

'That's Easter Monday. Three days after Mr Robbins was arrested?'

'Yes,' Claire said and then pulled in her top lip. As if she realised what this might look like, she arranged her features into a more assured pose.

Oh my lord, thought Norma. The conniving witch. What mother would be so considered in her actions as to try and cash in only days after hearing her only daughter may have been sexually molested? Surely this would be enough to see Dave go free. Surely?

'How did you feel, as a mother, Mrs Brown, to hear your daughter crying, to see her upset, while thinking that trauma had been caused by what might amount to sexual assault?'

'I was devastated.'

'So devastated you researched half a dozen literary agents and emailed them, citing a juicy celebrity link, only days after finding this out?'

'There's no law against making money is there?'

'Quite.' Bain looked to the jury members. 'And under cross-examination no doubt my esteemed colleague will have you repeat that assertion.'

'It was horrible to hear what my daughter had gone through. I needed to keep busy to distract myself from the disgusting thing that had happened to her. Yes, we're skint and we'll need to earn money to pay for the changes this thing has brought into our lives. Damaris can't go back to the same school. Everyone's different with her, so we'll need to move house. And she'll probably be in therapy for the rest of her life.' She set her jaw as if daring Bain to rip through her logic. 'All of that will need to be paid for.'

'I have to congratulate you on your perspicacity, Mrs Brown.' She looked at him.

'To make those calculations while in the throes of a horribly difficult time. You must be a great help in a crisis, Mrs Brown.'

'So I've been told,' she answered, defiance in the straight line of her shoulders and jut of her chin.

'Let's cut the sham, Mrs Brown. *All* of this was done with calculation. You hit upon the idea when Damaris came home crying after hurting herself in a delicate area when she fell off her bike.'

'Rubbish.'

'You picked up on that and ran with it. You needed the money.'

'No.'

'You were in great need of the money, and desperate times call for desperate measures. You were happy to sacrifice the freedom of Mr Robbins...'

'No.'

'...and the future mental health of your daughter...'

'No.'

'...in order to make a quick and shabby buck.'

'I've never heard such rubbish in my—'

'I find your machinations contemptible, Mrs Brown, and I wonder if you can sleep at night.'

'Mr Bain.' The judge looked over at him, her brows in a stern line. 'Cut the theatrics. The jury will disregard that last sentence.'

'Apologies, M'lady,' Bain said, but it looked to Norma as if he wasn't sorry in the least, and she exalted in the way her son's lawyer had torn a strip out of the woman.

'Mrs Brown,' Bain continued. 'I put it to you that your daughter has never been the object of any sordid attention from Mr

Robbins, and that this whole ... enterprise, and I use that word advisedly, was your way of cashing in on a little accident your daughter had with her bike, to make money from a celebrity connection to help pay your considerable debts.'

Claire Brown was shaking her head at almost every word Bain said. 'No, no, no. That man molested my child and I want to see him punished.'

'Very well, Mrs Brown,' Bain said. 'I truly hope your daughter gets all the help she needs after the way you've used her.' His tone suggested he was certain it wouldn't come from her. 'The defence rests, M'lady.'

Chapter 32

'Ladies and gentlemen of the jury –' the judge sat taller in her seat '– you have listened to the various witnesses as presented by the prosecution and the defence. I understand this case has garnered huge attention in the outside world, given the accused's association with Miss Hart...' At this Amelie felt every eye in the room on her. 'I urge you to ignore this and concentrate solely on the testimony delivered in this courtroom.'

As the judge continued in her summing up Amelie scanned the jury for hints as to what their decision might be. Most of them were now sitting impassively, eyes trained on the judge as if committing every word to memory. One or two were looking back and forth between the judge and her, and one woman at the end of the front row was staring at Dave as if she wanted to remove his testicles with a butter knife.

There was a loud noise as fifteen people stood up, pushing their chairs back, and they all trooped out of the room.

Dave was ushered out of his seat and all of those in attendance started to leave the room. Amelie felt a hand on her arm.

'What do you think, dear?' asked Norma. 'Is my boy going to be free soon?'

'Of course he is, darling,' Peter said. 'The jury will see through the lies from the prosecution. Give it an hour and the jury will be back with an innocent verdict, you mark my words.'

'I'd caution against thinking something like that,' Bain said as he walked alongside them. 'There's no telling how a jury will react to evidence. My advice is to go home and wait out the verdict callback as best you can.'

Norma stumbled. She managed to right herself and with a hand over her heart said in a near whisper, 'I'm not sure I can handle this.'

She looked even paler than normal, her lips almost the same colour as the skin of her face.

'Do you need a doctor, Norma?' Amelie asked. 'Should we get you a doctor?'

She shook her head resolutely, and Amelie could almost read her thought; if her boy was suffering, she would manage to endure until she knew he was safe.

'Did you take your medicine this morning, dear?' Peter asked. In his eagerness to reach his wife he all but shouldered Amelie to the side.

'Stop fussing, Peter.' She stood upright, but it was clearly an effort. 'I'm fine.'

'You don't look—'

'Peter, stop,' Norma said, and Amelie caught a little insight into their marriage in that brief interaction. It looked as if for the most part Peter was the one calling the shots, but the steel in Norma's response suggested whatever they did, they did only with her permission.

Outside the main entrance the press pack were hungry for a few words from her. So far she'd given them nothing, but from experience she knew that only made them more insistent, so she stopped for the first question.

'Confident of the verdict, Miss Hart?' A young woman she recognised as being from the BBC thrust a microphone in her direction.

'We have to be confident in the system; that a jury of ordinary members of the public will see the evidence and record the only proper verdict, that Dave Robbins is innocent.'

'You seem so sure, Miss Hart. What is that based on?'

'I trust in the system,' she replied with a certainty she didn't feel. It was only a couple of years ago that a dog had won a national TV talent competition for doing a few tricks while other huge talents had trained their whole lives to do incredibly complex things and failed.

A number of people fired questions at her.

'Miss Hart, will you be going back to work whatever the outcome of this case? There are reports that you have been offered a number of parts in Hollywood.'

'My only concern at the moment is hearing that my boyfriend has been found not guilty.'

'So you are concerned about the verdict?' someone else asked.

This was a mistake, she realised. Her thoughts weren't clear enough, the questions were coming at her too thick and fast.

'I'm sorry,' she mumbled while pulling her sunglasses from her handbag and putting them on. 'I have to go.' She pushed through the pack and ran down the stairs, saw that Peter had had enough time to bring his car round and ran towards it.

'Thanks,' she managed when she got in the back.

Faces and cameras were all round the car, peering in, mouths moving in shouted questions.

'How do you put up with this?' Peter asked. 'Parasites.' And as if he didn't care if he ran someone down he revved the engine and pulled away from the kerb. 'Do you want to come to ours, Amelie, or are you going back to your hotel?' Peter asked her as he looked in the rear-view mirror.

'The hotel, please, Peter. Thanks.'

'You sure, dear?' Norma said. 'It's no trouble.'

'Thanks, Norma.' Amelie reached to the front passenger seat and patted her on the shoulder.

'Hotel rooms are so impersonal, I find,' Norma said.

Amelie was so used to them in her old job, their impersonal nature sometimes suited her. Besides, once she'd disgorged the contents of her suitcase around the space it did sort of feel like her bedroom at home.

'I just need to close the curtains and crawl under the covers for a few hours,' Amelie replied. 'But thanks. I appreciate the offer.'

She pulled her phone out of her handbag and switched it on. There were two messages. The first was from the old lady with a cottage the other side of the courtyard from her: Mrs Thomson. She was seeing to George while Amelie was staying in town. Mrs Thomson let her know that George was fine and that he'd even mastered a new sound to let her know he was hungry.

Amelie smiled at this, and found a moment's relief in that simple pleasure. *Bless you, Mrs Thomson*, she thought.

Her next text was from Lisa, telling her to check what was happening on Twitter. Amelie sighed. She still thought of this as a 'new' online platform although Lisa had been using it, she said, 'for ages' and struggled with the point of the whole thing. Amelie replied with: *Really?*

Almost immediately a reply pinged on her screen.

There was a leak to the press re Mamma Brown. Would you believe it?

Realising what this meant, and wondering what it might mean to Dave, she brought the app up on her phone and started scanning through it.

People were talking about the migrant crises, the possible spread of Ebola into the West, and with Prince Harry turning thirty-one people were speculating if he'd ever get married.

What was she supposed to be looking for here?

Trending topics. That was the term Lisa had used during her short tutorial. She scrolled to where they might be and found her name was highlighted. With a surge of worry she tapped it and a long list of entries appeared. One was for an article from the *Telegraph*. The headline read 'Mother in Robbins Trial in Shock Literary Approach'. Below that it provided more detail, giving the date of the alleged assault and the date of the emails she sent out to literary agents.

The article had been shared over two thousand times and had a massive run of replies. The first one questioned Claire Brown's motives, so with that acting as a reassurance Amelie scrolled down. More tweets asking what kind of mother would be that callous. Then there were a few that echoed the prosecution lawyer's stance: it wasn't illegal.

Then the replies took a turn for the worse.

Momma Bear tweeted, *SFW, Robbins is a paedo. Deserves to be hung.*

Candy said, *Amelie Hart, movie star in a shit movie, knew what was happening. I betcha.*

DanTheMan asserted, *I'll shoot Robbins. Hart can fuck off and die for all I care. After she sucks my cock.*

She threw her phone onto the seat away from her.

'Everything okay, Amelie?' Norma asked.

'Fine,' Amelie replied. She was hit by a massive wave of fatigue. Closing her eyes against it she filled her lungs and found some energy to finish her answer. 'It's just people on Twitter being nasty.'

'I don't understand that twittering thing,' Norma said.

'Load of nonsense,' Peter echoed, and Amelie caught the look of concern he shot his wife, as if he was checking her to see how she was bearing up. Even from Amelie's angle, Dave's mother didn't look in a good way. Amelie hoped Peter would manage to persuade her to go and see her doctor.

The car pulled over to the side of the road, and aware of the movement Amelie looked around. They'd arrived. A small group of reporters were standing at the entrance to the hotel.

'Is there a back way?' Peter asked.

'There's probably going to be some there as well,' Amelie said. 'Don't worry I'll just barge through them. I've got sharp elbows, you know.' She managed a laugh.

'Give one of them a prod for me, dear,' Norma said.

'For sure,' Amelie replied and put a hand on Norma's forearm. 'It's a waiting game now, I guess.' Peter and Norma both nodded. 'Keep in touch, eh?'

She got out of the car and, head down, waded through the reporters, ignoring the shouted questions and the cameras. Once inside, she picked her key up from reception, all but ran to her room and flung herself on the bed.

Her phone rang. She fished it out of her bag to see Lisa's name appear on the screen.

'Well, did you see it?' her friend asked.

'I wonder where that leak came from?' Amelie replied.

'Heaven only knows,' Lisa replied in her butter-wouldn't-melt voice. 'Anyway, I doubt now that any self-respecting agent will touch her with the proverbial long pole. I hope the bitch loses everything.'

They were back in court. The jury had taken three days to reach a decision. Three days, during which Dave had no idea how he had managed to handle the tension. He couldn't stay still. In his cell he moved from his bed to the small chair at the desk, to the floor.

What if they found him guilty? Then he'd be in here, branded a convicted paedophile. What kind of sentence would he get? Bain told him the minimum sentence was twelve months, and the maximum was life.

'Life?'

'When it's a child under thirteen, yes. But don't worry; it's rare that a judge goes that long.'

'What determines the sentence length then?'

'Lots of things. The risk of reoffending, previous convictions – and your conviction for assault won't help here...'

'But that was years ago. I was a stupid lad and I've been a law-abiding citizen ever since.'

'Other factors could be remorse shown for the crime, pissing off the social worker who reports to the court...'

'Remorse shown? How the hell...?'

'Not going to happen, David. You're innocent and the jury will find in your favour.'

That was a conversation they'd had weeks ago when they were still preparing for the trial. Now, in the moment when he was waiting for the jury spokesperson to be called it seemed like a million years ago.

His pulse thundered in his ears. Every part of him trembled.

Someone was on their feet.

'Have you come to a decision?' the judge asked.

'We have, M'lady,' the woman answered.

'What is your verdict?'

Chapter 33

Dave felt like he was suspended in the air. Remote from everything. Noise was muffled, every breath came to him as if through a layer of cotton wool. He couldn't feel the slight cushion of his seat on his back or thighs, or the wooden floor under his feet. The edges of his vision were blurred as if he was viewing the world through some kind of filter. Everything looked as if the lights had been turned down.

He assessed the spokesperson for the jury. She was just an ordinary woman. Someone's mother. Someone's daughter. A touch of grey in her hair and a slight waver in her voice as if she had just become aware of the importance of what she was about to say.

'On the charge of sexual assault of a child under thirteen years old.'

She paused, eyes fixed on a spot in front of her.

'Guilty.'

The noise around Dave grew louder.

A roar.

People were gasping. Someone was crying. Someone was cheering.

'No, no, no, no, no,' a voice said. It might even have been him. It was him.

Reality slammed down on him like a hammer of thunder and light.

'On the charge of causing a child to watch a sexual act.'

Pause.

'Guilty.'

'No,' Dave shouted. 'No, how could you get this so wrong?'

'Mr Robbins, you will control yourself or you will be removed from my court.'

'Call this a court? It's a travesty. You've fallen for their lies.'

'Mr Robbins,' the judge said, shouting above him.

Dave felt strong hands on his arms. They pulled. He resisted. He heard cheers and jeers.

'No, no, no,' he shouted.

Hands on his shoulders and legs. There were too many of them to fight. He felt himself being carried off, and before the door slammed shut behind him he heard a noise that almost tore the heart from his chest.

A wail of pain and disbelief that could only have come from his mother.

Chapter 34

Amelie was sitting in another uncomfortable chair. This time in the waiting area of the intensive care unit of Glasgow's big, shiny-new Queen Elizabeth University Hospital.

Only now, as she waited while the medical staff worked on Norma, did she have the time to digest the verdict.

Guilty.

It was staggering. Beggared belief. Dave was a convicted paedophile. How could something like this happen?

No wonder Norma had collapsed.

Amelie had been sitting, stunned after hearing the words from the jury spokesperson's mouth, when she heard a wail from Norma and then felt her fall against her. She and Peter turned to her, his face a vision of panic. 'She's not breathing.'

'Clear the court.' Bain took command. 'Medical staff to me now,' he shouted.

They eased Norma to the floor. Bain checked her neck for a pulse.

'She's not breathing,' Peter said in a panicked whisper.

It occurred to Amelie as she sat in that sterile space that Dave wouldn't know what was happening. He was being all but carried out of the court when Norma collapsed, so he would have had no idea that his mother was having emergency surgery. Perhaps Joseph Bain had been in touch.

What would the protocol be there, she wondered? If Norma died would he get to the funeral? If she survived would he be allowed to visit her?

She cringed at the realisation that her first concern had been what would happen if Norma died, and sent a silent prayer skyward.

Hearing heavy footsteps, she turned and saw Peter coming towards her. He looked like a man at his own haunting. His eyes were heavy, his face the colour of bleached linen, and his suit, which earlier looked like it had been delivered direct from Savile Row, now looked crumpled beyond further outings.

He sat beside Amelie, exhaling as if the action of sitting had taken his last remaining ounce of energy. 'They're still operating,' he said. 'She can't die. She can't die.' He leaned forward, elbows on his knees, shoulders heaving with emotion.

At a loss as to what she should do Amelie placed a hand on his back. 'She's in the best place, Peter. This part of the world is like Heart Attack Central. They get loads of practice.'

'Dave won't know.' He pushed himself upright. 'We have to let Dave know.'

'I'll get on to Bain. Perhaps best to wait until we know the outcome of the surgery?'

He sat back in his chair. 'I can't believe he was found guilty.'

'Me neither.'

'My son's a convicted criminal. A convicted paedophile.' He looked in the direction he'd just come from. 'And then this...'

They each slumped into silence. Into a dead headspace where words were formless and fear chased them from one nameless emotion to the next. Where physical function was a matter of staying upright and in count with the breath.

How long they waited, Amelie had no idea. A clue perhaps in the slant of the shadows on the far wall from the large window behind her, had she the wit to read them.

A creak of a door. Heavy footsteps and an exhalation as weighty as the bearer's dolorous expression. The surgeon stood before them, shoulders rounded in defeat, removing the surgical mask from around his neck.

'Mr Robbins, I'm so sorry...'

Chapter 35

It was two weeks after he'd been found guilty, six days after his mother's funeral, and Dave was being guided into a small room where a woman was behind a desk.

'I'm sorry for your loss, Mr Robbins,' she said.

Dave sat on the seat opposite the woman. He crossed his arms and his legs, feeling that her offer of condolences were perfunctory. Just another box to be ticked.

'My name is Andrea Davidson. I'm a social worker appointed by the court to compile a report that will be used in your sentencing hearing.'

Bain had briefed him on this. Warned him to co-operate if he wanted to limit his eventual sentence, but confusion and resentment at being in this situation bubbled in his veins so much it was a wonder he could sit still.

'Do you understand this part of the process, Dave?' she asked.

He nodded.

'Any questions?'

He shook his head.

'I see from your records you were given a suspended sentence for assault in June of 2005. What can you tell me about that?'

'I was a stupid kid.'

'And?'

'And nothing. Lesson learned. I wasn't in bother ever again.'

'Until now. What happened to make you attack this other lad, Dave?'

Play the game, he told himself.

'It was a night at the local rugby club. Letting off steam after end-of-year accountancy exams. The barmaid's boyfriend took offence when one of my mates had a leer down her top. He pushed my pal. He was too drunk to defend himself. I stepped in.'

She read for a moment. 'It says here it took five men to pull you off him.'

Dave felt his face and neck heat at this. All these years later and he was still taken aback at the force of his anger. 'Not my finest hour, Miss Davidson.'

'Where was that anger coming from, Dave?'

He looked at her – really looked at her for the first time, trying to see the human being beyond the representative of the judicial system. He could smell cigarette smoke on her. She'd had a quick ciggie before coming in to see him. Was this an attempt at self-soothing before meeting someone she saw as potentially troubling, or simply an answer to a craving?

She was slim-shouldered, her wrists no thicker than a child's, a prominent vein stretching down the back of her freckled hand. Her nails were long, manicured, painted in a clear lacquer.

Her clothes were sombre, as if she was on her way to or from a funeral tea. Light-blue shirt buttoned to the neck, navy-blue cardigan. Was the cardigan an attempt to soften her look. Project a caring attitude?

Her long hair – light brown, threaded with grey at the temples – was pulled back in a ponytail at the nape of her neck. Femininity neither suppressed nor heightened, simply there, like ozone in the sky.

Was their calculation in any of this? Or did she simply get out of bed in the morning, see to her family – there was a wedding ring; did she have kids? And then see to her personal grooming in a way that was expedient? Whatever was in the wardrobe, cleaned and ironed, was enough?

She was eyeing him as if to ask, *finished*?

He offered her a small smile. How awful would it be to spend her working day, working *life* with people who'd committed some of the worst crimes imaginable.

'Throughout that whole period no one asked me about that,' Dave replied. 'They just sent me to a guy who was to help me control myself.'

'Where did that anger come from?'

'I was an angry young guy.' Memory presented an image of his father in his kitchen with another woman. The neighbour's wife. A betrayal he'd learned to push back into a dark space in his mind. 'When I was in my early teens I caught my dad with the neighbour.' He'd never told anyone this before.

'Did you confront your father?'

'No.'

'Did you tell your mother?'

'Jesus, are you kidding? You're only the second person I've ever told about it.' And why now, he wondered, in this place?

'Yeah, a death in the family can dislodge all kinds of things,' she said, providing a possible answer to his internal questioning. 'You didn't reoffend. The anger-management course worked then?'

'I think that explosion in the bar was enough. Got it out of my system. Besides, I was ashamed that I'd hurt that guy. He was just looking out for his girlfriend.'

She wrote something down on the pad in front of her.

'Back to the present.' She coughed into the back of her hand. 'You were working in your father's business at the time of your arrest. When you get out of prison do you expect to pick up where you left off?'

'I don't think I'll come away from this unchanged, do you?'

She gave a little smile as if acknowledging she'd framed her question in the wrong way. 'Will you go back to work as an accountant?'

'My father has lost some clients because of this, and that was before I was convicted. Provided the business doesn't haemorrhage clients that would be my plan.'

'If it would damage the business irreparably?'

Dave paused before answering. His father's firm was an established player in the financial world of the city of Glasgow. Peter Robbins had salted enough away over the years to give him a very comfortable retirement, but would his legacy suffer? Dave shifted in his seat, feeling the responsibility of that.

Realising that some kind of positive answer was going to help his cause, he replied, 'Dad is a creative thinker. If the business is in danger he'll find a way to appease the concerned.'

'For example?'

'Remove me as a partner and quietly bring me in to the back office. Perhaps work from home. Get me to work on internal audits. He'll keep me busy and employed, be assured of that.'

'Where will you live?'

'There's a small flat on the top floor of our business premises in St Vincent Street. Dad used to use that when he was in the city for posh charity dinners and the like.'

'Used to?'

'Mum didn't like it.' He stopped speaking. The mention of her caused a bubble of grief to work up from his chest into his throat. The muscles there tightened. He coughed. A tear slid down his cheek. 'She, eh, preferred to go home to her own bed after a night of wearing posh frocks and eating rich food.' He heard her voice in his head as he said this, remembering how she loved helping the charitable causes Dad's success enabled, but hating the waste and cost of bringing all these rich people together and cajoling them to donate. *How much did that dinner cost to put on? Bloody ridiculous*, she'd say each time.

'Do you need a moment?' Davidson asked him. In that moment, he appreciated that she was asking him as a fellow human being, seeing past the tag of paedophile. And that recognition was enough for the pressure to release, and for the first time since he heard his mother was dead, he cried. Hands over his face, bent over so that his elbows were on his knees, he gave in to the emotion.

Moments, or minutes, later he was aware that Davidson was rummaging in her bag. Then she was sliding something across the table top to him. A packet of paper tissues.

He pulled one out and wiped his cheeks and his nose. Then the corners of his mouth.

'Thanks,' he managed. It came out in a whisper.

'Do you need a break?' she asked, leaning towards him. 'I can book in to come back another day to finish this off.'

Dave shook his head and coughed as if he was trying to relocate his vocal chords. 'Please. Let's get this over with today.'

She sat back in her seat and her more business-like mask was on.

'In among that expression of grief for your mother was there any thought for the victim of your crime?'

'Her name's Damaris, and it's thanks to her lies that I'm in here.' Under the table Dave felt his fists clench. An involuntary reaction. And he was back in anger mode.

'In my experience little girls don't lie about things like this.'

'This one did.'

'The jury believed her.'

'Yeah, cos they never get it wrong.' Dave challenged her with his eyes.

She didn't flinch, she'd probably had years of dealing with bad men. Dave was just another one.

'Part of the process of your rehabilitation while you serve your sentence is for you to examine why you did this and to express your remorse.'

'Am I sorry?' Dave leaned forward. 'Yeah, I'm sorry. Sorry I ever moved in next door to her and her fucking awful parents. That little girl was coached to lie and you lot fell for it.'

She said nothing. Her head was inclined slightly to the left, her hand poised over her notepad.

Dave recognised the tactic of employed silence and decided at this point he couldn't – wouldn't – play the game. He wasn't going to fill the quiet with any dark, heavy secrets. He shifted in his seat so that he was side on to her. So that she was getting nothing but his profile and an elbow pointing back at her.

'Why do you think parents would use their child in such a way?'

'Why else? Money. I did not abuse Damaris. I was only ever a friend to that little girl...' His throat tightened with emotion again. He coughed, then swallowed, trying to release the feeling. Blinked back the tears that sparked in his eyes.

Dave thought about standing up and leaving. This woman wasn't interested in what he had to say unless it was to acknowledge his guilt. But if he did leave that would mean going back to E Hall and the beasts. As bad as this was, at least it was a break with being surrounded by sick and dangerous men. Besides, the outcome of this meeting could well determine the length of his sentence. He needed to get a grip.

'You're saying a mother and father would put their child through the hell of a court case and convince her she'd been sexually molested to make money?'

'It's the only reason I can think of. They are having serious money problems, as was documented in court. So, this day, Damaris comes home crying. She's all bruised down there after falling off her bike. Mummy dearest concocts a plan to cash in on the fame of her next-door neighbour.'

Hearing a crack and waver in his voice, he became aware that the deep unfairness of it all was leaking into his speech. He might say something that would make his situation worse. He clamped his jaw shut.

Davidson briefly scratched her pen on her notepad. He couldn't read her writing from where he was sitting but he could guess what she had written.

In denial.

It was clear on every line of her posture. The jury had found him guilty. Therefore he *was* guilty. The system was infallible or her existence came into question and that would be an intolerable position to be in. In her eyes he was guilty of a heinous crime and every thought or consideration she had about him flowed from that unassailable mindset.

Enough. His slender control on his emotions lost, he jumped to his feet, ignoring the squeal of the chair against the floor. 'Why don't we get to the part where you try to get me to demonstrate remorse and I reassert my innocence *for the millionth time*?'

Chapter 36

Despite her assertion she'd never leave her home, on the way back to her hotel from Norma Robbins' funeral Amelia was on the phone to Bernard asking him to find her a place for rent. Preferably in a hamlet somewhere the press would never think to look for her. The thought of going back to being neighbours with that couple was simply unbearable.

'And put the cottage up for rent. Fully furnished. Other than my clothes I can't bear to take anything with me,' she instructed him. What about the cat? *Oh George*, she thought. She'd really miss him. 'And make sure whoever arranges this, they only accept a cat-lover. George has to be looked after.'

'Won't old Mrs Whatshername across the yard want him?'

'She likes a visit now and again but she won't want the full responsibility.'

'Any ideas where this peaceful hamlet should be?'

She rubbed at her forehead, watching the grand buildings of Glasgow slide by the car window. 'I don't know, Bernard. I can't think. Somewhere unpronounceable. Ardnamurchan. It's difficult enough for the London press to get up to Glasgow. Let them wrestle with that one.' Where that name came from she'd no idea. Probably somewhere Dave talked about visiting.

'But that's in the middle of the middle of nowhere.'

'Exactly.'

'I'm sure the world's media would still find you there. Didn't you and Dave meet in the Highlands? That's part of your legend, they'll eat that up.'

Bernard had a point. She could see the headlines that would cause. 'Hollywood Star Retraces Paedophile Steps'.

'Did your French passport ever arrive?' he asked.

In the heat of the past few months, she'd forgotten about that. In a fit of anger over the Brexit vote she'd applied for her French passport. It had arrived some time ago and she'd stuck it in a drawer somewhere, realising it was an empty gesture and would change nothing about the political situation. She did get a thrill though when she plucked it out of the envelope and saw her real name on an official document: *Solange Amelie Meric*. Solange after her paternal *grand-mère*, with her father's surname, a name she hadn't used in such a long time, preferring her mother's maiden name, Hart.

'Yes,' she said. 'It's in a drawer back in the house somewhere.'

'Well, what about France? You've always talked about going back there, retracing the paternal line and all that.'

'But that would mean abandoning Dave.'

'How long would it take to get from Ardna-wherever to visit him in prison, supposing he changes his mind and puts you on his visitor list?'

Amelie wasn't exactly sure where it was but knew it was on the north-west coast of Scotland somewhere and suspected that narrow, winding roads and possibly even a short ferry journey would be involved. 'Ages.'

'And how long would it take to fly back from France to Glasgow? Supposing he changes his mind and puts you on...'

'Yeah, alright,' Amelie said. 'I take your point. But it still feels like I'm abandoning him.'

'He knew the relationship was over before this all kicked off.' And then, as if he sensed she was about to ask how he knew about the state of her relationship, he added, 'Sorry, darling, Lisa and I occasionally talk. Dave doesn't want you to stick by him out of some sense of duty or, God forbid, pity. He wants you to get on with your life.'

Peter Robbins wasn't so lost in his own grief that he didn't realise what a difficult situation she was in. When she called him the day after the funeral he offered her a place to live.

'I don't expect you can go back to Thorntonhall,' he said. 'You could stay at ours ... mine,' he corrected, 'until you get yourself sorted. There's the granny flat. Or if you prefer the anonymity of the city centre to our place here in Bearsden, you can have the apartment on the top floor of the office building. Have it for as long as you like, Amelie,' he said. And Amelie heard a faint note of desperation there. Now that his wife was dead and his son was in prison, perhaps she was a link to a better time that he subconsciously felt he needed.

With a massive sense of gratitude, Amelie collected her belongings from the cottage, at a time when she knew the Browns would be out, said goodbye to the cat, after she'd dumped a month's worth of cat food with her neighbour to tide George over until the new people were set up, and moved in to the city-centre apartment. It was well fitted out – a bit on the sterile side with barely a picture on the walls and no soft furnishings to talk of – but it had lots of space for her and her more personal belongings.

Then, without any real expectation that it really would happen, Amelie hoped that with the sentencing hearing over and a four-year sentence handed down, the clamour for all things Robbins and Hart would now die down.

If anything, it went up a notch. People were outraged about the length of the sentence and it seemed that every daytime TV host had an opinion about it. Then there was the petition started by one of the tabloids, apparently aimed at pressurising the Scottish courts into increasing the sentence, but of course, really aimed at increasing readership.

Every day, it seemed like a microphone was thrust in her face and the question was asked, 'Now that your lover is a convicted paedophile how can you still support him?'

Vanessa Court was a regular on TV now, boosting her acting

career with a running commentary on her relationship with Amelie Hart and her 'paedophile boyfriend'. If the TV was on and Vanessa's face appeared Amelie was quick to turn it off.

However, one morning she gave in to the impulse to listen, like a driver slowing down to get a good look at a mangled car.

'Didn't trust him for a moment. There was something that was just off about him. Everyone could see it,' Vanessa replied to whatever question she was asked. Amelie recognised the format of the show, she'd enjoyed this on many a lazy lunchtime. Four women at a large desk in front of a studio audience chatting informally to a guest, who always sat in the middle.

'So other people in your circle had concerns about David Robbins?' one of the women asked.

A nod. 'He was just, like, a bit awkward, you know? Anyone at these things who can't make eye contact is not quite right, in my humble... I mean, why else are you there, but to be seen –' she gave a little toss of her head and turned slightly to the left as if fully aware that was her best side '– and to network?'

Amelie tried to work out what event she could be referring to. Dave rarely attended any of them with her. There was only one she could think of, and he was only there because he was trying to raise money for a befriending charity. 'It was Children in Need, you dumb bitch.' She was on her feet shouting at the screen.

'And concerning these awful events, do you think Amelie Hart was aware she had a monster living in her house?'

Vanessa turned her face to the camera. Working her full emotional range, she looked down at the table top, over to the hosts, and then back to the camera. She swallowed, as if that would indicate her reluctance to betray a friend. And then, crossing her arms, as if bracing herself against a painful truth, she said, 'I have no doubt that Amelie Hart knew exactly what David Robbins was.'

The hate mail went up several notches after that, and every day it seemed someone spat on her. Refusing to hide from it all, she went out regularly, determined that the outrage wouldn't deter her from living her life, and when she got home it was to find that the back of her coat, and often her hair, was covered in spit.

She'd closed down her social-media accounts so people were driven into print. Letters arrived by the sack-load, all of them – all the ones she read, in any case – telling her what a foul human being she was. Many of them containing rape and death threats, and many of them were from other women, a fact that gave her much distress. How people knew where she lived now was a mystery. Often they were simply addressed to Amelie Hart, Glasgow. Many of them were even addressed to Peter's firm, in a desperate but scarily successful attempt to locate her.

Most days, after work, Peter would quietly knock on the door and enquire how she was. Every time, she would invite him in for a coffee or a glass of wine. Occasionally, he accepted, and now and again a glass of wine led to a simple meal. Judging by the way his suit was hanging on him he wasn't eating nearly enough food, so Amelie started a mission to feed the man. It hurt her to see how much he'd changed since they'd first met.

'You can't go on living like this, dear,' he said one day after manfully chewing through half a bowl of mushroom risotto. 'What are you going to do with the rest of your life?'

'I guess I was waiting to hear what the sentence was before thinking about that, but now I'm stuck in this state of inertia. I don't seem to have the energy to do anything, or make any decisions.'

She told him her thoughts about going to France.

He nodded. 'They have stricter rules about hounding famous people in the media. Worth more than a thought, I'd say.' He pushed his plate away from him. 'Would you go back to work? How would you support yourself?' She'd told him about her financial losses during a previous late-evening chat. 'I have plenty,' he added. 'You stood by our David, and Norma would want me to help you ... financially ... if you needed it,' he added with an apologetic smile.

'Thank you, Peter. That's very kind of you, but you've done enough.'

'It's no problem, really.'

'I've always stood on my own two feet. It's important to me that I carry on like that.'

'France is a good idea,' he said slowly as if continuing to think this through. 'How you can stand the attention every day is beyond me. People really are foul towards you, and you've done nothing wrong.' His eyes grew moist. 'Norma would be so angry.'

Chapter 37

'Who the fuck are you?' the young man sitting on the bottom bunk in his cell asked Dave when he returned from his session with the social worker.

'I should be asking you that question.'

'This your place then?' he asked, looking around the cell. 'I'm your new co-pilot, by the way. Angus.' Dave guessed if the man was over twenty years old it was only by a few weeks.

It had to happen at some stage, but Dave had become used to being on his own. His new 'co-pilot' obviously knew the lingo; did that mean he'd been inside before? As was his habit now, Dave looked him over, assessing him for danger. He had short blond hair, a carefully trimmed beard with a handful of acne scars peeping through. Under his red polo shirt, the sag of his man-boobs suggested the lad was a stranger to a press-up.

Angus's hands were clasped and rested on his knees as he sat there in a slightly crouched position, jiggling his legs. He was nervous then. The aggressive welcome merely a weak attempt at disguise.

'Here.' The guy stood up and Dave could see he was about average height. Shorter than him, then. 'Ah know you. You're that cunt with the movie-star girlfriend who was supposed to huv abused that wee lassie.'

Dave groaned. And was then on alert. He braced himself for an attack.

'Ma granny says you didn't do it. Says if you're guilty she's the Queen of Sheba. Whoever that is. Ma granny watches all they CSI programmes and guesses the murderer every time. It's like magic or something. Pure genius.' He held a hand out. 'I'm Angus, by the way.'

'Aye, you said.' They shook hands. 'Dave.'

'Ah know yur name,' Angus said. As he spoke he rubbed his scalp and his face pinked with pleasure. 'Ah'm dubbed up with a bona-fide celebrity. How cool is that?'

'Bin the celebrity shit, Angus.'

'By the way,' Angus looked at his face as if studying it, 'your scars are healing up nicely. That was a pure shame what they done to you. Imagine scalding somebody. That's pure evil.' Angus shuddered. Dave could judge by the careful attention to his beard and hair that Angus sported his fair share of vanity. Something like that would be his worst nightmare.

Dave climbed up on to the top bunk and lay there, both hands under his head. At least Angus had picked the free bunk. That was one less thing they had to negotiate.

'Is it cos you're a celebrity con, d'ye think, that they went for you?'

'I'm not a fucking celebrity, Angus.'

'Keep your hair on, mate. Just asking. And by the way, if we're going to be co-pilots let's at least be civil to wan another, eh? Space is a bit tight for any celeb tantrums.'

'For chrisssake.'

Angus laughed. 'Just yankin' your chain, mate.' The springs creaked on the bed below, suggesting Angus was changing position. 'It's a deal. No more mention of famous people. Except one last question. What was it like, sleeping with a proper movie star? You must have loads of stuff locked up in the wank bank, ya lucky bastard.'

Dave jumped off the bed and leaned into Angus's face. 'You want to be civil? Any more mentions of Amelie and I'll find a shank and have one of your kidneys out. Got me?'

'Got you. Jesus.' Angus held his hands up. 'Touchy or what?'

Dave climbed back up onto his bed.

Silence.

Dave turned to face the wall, pulled his knees up towards his chest and settled in to think through his conversation with the social worker. What would his reaction at the end of their conversation do for his chances of a shorter sentence? What an idiot.

'My bird's quite tasty as well,' Angus said. 'What a beautiful body. Gorgeous. Not in the same league as your...' He stopped. 'Just one of them head-turners you see every day in Glasgow. Lots of good-looking women out there, eh?'

Dave closed his eyes and hoped that Angus would read his silence as a signal to stop talking.

'That was my problem. Liked looking at women. Loved looking at pictures of Jenny. That's my hot girlfriend, by the way. Well, my hot *ex*-girlfriend.'

Despite himself, Dave found himself connecting the statements about looking at pictures and Jenny being his ex. 'Ex-girlfriend? You stalked her then?'

'No. What do you take me for?' he asked huffily. 'I'm no' a deviant. I had some pictures of her on my phone and when she two-timed me with a guy she met on a girly holiday I sent one of the pictures to her dad.'

'What was happening in this picture?'

'She was sucking my cock.'

'Bloody hell,' Dave said. 'Poor woman. What a horrible thing to do to her.'

'Well, she shouldn't have shagged that German guy in Ibiza, should she?' Angus lapsed into silence, but only for a moment. 'Yeah, lesson learned. One daft wee picture and I end up in this dump, locked up with the perverts ... no offence.' More movement from the bed below him and Angus was on his feet. He prodded Dave in the back.

'Can I get a wee bit of peace here, mate?' Dave asked.

'Sorry, just had a thought.'

Dave turned to face Angus, who was standing uncomfortably close. Dave pushed himself to a sitting position and flung his legs over the side of the bed, in the hope that Angus would move back and give him more space.

'You were an accountant or something, aye?' Angus asked as he stepped back to lean against the desktop bolted on to the far wall.

'Still am,' replied Dave.

'Means you're proper smart, eh? I need to write a letter to Jenny.'

'Not interested.'

'Wait a minute.' Angus held his hands up. 'I'm done with the revenge porn an' that. I want to send her a wee letter of apology. Ah done a horrible thing. Nae lassie wants her Da to see a pic of her with her mouth round a gerry helmet.'

'Shame you didn't realise that before you sent the picture.'

'Totally,' Angus agreed. 'What a bell-end. Anyway, if I write the letter, will you check it out? Make sure it's dead clever an' that?' His face was slumped in an expression of contrition.

'Yeah,' he replied, realising that Angus was genuine. 'I'll see what I can do.'

'Magic,' Angus said and rubbed his hands together.

Just then the cell door opened and Walker, one of the older guards, appeared. 'Letter for Robbins,' he said.

Dave jumped to the floor and stepped over to Walker.

'Cheers,' he said, wondering who it was from and if he would want to read it.

'Shit,' he said when he pulled the paper out of the envelope a couple of inches. Amelie's name and their old address appeared as the header. He pulled it out the rest of the way and read.

'What's up? Somebody die?' Angus asked and then covered his mouth. 'Sorry. Forgot about your ma. Ma granny was pure pissed off at that. Said it must've been the shock. I've got such a big gob at times. Ma granny says I need to think before I talk, but I said to her, how can folk do that and have a quick conversation? If you thought about everything afore you said it, every conversation would take hours.'

'Your granny's right,' Dave said.

'So? Whit's it say?' Angus stepped closer, his head tilted in an effort to read what was on the letter. 'Amelie, eh? Your ex? How's she been? Bet the press are pure giving her pelters.'

'She wants to come to see me before she leaves the country,' Dave said, feeling as if his stomach had plummeted all the way down to his feet.

Chapter 38

There was a little boulangerie tucked into the corner of the square just along from Amelie's new apartment in Bordeaux. She'd fallen into the habit of going there every morning for a baguette, croissant or, on the days when she felt she deserved a treat, one of their delicious pain au raisin. She took as long over her trip as she could, often going the long way around the park, through the ranks of trees, down to the junction where the fruit shop stood, then back past the little play park with the brightly coloured climbing frame and the side entrance to the Basilica de Saint Seurin.

Then she'd walk past the café with the red awnings, cross the road and stand in front of the boulangerie window to peruse the trays of bread, cakes and pastries, but only ever taking home the same items.

'*Bonjour, Madame,*' the owner said every day, her welcoming smile a rare human contact for Amelie in her first two weeks of living in the city. Indeed, in those two weeks the only conversations she'd had were with shop owners when she bought her food.

Two weeks that passed by at a tortuous pace. Every day she questioned why she was here, every day when she opened her curtains to look out over the little park across the road from her new home she felt guilty that she was among these beautiful surroundings while Dave was behind bars.

As she walked among the inhabitants of the city she tried to tune her ears in to the language. Her mother told her years ago that she had been fluent in French as a child, after various summers with her *grand-mère*, but disavowed everything *Français* after her father's string of affairs came to light.

It took a while to get her ear in. A word here. A phrase there, and it slowly began to make some sort of sense. While buying her groceries she would try to allow those forgotten words to tumble from her mouth, but then struggled to understand the response, the words bouncing off each other, the other person assuming she was a native.

'*Lentement, s'il vous plait*,' she would reply. *Slowly, please.*

As she moved among her new neighbours she tried to assess the reactions of everyone she came across. Maybe it was the new darker and shorter hair style – the 'pixie' look Lisa called it – or the large glasses, but it seemed like no one recognised her. Of course the Bordelais were blasé about so-called celebrities being in their midst. They were far too cool and Gallic to stand to the attention of her fame.

There were the usual glances she got from men, and some women, that she'd had most of her life, but few of them went beyond the quick appreciative glance. Those that did were easy to handle. Her well-practised responses ranged from a polite but distant smile to a withering look.

To limit her exposure she didn't walk much beyond her little circuit, more than a little afraid to walk down the Rue Judaïque, which led on to the Place de la Comédie and the Grand Théâtre in the city centre. There she was sure, with the number of tourists around, she was bound to be recognised. And they might not be so reserved as the locals were.

The apartment was her refuge. Bernard had outdone himself when arranging the lease. It was on the fourth floor – two bed-rooms, each en-suite and one large, open-plan living space with three plump-cushioned sofas squared off in front of a large, dec-orative fireplace and a kitchen with everything she could want in the far right-hand corner. All of this with the added bonus of a small, private rooftop garden, from where she could look over the red roofs and treetops of the city.

All this loveliness and she couldn't share it with anyone.

Sitting at her little green, wooden-slatted table in her rooftop garden, slicing and preparing her baguette with butter and jam, sipping fresh coffee that was brewed in her little moka pot, her mind often retreated from the guilty pleasure of it all and she'd think through that last meeting with Dave in prison.

'Thanks for seeing me,' she'd said while searching his face for signs of the attack. There was some scarring at the temple and hairline, and down the side of his face, but the beard he'd grown would disguise most of that.

'Good to see you,' he'd replied. And just as carefully as she'd assessed his skin, Amelie interrogated the tone of those few short words for clues as to his well-being.

'I'm liking the face fuzz,' she said. 'Suits you.'

He pinked a little and her mind flooded with memories. She always loved this about him: the vulnerability and the contradiction he offered when he was confident and capable and strong.

'There's a good barber guy in here.' Dave rubbed at his chin. 'I'll let it grow out a little and he can...' His sentence faded away as if he realised such a topic of conversation was trivial when held against all the things that had happened in the last few months. 'How's Dad? I'm glad he offered you the flat.'

'Yeah, that was very kind of him. He's been amazing actually. I don't know how I could have handled...' It was Amelie's turn to curtail what she was about to say. How could she possibly complain to this man when what he was facing was so much worse. And how much should she say about Peter? Dave would want the truth of it, but should she give so much detail that it would make him worry?

'He's doing okay,' she said, without any real conviction. 'I think work will be the saving of him. Keep him busy.'

Dave nodded. While she was talking his gaze was aimed down at his hands, the table-top, or over her shoulder at other people in the visits hall. He was yet to meet her eye.

'I'm so sorry about all of this. If it wasn't for me...' She slumped forward in her chair, momentarily overcome with emotion. She swallowed it down. She couldn't make a scene of herself in public.

Biting her bottom lip she straightened her back and squared her shoulders.

'Hey.' Dave reached across the table, and she felt the heat of his palm on the back of her right hand. 'None of this is on you. I don't blame you for any of it.'

'I'm...' Amelie's emotions threatened to bubble back up. 'But if I...'

Dave squeezed her hand. 'If pigs could fly they'd be dragons.' Then he pulled his hand away as if he just reminded himself he needed to keep his distance.

'What?' The nonsense of this disrupted her thinking, and she managed a laugh. And then longed for his touch again.

He worked on a smile. 'We were just minding our own business, getting on with our lives when that vicious woman saw an opportunity and ran with it.'

'Poor Damaris,' Amelie said. 'This is really going to mess her up.'

'I know.' Dave nodded his head slowly. 'I hope her mother uses the money from her book deal to pay for counselling. How's that going, by the way? Any word of a deal?'

'Nothing as yet. I'll need to check in with the oracle...'

'How is Lisa?'

Amelie laughed. 'Oh you know Lisa. Nothing bothers her. I did wonder if our connection would harm her, but she says she's Teflon. Last I heard from her she doubted any of the big publishers would touch Mother Brown ... but...'

'Money talks.'

'Yup. If someone thinks there's money to be made they'll snap the book up.' Amelie sat back in her chair, creating a little distance, and realising she'd done this because of what she was about to say next, she leaned forward again. 'I'm hoping my leaving the country will help the interest fade away, and she'll have even less of a chance of a deal.'

'I'm glad you're going,' he said. His smile was resolute, but laced with uncertainty. 'And to Bordeaux. Will you look up your father's family?'

'Last I heard *grand-mère*'s little vineyard was bought by a neighbouring concern when she died. Chateau Smith Haut-Lafitte, or something like that. Not sure if any of the family would have hung around.' She stopped speaking, realising that the conversation had mainly been about her. God, she was such a bitch.

'You bearing up?' she asked.

He shrunk a little, and then mirroring her earlier movements he sat up and set his shoulders. 'One day at a time,' he said, searching her eyes. And in his expression Amelie could read a litany of reasons why he was struggling. 'But I am genuinely happy for you. If one of us gets their life back together again that's a great big fuck-you to the Browns.'

'I still love you, you know...' Her turn for her face to pink. Why on earth had she said that? 'Sorry, I...'

She considered their relationship towards the end. At times she'd given him nothing but a cool indifference, blaming him for her confused state of mind. Then, feeling guilty, she'd accede to the limp plea in his eyes, and lie back, waiting for the passion to rekindle with each pant and thrust, feeling the slow rise of arousal, but pushing it down as images of that masked intruder in the corner of her room grew in her mind.

Then, his head was back on his pillow, and she was marooned on hers.

'I've been doing a lot of reading,' Dave said after a long moment's silence. 'There's a surprisingly well-stocked library in here.' He adopted a self-deprecatory expression before carrying on. 'He or she,' he added with meaning, 'that trusts in a lie shall perish in truth. And, a life well lived is the best revenge.' He ducked his head a little as if self-conscious. 'George Herbert's *Outlandish Proverbs* from 1694, would you believe.' It occurred to Amelie that there was a hint of desperation in his voice as he intoned these phrases. As if by repeating them over and over the wisdom might eventually sink in. He reached across the table once again, gripped her hands and looked her solidly in the eye.

'Please. Live well. Be my revenge, Amelie.'

Chapter 39

They were warned the day before that because of staff training they'd be confined to their cells for much of the day. All education classes and even any booked gym sessions would be cancelled.

'What do you think they're getting training in?' Angus asked. 'How to be even more miserable?'

'Wouldn't you be miserable working in a place like this?' Dave replied.

Judging from the movement of the frame of the bunkbed Angus was moving underneath him.

'Aye, true. It's just the whole beast thing. All I done was send a photo to my girl's da. I'm hardly a pervert, am I?' There was a low energy to Angus's voice that Dave recognised. Being locked up in this place was affecting Angus's mood on what seemed like a minute by minute basis. One moment he was laughing and talking non-stop, the next he was flat and crushed by his punishment. 'You're the only guy in here I can talk to. The rest of them pure give me the creeps. See that guy two cells down? The old guy with the walking stick and the thick specs? I swear if he looks me up and down one more time I'm gaunnae tear him a new arsehole.'

'I wouldn't,' Dave said. 'He might enjoy it.'

Angus snuffled a laugh.

Then there was silence, followed by a sob and some gentle shaking of the bed. Without looking, Dave could tell that Angus had stuffed his blanket into his mouth to try and hide his upset. He wondered about offering the lad some comfort but opted for distance instead. Often, Dave didn't have the spare mental energy to cope with the shifts in Angus's state of mind, he had enough internal torture of his own to deal with, and his responses would vary from 'bend over and take it like a man, dipshit' to 'you've only got a few more months, you've got this, mate'.

When the bed shaking subsided Dave waited for another few minutes before asking, 'You didn't mention if you got a letter back from your girlfriend...'

'Yeah, nothing yet,' he replied. 'I'm an idiot thinking Jenny'd be bothered. Probably still hates my guts. And why wouldn't she? I'm an arsehole.'

'Meant to ask. If you treated her like that...'

'Aye rub it in, why don't you.'

'Let me finish,' Dave asserted. 'If you treated her like that, why would the prison authorities let you send her a letter?'

'I sent it to her wee pal, Donna. I might be an arsehole, but I'm no daft, mate.'

'How do you know Donna handed it over to her?'

Silence.

'Right enough. I didn't think of that.'

'It's only a week or so, eh?' Dave asked. 'Maybe Jenny's on holiday? Maybe Donna's on holiday?'

'They haven't got the money for holidays at this time of year. They save up, get Christmas out of the way first and then they start saving for Spain in the new year...' his voice faded away and Dave groaned. That would just remind Angus of his reason for the revenge porn in the first place. Jenny's hook-up with a German in Ibiza.

'Do you trust Donna?' Dave asked.

'Aye, she's sound. Pure mental like, but sound.'

'In what way is she mental?'

'She's a right laugh. Doesn't take anything serious. Always up for a party.'

'And does she like you?'

'Now I think about it, she's done something similar. Sent a pic of an ex playing with hisself to his new girlfriend.' He laughed. 'It all kicked off after that, by the way. The new girlfriend was pure ragin". He paused, 'So, aye, she'll be less judgey than other people about all of this crap.'

Dave shook his head at this, glad that mobile phones weren't so ubiquitous when he was first out on the dating scene. God knows what nonsense him and his mates might have got up to.

'In that case, might she be understanding and more likely to pass on the letter?'

'Mibbe...' Angus sounded a little brighter.

'Give her a wee bit of time. You've got to wait for Donna to hand over the letter, and then for Jenny to take it all in and think about how she might reply.'

'Aye, true. And the letter you helped me write was a pure belter. She's going to be totally impressed' – he adopted a posh accent for the remainder of his sentence – 'by my command of the English language.'

They could hear doors opening and closing along the wing, and Dave realised the sounds were getting closer.

'What do you think that is?'

'Letters?' Dave replied.

Their door opened.

'Here's your tea pack,' a deep voice said. Excellent, thought Dave. Making himself a cup of tea and drinking it would use up a few minutes. But then the little plastic bag containing some tea bags, coffee sachets and UHT milk containers was dropped on to the floor and kicked along the ground towards them. The door slammed shut again before Angus or Dave could react.

'Bet that dickhead has done that in every cell in the wing,' Angus said.

Dave tried not to think too much about it, but couldn't help but sink into himself at the lack of human decency. Guards had said and done worse to him since he arrived, but this small act of contempt sent a signal that hurt him way into the depths of his mind.

He heard Angus get to his feet and walk over to the bag.

'Wanker,' he shouted. 'Anyway, there's the six-second rule. And the stuff is inside a wee bag. It's all good.'

'Isn't it a five-second thing?'

'Eh?'

'When something's safe to eat after you drop it. Five seconds.'

'I thought it was six.'

'Nah. Five.'

'I'm going for six.'

'It's five, mate.'

'Fucking six.'

'Your arse it's six. It's five.' Dave realised he was shouting, and he slumped back onto his bed amazed at how quickly his anger had flared up.

'Got your period or something?' Angus asked. 'Jesus. It's in a bag anyway so what's the problem?' With every word Angus was saying he was moving closer and closer to Dave's bed and his face was bright with irritation.

It dawned on him how ridiculous both the conversation and their response to it were, and he started laughing.

'What the fuck?' Angus said, his face a portrait of confusion.

'Five seconds, naw, it's six.' He ended with a shout and a snort, and then fell into laughter that verged into hysteria. Angus couldn't help but join in.

'What a pair of fannies.'

And they were both laughing, snorting, sides sore, eyes wet.

There was a loud familiar noise as the door was unlocked and opened.

'Letter for Angus Young.' A guard entered and thrust some paper into Angus's hand. He paused as if reading their faces. This wasn't the reception he expected when bearing 'gifts'. 'Want to share the joke?'

'Five seconds,' Angus shouted at him. They both started laughing again.

'Nutters.' The guard shook his head and left.

Angus waved the letter at Dave. 'What d'ye think?'

'Open it for chrissake,' he replied as he jumped off his bunk onto the floor in front of Angus.

There was a slight tremble in Angus's hand as he pulled the letter out of the envelope. He read, mouthing the words in a mumble, but not enough for Dave to comprehend. He didn't feel comfortable reading over Angus's shoulder. There might be something very personal on there.

'Well?' Dave asked when he finished.

'It's shite,' Angus said, crumpled the letter up and threw it on the desk before sitting on the edge of his bed. He was bent forward, elbows on his knees, face a slump of disappointment.

'What did she say?'

'Her da and her ma will never forgive me.' He looked utterly crestfallen.

'And?'

'I want to marry the lassie. How on earth is that going to happen if her parents can't stand the sight of me?'

'You want to marry her? Where's that coming from…?'

'I don't tell you everything, do I? Being in here's giving me lots of time to think.'

'Right,' Dave said and sat beside him. 'What else did the letter say? Can she forgive you?'

'Doesn't say. Just something about me getting a job when I get out and we'll see. What the hell's that supposed to mean? I've got a sex offence on my record. What employer's going to look at me twice?'

He had a point there.

'You've got to read between the lines, Angus.'

'What's that supposed to mean?' He looked angry enough to headbutt Dave, who moved back out of reach.

'She said her parents couldn't forgive you. She didn't say she didn't. What she did say was get a job and she'll reassess.'

'Aye?'

'Strikes me there's still hope for you two.'

'Aye?'

'Be serious about getting a job when you get out. Take all the help you can get in here and see what happens. What did you do before you got arrested?'

'Nothing.'

'You were out of work? How long for?'

'Six months.'

'Jesus, it's like drawing teeth. What work have you done?'

'I did some dog walking for my granny's mate. Worked in an office for a wee while. Had to wear a shirt and tie. Hated it. Did some courier shit with my bike in the town. That was cool, and I was fit as fuck cycling up all they hills.'

'What kind of office did you work in?'

'It was the city council's social-work department. Everybody was stressed out of their nut.'

'What are you like with numbers? Better than your English?'

'Cheeky basturt,' Angus said, but Dave could hear the humour in the response. 'What's wi' all the questions, by the way?'

'I know a guy,' Dave said, wondering if there was something his father could offer to help Angus out. 'I'm not promising anything, but, keep your nose clean and I'll see if he can help you.'

After a moment's pause, Angus asked, 'He's no' a paedo is he?'

A few days later, Dave was waiting for a shower. A couple of guys were drying off and dressing. One of them was Angus, the other guy was someone new to Dave. He had long, dark hair, a beard that reached his chest, and was so out of shape it looked like he hunted down every spare calorie he could find. The guy had his back to Dave but judging by the way Angus was inclining his head towards him he was doing all the talking. At one point Angus braced himself as if he was about to challenge the other guy, then whatever came next made him look towards Dave. It was a flash, but still long enough for Dave to spot the movement of Angus's eyes.

What on earth was going on?

Then, they both walked out of the shower area, fully dressed, towels over their shoulders, Angus in front and looking like he wanted to hurt someone.

'What's wrong?' Dave asked Angus as he walked past him.

'Nothing,' Angus replied without looking at him. 'Everything is fine. Just tickety-boo.'

It was clear to Dave that whatever had just transpired things weren't fine at all.

Chapter 40

Amelie was standing in the middle of the Place de Pey-Berland in the heart of the city. Using her phone she captured an image of a little girl in blue shoes in front of the series of arches before the Hotel du Ville, turned to her left and sighted a gothic buttress of the limestone magnificence that was the Cathédrale Saint André. Deciding that was too straightforward to work, she deleted the photo from her phone's memory.

Taking care not to step on the pigeons around her feet she made her way through the tourists and past the throngs enjoying the sunshine and a coffee in front of Café de France, and then paused, turning in a slow circle, taking in the buildings and people as she considered her next image.

Tired of having nothing to do and all day to do it, she'd found she had a good eye for a photograph, set up an account on Instagram under the name 'BordeauxGirl' and began to walk the streets, looking for quirky pictures of the city.

A man walked past, enjoying an energetic conversation on his phone, his free hand thrown out in extravagant gestures: a visual performance for an audience that could only hear. She caught him from the back, one hand planting the phone to his head, the other arm out wide, palm up as if offering a perch for a passing bird.

A tram swooshed past just ahead of her, then what looked like family, on their bikes in a cavalcade – mother, father, children – but they were past and away before she could capture them on her screen.

She turned again, saw what looked like a pile of old clothes situated between the entrances to the Cathedral to her right, and the café on her left. Moving closer she was able to make out a head. This was a man, on his knees leaning forward in supplication, a hat on the ground between his hands.

The number of homeless people had dismayed and surprised her when she first travelled through the city centre, but then, why should this city be any different to any other she'd lived near, like London or Glasgow? Architectural beauty may point to human ingenuity but certainly wouldn't preclude human misery.

As she approached him she plucked the ten-euro note she had earmarked for a late lunch from her purse and dropped it into his hat.

He lifted his head and she read the fatigue and gratitude in his expression. '*Merci, madame.*'

'What happened?' she asked as she got down into her hunkers.

'Life,' he answered as he got up onto his knees. She noted the shame that dimmed the already weak light in his eyes.

'Have you eaten today?'

He paused as if preparing a lie. 'No.'

Amelie brought out her purse. She hadn't been to the cash machine for a number of days and only had a two-euro coin left. 'Here,' she said as she handed it to him. 'It's all I have at the moment, but I'm going to the bank and I'll be back with more.'

'Thank you,' he said as if he didn't quite believe her.

'And I'll bring you back some water and some food.'

He held his hands to his chest and gave a little bow.

'Do you mind if I take your photograph?'

'Me? Why does a beautiful lady want to take a photograph of me?'

'Maybe if I post it online it might show people that we need to do more...' She tailed off, worried that she sounded a bit lame. Perhaps, she thought with excitement, this could be a new thread for her page on Insta, highlighting the less fortunate in the city?

'Okay,' he said and adopted his former position, bent forward so that his forehead was resting on the ground.

'Thank you,' she said and stepped back from him.

Waiting till the crowd thinned she got down to her knees and caught an image of him with the twin red doors of the cathedral towering behind him.

'I'll be back,' she shouted over to him as she got to her feet. 'With a sandwich.'

She found a little café up a side street where she ordered a ham-and-cheese baguette and a bottle of still water. Her stomach protested with a faint twist and she remembered she was yet to eat so she doubled her order. When asked for payment she handed over her card. The waiter popped it in the card reader. She keyed in her code.

And nothing.

'Do you have another card, madame?' the waiter asked.

'But there should be plenty of...'

'Let's try again,' the waiter said with a smile.

The same thing happened again.

Shit.

'Do you have another card, perhaps?'

Thinking there should be plenty of money in this account Amelie shook her head. 'This is the only card I can use.'

'Then I'm sorry, madame,' the waiter said and moved the food and drink out of her reach.

Face burning with embarrassment Amelie left the shop. What had just happened? And what about that poor guy? She'd promised she'd be back with food and now she was letting him down.

Resolutely, she made her way to her branch of HSBC, on the far side of the busy Boulevard du Président Wilson.

'Can you please check my card is working?' she asked the teller when she reached the front of the small queue. The badge on the bank worker's lapel read 'Alix'.

With a nod, the young woman took the card from her and slid it quickly through the card reader to the side of her computer terminal.

'The card is working, madame,' she said, her face giving nothing away. 'Let me give you a print of your balance.' Moments later she passed a slip of paper to Amelie through the small opening in the safety glass.

With a sinking feeling in her stomach she read that her balance was zero.

'This can't be right,' she said, realising there was an edge of panic to her voice. 'I have two other accounts linked to that one. Can you check them also?'

Claire nodded. Her expression calm and polite. She pressed some buttons, a printer clacked into life and then she passed another slip of paper across.

With mounting anxiety Amelie read the paper. All three of her accounts were empty.

'No,' she said. 'No. There must be some explanation. There should be at least...'

'*Je suis desolée, madame*,' Claire said: *I'm sorry*. 'If you would like to have a seat at the side, I have other people to attend to.'

'But...'

'Madame, please.' Claire was unruffled. She looked pointedly to Amelie's right where a couple of chairs were situated. 'I could get a colleague to check for you but the answer will be the same.'

'There was a lot of money in here last week. A lot.' Amelie was aware that other people around the office and in the queue were staring at her, but she didn't care. There was something very wrong here.

'And the balance now is as it is shown, madame.'

In a daze Amelie walked out of the bank and stood just outside the door. What the hell was going on? What was she going to do? There was nothing in her bank accounts. Nothing. Panic sparking in her chest, she pulled her purse out of her handbag to check the contents. She'd given the last of her cash to the homeless guy. She did have a little stash of money back at the apartment, though. Sixty euros. She could eke that out for a few days, but what then?

With care she closed her purse, planted it in the bottom of her bag and then pulled out her phone. She called Bernard. No answer. She cut the connection and tried again. Nothing. She tried again, this time leaving a message.

'Bernard, it's Amelie. It's urgent. Call me.'

The blare of a car horn and Amelie started. A hand on her shoulder and someone pulled her back from the edge of the pavement.

'Mademoiselle, are you okay?' an elderly woman asked her. She'd been standing behind her in the queue. 'You have to be careful of the traffic in Bordeaux.'

'It's been a long time since someone called me mademoiselle,' she managed to say, noticing the thump of her heart. She placed a hand over it as if that might calm its beat.

'There's a café just along the road. They have the best *caneles*,' the lady said, referring to the little cakes shaped like a cork that were on sale almost everywhere in the city. 'Perhaps a seat and some sugar might be good to help with your shock?'

'I'll ... I'll be fine, thank you, madame.' Amelie touched the woman lightly on the arm. '*Merci.*'

How she negotiated the streets safely and made it home, she had no idea. Her mind was full of doomsday scenarios. Someone had hacked into her accounts. She'd be thrown out of the apartment. She'd have to get a job. But who would employ her? She'd end up on the street.

Breathe, she told herself. *You've been poor before. You'll cope.*

She tried Bernard several more times through the day, but only received the same response; his answering service. Damn, this couldn't be right. Where had all her money gone?

Sleep was impossible that night. All she could think about was her missing money. Might it be linked to the scheme Bernard had invested her wealth in, which cost her the bulk of her earnings? Had they come back for more? Her phone was by her bed. She checked it regularly. Judging by the bars showing there was a strong signal so Bernard could get through when he got round to replying to her message. Messages. Each subsequent one probably sounding more anxious than the one before.

Light filtered in through the window, edging over the floorboards towards the bed as morning arrived. Feeling the weight of her worries amplified by her lack of sleep she groaned as she pushed herself up off the bed.

Had she eventually fallen asleep and missed any calls? Gazing at her phone she saw there were no notifications. She tried calling Bernard again. Nothing.

Perhaps Peter would be able to get in touch with him from the UK.

'Morning, Amelie, what a nice surprise,' Peter answered almost immediately.

'Peter, I need help. My money's disappeared. My agent's gone AWOL. I'm in this city alone, almost penniless and I don't know what to do, who to talk to...'

'Amelie. Tell me all of that again. But slowly.' His deep and calm voice eased her mind a little. She began again, slowly. Telling him about the failed investment scheme and her recent attempt to get some cash, and her failed efforts to reach Bernard.

'First things first,' Peter said. 'Do you have money to pay for your rent? We don't want you on the street.'

'Bernard paid six months upfront. So I have –' she made a quick calculation '– about ten weeks left.'

'Good. What about food, drink, utilities?' Peter's matter-of-fact approach simultaneously soothed and frustrated her. She was used to coping on her own. She shouldn't need to ask anyone else for help.

'The utilities are paid monthly from my main bank account...' Which is now empty, she thought.

'It's the middle of the month so you'll have a couple of weeks before you get into default, so we have time.'

'For what?' How was she going to get a job that quickly?

'I'll wire you some money across.'

'Peter, you can't.'

'I can and I will.' His tone brooked no dissent. 'You have a short-term emergency. Let's fix that and then you can concern yourself with paying me back once you are clearer about what you are going to do.'

'OK.' She felt better thinking that this was a loan. 'I *will* pay you back.'

'No rush. Just when it suits.' He paused as if something occurred to him. 'Open a new bank account, in another bank, with the money I send you.'

'Why?' She wondered what kind of hassle that might be.

'Someone's cleared out your cash, Amelie. If they see more in your account they might take that as well.'

'But how...?'

'Financial crooks are getting cleverer all the time. Who had access to your accounts?'

'No one. I'm the only one with the cards and the access.'

'Bernard acted as your agent? All payments to you came via him?'

'Yes.' What was he getting at?

'Bernard had full knowledge of your account details then.'

'But, no, Bernard would never steal from me. He's like a father to me.'

'Some fathers are dicks, Amelie.'

'No. I refuse to believe Bernard would do something like that.'

'You say he hasn't returned your calls...'

'It's only been just short of a day.'

'How long does it usually take him to get back to you?'

'Usually it's within the hour, but...'

'Does he have a full rostrum of clients? Might he be busy with one of them? Does he keep well?'

'You don't think he's ill, do you?' In her mind's eye she saw Bernard in a hospital bed, wired up to a multitude of machines.

'We have to discount the obvious before we move to the unthinkable.'

The unthinkable. Bernard stealing from her. No. She couldn't countenance that.

'Do you recall how much money you lost through this investment scheme?'

'It was a low seven-figure sum.'

'How much has gone missing from your bank accounts?'

'A low six-figure sum.' She cringed at the amounts. How stupid had she been not to take more care of that side of the business.

'I'm aware your financial situation ... didn't, ah, match your fame...'

'An accurate summary,' Amelie replied with a wry grin. The sums they were talking about were clearly way beyond the earnings of most people but, as Lisa had told her on numerous occasions, she should have been able to leverage her name for much, much more. There had been a few contracts signed with major film studios and advertisers that would have pushed her, financially, onto a whole other level, but that was all binned when she refused to distance herself from Dave.

'I'm also guessing, these financial troubles aside, standing by my son has cost you a great deal of money?' His tone was so worn through with sympathy that Amelie almost started crying. 'Anyway,' Peter continued as if he could read her silence. 'Let's get you sorted for now. I can transfer the money across. It won't take too long to organise. Anything else you need?'

'No, thanks,' she replied in a small voice.

'Do you want me to contact the police?'

'The police?' She flinched from the idea. If this got out, the press would have a great time. She could almost hear a grand chorus of 'Serves Her Right' ring throughout the world.

'If there's a crime here we don't want them to get away with it, do we?'

'Let's wait until I hear back from Bernard. I'm sure there's a perfectly plausible explanation.'

'I've been an accountant for decades, Amelie, and I've found that when money goes missing more often than not the explanation is greed.'

After she'd ended the call with Peter she felt so relieved and exhausted after a night of dire scenarios running through her mind, she fell asleep on the sofa.

She woke sometime later to a sore neck, dry mouth and the nearby church bells ringing twice. The screen on her phone continued to display a blank as far as Bernard was concerned, but there was an email from Peter. As she brewed a much-needed coffee she opened it to read his instructions.

A couple of hours later she was sitting on a bench in the park across from her apartment with two hundred euros in cash in her purse, and was the relieved owner of a new account at a bank just a few streets from where she sat.

From her bench she looked around herself and watched the Bordelais going about their business and wondered if any of them were suffering anywhere near the same amount of turmoil that she was.

To her left hunkered the limestone might of the ancient basilica. Ahead of her the children's park under the sheltering span of giant fir and oak trees. A woman strolled past with a small girl in a bright-yellow coat. 'Maman,' she chirruped. 'Can I play, can I?'

A couple walked just behind her. The man smiled at the woman. She raised an eyebrow and nudged him with her shoulder. He stuck his tongue out. They laughed. No words, but in those simple actions they managed to convey a symphony of affection.

And as the church bells pealed out four languid notes she ached for similar, simple interaction and wondered how she might look to these people, hunched over on the wooden slats of the bench. This stoop of bone. A semi-quaver on an empty fret. A melody whose movement had been stopped. A song of isolation.

Chapter 41

'Who was that guy?'

'What guy?' Angus demanded.

'At the showers yesterday. The guy with the hair. Looked like he was giving you grief about something.'

'I can handle myself.'

Many of their conversations in the cell were face to face. More than a few were held while they were each sitting on their bed, one above the other, both facing the opposite wall. This latter position was one they'd taken to adopting when one of them felt like they needed more space.

'I don't dispute that,' Dave replied, aiming his voice at the bed below him. 'It just looked...'

'What?'

'Uncomfortable. Who is he?'

'Just some guy.'

'What does he want from you?'

'Fuckssake, give it a rest, eh?' Angus's voice was high with irritation.

'Just asking. Jesus.'

The cell door opened. 'You two have got a library visit booked in,' the guard said.

'Great.' Dave jumped off his bunk and stepped across the cell to the desk where a book he had just finished lay. 'I need something different this time. I fancy something historical.' He was speaking needlessly in an attempt to lighten the mood. Aware that Angus was still lying on his bunk, Dave paused and looked over at the younger man.

'You not coming?' he asked.

'Cannae be bothered.'

'What?' Dave was astonished. Angus took up any reason to leave the cell. 'You feeling alright? Should I get the guard to call out the doc?'

'I'm fine. Just can't be bothered.'

'Who are you and what have you done with Angus Young?'

'Give it a rest, eh?'

Having spent so much time in close confines together the two men were well able to read each other's signals. Most times when the other's mood was edging towards hostile they knew to back down and let the other recover their equilibrium. There were times, however, when that spike of irritation was impossible to beat down. 'You've got a chance to leave your cell and you're just going to lie there? I'm not buying it, Angus. What's going on?'

'Away and get yourself some gay historical shite and give me peace, will you?'

'Wanker.' Dave picked up his book and his prison-issue fleece jacket, and left the cell. As he was escorted across the open yard to the building that housed the library he cursed himself for his reaction. He should know better. He should be the bigger guy, but sometimes, too many times, he simply couldn't control his frustration. On the outside, since his one rampage in his late teens he rarely lost his temper and was always the one to talk people down from theirs, but here, in this place he was becoming something else, someone else, and he hated himself for it.

Dave was instantly awake. Senses on high alert. Not his usual reluctant, slow climb to awareness.

He turned from his position facing the wall and saw in the dark of the cell Angus's profile. His co-pilot was just standing there, facing him. Frozen.

Dave's body prickled with adrenaline.

'Angus?'

Nothing.

'Angus,' he said a little louder. 'What are you doing?'

Angus coughed. 'Just going for a piss.' Then he moved over to the tiny toilet in the corner. There was no sound for a long moment. Then Angus's feet shuffling back along the floor as he made the return journey. 'Didn't need a piss after all.'

The bunk bed shifted under Dave as Angus climbed into the bed below him.

'What were you doing there, Angus?'

'Gimme peace,' he replied. 'Told ye, I was going to the loo.'

'You were standing staring at me, you dick. What were you doing?'

'Fuck off and let me sleep.' The bed shifted again as if Angus was moving onto his side.

It felt like an age before Dave got back to sleep. In his mind's eye all he could see was Angus's outline in the gloom of the pre-dawn room, as if he was locked in indecision.

Chapter 42

The office was in a giant, grey brutalist building near the Rue Georges-Bonnac, a structure that didn't feel in keeping with the splendour of the majority of the city. As she was directed to the waiting room of the job agency she was visiting, Amelie hoped this wasn't a sign. She shook her hair free of raindrops, and using her bare hand swiped them from her shoulders, arms and thighs. She took a seat, making a mental note to invest in an umbrella. For a warm part of the country Bordeaux had a surprising amount of rain, although, if this is what passed as January weather she was fine with it.

'Solange Meric,' the woman behind the reception desk called her moments after she had sat down. Temporarily forgetting that was the name she'd booked under, Amelie looked to the other women sitting around her. Then she realised the receptionist was looking straight at her.

She stood up and smiled. 'Sorry, I was...' she considered how she might explain herself; '...elsewhere.'

She had really been lost in thought about Bernard. Where was he? Was he avoiding her calls? Was he behind her missing money? No, she couldn't believe that, he had always been so supportive of her. Why would he suddenly change now?

She was guided into a small office where a woman in a navy suit was sitting behind a white desk. The desk was clear apart from a small plant on the far-right corner and a paper folder in front of the woman. When she heard Amelie enter, she looked up and greeted her with a smile. She introduced herself as Nicole and without much preamble got down to the task in hand.

'What kind of work are you looking for?'

'I'll consider anything really. As you can see from my CV' – a document that was light on detail for the last few years, concentrating mainly on her employment when she was in her late teens and twenties – 'most of my previous work was in retail and hospitality. And I've also done...' She stopped talking when she was aware Nicole was staring at her.

'Do I know you?' Nicole asked.

'I don't think so. I've only been in the city for a few months and I've mainly...'

'Are you sure? You look very familiar.'

'Impossible,' Amelie answered, worried that Nicole might work out who she was. Aware how brusque her response must have sounded Amelie attempted to soften her tone. 'I haven't been to France for years. Since my father cheated on my mother when I was a girl.'

Nicole gave her that look. *Men, eh?* And another, more questioning look that Amelie read as a curious thought. Why come back to France now? But as if she remembered this was a professional meeting, Nicole returned to the reason for their meeting.

'At the moment most of our retail jobs are temporary. I expect things to improve in the next couple of months, perhaps in April and May as more tourists start to arrive. I can see you in a classy department store, or a high-end fashion shop. We have lots of designer shops in the city. Have you been along Rue Saint Catherine?'

'No. Too busy for me.' And too many tourists. Someone was bound to recognise her if she went down there.

'Mind you the more exclusive names are on Cours de l'Intendance or George Clemenceau ... Are you sure we haven't met?'

'I'm sure.' Amelie bit down on her lip. Surely this woman wasn't going to recognise her. Please God, no.

'You are so familiar. There's something of that actress in you. Her name escapes me at the moment.'

'I have one of those faces.' Amelie realised she was twisting her fingers together and made herself stop. 'You were talking about exclusive shops?'

'Amelie Hart,' Nicole said. 'How could I not have seen it. I loved that movie. I saw it three times.' Nicole studied her face, her head cocked to the side. 'She's my favourite actress. WOW, grow your hair out, some blonde highlights and you could be her twin.'

Feeling the heat of panic in her throat, Amelie jumped to her feet. 'Sorry. I have to go. I suddenly feel awful. I didn't eat breakfast this morning. Slept in and didn't want to miss ... be late. I'm so sorry,' she garbled on. 'Please forgive me.'

'Oh,' Nicole stood. 'Can I get you a glass of water?'

'No, thank you. You are kind.' Amelie backed out of the room. 'Thank you.' Then feeling as if everyone was staring at her, she walked through reception, through the main doors of the office and out onto the street.

Once there she stopped, leaned against the building and took a breath. What was she thinking, dressing up and putting on her make-up for this meeting? A haircut, ill-fitting clothes and flat shoes would have to be her uniform from now on.

She began walking, her mind choosing a pace that would take her away from the employment agency's doors quickly. A cool wind in her face brought with it sparks of sullen rain. She screwed her eyes against it, walking faster, sightless, anxiety a weight in her gut.

Breathless now. Almost at a run, she was a leafless branch being swept along in a silt-laden stream.

A sound broke through. The whoosh of the tram. Just ahead, she saw the low shelter of a tram stop and a collection of people waiting to get on. She was sure they were all staring at her. And just as sure they were as harsh in their assessment as a hanging judge.

She turned back on herself, unsure of her direction but knowing she needed to get away from people. Past the brutal grey of the building she had just been inside and she was drawn up some steps, and there found her reward. A little square was tucked away within the concrete, edged with small trees and bushes, like a cloudless patch in a storm-strewn sky.

She saw another set of steps that led down to a short avenue of trees and beyond them, across a busy road, the gilded railings of a building she guessed might be a museum. She sat on the edge of the top step, the stone edge hard on her sit bones, and took a breath. Anonymity resumed.

From habit, she took her phone from her bag, set it to camera mode and found some distraction and a sense of distance in viewing the world through a lens.

Her phone began to vibrate and the call tone sounded. She looked at the screen. When she saw who was trying to get in touch she answered immediately.

'Bernard, where the hell have you been?'

Chapter 43

As usual it was dull with drizzle, so Dave pulled his fleece jacket over his head to stop his head from getting soaked as he made his way back to his prison block. Another visit to the library and a change of reading material. As he walked he realised his thoughts that morning had been dominated by the change in Angus's demeanour. The guy had been all over the place since his arrival – so had he; but in the last few days and weeks the man's mood had been all the way down. And when he wasn't monosyllabic he was spiky with irritation, so much so they'd almost come to blows on a couple of occasions.

Living in such close confines with someone amplified everything. Even a slightly brisk reply to a harmless question could take on nuclear proportions. That morning he'd asked Angus how his Weetabix was.

'Wish they'd give us that more,' Dave said. 'Instead of that cardboard muck, cornflakes.'

'Bollocks. It's just a different kind of cardboard muck,' Angus replied. 'With a different flavour, for chrissakes.'

Dave had ploughed on, unusually mindless, or, to be more accurate, for once not taking on board how Angus's tone had climbed through the anger scale from the start of his sentence to the finish. 'No, it's not. Weetabix is actually good for you,' Dave said. 'Did you know that Kellogg guy came up with cornflakes as a way to stop folk masturbating? Tasteless and totally devoid of nutrition is the way forward, apparently, if you want to stop guys knocking one out.'

'Give it a rest, will you?' Angus all but threw his plate of cereal on to the desk. 'I'm sick of you and your opinions. Just shut the fuck up.' His face was puce, saliva spraying from his mouth.

'You on the rag, pizza-face?' Dave had had it with the boy's dark moods.

He was on his feet and both men were face to face, inches apart, snarling.

The door opened.

'You guys having a lovers' tiff?' the guard asked.

They stepped apart.

'Young, you've got an appointment this morning. Robbins, library,' the guard said and walked out.

Normally Dave would have asked Angus who the appointment was with. The lad was almost halfway through his one-year sentence so he guessed it might have been to discuss his release date. A conversation he would be desperate to have. But to hell with him.

None of the novels he saw on the shelves talked to him that morning so he'd pulled out a collection of poetry: *Being Human: More Real Poems for Unreal Times*. That was about right, he thought. *These* times were for sure unreal. Perhaps pouring over brief insights might be more involving than a long narrative? Would be a change anyway. And God knows, he needed a mental shift. The written word was one of the few ways he could lift himself out of this place, a refuge for his mind, before his reaction to Angus's moods and aggression became dangerous to one or both of them.

When Angus returned his mood was no better. If anything it was slightly worse.

'How did it go?' Dave asked as he set his book on his bunk.

'Okay, yeah, okay, I suppose.'

'What does that mean?'

A moment of silence.

Dave sat up and swung his legs over the edge of the bunk so he was facing Angus. 'What? They keeping you in longer? Not getting out on a tag or anything?'

'Yeah. Sorta.'

'What do you mean, sorta? You getting out or not?'

'I've got two weeks left,' he said, and a flicker of a smile formed on his lips before failing altogether. 'Getting out on a tag.'

'Man, that's brilliant. Why aren't you…? What's up, Angus? Did you propose to Jenny already and she said no?'

'Just leave it, eh?' Angus snarled.

'Thanks be to Christ it's only two weeks, cos you are doing my nut in,' Dave said. He lay back in his bunk, picked up his book, stared at the pages but really saw nothing. What was going on here? He couldn't follow this guy with radar.

The rest of the day followed the set pattern of mealtimes, recreation and a shower. Then it was back into the cell, where it was Angus's turn to choose what they watched on TV. And that evening it was a diet of the soaps, and a crime drama where a child had gone missing and the neighbour did it.

Dave spent most of the evening with his back to the small screen and his book over his face.

Just before lights out he heard Angus cough below him.

'Just want you to know, big guy, you've been a good mate.'

'Eh?' Dave asked. 'What?'

The frame of the bed moved as Angus turned on his side.

'You alright, mate?' Dave asked.

Nothing.

Eventually, Dave fell asleep. When he set his head on the pillow initially all he could do was worry about Angus. Had he sent a letter to Jenny without asking him to review it? Might it have been a proposal that she rejected? Why else would the young man be unmoved by the fact he was soon to be released. Fair enough it was on a tag, but still, he would be away from this place.

Something pulled him from a dream.

Angus was standing by the side of his bed, and the moonlight picked out the silver sheen of tears running down his cheeks.

'I've got to do it, man. I've got to.' He held up his right hand. And paused. And in that frozen moment, Dave could see a line of darkness pointing from Angus's hand. 'They'll hurt her if I don't.'

"What the...?'

With a scream Angus brought his hand down towards Dave's chest.

Hard and fast.

Chapter 44

'My apologies for not returning your call sooner, dear,' Bernard said. He sounded a little breathless.

'Have you been running?' Amelie asked. She was so relieved to hear from him she felt about ten kilos lighter.

Bernard snorted. 'I never run, darling. Unless it's after a good-looking waiter and he's holding a giant bottle of champers.'

'What happened to you? I was so worried.'

'I'm fine now, Amelie. There's no need to worry.'

'What do you mean you're fine *now*?'

'I had a little heart attack, sweetheart. But I'm fine. I've got all these lovely doctors and nurses running after me and my –' Amelie heard a slight clanking noise as if Bernard was tapping something large and metallic; '– oxygen tank new best friend.'

'Oh my God,' Amelie said. 'I'll get the next plane. You can't be on your own.' She knew Peter's suspicions about him had to be wrong.

'You'll do no such thing, Amelie. I'm getting the best of care here, and besides, the world thinks you're in Latin America so don't be spoiling that for me.'

'America, where? What on earth are you talking about?'

'When you left the UK the newspapers asked for sightings, so using some snaps of you I have on file I anonymously send them pics every now and again.' He cackled, coughed and then cackled some more. 'You've had a lovely time in Mexico City, Rio, Buenos Aires...' Amelie recalled a tour she'd taken for the movie that involved those cities. 'And if you come back here you'll waste all my hard work.'

'What has been the reaction to my *travels*?'

'Do you really want to know?'

'I'll be like super bitch or something. Off sunning myself while that poor girl and her family deal with the after-effects of her abuse.' She paused. 'Shouldn't you stop sending out those pictures? Isn't it keeping me in the public eye?'

'Darling, you never left it. And in the absence of any real news they make up all sorts of nonsense, so at least this way I've been keeping some sort of control. And making you look fabulous while I'm doing it.' He paused. 'What was so urgent anyway, Amelie?' Bernard asked. 'I only listened to part of your first message. You sounded so worried I cut it off and dialled you straightaway.'

Amelie told him about her missing money.

'Dear God, that's horrible. What are the police saying?'

'I haven't reported it to them yet.'

'Why on earth not? Have you taken leave? You can't just let that kind of thing slip.'

'It's so difficult to do things from over here, and I didn't want to go back to Glasgow and then word would get out and...'

'Amelie, you're talking about over a hundred thousand pounds. That kind of money just can't go missing.'

Amelie bit back a retort about the much bigger sum that had gone missing under Bernard's less-than-watchful eye.

'Dave's father, Peter, is on stand-by. He's an accountant, as you know. I'm sure there's a reasonable explanation.' She *hated* thinking about the money, and, besides, cash had never been a motivator for her. They could take the money and rot for all she cared. As long as she had enough to pay for essentials, that was good enough for her. She'd known real poverty in her life, when her father left, and this moment in time was more than comfortable by comparison.

'Do you want me to fly up to Glasgow to meet him?' Bernard asked, and she felt a surge of affection for him that in *his* moment of need he was thinking of her.

'Will they let you on the plane with your oxygen tank?' she

asked while wondering if it was a good idea to have Bernard and Peter in the same room. She'd found Peter's suspicions of her old friend so unlikely she'd dismissed them with little more than a momentary pause, but she certainly didn't want two of the few people who were actually on her side to be at odds with each other.

'I'll paint a face on it and say he's my carer.'

'Idiot.' Amelie laughed and enjoyed the feel of it as sound vibrated up from her lungs to her throat. It had been so long since she'd managed to find something to laugh about. Or someone to laugh with.

Bernard joined in, but it set off a coughing fit that sounded so harsh Amelie thought about going straight to the airport.

Eventually he stopped. 'God,' he managed. 'You should see the other guy.'

'Any word on a book deal for Mama Brown?'

'Isn't Lisa keeping you up to date on that?'

'She's away on a shoot in the Far East somewhere,' Amelie replied. She hadn't heard from her friend for a few months, but she wasn't concerned. The pattern of their friendship over the years was long absences followed by unannounced and dramatic drop-ins.

'I'll put some feelers out. See what's what, but Claire Brown has been absent from the public eye of late. She did all those late-morning and lunchtime talk shows, playing the victim card in the first few weeks after the trial. Since then, nothing. The latest word, which might be stale now since my little contretemps with the surgeon's knife, was that the expected windfall didn't arrive and they had to move out of their home before they were evicted.'

'Really?' Amelie fervently hoped that this was true. She then felt a churn of concern for Damaris. How would all of this upheaval affect her?

As she'd been talking to Bernard, Amelie had been walking. When she ended the call she looked around to see where she was, and with a start of pleasure she saw the trees in the centre of a large square, recognised the awnings of a couple of cafés as being at the end of Rue Judaïque, and realised she was on the Place Gambetta. Only a few minutes' walk from the Saint-Seurin and home.

Someone barged in to her. She turned to face them. 'Pardon,' she said automatically.

A young, dark-haired man faced her. Raised an eyebrow and then walked away.

How rude, she thought. It occurred to her that he was wearing a slight, black leather jacket, which at this time of year would be rare for a local. The temperature must be around 14 or 15 degrees Celsius, which would be considered to be positively balmy back in Glasgow, but here in Bordeaux had the locals out in their woollen coats, puffy jackets, scarves and hats.

Dismissing him as a tourist she continued on her way home, going on a little detour past the front entrance to the basilica, which faced on to Place du Pradeau. The sight of the building from this angle never failed to move her. The pale-yellow lime-stone edifice always seemed to pick up on any sunshine available and beam it back to her. Feeling that she needed the sense of calm it always provided, she made her way inside the church and sat in the back row. When she'd first visited this place she was surprised that instead of pews there were rows and rows of wooden chairs, but they looked almost as old as the stone of the basilica itself.

Sitting there she allowed the hush and awe of the place to settle on her, feeling it work its way through her skin, her muscle and deep into her bones. Looking around, she took in the giant pillars, wondering how many people it would take to circle one of them. A few rows ahead of her, on the right, an ornately carved pulpit, darkened with age to walnut, stood high against a pillar, complete with its own little winding staircase. To preach from a pulpit like that with its own gothic spire pointing to the vaulted ceiling would surely make any priest feel full of the word of God.

She heard a muffled cough to her right. And then again.

Turning, she recognised the figure hunched there.

It was the man who'd bumped into her over on the Place Gambetta.

Before he could notice her looking she turned back to face the front. She ran over the moment when they collided. He was walking in a direction that would take him further away from here. Had he followed her?

Was she being paranoid?

Looking over her shoulder again she saw that the man's head was tilted as he gazed up to the ceiling, one arm draped over the shoulder of the chair at his side, his left foot resting on his right knee. A typical tourist. Or was he just acting the part?

As if he was aware of her scrutiny he faced her and offered her a nod. But there was something in the directness of his gaze. This was more than the usual looks she got from men. There was an intensity in his eyes that set off a flare of worry in her gut.

She was back in her London home that night more than five years ago. Fear prickled through every cell in her body and robbed her of breath.

She rubbed at each of her wrists as if the bruises were still there after all this time.

Holding herself rigid and moving slowly so as not to give anything away, she stood and walked to the door, her footsteps echoing in the great chamber. Outside the main entrance she all but ran to Le P'tit Bar and in through the door. Picking a stool just inside the entrance with a view of the church she sat and waited and watched to see if he would follow.

Sure enough, the dark-haired man appeared. He looked around, not observing his surroundings as a tourist might, but scanning the people.

'Here's your *café allongé*, madame.' A waitress was at her side, an oddly knowing look in her eyes. 'Can I get you something else?' she added under her breath. Amelie had only been in here a couple of times and only ever had this drink. She was impressed that the woman remembered. But then she looked at the waitress properly and saw that her expression articulated what she really meant: it was an offer of help.

Forcing herself to appear casual, she picked up the coffee, fought to control the shaking of her hand, and just managed to sip without spilling any.

'The man, over there, at the church door, have you seen him before?' she asked.

'No. But that is no surprise.' Shrug. 'The basilica attracts a lot of people.' The waitress placed a light hand on her shoulder, an offer of support and solidarity. Her eyes questioning.

Amelie shook her head. This was fine. She was fine. She was over-reacting. She was imagining a threat where there was none. She didn't want to cause a fuss. It was fine. No, really. Fine. All the things women told themselves when a predator was nearby.

Was he a run-of-the-mill predatory male, or something more? She ran over their brief meeting in Gambetta, and the one in the church. His eyes. There was something about them. Something familiar. *Someone* familiar. She couldn't shift the thought that he wasn't just on the prowl for a woman, any woman, he was looking for her.

The figure in the gloom at the top of her stairs, could this be him? She held herself tight against the thought, aware that every part of her was trembling.

Although she'd managed to rebuild and get on with her life with little impediment, it dismayed her that the terror that man caused her had never really left.

Chapter 45

The governor looked across the table and explained to Dave what was happening. This was called the Orderly Room and was in effect a mini court inside the prison. He was being placed under a Rule 95 for fighting, and the meeting today was to apportion blame and set the necessary punishment. Did he understand?

Dave nodded. He understood. Without thinking, his hand strayed to his left ear and the earlobe that had to be stitched back on. He'd thrust his arm up just in time to deflect Angus's blow. The small blade was aimed at his throat, but ended up cutting his arm, cheek and earlobe.

'Are you comfortable, Mr Robbins?'

'Yes.' His hands were resting on the table in front of him, and he could see the clean bandage just under his wrist. He shuddered. He had been so lucky. If he hadn't woken up. If his arm hadn't been outside his blanket.

'What can you tell me about the night of the fifth of February?' the governor asked.

'Nothing.'

'You won't or you can't?'

'I can't,' Dave replied. 'I can't remember anything.'

'The screams of your cellmate alerted the staff, Mr Robbins. They entered your cell to find you both on the floor. You straddling Mr Young, him covered in blood and you with your hands around his throat. You have no memory of this? Forgive me if I don't believe you, Mr Robbins.'

Before the attack Angus was crying, pushing himself into a fury, working himself up so he could carry it out. In the week since it happened Dave had thought through the events of that night over and over. Angus's words:

I've got to.

If I don't they'll hurt her.

That could only have been about Jenny.

Who was 'they'? And what kind of threat had they asserted that would persuade Angus to try and kill him?

'I went to sleep as normal, boss,' Dave said. 'And woke up in a hospital bed. The rest is…' he shook his head '…a mystery.'

'If not for the fact that you were cut, and the blood all over Mr Young was yours, you would be in much more serious trouble, David. Do you understand?'

'Yes.'

'Help us get to the bottom of this then. What happened?'

'I don't remember, sir.' Dave knew that the law of this particular jungle was that you said nothing. Snitch and your life would be even more of a misery. Besides, he had no idea what punishment Angus might get if he told the truth. Would his sentence be increased? Despite everything he didn't want the boy to spend any more time inside.

'Where did the blade come from?' The governor picked up a clear plastic evidence bag by a corner. Dave could see the knife inside weighing it down.

'No idea, sir,' Dave said, thinking at least he could be honest about this.

'My officers tell me there was an air of acrimony between you and Mr Young in the days leading up to the incident. What was happening? I'm assuming you can remember that?'

'Nothing more than two men being held in close confines for too long. You've periods where you get on fine, and then periods where you annoy the hell out of each other. What your officers are telling you about is … sorry, was, nothing more than that.'

'So how did you end up almost missing an ear lobe, and bleeding all over your cell-mate while you attempted to throttle him?'

'Can't remember, sir.'

'Strikes me that this memory loss is very convenient, Mr Robbins.'

The governor asked more questions. Ran through events of that night over and over again, trying from different angles to trip Dave up. He simply zoned out the man in front of him with the white, freshly laundered shirt, and whenever there was a silence, assumed that it was left for him to fill. He answered with the only phrase he could.

'Can't remember.'

The governor threw his pen down on the pad of paper in front of him. 'I will not tolerate violence in my prison, Mr Robbins. Am I understood?'

'Yes, sir.' Dave studied his hands.

'Seven days of no TV, no library access and you're on your own for two weeks.' The governor looked to the guard who was standing just behind Dave. 'Take him out of my sight.'

Dave was escorted in silence back to E Hall. When he arrived back in his cell he asked the guard, 'Angus – is he alright?'

The guard looked at him with disbelief. 'The guy shanked you and you're asking after him?'

'There's something else going on there. Angus didn't have a violent bone in his body before he came in here.'

'He gets out next week.'

'Good.'

'Listen, Dave.' The guard put a hand on his shoulder and stopped him before he entered his cell. Dave noticed the cotton of the guard's shirt was so thin he could clearly see the design of the man's tattoo on the skin of his upper arm. Quite a difference from the quality cotton of the governor's shirt. 'The boss will do what he can to keep you on your own for as long as possible, but an empty bunk isn't going to stay empty for very long. You hear me?'

Dave nodded.

'Word will get out that you kept schtum. That you're a stand-up guy.' Notes of fatigue and frustration trailed through the guard's words. His tired expression said that the same discordant song was being played over and over again on a battered guitar and nothing was ever going to change. 'But be careful. As long as you're still in here you're going to be a target for any nutter who wants to make a name for himself.'

Chapter 46

London 2010

The first thing she became aware of was that her wrists hurt. And her arms had been pulled back over her head.

They were tied to the bed.

She kicked out in weak protest. Her feet barely moved. Binding around her ankles let her know they were also tied.

'Help,' she croaked. Her mouth was so dry.

Why was she so tired? She could barely sustain a thought.

Had she been drugged?

Then she became aware she was being watched. An outline in the dark. Someone was sitting in the corner of her bedroom, on the sheepskin cocktail chair she'd found in a local market. And why had that random fact popped in to her head in this moment? Was she seeking some sort of normality? Because this was as far from normal as you could get.

'What do you want?' She could hear just from those four syllables that her voice was fractured, as if her mind sent the signal, but someone else did the work.

They said nothing. Weak light from the streetlamps filtered in through a crack in her curtains, picking out a line from his knee to the black leather shoes on his feet.

'Let me go, please...' She hated herself for begging. 'Please.'

Silence.

Then: 'Do you like the dress I bought you?' His voice was deep, the accent English but enunciated in a way that made it difficult to pin down the exact location. 'I managed to work out your size.' There was pride in his tone.

Sensations began to emerge through the fog of fear. A scratch of lace at her throat, a weight of fabric over her legs and something pinned to her hair.

She lifted her head from the pillow and scanned the length of her body. Her answering scream rent the room.

He had put her in a blood-red wedding dress.

Amelie waited until the man walked away before leaving the café. She had lost years of her life to fear; she was not going to allow that to happen again. Gathering every last piece of her courage, she got to her feet and followed him at what she hoped was a safe distance until he reached the fringes of the Place de Martyrs de la Résistance, and then, from behind a queue of people waiting at a bus stop, she watched as he sauntered across Rue Judaïque towards Rue Pierre Charron in the direction of the multi-screen UGC cinema.

Only when she was sure he was safely on his way did she double back and go home to her apartment. Once inside she checked every room, and even went up to her little rooftop garden to make sure no one was there.

Then with a glass of wine she sat on the sofa, facing the door, thinking through a rushed exit, and considering her next move. This was her sanctuary; there was no way some random stranger was going to make her leave. Not a chance.

How dare he follow her?

Lifting her glass to her mouth she noticed the tremble of her muscles was making the deep-red surface quiver. She put the glass on the side table and took a breath, forcing herself to stay calm.

She was fine.

Everything was fine.

This man was a nobody.

Enough.

Time to take back some element of control. Time to get her big-girl pants on. She picked her phone out of her handbag. Peter answered straightaway.

'What do I need to sign to have you act on my behalf?' she asked.

'I'll email you the forms right now.'

'I've been an idiot, Peter. I've buried my head in the sand long enough. Someone stole from me and I want them to be found and to pay.'

'Leave it with me. I may need other stuff and the police will want to talk to you. Just stand by.'

'Okay.'

'Do you need any more money in the meantime?'

'I'm fine, thank you.' She couldn't take any more from him. He'd been too kind as it was. She needed to stand on her own two feet again.

'And don't worry, Amelie. Greed makes people stupid. I'm sure we'll get to the bottom of this.'

She repeated her thanks, ended the call, scrolled through her phone and with a hard certainty in her stomach she pressed the green button.

'*Bonjour! Agence du Personnel.*'

Amelie explained she'd been in earlier and asked if Nicole was available. The young woman's voice filled her ear a moment later.

'Are you okay, madame?' Nicole asked. 'I was so worried for you.'

'I'm fine,' Amelie replied, and then, aware that she'd perhaps sounded too brusque, she modified her tone. 'Thank you. I just wanted to get in touch to ask if you had any ideas of work I might be able to apply for.' She paused. 'I'm willing to consider anything.'

'How much do you know about wine?' Nicole asked after a pause.

'My *grand-mère* had a little vineyard outside the city, to the south I think. When I was a little girl I used to visit her. I'm sure I picked up a lot without knowing.'

'When I say the word *terroir* to you, what does that make you think of?'

Amelie could feel a half-smile flit across her face as she heard the words of her *grand-mère* from what seemed to be a hundred years ago.

'It's the soil, the earth,' she replied, as her mind, rusty with distance, tried to formulate an answer that would satisfy Nicole. 'But it's more than that. It's what marks a place out as specific. Everything that affects the wine. The weather, the climate, the aspect of the vineyards.'

'Wonderful,' Nicole said. 'Chateau Smith Haut Lafitte is a vineyard that is one of the best in its class so I wasn't sure if you would fit. But your response...'

'Excuse me. What did you call this place?'

Nicole repeated the name. 'Why? Do you know it?'

Amelie held a hand to her heart. 'My *grand-mère* sold up to them years ago, I believe.'

'Wonderful. This is meant to be, madame.' Her voice was full of excitement. 'They are interviewing tomorrow. Do you have a car?'

'No.'

'Well, as you may remember, this chateau is about half an hour from the city, so public transport may not suit for the hours you may be working.'

'Let's jump off that bridge when we come to it,' said Amelie. 'If you think I'm suitable, please set up the interview. I'll worry about transport later.'

Amelie climbed out of the taxi and immediately fell in love. Ranks of vines spread out on all sides, reminding her of happier times. Turning in a slow circle she could see that the vine-filled plain around her was edged with trees on all sides, and there in the centre a series of low, red-roofed buildings, ivy-covered walls, and here and there tall cypress trees. And to her right, a stone tower weathered by centuries of warm wind from the coast, built in a style that clearly pre-dated the architecture she was used to in the city.

'*C'est beau, non?*' the taxi driver said.

'*Oui,*' she agreed, paid him and asked him to return for her in two hours. Even if the interview didn't work out, that would give her a little time to walk around this wondrous place.

A cobbled pathway, just wide enough for two people to walk shoulder-to-shoulder, led through a field of vines up to a courtyard. In one corner stood a sculpture of a man outlined in tiny sparrows, and under a canopy sat an antique car. The front chassis and the cabin were cream, and a wagon frame of dark wood covered the back. The door wore a coat of arms and the words *Chateau Smith Haut Lafitte.*

She walked through a set of doors and out into another courtyard. To the right a stone stairway flanked with a pair of weather-worn, carved lions led up to a small ancient tower, and to her left, at the end of another wing, stood a wooden clocktower stretching into the clear sky.

Imagine having this view every time she came to work.

She felt her spirits rise at the thought.

'Solange Meric?' she heard someone say. There in front of the clocktower stood a young woman in a yellow coat. 'This way, please.'

Amelie followed her, walking past a bronze statue that looked like a giant wedge of crumpled-up newspaper, and round to a glass-fronted reception area.

The woman led her inside, past a seated area and over to a large leather chair in front of a massive fireplace. 'Please have a seat. Valérie will be with you in a moment.'

Amelie sat down and looked around. This was not what she imagined. Everything was in its place, sparkling but homely. Pristine.

'Solange?' A voice interrupted her reverie.

She stood. 'Bonjour.'

'My name is Valérie,' she smiled, and Amelie immediately felt at home. 'Please come into my office.'

∞

The following couple of days passed in a long, slow blur of waiting. Nicole called with another couple of opportunities, both in the city, but Amelie wanted the job at the vineyard. Being surrounded by so much natural beauty in combination with the quality of the entire operation sang to her.

During those two days she barely left the apartment, and when she did she wore a long, shapeless coat and a baseball cap, on high alert for a return visit from the man in the leather jacket. The fear was still there in the dark corners of her mind, like smoke from a distant fire, but she refused to give in to it.

The more she thought about that whole incident the more she was certain he was looking for her. It was no random occurrence. But if she was correct how did he know where to find her? Might it be linked to her missing money? The two things happening so close together might suggest that was so. In any case she had something to be grateful to him for; he'd woken her up from her hibernation. Made her realise going through the motions was not good for her. She needed a purpose, something meaningful to occupy her time. And she prayed that came at Chateau Smith Haut Lafitte.

As a distraction she researched the vineyard and learned all she could about the history of the place. Wine had been made there since the fourteenth century, which explained the architecture; and the 'Smith' part of the name came from an Edinburgh merchant who travelled there in the eighteenth century, fell in love with the place and bought the entire operation. Learning this, she hoped that her own Scottish connection might help with her application.

Needing something for dinner she went along to one of her favourite takeaway places, Le Poulailler d'Augustin on the Place du Pradeau, for some of their delicious roast chicken. She was eyeing up a little glass pot of crème brulée for dessert when the phone in her pocket rang.

She didn't recognise the number showing on the screen alert.

'Hello,' she said.

'Solange, it's Valérie at Smith Haut Lafitte.'

'Oh, hi,' Amelie replied as she stepped outside the shop onto the street. She didn't want her disappointment at what she was sure would be a rejection to be seen by the other people in the queue.

'Okay,' Valérie said. Amelie read her tone and her heart sank. 'There are other people who applied for the job who have better qualifications than you.'

'I understand, but thank you for letting me know so quickly.'

Valerie laughed. 'No, no, no. What I was about to add was that despite that, there is something about you that we like and we want to offer you the job.'

'You do?' Amelie asked. Then squealed. *'Vraiment?'*

'When can you start?'

'Oh my God, this is wonderful. Thank you.' Amelie couldn't remember being this excited when she won the part in her breakthrough movie. At last. Something good was going to happen in her life.

Chapter 47

Damaris was fine with her new house – well, flat – in the West End of the city. It was near her new school and she could walk there and back on her own, despite her Uncle Cammy's protests. She'd heard him a number of times arguing with her mum in the kitchen, which was right next door to her bedroom. He couldn't believe after everything she'd been through that her mum was relaxed about letting her walk about without someone to protect her.

Uncle Cammy needed to chill.

She was also fine with her new bedroom, even though it was tiny, with barely enough room to walk around the bed, but when she was lying there watching a movie on her wall-mounted TV, and all the fairy lights draped around the room were switched on, it was lovely and cosy.

Also, she was fine with the new school. A couple of the girls were nice. Some of them were proper bitchy but she knew how to zone them out now. Only the head knew she was the girl at the centre of the Amelie Hart case, which was what it had become known as on the TV and in the newspapers. Which was weird because Amelie had nothing to do with anything really.

What she wasn't fine with was that her dad had moved out. And she wasn't fine with the stinking flat he'd moved into. There was stuff growing on the walls, the next-door neighbours screamed at each other constantly, and kids were always hanging about at the end of the street calling her names.

'Thinks she's better than us.'

'Why you got your nose in the air, posh bird?'

'Bet your maw nicked those trainers.'

They'd been evicted because of financial stuff. Not that Mum or Dad told her that was what was happening. One of her friends showed it to her in a newspaper. Her parents told her it was because they weren't in love anymore. They'd also decided that she was going to live with Mum, so agreed that her and Mum would get the bigger new place. To be honest it was a bit of a relief in a way. Before they broke up, her mum and dad argued so much Damaris wouldn't allow herself to sleep. She was sure one of them was about to kill the other. Her money would have been on her mum being the last one standing; it was always her making actual threats, while her dad resorted to name-calling.

'Mad bitch' was his go-to now. She visited him every other weekend, which was a major source of argument for him: 'Imagine only being allowed to see your daughter twice a month.'

'Has the mad bitch finished that book yet? Nobody told her it would be so difficult to write one or to get it published, did they?' he'd asked her during her last visit, his voice loaded with angry sarcasm. 'Tell her I want some of the money when it eventually arrives.' He'd then looked around, his eyes weak with loathing. Whether that emotion was aimed at her mother or himself she couldn't say.

Damaris loved her dad and loved seeing him, but she wished he would snap out of that dark, heavy mood that seemed to pull his eyes three inches lower in his face. It meant there was something else to worry about: what if he killed himself? Some men did that, didn't they? One of her friends at her old school found her dad dead in their car. Another boy found his oldest brother hanging in his bedroom.

And if that did happen it would all be her fault. She shouldn't have gone to play with Dave. Shouldn't have pestered him for some attention. If she hadn't done any of that everything would still be fine. Her life would be normal.

At least they had Cammy. He was the one pleasant figure in her life. Her uncle was always up for a laugh, always interested in what she had to say, always listened to her with that soppy smile on his face. Always brought her some kind of gift when he visited. Chocolates, movies, or even clothes and designer trainers. And when he was away for a few days he usually brought her something extra nice.

'I know you're dealing with your own stuff, Cammy. But will you please stop spoiling her?' Mum said to him each time.

His own stuff?

Damaris asked what she was talking about after Cammy left. Her mother looked at her, making that face, as if she was trying to judge if Damaris was old enough to be told something.

'Godssakes, Mum. I'm not a baby.'

Her mother reached for her hand. Damaris read the movement and thought, oh no, this is serious.

'You know that Uncle Cammy was in America.'

'Uh-huh.'

'And you know he came back after his wife and daughter died in a car crash?'

Damaris nodded. That was so sad. Now and again she'd catch Cammy in a moment when he thought no one was looking; he looked so lost.

'Well, what I didn't tell you was that Cammy was driving. And he was over the limit. He hasn't told me all the details. Only that it wasn't just alcohol.'

'What?' Damaris sat bolt upright.

'I don't know what kind of shit ... sorry, stuff he was into over there. And it's horrible and everything, it really is, but I don't want him spoiling you and treating you like some kind of proxy for Mindy.'

Damaris didn't want to look stupid, so didn't ask what proxy meant, but she could make a good guess. 'What age was Mindy?'

'A year or two older than you, babes.' As Claire spoke she reached out and stroked Damaris's cheek, as if she was contemplating that loss for a moment. She shivered. 'Anyway, the point is your uncle is going through a hard time and I don't want you taking advantage.'

'I don't do anything,' Damaris protested. 'He just gives me stuff now and again.'

Of course, Cammy ignored his sister, told her to shut up and insisted he only had one niece and he was going to spoil her like crazy, which was fine with Damaris really. But she would be happier if they didn't argue about it.

All she wanted was for everyone to get on and stop fighting.

All she wanted was everything to go back to normal.

All she wanted was for everything not to be her fault.

Chapter 48

Amelie was initially nervous about taking guests on a tour of the vineyard, but Valérie was patient in her coaching and persuaded her she was a natural. It helped that her knowledge of the process of wine-making was growing, and her everyday use of the language was improving her conversational skills. She could now understand what people were saying when they responded to her.

Because the bus services from the city didn't always suit her working hours she used some of the money Peter had given her and bought herself an old Renault Clio. And each day, driving into work, when the stretch of vineyards appeared before her she felt a huge thrill of appreciation that she got to visit here every day.

On her lunch breaks, after a hastily eaten meal, which was an idea that her colleagues abhorred – lunch was to be savoured in France, she was reminded – she loved nothing more than to borrow one of the estate's bikes and cycle the lanes between the vines, visiting each of the monumental sculptures that were deposited here and there, like blessings from an art-loving god. Her favourite was The Hare. The bronze was set on a plinth so that it was visible above the vines – a giant animal stretched out at the gallop, over four metres in length from the tips of its eager front paws to the ones at the back, its ears trailing high and happy in the breeze.

Thankfully, she'd not come across the strange man who had followed her in the city, and she felt confident that now she was spending more and more time out in the country it was less likely their paths would cross. She was, however, on high alert every time she left her apartment building and stepped out onto the street. Looking either way, searching for that short dark hair and black leather jacket in every male figure around her.

Even here when she greeted each new group of wine tourists she would scan them for threat, only relaxing when she was confident he was not among them. There was also a worry of recognition when the guests were English-speaking, but she kept her hair short and dark, and had taken to wearing large-framed spectacles as part of her disguise. Also, when none of her colleagues were about, she adopted a more French pronunciation to her English. Try as she might she couldn't completely excise the hard, sharp consonants and snappy vowels of her Scottish heritage, but she hoped the addition of some Gallic flavour might put the more curious off the scent.

Despite a twinge of guilt, like a daily stitch in her side, that she got to enjoy this wonderful lifestyle while Dave was locked up in prison, she savoured the fact that Solange Meric was a world apart from the movie star Amelie Hart, and she prayed fervently it would stay that way.

It was late March. Having just guided some visitors to the entrance to La Foret des Sens – an enchanting woodland walk on the estate – she was perched on her bike, face to the sun, enjoying the first real heat of the year, when the phone in her pocket sounded an alert.

'Bonjour,' she said.

'You sound well,' Peter replied.

'Sorry.' Her response was automatic. She'd found a level of happiness here she didn't quite feel she deserved and consequently wasn't sure how to speak to people who were elbows deep in their own troubles. 'I'm just ... enjoying a moment of sunshine.'

'Please don't apologise for enjoying a nice moment, Amelie – sorry, Solange. I'll have to get used to calling you that.' He paused as if reflecting for a moment. 'It would be nice to feel some sunshine on these old bones of mine.'

'How's Dave?'

'Yeah, he's keeping his head down. Getting a lot of reading done, apparently.'

She could tell from his tone he was keeping something back.

'What are you not telling me, Peter?' she asked.

'Nothing,' he replied. 'Things have settled down since that last ... escapade.'

'And?' After some persuasion, and against his better judgement he'd told her about Dave being attacked by Angus in his cell.

'He's still on his own, but eventually they'll have to put someone else in with him.'

'Hopefully it will be someone less murderous.'

'Angus isn't a bad lad, not really. He was put in an impossible situation.'

'What do you mean?'

'Someone threatened to rape and kidnap his girlfriend and turn her into an addicted whore if he didn't kill Dave.'

'What the hell...?' It was like something out of a movie. 'How did you...?'

'Angus told me himself. He ... He's working for me now.'

Amelie was aware of Peter's kindness, having been a recipient of it, but this seemed above and beyond even for him. 'Really? What were you thinking?'

'Dave,' he answered, as if his son's name was the only explanation possible.

'I'm sure he had a good reason.' Amelie was shaking her head. The last thing she'd do if someone tried to kill her would be to help them into a job.

'It's all very complicated and I can't begin to understand it myself, but Dave promised the guy, vouched for him despite everything, and I have to say he's grabbed the opportunity with both hands.'

'Isn't there still a risk to his girlfriend? After all, he didn't succeed.'

'He did make a good stab at it,' Peter said. Then as if realising what he'd just said, he croaked out a tension-minimising laugh. 'Angus has been hyper-vigilant, and so has the young lady in question, but there's been nothing. Not so far.'

'I know that sex offenders get a difficult time in prison, but this seems driven by something...' she struggled to find the right word; '...more.'

'What are you suggesting?'

'Is Angus able to tell you who set it up?'

'He said it was another prisoner who passed on the threat, and the weapon, acting on someone else's behalf.'

'Another prisoner?'

'He can't say for sure.'

'Are you being too trusting here, Peter?' Amelie was suddenly fearful for him. 'What if there is no other actor in this? What if Angus is playing you?'

'I believe him, Amelie. I really do. Besides, who in their right mind is going to try and kill someone who offered them a chance at a job on the outside and then actually go for that job? It just doesn't make sense.'

Amelie felt a gust of wind brush past her face, bringing with it notes of pine and damp earth. Then a cold spark of rain on her cheek. She looked to the sky and saw how the cloud cover had increased since she'd been talking. She got off the bike, kicked out the small metal leg from the frame and set it to stand, then she stepped under the little white stucco shelter at the side of the entrance to the forest. She took a seat on the wooden bench inside and pulled her rain jacket around her, now aware of a slight chill.

'Anyway,' Peter said. 'That wasn't the reason for my call. Your missing money...'

'Yes?'

'My forensic accountant has been beavering away in the background, liaising with the bank and the police.' He lifted the phone away from his mouth and spoke to someone else as if they'd just appeared in his office. She heard a muffled 'Please. Have a seat.' Then his attention was back to her. 'Tell me, when you moved abroad did you redirect your mail?'

'Of course,' Amelie replied. 'Or I should say, I got Bernard to do it.'

There was a pause on the line at the mention of Bernard's name. She waited to see if Peter would repeat his concerns about her friend. Instead he simply asked, 'Do you know when?'

'I'll ask him to give me dates. Why?'

'We haven't traced the bulk of your cash, but there were a series of withdrawals from your account. A couple of hundred pounds at a time. All of them in Glasgow city centre. And a few of them on the same day you were withdrawing cash, albeit from a different bank account, from a machine in Bordeaux.'

'Sorry?' Amelie struggled to compute Peter's meaning. 'Someone was using my card in Glasgow while I was in Bordeaux?'

'As you haven't mastered the art of being in two places at the same time we are able to prove to the bank that one set of withdrawals is fraudulent.' At this she felt a tremor of concern that there were people in the UK who knew exactly where she was. She hadn't considered that it was right there on her bank statements. The exact time, date and place noted every time she withdrew some cash.

'But...' Then Peter's question about redirecting her mail hit her. 'The bank sent something out – a new card, a statement, or something?'

'Yes, exactly,' Peter said. 'It wasn't redirected and the wrong person somehow got their hands on it.'

'What do we know about my lodger?'

'We know it wasn't them,' Peter answered. 'But we have a working theory who it might have been. These small regular withdrawals amounted to only a couple of thousand pounds, but, as I said, we're still looking for the bulk of your money. The person who got their hands on that is much less amateurish.'

Amelie thought about her accounts, yet again cursed her tendency to bury her head in the sand when it came to financial matters, and thought about the set-up Bernard had suggested to her years ago: one main account for the big sums, with regular movement from there to another account for everyday cash, then a third emergency-style account. She heard his voice in her ear, a replay of their last conversation, when they'd eventually caught up with each other; his assertion that he'd been in hospital. She wondered if that was all part of an elaborate swindle.

Enough, she told herself. Bernard was her friend. One of the few remaining. He wouldn't do that to her.

'You heard me speaking to someone else a little earlier on?' Peter said.

'Yes...'

'I'm with Detective Sergeant Campbell. I'm going to put her on the phone.' Amelie could hear a tremor of excitement in Peter's voice.

A pause, and a woman came onto the line: 'This is Amelie Hart, yes?'

'Yes,' Amelie replied.

'DS Campbell here. We have a CCTV image of someone withdrawing cash from your account from a machine in the city centre. We're wondering if you know this person.'

'Okay.' They were that far advanced in the investigation? Amelie didn't pick that up from what Peter said.

'Be prepared to come back to the UK, Miss Hart. You'll probably be needed to testify if, or when, this comes to court.'

'What have you found?'

'I'm going to have Mr Robbins send a CCTV image to your phone.'

A moment later she heard an alert as an email landed in her inbox. She removed the phone from the side of her head, went in to her email app, saw the mail from Peter and thumbed the attachment. An image bloomed onto the screen. A woman's face in grainy black and white, taken from above, one hand frozen in the moment she put out a hand to pull the cash from the machine.

It was Claire Brown.

Chapter 49

There was a knock at the door. Loud and firm.

Damaris was in the kitchen with Cammy. He'd brought a massive birthday cake with him. Tiny, pink icing roses covered the sides and it had twelve candles and a large capital D on the surface. Her mum had asked Cammy to light all the candles while she went to the toilet.

'And don't blow them out till I come back, birthday girl,' Claire said as she tweaked Damaris's nose.

The door sounded again.

'Will you get that, Cammy?' Claire shouted from behind the toilet door. 'Kinda busy here.'

''Sake,' Cammy grumbled. 'Who could that be? Is your dad coming over, Damaris?'

'No,' she said, trying to hide her disappointment. Her father told her that he and her mum were unable to share a civil word and it would only spoil her birthday if he turned up. His plan was to have a separate celebration for her: 'Just you and me, doll. It will be magic. And we can go to the pictures, or the ten-pin bowling, or a concert. Is there a concert on? There's bound to be, eh? Kylie or Madonna or somebody. Just think, it will be like you have two birthdays. How lucky are you?'

Damaris was glad this conversation happened over the phone, because then her dad wouldn't have seen the disappointment on her face. She'd had it all planned. Dad would come over. They'd have cake, drink lots of fizzy stuff, remember the good times and Mum and Dad would fall back in love again. She was to blame for them splitting up, so maybe she could bring them back together?

In that moment, watching each candle puff into light, while her mother was in the toilet and someone was banging on the door, she realised her hope was silly. It would take way more than a slice of cake for her parents' attitude towards each other to soften.

'Coming,' Cammy shouted in the direction of the door. He looked down at the cake. 'Just one wee candle to go, babe. I'll get that in a second.'

He charged along the long corridor to the front door, yelling, 'Hold your horses, will you?'

Damaris was wondering if she should light the last remaining candle when her mother eventually came out of the toilet, wiping her nose with the back of her hand. 'Who was it?' she asked Damaris.

The girl shrugged. They heard a grumble of voices from the door. Claire cocked her head when she recognised her name.

'Who is it, Cammy?' she shouted through.

'You can't do this, guys. Not on the wean's birthday,' Cammy shouted.

Then there were footsteps, and a man and a woman appeared at the kitchen door. They were both in dark suits and there was something very official about them.

'Claire Brown?' the woman said. 'I'm Detective Sergeant Marjorie Campbell. We have some questions we need to ask you. Would you mind coming with us to the station?'

'It's no' exactly a request though, is it?' Cammy accused.

'Zip it, Cammy,' Claire said.

'On the wean's birthday? How sick are you guys?' Cammy said.

'What's happening, Mum?' Damaris felt small and afraid. 'Mum?' She did her best to hold back her tears, but she was very, very scared.

'Cammy, leave it,' her mum said. Then she looked at Damaris, and the cake. 'You two have a wee slice, but don't eat it all, mind. I want a massive chunk when I get back.' She bent down so that her face was level with Damaris. It was one large smile, a smile that Damaris could tell was fake.

'Let me get my coat,' her mum then said to the man and woman.

'Want me to give Roger a call?' Cammy asked.

'How long can you stay for?' Claire asked.

'As long as you need me.'

'Great.' She approached Cammy, leaned in to him, whispered something short, and then putting on what even Damaris could see was a brave face she turned to the police officers. 'The sooner we get on with this, the sooner I get back. I've got a wee girl's birthday to celebrate.'

Damaris ran to the window in the front room and waited for them to appear on the street below, then watched as they walked out of the communal doorway, up the path and along the road to a car. There her mother was directed into the back seat. Before Claire ducked inside, she looked up at the window and gave a bright wave as if she was just off to the supermarket.

Damaris sensed that Cammy was at her side. He handed her a large slice of cake on a pink paper napkin.

'What's going on, Uncle Cammy?' she asked, holding herself tight as if that might contain the mess and confusion of her thoughts.

'Nothing, doll. Everything will be fine. Just eat your cake.' He left the room, and came back moments later with a slice for himself. He put his face down to the cake and rammed as much as he could into his mouth. He looked so ridiculous when he lifted his face back up, sponge and icing stuck to the stubble around his lips, that Damaris laughed. Cammy brightened with the sound of her laughter, so she forced out some more.

'That's the stuff, D,' he said. 'Nothing's going to spoil my girl's birthday. Now...' He took a more delicate bite of cake this time, chewed and swallowed. 'Movie night?'

Putting on what she thought was perhaps the performance of her life Damaris pushed a smile onto her face and made her eyes bigger. 'Yay,' she said, and felt a weight solidify in her stomach and slowly move up to her heart, as if something had died inside her.

Laughing in all the right places, groaning, and then jumping in fright when it was expected, with her uncle as the conductor of her responses, she watched the movie. And just as the closing credits were rolling on the TV they heard the front door open.

'Mum.' Damaris ran to her and gave her a hug. 'Uncle Cammy and me watched this movie. We were going to watch the Disney Channel next, want to join us? Can I get you some cake? It's delicious.' When she was hugging her mother it occurred to Damaris that she'd never felt so much heat come off her.

'Whoa, whoa, Damaris. Let me get my coat off.'

Looking up at her mother's face Damaris caught a glance that passed between her and Cammy.

'I'm thinking a large glass of wine might be preferred,' Cammy said.

'Wine and cake,' Claire said with a tight smile. 'A winning combination.'

Damaris wasn't stupid. She could see her mother was struggling with something. And knew her mother couldn't wait for her bedtime so she and Cammy could talk. Really talk.

She faked a yawn. Compliance with the adults meant an easier life, right? It meant she was a good girl and nothing would go wrong. Nothing more.

'I'm tired, Mum. Can I go to bed?'

'Wait. You sure, baby?' Damaris felt the heat of her mother's hand on her head and sensed relief.

Damaris nodded.

'Alright, then. It's your birthday, we do it your way. Give your uncle Cammy a kiss and go and brush your teeth.'

Damaris dutifully did as she was told, kissed both the grown-ups, changed into her pyjamas, brushed her teeth and, making sure the nightlight was on in her bedroom, she climbed under the covers.

Once there she listened to the muffled voices coming from the living room. Then it sounded like her mother was crying. Moving as silently as she could, she got out of bed and moved to the door. She pulled it open, just a little, slowly so it wouldn't creak, and placed her ear to the space.

She heard her mother trying to shush Cammy.

'I'll kill her,' he said. 'I'll fucking kill her.'

Damaris shrank back from the threat and the violence in her uncle's voice. He was her fun relative. She'd never heard him speak in such a way before. It frightened her.

How long she stood there she had no idea, but her feet were getting cold. Then she heard Cammy groan as if he'd pushed himself onto his feet.

'I need to go. I'll just give the birthday girl a goodnight kiss first.'

Alarmed, Damaris jumped back into bed, lay on her side and pulled the covers up to her neck. The door opened and Cammy entered. He sat on the side of the bed and she felt his fingertips brush across her forehead as he moved her long fringe to the side.

'Stop pretending you're asleep, D.' There was teasing humour in his tone. He bent forward and kissed her in the same place his fingertips had been moments before.

'I love you, little girl. So much. You know that right?'

Damaris opened her eyes and nodded.

'And nothing is going to happen to harm you or your mother, okay?' he said quietly, and with a coldness that was at odds with the warmth of his message.

Damaris nodded again.

'Uncle Cammy's here and he protects his family. You got that?'

Another nod. There was a fierceness even in those almost whispered words, and a cold, sterile light of determination in his eyes. 'Okay.' He kissed her again and stood up. 'Go to sleep, and you have my permission to have cake for breakfast.'

'Thanks, Uncle Cammy,' she said. 'I loved my presents. And the cake was delish.'

'Aww, wee girl, you are so welcome.' He ruffled her hair, and was gone.

⊙⊘

Damaris woke sometime later. Her bedroom was in complete darkness. Feeling pressure in her bladder, she climbed out of bed and padded across the narrow hall to the bathroom. She didn't need to put the light on in there to use the toilet because the streetlight outside the window painted everything a joyless mustard.

Worried it might wake up her mother, she didn't flush, and then gently closing the bathroom door behind her, in that way she'd learned, moving slowly, so slowly so that there was only a little click when the door was properly shut.

A sound issued from the living room. Still on tiptoes she moved to the doorway and saw her mother slumped on the sofa, head back, eyes closed and mouth open. There was an almost empty bottle of wine on the floor at her feet and an empty glass in her hand.

With care, Damaris approached the sofa.

'Mum,' she whispered. 'You okay?'

Her mother mumbled something. Damaris wasn't sure whether this was a reply or a dream her mother was having.

She leaned over and gently pulled the glass out of her mother's hand. Didn't want her to cut herself. She put the glass in the kitchen sink and went through to her mother's bedroom. There she gathered a soft, grey fleece blanket into her arms and padded back to the living room to drape it over her mother.

Her mother mumbled something. It sounded like *Leave me alone*. Then she curled up, pulling her knees to her chest, and in doing so knocked over the wine bottle. Damaris picked it up and took it through to the kitchen.

There she could see the cake on the table, the knife, its blade crusted with icing, and her row of twelve little candles. The one at the end with its sad, pristine wick.

She bit her lip as she felt all the emotion of the day build up in her. Voices filled her head. Unnameable emotions charged against her ribs and she thrummed with the tension of it all. She wanted to throw the cake out of the window, she wanted to scream until her throat was ablaze, she wanted it all to stop.

Without articulating what she was doing, why she was doing it, or how she knew it would help, she picked up the knife in her right hand, licked the icing from it and then placed it against her left wrist. She pushed. And as her blood welled on to the blade she heard the voices in her head go quiet and felt a release, like a pop, in her chest.

For a moment. For a delicious, light-filled moment everything stilled.

Everything was silent.

Everything was better.

Chapter 50

Amelie flew back to Scotland for the trial via Lisbon. It meant a longer journey but she hoped if the press got wind of her arrival they would be diverted away from her actual home. The first thing she did when she got through passport control and picked up her luggage was to go into a toilet and put on her disguise. Which consisted of a blonde wig she'd bought in Bordeaux to make her look more like the Amelie Hart the British public would be expecting.

Peter was waiting for her in the arrivals hall. There was a stoop to his back that hadn't been there before and a weariness in his face. But as soon as he saw her walking towards him, he lit up with a large smile.

'Hey,' he said, and gave her a surprisingly strong hug. 'Great to see you.' All the tiredness was wiped away by his smile of welcome.

'Let me.' He reached across and took the handle of her suitcase. Amelie was more than capable of pulling the case along herself but Peter seemed keen to be of assistance, so she let him.

'You're looking good,' she lied. 'How's Dave?'

He squared his shoulders as if it might help him bear his burden. 'Keeping his head down, love. Biding his time.'

'No more incidents then?'

'All quiet on the prison front. Thankfully.'

'Do you think he'll want to see me?'

Peter gave her a sad look. 'He asks about you. All the time. But I don't think he wants you to see him in that place.'

'That's so silly.'

'He's an idiot. What can I say?' He looked around. 'I think we should be going.'

Amelie became aware that they were attracting attention.

People were whispering in clusters, sending lingering stares, mobile phones aimed in her direction. All the things she once barely registered now felt like a painful intrusion.

In the car, as he buckled his seatbelt, Peter told her he had news.

'I expect your money will be replaced in your bank account very soon.'

'What? All of it?'

'We were able to show that you had no part in the theft of your cash.'

Amelie relaxed a little in her seat. 'I'll return your money to you first chance I get.'

'No rush.' Peter drove off.

'Thank you, Peter,' Amelie said as she put her hand on his for a moment. 'You have been so very kind. I don't know what I would...'

'You're family, Amelie. Despite how things are with you and Dave. Besides, Norma would be giving me a tongue-lashing from the grave if I didn't help you out.' A little bit of tiredness slipped into his voice when he mentioned Norma, and Amelie was struck by how much this man had changed since she first met him. Always polite, slightly stiff and formal was how she first thought of him. Recent events had scrubbed that stiffness from him and he looked older – much older – and his formality had been replaced with a vulnerability and human warmth that she couldn't help but respond to.

'It is appreciated,' she said. She looked out of the window as they joined a slipstream of traffic heading for the city centre. The familiar cityscape unfolded in front of her: the long, wide motorway full of traffic snaked ahead of them, crowded by buildings on either side. The sky held a vista of clouds in a uniform grey. Just ahead, a gull appeared to float past, then, as if lifted by a strong breeze, it veered off sharply to the right. Raindrops scattered across the windscreen. She turned and looked out of the window at the spread of hills beyond the sprawl of buildings. Familiarity unwound in her, but it was tainted, as if entwined with a snake of discomfort. Until this situation clarified itself, until Dave was free, she'd never feel completely at ease in this city.

'I thought it might be nice if you stayed in the granny annexe at the house, rather than that big lonely flat in the city,' Peter said.

'Lovely,' replied Amelie. She had wondered, but was afraid to ask when they'd made arrangements for her visit. A hotel in the centre would have been fine, but she knew Peter would want to provide. She had hoped that he might offer her the flat, but now they were on their way to the house in Bearsden she realised it would indeed be lovely to share the space with him. And besides, the house was surrounded by a large wall and had security gates. Not enough to deter the determined but it would offer some privacy from the more casual observer.

'What time are we due in court tomorrow?' she asked.

'Ten am.'

'Good. We get a lie in then.'

'Can't remember last time I had a lie in,' Peter said. In his tone Amelie read that what he couldn't remember was the last time he had a good long sleep.

'You sleeping alright?'

'Whisky helps,' he replied with a self-deprecating smile. 'Are the folks at the chateau happy to give you the time off?' He changed the topic smoothly.

'I've worked six days a week without any time off since I began there. It wasn't a problem.' She didn't add that she'd concocted a lie about going back to Scotland to spend time with elderly relatives.

Peter's phone rang. He answered hands-free.

'Mr Robbins,' a woman's voice sounded through the speakers. 'It's DS Campbell here. Are you free to talk?'

'I'm in the car with Amelie,' Peter replied.

'Even better,' Campbell said, all business. 'We've just received word that Claire Brown has changed her plea to guilty.'

'What?' Amelie and Peter said at the same time.

'I'm so sorry, Miss Hart, your journey has been unnecessary,' Campbell said.

'I wonder why she waited until now,' Amelie thought out loud.

'I've given up guessing why people do the things they do,' Campbell replied.

'I bet this was part of her thinking all along,' Peter said. 'She always had the intention of pleading guilty. The evidence was too strong. She just wanted to make life as uncomfortable for Amelie for as long as she could.'

'I couldn't possibly comment,' Campbell said in a tone that suggested she was in agreement.

'What happens now?' Amelie asked.

'There will be a sentencing hearing, and my feeling is that she'll get a suspended sentence.'

'What? No prison time?' Peter said. Amelie looked across at him; his lips were a tight line of anger. 'What a joke.'

'In the scheme of things she didn't steal that much money. It was an opportunistic crime. And she has a child to look after so I think the procurator fiscal will take the view that a custodial sentence isn't in the public interest.'

Amelie said nothing as she allowed what DS Campbell was saying to sink in. Disappointment and anger built in her. She wanted that moment in court when she could look across at the dock and see Claire Brown there, in that same position she'd forced Dave into. She wanted to observe the other woman's discomfort, see her reactions as her crime was read out in court. See how she acted when the moment she stole the money played out in front of the public eye.

'What do we do now?' Amelie asked. 'And what about the larger sum? Someone has stolen my money, DS Campbell, and it looks like they're getting away with it.'

'That is part of another investigation, Miss Hart. We can find no link between those monies and Claire Brown. My advice is to go back to your life in France and leave all of this behind you.'

∞

Later that evening Bernard called. When she saw his name on the screen she felt a twinge of guilt that she hadn't let him know she was in the country.

'Good evening, my dear. How is sunny Glasgow? You're on the news.'

'Sorry, Bernard. I should have let you—'

He tutted. 'Not a problem. You have enough on your plate without having to concern yourself with me. Although a cocktail session at The Groucho Club wouldn't have gone amiss.'

'You know I can't face the public scrutiny, Bernard.'

'I know, dear. Just missing you, that's all.' He sighed. 'How are you?'

'Looking forward to going back to France.'

They chatted for a little while about nothing important as if each recognised there was some distance between them and as if they were trying to work on the fraying fabric of that old connection.

'I know you're enjoying a life of anonymity over there in *la belle France*, but do you ever hanker for the roar of the greasepaint, the smell of the crowd?'

She managed a chuckle at the old joke, while wondering if there was some self interest in the question. After all she had become his biggest earner. 'Honestly, no, Bernard. I prefer to be real in a real world, if you know what I mean? Being part of the smoke in that mirror, and yet being so reliant on what other people think of me?' She shuddered. 'Sometimes I think that horrible man did me a favour.'

They both knew who she meant by 'that horrible man'.

'I should have insisted we put a pause on the filming, got you some help. Instead you went straight from that nightmare into a high-pressure major part in a movie, and all that entailed.'

'I wouldn't have listened to you anyway,' Amelie said. 'I was hungry for the success.'

'And then you have all of this with Dave, and the theft ... I don't know how you're still standing, my dear.'

There was a long moment's silence as they both fell into their own thoughts.

'I just feel so bad. I could have been more of a support back then. I mean, waking up in your own bed in that dress. He even made you a wedding cake, for chrissakes. How you got past that and retained your sanity I'll never know.'

Amelie was back on the bed. Light from the street picking out the odd detail in the gloom of her bedroom. Lace catching on the skin of her neck. Numbness growing from the restraints on her wrists. Unable to obey any of the commands from her brain.

Paralysed with fear.

Chapter 51

London, February 2010

'I have a surprise for you,' the man said as he got to his feet. It was still dark outside and Amelie frantically tried to work out how long she might have been out. 'But you won't get it if you scream. Do you promise me you won't make a noise?'

Amelie nodded.

'Let's just make sure about that, shall we?' He walked towards the bed. She shrank from him, but her restraints made any movement all but impossible. She felt something being pushed into her mouth. A ball of some sort. Then she felt her hair being tugged and heard a small metallic jingle as whatever he was using was fastened at the back of her head.

As he worked his breath felt like a hot souring on her cheek. Certain that she was about to be sick she tried to turn away from him.

'You'll be fine,' he said, and through her fear Amelie could hear a genuine note in his tone. He really thought she would be fine? Instead of being reassured this frightened her even more.

'Now, we'll just loosen you from the bedposts and take you downstairs, cos I have a lovely surprise for you.'

After he had untied her, he helped her to her feet.

'Take it easy now. You've had a lovely sleep and sometimes we're a bit woozy after a lie down.'

She rubbed at her wrists, but the relief was short-lived, because he re-tied her hands together in front of her. Then he led her out of her bedroom, down the stairs and into the sitting room.

Her heart quailed at the sight he had prepared for her.

'While you had your little nap I was busy,' he said. 'I hope you like it.'

A table had been placed in front of the fireplace. On it was a three-tiered wedding cake, complete with tiny bride and groom on the top. To the side of the cake was a large knife, a black leather bible and a bottle of champagne with two glasses.

Trembling, she made herself turn to face him.

He was very thin, just a few inches taller than her, his short, dark hair was glossed back, and he was wearing a red dinner jacket, a dog-collar, and a red lace eye mask.

'I know, it's all a bit much, but I do love the drama of a wedding, don't you?' His smile displayed a top row of perfect teeth.

This guy was deluded. Did that mean she was in physical danger, or once this charade was over, would he leave her be?

'And the dog-collar is weird I know, but who else – ' he reached for the bible '– is going to perform the ceremony.'

She stared at him, taking more care this time: his body shape, his movements, his forehead, his nose and chin. Did she know him? Had their paths crossed before? Could he be an old boy-friend? But there was nothing familiar about him.

'Now.' He moved closer, using his extra height to try to intimi-date her. 'I'm going to take the ball-gag off. How else are you going to say "I do"?' He nodded his head in the direction of the knife. 'You're not going to shout for help are you?'

He loosened the gag, placed it on the table beside the cake and handed her a glass, then he stepped back as if he was worried she might use it as a weapon. 'Have a sip. Your mouth will be dry.'

She sipped, felt the welcome moisture in her mouth. 'Please don't do this,' she said. 'Let me go. I won't tell anyone this hap-pened. We can pretend it never happened.'

The doorbell rang.

They both turned. He stepped towards her, his hands up in a warning gesture. Must be her taxi driver, she thought.

And she screamed with every ounce of energy she possessed.

Chapter 52

Glasgow, September 2019

Every now and then Dave would get a book of inspirational quotes out of the library, Anything to distract from the clench of his fists, the weight on the back of his neck, the permanent cloud over his mind and heart that soured everything he tasted, touched, heard or saw. The constant fight-or-flight mode was exhausting. Continuously over-reacting and being unable to control those reactions was an ever-present worry. There was a better man than this inside him, but he was lost in a mental maze of recrimination and resentment.

He was sure he was going to hurt someone, or they'd hurt him and he'd never get out of prison.

That morning's quote came courtesy of the *Talmud*: 'He who controls his thoughts, controls his destiny.'

Yeah.

Right.

His thoughts were a free-wheeling, toxic jumble of self-and-everybody-else-loathing, and even the knowledge that he was about to get out didn't offer any peace. In fact it made it worse. Inside he only had the other prisoners and guards to worry about. Once outside he would have to add the world's population to that list, because how could he ever trust anyone again?

A thought that churned through his mind every hour of every day he'd been inside these walls. He simply couldn't get past the unfairness of it all.

Dave didn't sleep during his last night in prison. Nor did he relax for a moment the day before. Things had been mostly incident free since the attacks near the start of his sentence, but he wouldn't put it beyond whoever was behind them to have another go while he was still in prison.

That was, if the threat to him would only come from within these Victorian walls. From the first it seemed to Dave that the orchestrator of the violence was in the outside world. There was any number of willing participants in prison, prepared to act on instructions, or to make a name for themselves.

On the morning of his release Dave was on high alert. Anything that could go wrong would surely go wrong. He was sure the Parole Board would get in touch and say they'd made a mistake; that he should have had time added on for violent conduct.

To make the time pass quicker that last day, at rec time he went round the guys with whom he had been on nodding acquaintance, and doled out his meagre belongings – toiletries, books, and the few food items he had left from his canteen. He was aware that some guys made friends in prison, but aside from the fact that most of the prisoners around him were sex offenders, since the incident with Angus he'd stopped himself getting close to anyone. He didn't want them to be used against him.

Angus himself had visited only a couple of times since his release. It had been good to see him again, and he couldn't blame the lad for visiting so rarely; why on earth anyone who'd been in here would voluntarily come back, even just to the Visits Hall, was beyond Dave. The job with Robbins Accountants and Co. had only lasted a few months. Peter had reported to Dave that he was sure the boy's guilty conscience stopped him from relaxing into the work, and he'd left as soon as he was legally out of the reach of his parole officer.

At lights-out Dave lay back in his bunk, eyes open, staring into a darkness that seemed to lie heavy on his chest, aware of his pulse and sure that everyone in the building could hear it pounding. He listened for every movement beyond the walls of his cells. The clink of keys as a guard walked near his cell; he was sure he heard stealth in that movement, an intent to do him harm. A cough from the next cell and his imagination provided an image of someone crouched over him ready to strike.

Calm, he told himself. *Breathe. It is going to happen.* At long last he was going to get out of here.

But what was his life going to be like outside?

He was an offender. A *sex* offender.

A convicted paedophile.

His days as a member of polite society were over. He may have served his time but people would never forgive him. If it weren't for his father he was sure he'd never be able to work again and would spend the rest of his life on the street.

No, he decided, he'd leave, get away from Glasgow as soon as his parole visits were done. A cave facing onto a deserted beach. A hut in a forest. Somewhere people didn't visit. Because the wrong look, the wrong word, and he'd surely end up back in here.

Best to put up with the bullshit sex-offender rehabilitation sessions, or whatever they were called, for as long as he had to, and then move into the wilds somewhere and get the fuck away from everyone.

Chapter 53

Damaris had come to associate birthday cakes with knives. Take your cutesy little candles, pink icing, your velvet sponge with its jam-and-cream filling and shove it, she thought each year. Leave her the knife, make sure it was deliciously sharp, and give her the peace and quiet to put it to good use.

This year's had fifteen of the little wicks, and she'd groaned when Uncle Cammy brought the massive white box into the house.

'Really?' she asked.

He ruffled her head. *Actually* ruffled her head, and said, 'Don't be acting all grown-up with me, D. You'll always be my little girl.'

She shrunk away from his touch, said, 'Whatever.' Even though she knew that no one said that anymore.

'And why are you always wearing black?' Cammy asked. 'Hiding behind those shapeless tops and long sleeves. You're a pretty girl. Don't hide it.'

'Leave it,' Claire said, shooting him a warning look from her position on the sofa, nursing her ever-present glass of wine.

Her mother and uncle talked about this subject a lot. Her mother opined that Damaris did it to hide her burgeoning sexuality after what she'd experienced as a little girl – she actually used the word 'burgeoning'. She probably heard it on one of those TED talks she was always listening to, after which she'd subject Damaris to an interminable lecture. *Interminable.* A word Damaris got from, like, a proper book instead of doing it the lazy way.

Even now that she was older they still talked about her as if she wasn't there.

'Just trying to be nice, sis.' Cammy dropped onto the sofa beside his sister. He looked at her glass. 'It's five o'clock somewhere, eh?'

Claire stuck her tongue out at him. 'Whatever,' she said.

'I know it's D's birthday,' Cammy said while staring at the glass. 'But is there another reason why you're drinking in the afternoon?'

Claire looked at Damaris. Then her brother. She opened her mouth, but before she could say anything Damaris walked out of the room. It was all her mother had talked about that day.

A letter arrived in the morning post from the Scottish Prison Service telling them that David Robbins had been released.

'On my wean's birthday,' Claire had said when the mail arrived, and what felt like every hour since, so angry that saliva had flecked Damaris's face as her mother raged.

Way to make it all about you, Mother, Damaris thought. 'My wean'. She said nothing. Of course. That pattern had been laid a long time ago and would take something major to shift. But the words lay coiled and heavy in her heart and on her tongue, tainting every mood, every moment.

'Hey,' Cammy yelled after her. 'Where are you going? Not want to open your presents?'

'Sorry, Uncle Cammy.' She came back into the room.

'That paedo getting out has got us all flustered,' Claire said.

No, Damaris thought. *It's got you all flustered*. She didn't know how she felt. She'd spent the last few years hiding from her feelings, only feeling a flicker of relief when thin, sharp metal scored some blood from under the gauze of her skin.

'Here.' Cammy thrust an envelope and a small box into her hand, his face bright with an expectant smile.

God, please be something good, Damaris thought. She was exhausted from acting in a way that would suit her mother all day. Please let this envelope contain something she could be genuinely pleased about.

She peered inside the envelope. Then thumbed through a collection of notes. There had to be hundreds in there. 'Wow,' she said.

'Thought, seeing as you're an ancient teenager, you'd want cash so you could spend it on what you want, rather than me buying what I think you want.' As Cammy spoke he looked at her. That look he gave her that made Damaris feel that he could read every thought as it scrolled through her mind.

'Go on,' Cammy said. 'Open the box.'

She did. And saw that it contained an iPhone. The very latest model.

'Wow, Uncle Cammy, that's so cool.' Damaris gave a little squeal and then gave her uncle a big hug.

'That's very generous,' Claire said using a tone that sounded to Damaris like a warning: *Stop spoiling my daughter.* 'Too generous, Uncle Cammy. And D, you can get to your bank in the morning and deposit the cash.' Was she jealous because she couldn't be so kind? Damaris wanted to tell her it didn't matter, that she didn't care about that stuff, but she couldn't find the energy.

'Sure,' she replied, thinking, *as if.* First chance she got she was heading down the town with Chrissie and scoring the best quality weed she could find.

'I've only got one niece,' Cammy said. 'I've got to spoil her. It's the law.' He leaned forward and kissed her forehead. He whispered, 'And spend any of it on that shit you smoke and it'll be the last thing you get from me.'

With an effort, Damaris managed to hide her reaction.

'What was that?' Claire asked.

'Uncle and niece stuff, Mum,' Damaris managed to say, ignoring the shift of the pulse in her throat. How did he know?

'Yeah, uncle and niece stuff, Claire Bear. Just you stick with the vino and leave the parenting to the real grown-up in the room.'

Ouch, thought Damaris, her face still warm from Cammy's whispered comment.

'Arsehole,' replied Claire.

Once Cammy left her father came over and took her out for dinner. They went to a posh little restaurant in the West End, up some cobbled lane near a cinema.

'Nice, eh?' her dad asked, watching her as she looked around them.

'Sure,' she replied.

'Have anything you want,' he said. 'Steak, cheesecake, chips, whatever.'

Damaris made a face. 'Cheesecake and chips. Gross.'

Her dad laughed and Damaris's heart lightened a little. She loved it when her father laughed. It happened so rarely.

Life appeared to have improved for him over the last year or so. He'd met a new woman, Lucy. She was nice. Didn't fuss. Didn't try to be another mother. And he was living in a proper house now in a nice area.

But still, despite all of this, there was a heaviness in him, and he drank way too much. He had a whisky in front of him now. And a pint of beer. She was never going to drink. Alcohol was for losers. Then, realising what a harsh judgement this was of both her parents, she felt her face heat.

'I'm only having the one,' he said as if he'd been watching where her eyes were going.

She shrugged.

'So, I hear Dave Robbins got out today,' he said.

She shrugged again.

'How do you feel about that?'

'It's alright, Dad,' she said. 'Mum and I have already had the talk.'

'Cool,' he said. 'Just checking.' He pretended to read the menu. 'Are you okay? You can tell me if you're not.'

'I'm fine, Dad,' she replied. 'Really.'

Her turn to pretend to read the menu, and as her eyes roamed sightlessly over the page she wondered about her lack of feeling about Dave's release. She wasn't worried, or scared. Should she be?

She only knew that she wanted to see him. Make sure he was alright. All those years in a prison couldn't have been very nice for him.

How weird was that?

∂‰

Next day was a Saturday so Chrissie came over with her present – a bottle of Guess Girl, which Damaris thought was lush – and they spent the afternoon side by side on her bed, re-watching the *Twilight* movies.

'I thought we were going into town … for some stuff,' Chrissie asked at one point.

'My uncle Cammy told me not to.'

'Eh?' Chrissie's head shot up from the pillow. 'He knows you smoke…?'

'He totally called me on it.'

'How does he know?'

'Freaks me out. Feels like he knows everything about me.'

'He's proper hot,' Chrissie said. 'I wish I had a cute uncle like him.' She scooched up on the bed so she was sitting upright. 'But how does he know? That's weird. Is he following you?'

'He knows so many people,' Damaris answered. 'I bet one of them saw me buying the stuff and grassed me up.'

'*Grass*-ed you up.' Chrissie prodded her. 'Get it?'

'Moron.'

Chrissie laughed. But it wasn't her usual full-bellied chuckle, and Damaris realised her friend was a little off today. She'd been so full of her own stuff she hadn't spotted it until that moment. She felt like a bad friend and sunk a little into the bed.

'Your uncle bought you your phone, yeah?' Chrissie asked as if a thought had just occurred to her.

'And?'

'And he got you your last one as well?'

'What are you getting at?'

'I bet he put you on one of those tracking apps, so he can, like, track you.'

'He's a bit of a control freak but even that's too much for someone like him,' Damaris replied while wondering if it might be true. Cammy did seem to know more than was healthy about her. 'Anyway, I totally love my phone so I'll forgive him.'

Chrissie lapsed into silence, as if she was wondering how to say something.

'What's up, sis?' Damaris asked. Sis was a title they gave each other, because they totally felt like they were sisters, but they only tended to use it in moments when they felt some tenderness was needed.

Chrissie shook her head. She was leaning forward, legs crossed, head down, her long dark hair falling down either side of her face.

'Come on.' Damaris reached a hand out and touched one of Chrissie's. 'Spill.'

'You've got to promise not to say.' Chrissie's eyes were large and there was a suggestion of impending tears in the corners.

'Pinkie promise.' Feeling a charge of worry for her friend, Damaris held up her right hand, pinkie prominent.

'I'm only telling you this because, you know, what you went through, like, when you were a kid.'

Damaris crossed her arms. Chrissie was the only person in her new life who knew about any of that, and she wasn't comfortable with it being referred to out loud, even though they were alone in the room.

She waited for her friend to speak.

'My big sister, Selina? She was attacked last month. Raped.'

'Last month? Oh my God. Why are you only telling me now?'

'We were told to keep quiet about it. Mum didn't want anyone to know.'

'Secrecy's not good, Chrissie. It only helps the rapist.'

'Selina's in a state. Won't come out of her room. Doesn't eat. Sits in the bath for ages.'

'Did they catch the guy?'

Chrissie nodded. 'She was in a club. He must have roofied her drink. Next thing she knows she's in a disabled toilet and ... apparently there's a whole load of girls he attacked.'

'Oh my God.'

'I'm so worried about her.'

'Poor Selina. That's awful.'

'Mum got her some counselling and stuff, but nothing's helping.' Chrissie was fiddling with her false nails as she spoke, pulling one up from the nail it had been glued to. Then she looked up at Damaris. 'Could you speak to her?'

'Sorry?'

'You know what it's like. I wondered if, you know, talking to someone who's been there might be better than some woman with a big blouse and a chiffon scarf.'

Wondering what the blouse and scarf had to do with anything, Damaris hesitated before answering. Did she want to go into that sort of headspace?

'Don't worry, I haven't told Selina anything about you, in case you said no. We can say it happened when you were wee. We don't have to tell her you're the girl in the Amelie Hart case.'

'Yeah. I'll do it,' Damaris said. 'I'll do it,' she repeated.

Maybe speaking to someone else who had been through this might help her sort out the mess in her own head.

Chapter 54

Dave walked through his parental home feeling like a tourist in his own life. His parents had bought the house when he was in his early teens, when his father's business really started to take off. He'd spent years on that bed, staring at the ceiling worrying about girls, exams, other boys, his parents, getting enough game time for the school rugby team. Watched TV on that very sofa with his parents. Played in that long, sloping back garden with his mates. Ate porridge at that pine breakfast table every morning for years and years. But the memories came at him as if at a remove. As if they happened to someone else and had been somehow transplanted into his brain.

There was so much space. It all felt so big. The quiet rang painfully in his ears.

'You alright, son?' his dad asked.

Dave tried on a smile of reassurance and realised it had faltered somewhere between his eyes and his cheek muscles. 'I'm good, Dad.'

'I expect there will be a period of adjustment after prison.'

Dave pushed his hands deep into his trouser pockets.

'When Amelie moved out of the mews at Thorntonhall, I arranged for all your stuff to be brought over here. The boxes are in the granny flat. I'll help you sort them out if you want.'

'Don't fuss, please, Dad,' Dave said, and then realising his tone was a little harsh he apologised.

The granny flat was a studio above the giant double garage. It had one bedroom and a large living room with a galley kitchen tucked away into one corner. It had never actually been used for anyone's granny as far as Dave knew, but his mother used the term once and the name had stuck.

Mum.

Dave felt a pang of missing. His eyes sparked with tears.

His dad put a hand on his shoulder, but Dave shrank from both it and the care in his father's face. He didn't want sympathy, didn't deserve it. He worried that if he started to cry he wouldn't stop.

'Why don't you go and get settled in, and meet me back here when you're hungry? I've got lots of food in for you. I can make you a sandwich or heat up some soup. Or do both.'

'Dad...'

'Or, whatever you want, son. Just let me know,' his father said, as if he too was lost and anxious to work out what their new 'normal' should look like.

Dave stood in the middle of the large kitchen as if set adrift from his own mind. He didn't know who to be. How to be. Where to put himself. What do to.

'Hey,' Peter said and stepped closer. 'You're home now, son. You can start to put it all behind you.'

He opened his arms and Dave stepped inside them, placed his head on his father's shoulder and allowed the tears to take him.

An hour or so later he was in his new bedroom. The wardrobes were full of his clothes, the bathroom shelves studded with his toiletries, and his other belongings placed into workable spaces around the flat.

He'd changed his clothing. He'd taken off the chinos and T-shirt that he'd been wearing the day he was arrested and that had spent the subsequent years in a bag in the prison, waiting for his release date, and threw them in a bin. The prison had also returned the more personal items he'd been carrying on his person that day. Wallet, watch, and a certain little, black, velvet box.

That proposal worked out well, he thought, and with a pang of missing he opened the lid. The little diamond caught the light, fractured it and bounced it back at him. Emotion tightened his chest, setting the air to a quiver in his airways. How could he have thought a marriage proposal would have worked given their situation at the time? It was a desperate act from a desperate man.

Idiot.

With a sigh he closed the lid and put the box in the little drawer of his bedside cabinet. He'd wait until his father was out and return it to his mother's jewellery box. Where it would likely stay until the end of time.

Back in the living room he threw himself onto the sofa, luxuriating in how much space he had, and switched on the TV. With a small thrill he realised this TV had its own satellite subscription. With a mental thanks to his father, he scrolled through some channels, landing on sports. All this choice was amazing after being limited to terrestrial TV for so long. He lay back on the soft cushions, watching the screen as a man in a suit jacket talked about the English Premier League. As he shifted, a scent lifted from the cushion and he recognised it instantly. It was Angel, Amelie's favourite perfume. Of course. His father told him she'd stayed over for a few days when she visited for Claire Brown's trial.

He wondered what she was doing, where she was, who she was with, if she ever thought of him.

That's your old life, he told himself. *Don't go there.* But the thought was trailed by an ache in his heart. He saw her face, her smile, felt a ghostly imprint of her hand in his. Heard her laughter.

He buried his face in the cushion and breathed in deeply, her scent filling his nostrils. Then he sat up briskly. Not a good idea. His life was going to be difficult enough without pining for a lost love.

Noise sounded from outside his window. Someone was shouting. He got to his feet, walked to the window and looked out. His father was at the gates, face almost purple with rage, gesticulating wildly at a group of people standing there, all bearing cameras.

Before he knew it he was out there with him, pulling his father away, worrying that if he carried on like this he was heading for a heart attack. Then he noticed a man standing at a distance from the paparazzi. Something about him – his stance, his stare – drew Dave's attention, and the danger-alert system he'd built during his time in prison turned on, full beam.

When he'd pulled his father back along the drive to the front door he paused.

'Did you see that guy, at the back? The one with the black leather jacket?'

His father was breathing heavily, his white hair sticking up all over his head, face deathly pale, his shirt untucked. 'Who? What guy?'

Dave stepped forward and looked around. There was no one there.

'Probably some weirdo,' Peter said. 'We get them every now and again. Don't know what the hell they are looking for.' He stiffened his back, tucked in his shirt. 'Sorry you had to see that, son. Word is clearly out that you're home.' He forced a smile. 'Soup?'

Chapter 55

Selina, Chrissie's oldest sister, was curled up on the sofa. She was wearing grey baggy sweatpants, a navy wool sweater with too-long sleeves and her brown hair was pulled back from her face in a ponytail. When Damaris walked in the room what struck her most was Selina's eyes; they were red-rimmed, puffy and looked as if they were shrinking into her head. This was so far from the vibrant, fun-loving woman she'd met countless times when she had visited Chrissie. Usually on those occasions Damaris caught only glimpses of Selina, as she sailed out of the door in a variety of fashionable clothes, a cloud of perfume and good humour.

'I'll, eh, leave you to it,' Chrissie said, shooting Damaris a look of thanks as she stepped back out of the door.

'Hi, Selina,' Damaris said as she sat on the far edge of the sofa, unsure what to say or how to be in this moment. Regret that she'd agreed to come over and talk to Selina was a heavy lump tucked under her heart. What did she think she could achieve?

'Hey,' Selina said and wiped at her nose with her sleeve. She looked away out of the window, then her gaze darted back to Damaris, then to the floor, then to the TV, which was on mute but showing some sort of shopping channel. 'Did Chrissie get you a cuppa or some juice or something?'

'I'm fine, ta,' Damaris answered. As she did so she lifted her hand to put her hair behind her ear. Then aware that her sleeve had fallen down a little she hastily brought her arm back down and tugged at the material, making sure her wrists were not on display. But she was too slow to hide her scars.

'You cut too?' Selina asked in a quiet voice.

Damaris's mouth fell open. Her face and neck grew warm.

'Don't worry. I won't say.' Selina pulled a sleeve up quickly and

Damaris caught a glimpse of familiar, pale, jagged lines across her wrist. 'I stopped a year ago.' Selina bit down on her lip. 'It's all I can do not to start again now.'

Damaris didn't know what to say, but felt a little lighter now that she realised she and Selina shared some other common ground.

'Chrissie told me your secret.' She shook her head. 'I won't tell.' Selina looked into her face, as if searching her eyes for something. Something to hold on to. Something that might stop her from drowning. 'You were the kid in the Amelie Hart case?'

Damaris exhaled. 'Yeah.'

'God,' Selina said. 'Poor you.' She paused. 'A few of my girl-friends have been pawed at by men, groped and stuff.' She said this with a cold, matter-of-fact voice that chilled. 'But I don't know anyone else who's actually been...' Moisture gathered in the corner of her eye. Leaked onto the skin at the side of her nose. 'You were only a wee girl, eh?'

Damaris nodded.

'And you're still only a kid really,' Selina said as she wiped at her face.

They talked for a little while longer. Inconsequential things. Movies, celebrity gossip, and the good and the bad around social media, as if Selina wasn't quite ready to talk about *it*.

'You should stay away from all those things,' Selina said. 'I hate them and love them at the same time. I see people with these perfect lives and get so jealous I want to scratch their eyes out, you know? Cos they haven't gone through what I've gone through. And I know it's not real. It's only edited highlights. Nobody shows the pile of dirty laundry in the basket, or the dishes piling up in the sink, or the bruises...' She trailed off. Eyes staring into her recent past, the horror of it twisting her delicate features into a mask animated by self-loathing and shame. 'I can never get clean,' she added. 'It doesn't matter how long I sit in the bath I just can't get clean.' She scratched at her right forearm, her fingers working so hard that Damaris was sure if she wasn't wearing a thick wool cardigan she'd be drawing blood.

Selina held herself tight, staring into space, a trail of tears on the silk of her cheek. Damaris was caught up in the other girl's pain. She reached for her hand and gripped it tight.

'You'll get there,' Damaris said, hearing the tremble of uncertainty in her voice. 'It's not easy. You'll get there, cos if you don't the bad guy wins, right?'

As she spoke she had no idea where the words were coming from, or even if they might help. What did she know? She was only a little girl when *it* happened.

In this moment, watching Selina, observing her pain and drive to be scoured clean of the event, but recognising the emotion at a remove, as if she'd only read about it in a book, she wondered about her own experience, and why she had never felt any of that.

After supper, Damaris had developed a habit of sitting on the sofa to watch some TV with her mother, but only for a short while. As if there was a prescribed amount of dutiful family time before she could escape to her bedroom sanctuary, and her cutting kit. That evening as her mum watched another one of those dumb cop shows, this one with a snowy background, she itched to leave.

'You're even more quiet than usual,' Claire said without taking her eyes off the action.

'Just tired, Mum. Alright if I...?'

'Sure, baby.' Claire shot her a smile and held her hands up. 'A quick kiss and a hug first?'

Damaris untangled her legs from the faux fur blanket she'd been seeking comfort in, and allowed the kiss and hug from her mother to happen.

In her bedroom she pulled a small tin from under her mattress and held it in her hand. Just knowing the ability to cut was within her grasp was sometimes enough for her, and she willed the hard coolness of the metal to seep from her palm, up her arm and into her heart, because then the feelings might dim.

She curled up on top of her quilt, holding the tin to her chest, just as another girl might with a cuddly toy, and she allowed her emotions about her visit with Selina that afternoon to unspool.

Hours later, during which she heard her mother's tell-tale footsteps through to the kitchen, and the clink of glass on glass, she was still there, her lights off, staring into the darkness. Her mother had been on the phone for much of that time. On other occasions Damaris would have crept to her door, opened it a little and listened in, just as she had done many times throughout her childhood.

When did that habit start, she wondered?

And why?

Eventually, just before sleep took her, the deep, velvet curtains of memory opened and a long-forgotten conversation slipped through.

They were back in Thorntonhall as if the intervening years had never happened. It was the evening after Dave had been driven off by the police. Concern about who she thought until then was a nice guy, combined with a need to make sense of what had happened, had her eavesdrop on her parents. Hearing her father cry almost made her run into their room and give him a hug, but something held her back.

'Your little girl will get over this,' her mother was saying in a cajoling tone. 'What doesn't kill you makes you stronger, right? You're always saying that.'

There was a pause, and Damaris tried to imagine what her parents were doing. What their faces were like. Had Daddy stopped crying? Then her father spoke as if his emotions had been placed on hold. His tone was weird. Quizzical, as if something strange had just popped into his head.

'Why aren't you more angry?' he asked.

Silence.

'I am. I'm furious.'

'You don't actually sound furious. You don't sound much of anything. What are you not telling me, Claire?' He sounded on the verge of anger now.

'You said it yourself, Roger. We're skint. We're out of our house if this thing of yours doesn't work out.'

'Jesus, kick a man while he's down, won't you?'

'So, butter-wouldn't-melt Amelie Bloody Hart is loaded. Bound to be.'

There was a long silence.

Then her father spoke. His voice an accusation. 'What have you done, Claire?' There was anger there in the gruff tone. Like that time Damaris had left the rabbit cage open and the rabbit had escaped and done little drops of poo all over the living room.

Damaris could hear a shuffling sound, as if one of her parents was moving across the carpet towards the other on their knees.

'Damaris is fine...' Her mother's voice grew so quiet that Damaris couldn't make out the rest of her words.

Then.

'Oh my God.' Relief. Even from where she was listening Damaris could sense it. 'But that's ... that's...'

'No harm done. We get some cash, save our home. Then that daft prick gets out of prison. Everyone's happy.'

'I don't know, honey. That man's reputation is ruined for life. He'll never get work.'

'Yeah, but his girlfriend will keep him. He'll be fine.'

She slept in the next morning and had to rush to get ready for school, a sense from the previous night's memory tainting her mind, like the taste of butter on the turn. Was it a memory or a strange dream? Had her parents even had that conversation? The replay, if that was what it was, seemed so real.

After school she went to her father's, even though it wasn't his night to have her. He opened the door before she had the chance to place a knuckle to the wood.

'Hey, baby,' he said, his face large with smiles. 'This is an unexpected pleasure.' He paused as if a thought had interrupted the words queuing on his tongue. 'Everything alright?' He drew her into a hug. She closed her eyes for a second, enjoying the weight of his arms on her shoulders, across her back.

'I'm good, Dad,' she said, reluctantly stepping back from the security of him. 'Got any chocolate biscuits in?' This was a ploy. He always complained she was too thin and should eat more.

'Hungry?' he asked, his eyes showing his pleasure at the thought of feeding her.

'I could eat.'

'C'mon through to the kitchen and I'll rustle you something up. I've got some tomato soap and I got some fresh bread from the deli down the road that you like.' He raised an eyebrow. 'And then we get out the biscuit barrel.'

After she finished her soup he asked, 'You staying over?' and something in her curled up against the hope in his voice.

'Nah, Mum doesn't know I'm...' The thought of being away from her kit drove her response; in truth her mother would have been fine with her staying over at Dad's. Provided she let her know, of course. 'But I can stay till bedtime if you want?'

'I always want,' her father replied and pulled her into another hug. She felt the pressure of his head on top of hers. 'Not sure if that sounded right.' He laughed. 'I have some work to catch up on.' He pointed to a laptop resting on a little table to the side of the sofa. 'Give me an hour and I'm all yours?'

'Sure,' she replied. 'Is your tablet charged?'

He nodded, jumped off his stool, left the room and returned a moment later carrying his tablet. Holding it out to her he said, 'The pass is...'

'I know your pass, Dad.'

'You do?' he asked mock sternly.

They settled down to some electronic time. Her father clacking away on the keyboard of his laptop, while she positioned the tablet in a way he couldn't easily see what she was looking at.

It wasn't the first time since his release that she'd googled Dave Robbins. If her parents knew how often she brought up his face on her phone they would probably confiscate the thing from her.

A row of images of him appeared on her screen. She touched one and it enlarged. There was a sign behind him suggesting this was taken as he was released from prison. He looked smaller than she remembered, thinner, and his complexion was grey. This was not how she remembered him at all. Her memory presented a moment in her garden. Dave leaning down to speak to her, his complexion tan and eyes bright with good humour.

She screwed her eyes tight against it.

He'd hurt her, hadn't he? And the ghost of the bruising on her upper thighs and between her legs momentarily ached as if they'd only just healed.

'Got to go, Dad.' She shut down the screen and jumped to her feet.

'What?' Her dad's face was a picture of confusion.

'Forgot about something.' She was at the door now. She waved. 'See you tomorrow.'

Damaris ran almost all the way from her father's to her mother's, a trip that would normally require a short bus ride. She didn't know what she was running from. The past, or the present.

Chapter 56

Her sleep was fractured and fevered that night. She woke up several times, twisted in the quilt, a pool of sweat in that tiny bowl of skin at the bottom of her neck, between her collar bones.

Dreams presented her with many faces; Mum, Dad, Dave, Amelie, and a strange woman sitting in her old living room. She was nice. Caring. And she kept sending her mum out of the room so she could talk to her without interference. Did that really happen?

There were so many questions. Cringy questions that made every part of her want to curl up into the tiniest ball. If only sitting incredibly still and very quiet actually made you invisible. But the questions kept coming. For hours.

'But it was the bike. My wheel caught in the wire thing and I fell,' Damaris said. At first.

The questions kept coming.

'I know this is confusing.' A warm hand on hers.

'He touched you where he shouldn't, didn't he?'

'You know it's called a penis, don't you?'

'It's alright, you can tell us. We need to know so we can help other little girls.'

'Hey, you don't need to feel ashamed. This is all on him.'

This woman was a grown-up. Mummy said she was an expert. She had to know the truth, right?

At breakfast, while she pretended to eat, she was aware of her mother's scrutiny.

'What?' she demanded.

'Swirling the cereal around the plate like that doesn't fool me, D. You need a good breakfast. Eat it up,' her mother replied.

Damaris took a mouthful. Chewed. Swallowed. Then jumped to her feet.

'Oops, I'm late. Got to go. And I'll be at Dad's after school.'

All day at school the words falling out of her teachers' mouths came at her as if through a fog. At one point, in the loos, Chrissie pulled her up.

'What's with you today? You on something?' She pulled at Damaris's lower eyelid.

'Hey. Leave me alone,' Damaris said, shoving her away.

Eventually the bell rang; the last class of the day was done. She gathered her things together and rushed out of school, past the gates and down the road to her father's.

'Two days in a row?' As always he was delighted to see her. 'To what do I owe this pleasure?'

'A daughter just wants to hang out with her father. Nothing wrong with that, is there?'

'Speaking about yourself in the third person? Is that a thing now?'

Hoping the turmoil of her thoughts weren't obvious to him she brushed past him and made her way to the kitchen. 'I hope that biscuit barrel's full today.'

After a meal of soup and crusty bread, and some biscuits, they sat in companionable silence while her father finished up some work on his laptop and she did some more scrolling on his tablet. After several minutes she became aware that her father had edged closer to see what she was doing.

'False memories? Why are you looking up something like that?' he asked.

'It's for a school project.' She feigned boredom and closed it down. 'I swear our teachers are weird.' She paused and looked out of the kitchen, down the length of the garden to the little shed at the end. The real reason she was here today. Her father stored some of her old toys inside it, still reluctant to throw them out. Something had been nagging in her head all day, telling her she needed to get in there. That something inside would help make sense of whatever was going on in her mind.

'Hey,' she said, trying to sound casual. 'You still got my old stuff in the shed?'

He followed her gaze. Smiled. 'Yeah. Haven't had the heart to chuck any of them out yet. Was working up the courage to give it all to charity. Want to go have a look?'

In the garden, as they walked down the long path to the shed that backed onto a tall conifer hedge, her dad kicked at a small stick and asked, 'Has your mum got a new man yet?'

She gave him an assessing look. Why did he want to know that? Didn't he have a new girlfriend? 'There's been one or two dates recently. Nothing serious, I don't think.' As Damaris answered she had a mental image of her mother returning around midnight, creeping into her bedroom, slightly drunk, and sitting on the edge of her bed as she slipped off her high heels. 'You awake, babes?' she'd asked.

'Am now.' Damaris rubbed at her eyes.

'Men are a waste of space,' Claire said. 'Wide berth, sweetheart. Give 'em all a wide berth.' Then she'd creeped back out again, leaving her shoes behind her. Damaris told her father none of this. It would have felt disloyal.

They walked into the shed and over in the far corner Damaris saw a small bike leaning against the wall under the window.

The bike. Now she realised why she had to get into this shed.

'My bike,' she asked while her stomach twisted. 'You've still got this?' She moved over to it, plucked it from its resting place and forced herself to sit on the seat. It was the first time she'd been on any bike since that day. 'Why did I have a boy's bike?' she asked.

'You remember your big cousin, Ricky? Ricky Hirst?'

She shook her head. 'Vaguely.' She remembered an uncle. Her dad's brother who had died of a heart attack when she was little. The family had moved away shortly after. 'Why don't we keep in touch with them?'

'They moved to Australia. They send emails and Christmas cards and stuff. Anyway –' he cleared his throat '– you kinda doted on Ricky, thought he was so cool...'

Damaris had no memory of whoever this boy might be.

'And when he grew out of this bike and got a new one you demanded he give it to you.'

'I did?'

So much of her life felt like it had happened to someone else. A fictional someone else.

'Dad?' She gripped the handlebars. She had to ask, while simultaneously hoping her father would change the subject.

'Yes, honey?'

'That day...' She didn't need to explain any further which day she was talking about. 'What really happened?'

Chapter 57

Dave was in the social worker's office for his weekly assessment – criminal justice social worker to be more precise. Giving the woman the benefit of the doubt, he guessed that she might even be a nice person underneath the dust of her occupation. Besides, whose attitude wouldn't be curdled by working with dangerous and disturbed men every day?

But the questions set his teeth to grind, and brought bile flaring up in his gullet.

'Have you had any sexual intercourse over the last week.'

He crossed his arms. 'No.'

'How many times have you masturbated?' She asked this with a tone that someone might bring to a discussion about dishes being left in the dishwasher.

'None.' It was truly the last thing on his mind. He doubted he'd ever have any sexual feelings ever again.

'You're sure?' She didn't believe him. Nor did she quite believe him every other time she'd asked.

'I think I'd know.'

She scribbled something on her notebook.

'Let's go through your movements this week. What have you been doing?'

'Nothing. I've barely left the house.'

'Aren't you working for your father?'

'Yes, but he brought me an office laptop and a bunch of files to work on so I don't have to leave home.'

That also went in the notebook. 'I'll need to have a look at that laptop.'

'Fine.' He'd already had one unscheduled visit from a social worker at the house, but that was before the laptop arrived. 'Understood.'

She looked at him as if checking for sarcasm. Then satisfied there was none she continued. 'You say you barely left the house. When you did leave where did you go?'

'Just to the corner shop. For some bread and milk.'

'Did you meet or speak to anyone?'

'Just the old guy behind the till.'

'There was no one else in the shop?'

'A woman was leaving as I walked in. I didn't get her name.' He paused. *See, I can do sarcasm.* 'Other than that, no one.'

'Must be lucky to stay in business if they've no customers.'

'They open at six am. That's when I went.' He still wasn't into a proper sleeping pattern so it wasn't an issue to be up and about that early, and, besides, he'd calculated that there were likely to be fewer people around at that time. And even less likely that there would be any children.

He'd be avoiding them for the rest of his life.

He couldn't face public transport so he got a taxi to take him back home.

When the taxi drew up at the bottom of his drive, with a start he saw that there was an ambulance parked by the front door.

'Oh God.' He threw some money at the driver, jumped out, and ran up the drive shouting for his father.

The brake lights went on in the ambulance and a man in a green paramedic suit stepped out of the driver's side.

'Sir.' He held a hand up. 'Before you go any further can you tell me your name?'

'Where's my dad?' Dave felt his panic rise.

'Are you Mr Peter Robbins' son?'

'I'm Dave.' With a sense of dread, Dave walked closer to the back of the ambulance. He put a hand out to pull the door open, but the paramedic put his hand on his.

'Dave.' His voice was heavy with a warning. 'We got a call from a neighbour. There were photographers. A bunch of them. Apparently your dad came down to try and get rid of them...' His father must have been trying to clear them away before he arrived home from his social-work visit.

'Is it his heart?' he asked, hand over his own.

'I'm so sorry, Dave.'

In that moment Dave realised that was why there was no siren. That was why the man had taken the time to speak to him rather than drive off in a rush.

It was too late.

Chapter 58

Damaris ran all the way home, thundering along the street, fuelled by fury.

Her father had reeled away from her when she asked the question. He'd stared at her with his mouth hanging open, as if he'd mentally prepared for this moment for years and still couldn't figure out what his response should be.

Then a tear began a slow slide down his cheek.

He put a hand out towards her. 'I'm so sorry.'

She stepped out of his reach. 'Don't.' She held a hand up to ward him off. With those three words and the look of shame on his face he'd confirmed her worst fears.

'Honey...'

She was holding herself so rigid it felt as if a whole mix of unnameable emotions were fusing her bones together.

'I only just persuaded myself that everything was fine,' Roger said. 'When Dave Robbins got released. But it's not. It never will be.' His eyes searched hers. For what? Forgiveness? A sense of what was going on in her head?

How could he read any of that if she didn't know?

'I ... I...'

She was in shock. Her tongue was gummed up, lying in the bed of her mouth as if cut off from her brain and her ability to reason. Her father reached for her again. She moved towards the door of the shed, staying beyond the span of his touch.

'Honey, it was a despicable thing to do. If I could take it back. If I could turn back the clock...'

'So, he didn't touch me?'

Roger shook his head.

'The bruising between my legs was from the bike, wasn't it?'

'Yes.'

'When I saw Selina ... watched her and saw what she was going through, I didn't feel any of that. I've never felt any of that.' When she realised she was thinking aloud, she put a hand in front of her mouth.

She wanted to scream. She wanted to bash her head on the wall. She never wanted to see her father ever again.

When she finally arrived home, legs aching from the unaccustomed effort, breath a harsh rasp in her throat, she threw the door open and marched into the living room. Her mother was in the act of getting to her feet, her phone to the side of her head.

'Honey...' Claire said. She knew. Damaris guessed her father was on the other end of the call.

'What were you thinking?' Damaris demanded.

'It's not how it looks.'

'How is it then? Tell me.'

'He did hurt you. That man.'

'How? By playing with me when you were too busy?'

'There was the bike ... and you were crying and hurt and I was angry and...'

'And what, Mother? You saw a chance to make some money?'

'That's not what happened.' Claire reached for her. Gripped her arm.

Damaris wrenched her limb free. 'Tell me the truth, Mum. Please. I deserve that, don't I?' Damaris became aware she was crying, and hated herself for it.

Then her mother started crying too. 'I love you, baby. You know that, don't you?'

'You don't get to play the teary mother. Tell me the truth. What happened?'

Claire's crying hiccupped to a halt. She slowly sat down, and Damaris could see that she was preparing some sort of speech.

Forcing herself to be calm, Damaris sat beside her mother, unsure where this version of her was coming from, when all she wanted to do was smash everything in the house. She had to get to the facts, and something told her this was the best way to achieve that. She could go on a rampage later.

'Mum, you need to tell me exactly what happened, or you and I...' She paused and poured as much determination into her expression as she could. 'Or you and I are finished. I will never see you again. I'll never come and visit. I'll never speak to you ever again.'

'You can't say that. Where will you go? Where will you live?'

'Cammy will help. I'll live with him.' A thought. 'Unless he was in on it.'

Claire shook her head. 'He doesn't know anything.'

Something she'd heard from her bedroom door all those years ago sprang into her mind. 'But he helped you steal some of Amelie's money, didn't he?'

'How...?' Claire's eyes were large with surprise.

'I was eleven, Mum, not moronic.' Damaris got to her feet and pointed towards her bedroom. 'I heard you guys talking.'

'Oh, so you're some sort of superspy now?' Claire bristled.

'Really?' Damaris stared her mother down. 'That's the response you're going with?'

'I'm human. I made a mistake. A mistake I'll have to live with for the rest of my life.'

'The rest of *my* life, Mother. You made the mistake.' She imbued that last word with as much sarcasm as she could muster. 'I'm the one who'll pay the price. Me and that poor guy, Dave Robbins.'

'Och, he'll be fine.' Claire waved a hand in the air, as if dismissing any concern on that score. 'A couple of years in the clink. It's nothing. In fact, it will be the making of him.'

'Are you for real?' Damaris let out a little scream of frustration. 'Sex offenders are the lowest of the low in prison. Even I know that. He was a target every day he was in there. He was scarred with boiling water. Nearly murdered by a cell mate...'

'How do you know that?'

'There's this new thing, Mother, called the internet...'

'Don't you use that tone with me.' Claire was on her feet.

'What tone should I use to a liar and a thief?' Damaris shouted.

They were face to face and it was all Damaris could do not to strike out at her mother.

Footsteps sounded behind them. Then she heard her father speak, his voice a little breathless as if he'd run up the stairs.

'Claire,' Roger said as he walked into the room. 'It's time for the truth. Damaris deserves that, doesn't she?' After the recently raised voices, his quiet tone brought the energy in the room down a notch. 'If we want to move on as a family we have to talk about this. Truthfully.'

They all sat.

'I hated that stuck-up bitch,' Claire said quietly. 'She always ignored me. Nose up in the air like she owned the world. She blanked me too many times to mention.'

'Claire,' Roger said with a hint of warning.

Claire took a deep breath, as if fighting for control. 'When you came in that day you were crying. Sore. Upset. And at first I really did think Dave had ... hurt you. Even the doctor said your injuries were consistent with a sexual assault. I was furious that man had hurt my little girl. Made you cry so hard. I phoned the police without thinking. And then ... it all kind of spiralled.'

'It all just grew and grew,' Roger said. 'It was terrifying how fast it all happened.'

'And then we couldn't stop it. Couldn't tell the truth or we'd be locked up and lose our house, and lose you.'

Damaris looked from one parent to the other, feeling utterly betrayed by them and wondering how much of what they were saying now was real.

'But you did lose your house,' she said.

'Business was bad,' Roger said, his head low with shame. 'We over-reached with the mortgage, and the holidays.'

'And I just loved that place on first sight. I had to live there,' Claire added.

'One of the newspapers reported that you had plans to write a book,' Damaris said. 'What happened to that?'

'How...?'

'The internet really has everything,' Damaris said, and cringed at how much of her young life was detailed there. It amazed her that it wasn't widely known that she was the girl at the centre of this event that just a few years ago had the whole world talking. Although she was never mentioned by name, her mother was, and it wouldn't take a genius to make the leap from mother to daughter.

'I ... couldn't.' Claire was staring down at her hands. Twisting her fingers.

Damaris had a flash of insight. 'That's the first time in this conversation I've seen anything from you that might resemble a guilty conscience.'

Claire looked over at her, and in that moment Damaris read her mother's reaction as she slowly turned from her, cringing away from her past actions, unable to bear her daughter's scrutiny.

'I'm a horrible woman. A truly...' Claire started sobbing. Neither Damaris or Roger moved to console her.

Damaris left the room and came back minutes later with a couple of full plastic bags.

'What are you doing?' Claire looked up at her, and Damaris was gratified to see that her eyes were puffy and red.

'I can't be with you. Either of you. I'm going to live with Chrissie for a little while.'

'But ... honey...' Roger began.

'Please. Don't.' Damaris looked over at her parents. They bookended the large sofa, both wide-eyed and open-mouthed. Faces heavy with regret and contrition. And fear at what might happen next.

'Don't get in touch. I don't want to speak to either of you. I can't even look at either of you.'

'Honey,' Claire began.

'Leave her, Claire,' Roger said. 'She needs the space.'

'And I'll tell you what else *she* needs,' Damaris said. 'To clear Dave Robbins' name. Either you guys go to the police or I will.'

Chapter 59

While Dave stood at the door of the crematorium, bearing the good wishes and condolences from friends and colleagues of his father, Amelie stood quietly at his side. Every now and then he'd feel her there; a touch on his back, a hand on his shoulder, as she helped him deal with all the people who had attended his father's funeral.

Dave was gratified at the turnout. He was aware his father was widely admired, and as the service progressed he could feel there was a lot of love in the room for his old man. Despite Dave's infamy people wanted to show their appreciation for the kind of man his father was. Only a few of them were willing to shake Dave's hand, though.

'I'm going to miss him.' An old man was now in front of him. Dave recognised the hook nose, heavy-framed spectacles and wild brush of white hair. Martin Walker. This guy had known his father through the city's Chamber of Commerce.

'Thank you.'

'He had a lot to bear in these last few years.'

Dave heard a tiny gasp from Amelie but took the comment on the chin and moved to the next in line. Margaret Brady. She'd been with his father in the firm for years.

'I'm so sorry for your loss, Dave. If it hadn't been for your father I don't think I would have got through to chartered status. I owe him so much.' She wiped a tear from her face with a white cotton handkerchief. 'Stay strong, son,' she said quietly. 'Your father believed in you and that's good enough for me.' She gripped his forearm pushing a wave of loss up from his heart.

'Thanks,' he managed to whisper through the grief clenching this throat.

Dave noticed with immense relief that he was coming to the last of the mourners. A man stepped in front of him. He was tall, bald, and was wearing a dark overcoat. His tie was at an odd angle, like a child who had just come home from a hard day in school.

'John Warner. *Daily Observer*,' he said. He raised his hand and Dave automatically held out his. But then he realised this man wasn't looking to shake hands; he was holding out a mobile phone. 'Do you think your father's heart attack was a result of your conviction for paedophilia?'

'Sorry?' Dave was momentarily confused.

'Enough,' Amelie said, stepping between Dave and the journalist. 'This is a funeral service. How dare you?'

'And you, Miss Hart,' Warner said undeterred. 'Where have you been? You weren't standing by this convicted sex offender for years. But now you are?'

'Okay.' Margaret Brady had returned. She took Warner by the arm and led him away while speaking in a determined voice. 'You're going to leave. You're going to write your shitty column in your shitty rag and you're going to leave this man alone.'

'You alright?' Amelie asked Dave.

He gave a small nod, although he certainly wasn't. 'Not looking forward to the funeral tea, to be honest.'

Amelie took his arm. 'Come on. Let's go to the car.'

They left the crematorium building and walked down the steps to a black limousine. The moment that the red, velvet curtains had closed played again in his mind. A heavy bullet of grief shot through him. He stumbled. Almost fell.

This was so unfair. What had his father ever done to anyone. A sob burst out of his mouth.

'Hey,' Amelie said, holding a hand out for him.

Dave looked up at her, but his attention was snagged by something across the street, beyond the cars. A young girl was standing there, hands clasped in front of her, head bowed. Her stillness and her evident posture of respect surprised him. Did she know his father? She lifted her head up and met his gaze, and with a start Dave recognised her. Of course, she was a little taller now, but that had to be Damaris Brown.

'Sir,' the driver said. 'Are you ready to go?'

'Sure.' He looked to the driver, and then back to the girl.

She opened her mouth, just a little, as if she was about to shout something across to him, but stopped herself. She held a hand up, and in that simple gesture she looked so forlorn and lost. The movement bore a deep sympathy that almost had Dave sob again.

She turned and walked away.

In the backseat they held hands. The warmth of her skin, the strength in her grip, and the ballast of her affection added layers of confusion to Dave's care-worn mental state.

How was he going to bear this additional assault on his life?

'Thank you for being here,' Dave said, afraid to look into Amelie's eyes in case his love for her was too apparent.

When she'd turned up at his door the day before all his old feelings for her had crashed through him like a tidal wave. He'd asked her how she knew about his father, while feeling a burr of shame that he hadn't been the one to tell her.

'I have an alert in my emails. Set it up years ago when I was searching for fame.' She gave a small self-deprecating smile. 'Whenever I'm mentioned I get a notification. Don't know why I keep it going, it's been nothing but bad news for years. Anyway...' She shook her head a little, flicking her hair away from her face in a gesture he knew so well. 'I read that Peter had died. Contacted the office and they let me know about the funeral.'

'You should have phoned. I would have picked you up at the airport.'

'I wasn't sure,' she looked into his eyes, 'what kind of reception I might get.'

'Have you booked into a hotel? Cos you're welcome to stay...'

'I'm at the Hilton.' She smiled, and there was a wariness there. 'But thank you.'

Now in the backseat of the limo, on the way to a local hotel for the funeral purvey, he felt overwhelmed with loss and confusion. What he'd gone through the last few years was surely more than any one person should have to deal with.

He sneaked a look at her, saw the light tan and glow of her skin, the clearness in her eyes, and thought she looked better than ever. There was no way a woman this beautiful didn't have anyone in their life. He moved his gaze to her hands. No ring.

He thought about the little black box in the cabinet at the side of his bed, and felt his neck heat with embarrassment that in a moment of desperation back then, he was prepared to propose to her.

Then he remembered why he'd forced a distance between them; refused to allow her to visit the prison. The relationship had been over. She had moved on emotionally, and had surely only kept in touch with him, and then his father, out of some sort of guilt or misplaced sense of duty.

What an idiot. He should forget about looking for any possibility of a reconciliation.

Friends.

That was all they'd ever be now.

Dave got through the tea as best he could. Watched people as they ate the sandwiches and sausage rolls, and drank anything from coffee to whisky. Thankfully only a handful of people came. Most of them who'd attended the service were there in memory of his father and the impact he'd had on their lives. He was sure most of them thought his father's abrupt death was a result of his conviction and despised him for it, so he was grateful that most had decided not to come along to the hotel afterwards; it would only have caused friction.

After allowing for a decent interval he went around those who had attended and thanked them. Then, spotting Amelie being all but pinned to the bar by Martin Walker, he went over to them.

'Thanks for coming, Martin,' he said and shook the man's hand.

'The world's a sadder place the day, son,' Walker said, barely taking his eyes away from Amelie's face.

'It sure is,' Dave replied and then, hands in his pockets, just looked at Martin, waiting for him to walk away. When he did, Dave turned to Amelie.

'I need to go. This is...'

'You shouldn't be on your own,' she replied, reaching across the space between them and touching his forearm. 'I'll come home with you.'

'You don't need to.'

She smiled. 'Sometimes you just have to accept help and support whether you want to or not, Dave Robbins.'

Back at the house, Dave noticed the large gate to the drive wasn't closed properly, but he dismissed it, thinking he'd had too much on his mind when he left that morning to be worrying about gates.

In the living room Dave sat on an armchair, Amelie on the sofa. He noticed her shiver.

'I'll turn the heating up,' he said, thinking how awkward he felt and wishing she hadn't offered to come over. He just wanted to go through to his bedroom in the flat with a large whisky. This house was just too big without the energy of his father.

Turning away from the thermostat, he offered Amelie a drink.

'Any wine?' she asked as she followed him into the kitchen.

'Nothing that will be anywhere near the standard you're used to,' he replied. He'd heard about the vineyard she'd been working in.

'As long as it's wine-flavoured and red, that's good enough for me.'

Dave stopped so abruptly that Amelie almost walked into him.

He turned to her, tearing his eyes away from an object on the kitchen table that shouldn't have been there. That just that morning had been in pride of place on the mantlepiece. Before leaving for the service, he'd touched his lips, then briefly pressed his fingertips against its polished surface.

'Have you...' He was confused. 'Have you been in here, Amelie?'

'What?' she asked.

'Have you ... did you move anything?' He was aware of the rising panic in his voice.

'What are you talking about, Dave?' She touched his shoulder. 'I came in. Sat in the living room with you and I've only now walked into the kitchen. With you.'

'Oh my God.'

'What's going on, Dave? You're freaking me out here.'

He looked around wildly. Walked over to the kitchen window, and looked around outside.

'Dave?'

'That. There.' He turned and pointed at the kitchen table. 'It was on the mantlepiece when I left for the service this morning. Some bastard broke in here and is playing with me.'

In the middle of the kitchen table was his mother's small, polished-oak funeral urn.

Chapter 60

Damaris couldn't stand seeing the sadness that lay so heavily over Dave Robbins. He'd suffered so much and it was all because of her and her family. She had to do something about it. But what? She was only a girl.

She'd walked to school with Chrissie that morning. Pretended she was going to the toilet before class and then doubled back and walked out of the school gates.

It had been easy to find his father's house. And she'd gone there, taking several buses, stood at the locked gates, looking up towards the house and wondered if she should go in.

Two massive black cars were at the door, one with its nose pointing down towards the road.

A hearse. Through the glass she could see polished wood and a wreath of white flowers formed into the word 'DAD'.

A grey-faced man in a dark suit and a black tie came out of the front door with a small group of people.

Dave.

She stifled a sob at the open grief in his face.

A couple walked down the path and out of the gates. The woman fished in her handbag and pulled out a set of keys as they walked towards a car.

'Excuse me,' Damaris said. 'The funeral?'

The woman looked at her black clothes and then up at her face. Clearly assuming she was another mourner she said, 'At the crematorium, dear.'

Damaris must have looked confused because the woman elaborated. 'At Lambhill.'

Damaris nodded and made a noise as if she understood. The woman frowned at her, looking as if she was going to ask something, so Damaris added a quick thanks, turned and walked away.'

As she walked back to the bus stop she opened up her phone and worked out which bus routes would get her to the crematorium at Lambhill, wherever that was.

What she intended doing once she was there she had no idea. She only knew she had to offer some sort of ... what? Penance? Solidarity?

∞

Amelie looked just like she remembered. Lovely and stylish, and for a moment she felt it was a shame she couldn't tell people that the actress used to be a neighbour and was always nice to her.

She would never forget the moment Dave spotted her. It was all she could do not to run across the road and throw herself at his mercy; say how sorry she was, swear how much she hated her mum and dad, and promise to go to the police and make it all go away.

Instead she stood there like a lump, caught up in the poor man's misery and offering nothing but a pathetic little wave.

Heart like a stone in her chest she walked away towards the nearest bus stop. From there she went back over to the West End of the city and wandered the streets. She could go back to Chrissie's house, but Selina's pain and upset was so visible she couldn't handle it anymore.

Instead, she went into a café and pretended she was meeting her mother there so they would let her have a seat.

'You alright, honey?' the woman taking the orders asked her.

'I think my mum's held up at work,' she replied.

'Want anything while you wait?'

Damaris considered how much money she had in her purse. She still had lots of her birthday money left over. Way more than enough for a drink, and whatever bus trips she might need to take next.

'A Coke, please?'

'Fancy a cheeky wee scone?'

'No, thanks.' She hated scones, but appreciated that the woman was trying to be nice.

'Drink coming up,' the woman said breezily, and Damaris wondered about the parallel world this woman lived in, where people had nothing to worry about and could actually be cheerful.

The drink arrived. A tall glass, lots of ice and a red-striped straw. She sipped and felt the sweet bubbles hit her tongue. It revived her a little. Helped her to think.

If she went to the police who would she talk to? What would she say? And then, what would happen? Would her mum and dad end up in prison? And if they did what would happen to her? Some kind of foster home?

She pulled her phone out of her pocket. The screen lit up, showing her she'd had some missed calls. Again. Mum had been calling her every day since she moved to Chrissie's.

Take the hint, Mother, she thought.

Dad had sent her a few texts. Saying he was sorry, how he understood he had let her down badly, and hoping they could mend things eventually.

Chrissie had sent her a couple of texts as well. Wondering where the hell she was and why she wasn't sitting in French class that very second.

When her drink ran out the server noticed and came back over.

'You been stood up, wee pal?'

'Looks like it,' Damaris said.

The woman cocked her head and placed both hands on her hips. 'Should you not be in school?'

'Study time,' she lied and was impressed by how smoothly the words came out of her mouth.

The woman waited as if expecting her to get up and leave. When Damaris stayed in her seat she asked, 'Are you needing help?'

Damaris shook her head, finding the strength from somewhere not to unload everything onto this kind woman. How good would it be to get all of this off her mind?'

'Do you have somewhere to go to, dear? Someone to talk to?' The woman sat in the seat beside her.

'I'm fine,' she lied. Then she pulled a five-pound note out of her purse, put it on the table and by way of reassuring the woman, said, 'Keep the change.' And left.

Outside the café she wondered what she was going to do next. Mum usually had her book group on a Monday afternoon. She looked at the time on her phone. And usually around now. There was enough time for her to wait at home until school was out and then go back to Chrissie's. Fifteen minutes later she was standing just down the street from her mother's. Her white Range Rover wasn't in its usual place, so she made her way inside. As she walked past the space where the giant machine usually sat a thought crashed in. How could her mother afford a car like that? She remembered all those years ago that her mother had used Amelie's cash card to withdraw money. Every time she thought about that her toes curled up with embarrassment. But the money needed for the Range Rover would be on a whole other level. Did her mother steal more money? What was Cammie into and did he pass some of that on to his sister? Or was her mother's work as a bookkeeper that lucrative?

Inside, curled up on the sofa, she mindlessly scrolled through the television channels. She needed to stop thinking; it was hurting her head. There was so much she didn't know and jumping to conclusions wasn't helping. Unable to settle on anything on the TV she turned it off, and went into her bedroom. There was a pile of folded laundry on her bed. She needed clean clothes so she took her small suitcase from the floor of her wardrobe, carried it to her bed and filled it up. It occurred to her as she did so that her mother would now know she'd visited.

Too bad. She really didn't care what her mother or father thought.

Looking around she thought about the nights she'd spent in this room completely unaware of how her mother had betrayed her. As she scanned the room she noticed that the top drawer of her bedside cabinet was slightly open. She pushed it shut; Mum had obviously been in here for a nosey. Then with a sharp charge of worry, she wondered what her mother had found.

She got to her knees and looked under the bed. With a sense of relief she saw that the small box, holding what she thought of as her 'cutting set', was still there, tucked behind the leg of the heavy-framed bed. She'd chosen her hiding place well. It looked exactly as she'd left it.

Pulling the box out, she got off her knees and placed it in the middle of the bed. With a shock of surprise she realised she hadn't missed it at all. For the last few years she'd barely gone a week without thinking of placing a sharp edge to her skin, or a month without actually doing so. Yet, since she moved over to Chrissie's a couple of weeks ago it hadn't entered her head.

Opening the box she assessed the contents. The sharp little knife, the razor blade, the antiseptic wipes and the plasters. Looking down at them, neatly arranged, it felt like the kit belonged to someone else.

She pulled her left sleeve up a little, plucked out the razor and held it against the tender pale of her inside wrist, lining it up against the pucker of an old scar. Even then there was no urge to press the blade into her flesh, to see the blood well onto her skin.

There was a sound at her doorway and a deep male voice boomed, 'What the hell are you doing?'

She jumped in fright, accidentally applying pressure to the blade. Looking up she saw Uncle Cammy standing in the doorway.

'What are you doing?' he asked again. He reached her in a couple of steps and took a grip of her arm, holding it in the air. 'You're cutting yourself? Why?' His brows were tight, his mouth a thin line of anger. This wasn't the Uncle Cammy she knew so well, and looking at the fury in his eyes she was suddenly scared of him. Sure, she'd heard the rumours, but dismissed them as just that: rumours. He was her uncle. He loved her. He could never harm a fly. But looking at his face as he shot hot shards of disgust at her she shrank from him.

'Look. You're dripping on to the carpet.' He started tugging at her arm. 'Right. Bathroom. Now.'

Once there he turned on the cold tap and pushed her wrist under it. Then he picked up a small towel and clamped it to her skin. 'Sit.' He pointed to the bath. She sat on the side as ordered.

'When did you start doing this?'

This was her worst-case scenario. One of the grown-ups in her life finding out about her compulsion. She hung her head, her long hair falling to each side like curtains.

'Talk to me,' he shouted.

'I ... I...'

Cammy pulled at her other arm, and lifted up the sleeve. When he saw the scars he dropped her arm.

'You stupid little bitch. You've been doing this for years, haven't you?'

She could only nod, her face so hot with shame she was sure it would combust.

'Ever since...?' A realisation, and the hinge of his jaw relaxed leaving him open-mouthed. Anger clouded his eyes. 'I'll kill him. I'll fucking kill him.'

Chapter 61

'You're sure you didn't put the urn there?' Amelie asked Dave.

'Why would I put it on the kitchen table?'

'Who would move it then?'

Dave slumped onto one of the kitchen chairs as his mind chased down one theory after another. 'The cleaner isn't due in until Friday. There's been no one over from the office.' His words tailed off. He was at a loss as to how he could explain this. Unless he was mistaken and it was there, on the kitchen table, when he left for the funeral service that morning.

He gave that some thought. Recalled the moment he'd thought of his mother, how much he missed her, and caressed the polished wood with a fingertip kiss just before he left.

'No,' he asserted. 'It was definitely on the mantlepiece this morning.'

'Maybe you should call the police?'

'And say what? Someone sneaked in my house and moved an ornament from the living room to the kitchen?'

'No need to be snide, Dave,' Amelie replied. 'I'm trying to be helpful.'

He bit down on his next response. 'Sorry.'

'This is freaking me out,' she said as she crossed her arms. She told him about being followed when she first moved out to France, and as she spoke it was all Dave could do not to take her in his arms. 'It's been such a long time since that stuff happened, I thought I was over it.' It looked to Dave as if every part of her was now vibrating with tension.

'Why didn't you tell me?' he asked. 'That's horrible.'

'Yeah, tell the guy who's had an attempt on his life while in prison that I've been followed into a church by a good-looking guy in a leather jacket.'

'Oh, you had time to notice he was good-looking, did you?' Dave asked with a mock serious voice.

Amelie dutifully laughed, but there was little real humour in her response.

'Do you want to go back to your hotel?' Dave asked, simultaneously wanting her to leave and stay.

There was a knock at the door, and then the doorbell rang.

'Who could that be?' Amelie asked.

Dave remembered the last time they were together and the door had sounded. He shuddered, but got to his feet. 'Better see who it is. Probably one of Dad's old buddies who couldn't make the service.'

Another loud knock as he walked down the hallway, and a man shouting. Then the door burst open.

'Who the hell are you...?' Dave demanded, looking around for something he could use as a weapon.

The man was in his early thirties with dark hair, and was wearing a black leather jacket. Something about him was very familiar. He was holding an arm up, pointing at Dave.

Amelie appeared by his side.

'You,' she hissed. Then she gasped. 'What are you doing with that?'

Dave looked at the man's hand. On delay, as if his brain was just catching up, he noticed the man was holding a small gun. 'Okay,' he said, taking a step forward and holding an arm in front of Amelie. 'Whatever you want, leave her out of this.'

Then finally he realised who this man was.

'You're Claire Brown's brother.'

'What?' Amelie said. 'This is the man who was following me in Bordeaux.'

Amelie and Dave glanced at each other.

Fuelled by a sudden anger, Dave stepped closer to Cammy, his arms spread wide. Cammy whipped his arm round. A metallic taste in his mouth and immense pain bursting across his head, Dave fell to the floor.

Move, he urged himself, *do something*, but the commands he sent to his muscles didn't, couldn't, get there. He was aware of Amelie shouting, of the sounds of a scuffle. Then someone tugging at his feet. He was powerless to do anything.

Then darkness took him.

When he regained consciousness, he was sitting on something soft, his neck lolling so deeply his chin was almost on his chest. The sofa. He must be on the sofa. The heavy throb in his head…

Gritting his teeth against the pain he managed to set his head upright. He could feel that something was binding his feet and hands together. Amelie was on the sofa beside him, and he could see her hands were also tied.

'Good, you're with us,' Cammy said.

He had pulled a chair over and sat in front of them, elbows on his knees, the black hole of the gun tip unwavering. 'I've just been getting to know your lovely ex-girlfriend a little bit better. She is your ex, right?'

'Just let her go. She's done nothing wrong.' Jesus. Even speaking caused pain to explode in his skull.

'And neither has Dave,' Amelie said.

'Shut up, the pair of you.'

'Let her go. She won't tell anyone. Will you, Amelie?'

'Yeah,' said Cammy. 'A woman with the press at her beck and call is going to quietly go back to France and leave you here facing a gun.'

'If you leave him alone, I will,' Amelie said.

'Not happening,' Cammy said. 'I've got a plan for you two.'

'Why don't I know you?' Amelie asked. 'Your family lived next door to me for ages.' She turned to Dave. 'Did you ever see him there?'

'Didn't see him at Thorntonhall, no.' Dave could see that

Amelie was trying to distract their intruder. Playing for time. 'I think I saw him in town with Claire a couple of times. That must be it.'

'And Roger's uncle's in the police. Quite high up. Must have been awkward for you,' Amelie said. 'You loving your family so much and having to keep your distance.'

'Fucksakes, shut up the pair of you, or I'll end this right now.' He waved his gun.

'It was you at the prison, wasn't it?' Dave asked, one part of his mind feverishly trying to work out how they were going to get out of this safely. 'You were behind those guys who attacked me.'

'Do you think you were going to get away with molesting my niece, you pervert?' His face was inches away from Dave's now. The force of his anger so strong, saliva was spraying Dave's skin. 'You hurt mine. I hurt you. It's that simple.'

'Why go after Amelie in France? She had nothing to do with anything.'

'Pull the other one, arsehole. Expect me to believe that you were grooming Damaris and she knew nothing?'

'Dave wasn't grooming anyone. Damaris was just a lonely little girl he passed the time of day with.'

Cammy laughed, but there was no mirth in it, only menace. 'Is that a French euphemism, or something – "passing the time of day"? I'm glad we stole your money, you whore.'

'You stole my money?' The insult meant nothing to Amelie. 'That was your sister.'

Cammy crossed his arms, pleased with himself. 'She didn't even think about using your card until I put the thought in her head.'

Dave felt Amelie stiffen in the seat beside him. The heat coming off her body was incredible. He felt her shift position, and then she screamed, 'Help. Somebody. Help.'

Cammy laughed. This time for real. 'This is a big house, with thick walls, set back from the road. No one can hear you, doll.'

Amelie shouted again.

'Shut up.' Cammy was on his feet. He reached her in a stride, and slapped her.

'Touch her again and I'll kill you,' Dave raged.

The insults life had heaped on him over the last few years tore through his mind. Enough. He'd had enough. Somehow he got to his feet, but Cammy simply prodded his chest hard enough that Dave lost his balance and fell back onto the seat.

'God, you're pathetic,' Cammy said, and moved back to his chair, Dave staring up at him with impotent rage. 'So, here's what's going to happen. Or, I should say, what it will look like happened. Dave's going to kill you, Amelie. Sorry, *Solange*.' He tapped the barrel of the gun against the side of his head. 'You should have stayed away. I can't let you go now.'

'You're never going to get away with this,' Dave shouted.

'Where was I? Right. Yes. Dave, driven mad by grief and knowing Amelie doesn't love him anymore...' He looked at Amelie. 'She doesn't, right? Else, why did she stay away so long?'

Dave flinched.

Cammy spotted the tiny movement. 'Yeah, shitty, right? So, as I was saying: the newspapers will state that mad with grief, etc., Dave Robbins killed movie star Amelie Hart before turning the gun on himself.'

Chapter 62

Without a word, Cammy had turned and left Damaris with her wrists and shame bare.

'Uncle Cammy, no,' she shouted. She ran to the living-room window and watched him charge towards his car and drive off. She knew exactly where he was going, and she had to follow him and stop him.

Her only problem was that Cammy was already on his way and she had to get the bus.

Grabbing her jacket she ran out of the door, down the stairs and onto the street. Just in time to see the brake lights on Cammy's car as he reached the junction at the top of the road.

Lungs bursting and panic sparking in her mind, Damaris made it to the nearest bus stop. Ignoring the strange looks from a couple standing there, she brought out her phone. Her hand was shaking so badly it took a few attempts to key in her passcode. She lifted her head to look at every passing vehicle, praying it was a bus that would take her where she needed to go.

Eventually, just when her phone said it would, the right bus arrived. She chose the closest available seat to the door, judging that every second was crucial. And from this vantage point, she stared at the bus driver's back, willing them on, swearing at each red light, and every passenger that stopped the bus so they could get on.

As she travelled across the city she cursed herself. When she was *actually* cutting herself, she would have never been caught out like that. She should have heard Cammy walking in. And then she could have safely hidden her stash, and not put Dave and Amelie in danger.

Because, judging by the look on Cammy's face, danger was very definitely heading their way. Every time she closed her eyes she saw his; those long, dark lashes, the dusted amber. And clearly readable, even to her, the threat and purpose. The will and certainty. And most scary of all, the anticipated pleasure. In just a few seconds she'd read all of that in his face. And more.

She crossed her arms against the realisation that he'd really just been waiting for the excuse; and like an idiot she'd given it to him.

Maybe she was wrong. She tried to tell herself she was over-reacting. Maybe he was just going over there to give them a talking to. Maybe shout at them a little. Having said his bit, he'd leave them in peace. That's what Dad would do.

Dad.

She should have gone to his and asked for help. He would have come over with her, and told Cammy the truth. Because he sure wasn't going to listen to her.

Looking out of the window, she judged her whereabouts, and whispered, 'Shit' to herself. Dad's house was now well behind her. If she got off the bus, to get another bus back to his, it might be too late.

She fished her phone out of her pocket and dialled him.

It went to his answering service. She ended the call. Then, reconsidering, she dialled again, this time leaving a message.

'Dad, I'm going over to see Dave Robbins and Amelie.' She spoke just above a whisper, mindful of the people around her. 'I think Cammy's going over there and I'm scared about what he's going to do.'

She stared at her phone for a moment. What if Dad didn't get there? What if he didn't check his messages until it was too late. The police. She had to call the police.

'999 – what's your emergency?'

She blurted everything out. 'Hurry. You have to send someone out there. Now. Hurry.'

As she remembered the look on her uncle's face before he charged away, all the veiled warnings her father had given her about Cammy edged into her mind. 'Just be careful,' he'd said so many times, then refused to say why. There was one Christmas dinner the year before Dave went to prison. Her gut twisted. How could she have seen this event any other way? She'd allowed the time of year, the number of presents piled on the table to distract her.

Her grandparents had invited them all out to a local hotel for dinner, and even insisted they'd pay. Dad had been unhappy about it from the moment it was suggested. Damaris overheard him say to her mother that he knew who was really paying and no way was he taking money from a crook.

Mum managed to placate him and they'd gone. But between courses, Damaris had gone to the toilet, and while washing her hands, she'd heard shouting from the other side of the wall, and then a crash. She walked out of the ladies in time to see her Uncle Cammy leave the gents, a dark look on his face. He was followed moments later by her father, squaring his tie and tucking one side of his shirt back into his trousers. In the moment she'd read the look on his face and saw only irritation; but now, she recalled that expression and could only translate it as fear. Whatever Cammy had said to Dad in that toilet he'd interpreted it as a threat.

She was at Dave's gate and with relief saw there was only one car in the drive. A white one. Maybe Cammy wasn't here. Maybe he didn't know where Dave lived.

Shaking her head, she dismissed that as a faint hope. When Cammy had left her mother's there was no doubt in his movements. He knew exactly where he was going. And if she'd found Dave's house easily enough it wasn't going to present any difficulty to her uncle.

She looked up at the house. There was a lamp on in the porch, and over to the right, light shone through the closed curtains of a large bay window. Someone was inside, but she couldn't make out who.

From this vantage point, the house and the neighbourhood all looked calm. Just like any other street, in any other town. She turned to the left and looked back down from where she came. A car was approaching. She shrunk from it, afraid it might be Cammy and that somehow she'd made it over here before he did. All but hugging the wall at the side of the gate, with relief she noted that the car's speed remained steady and as it passed she saw that it held a female driver.

Then as she watched the car, she saw, parked just a few houses down, Cammy's Range Rover.

Shit.

She took a few tentative steps towards it. Craned her neck. It looked like it was empty.

He was here already.

Who knew what he was actually capable of? She checked her phone again for her father. No response. Thought about calling the police again. They'd said they would send someone over here. If she called again might they think she was just a crank and cancel their call?

She couldn't risk it. It was up to her.

All of this was her fault and she'd have to fix it.

With that thought, she set steel to her spine, clenched her teeth and braced herself for whatever she might find. Opening the gate, she prayed that she was going to be on time.

She'd just reached the front door when she heard a scream. A woman – in pain or fear, she couldn't tell.

Amelie.

Without a further thought she pushed open the door.

Another scream.

It sounded like it was coming from behind a door at the other side of the large hall. Her heart about to burst out of her chest, she crossed the tiled floor, and girding herself against what she might find, she pushed the door open. What she saw was worse than anything her imagination could have invented.

Dave was on the floor, curled up on his side, hands behind him as if he was tied up. Amelie was on her knees beside him, hands thrown up in a defensive gesture. Her uncle Cameron was holding something to her head.

A gun.

Chapter 63

Damaris took in the scene with a detached sense of horror. This couldn't be real. Dave was on the floor, deathly still. Amelie looked up from him to Cameron, then to Damaris at the door. Her mouth moved as if in slow motion. She was saying something that Damaris's mind couldn't compute.

Then Damaris's mind snapped back into reality with the power of a lightning bolt.

'Uncle Cammy,' she shouted. 'Stop.'

He turned to look at her, his face long with surprise. 'D! Get away from here.'

'Stop.' She charged across the room. 'You can't do this. They did nothing.'

'Damaris, doll. I know you've got a kind heart and everything, but you can't be here,' Cammy said. To Damaris's relief, he moved the gun behind his back.

'Damaris, phone the police. Please,' Amelie cried.

'Don't do anything, D. Just leave,' Cammy said as he stepped towards her.

Dave was very still. Not caring how Cammie might react, she ran over to him and knelt by his side. There was blood just above his right ear, his face was the colour of putty and his eyes were rolling back in his head.

With a charge of relief she noticed his chest was rising and falling. 'What did you do to him?' She turned to her uncle.

'Get the hell out of here,' he snapped. In a flash he was by her side and pulling her to her feet. 'Go,' he shouted and shoved her towards the door.

She stumbled with the force of his push, but corrected herself and turned, mustering as much defiance as she was able. 'No. You can't do this. Dave did nothing wrong. He never touched me. Ever.'

'Enough,' Cammy shouted. 'You're leaving if I have to drag you out.' He reached for her again.

'No,' Damaris screamed, and as she did so she stepped towards him and stamped on his foot with her heel.

Cammy yelled, dropped to one knee and as he did so the gun fell from his grip. Damaris dived and got to it first. Cammy lurched towards her. She jumped out of his reach, and feeling the weight of the weapon in her hand she pointed it at him.

'Whoa,' he said. 'Hang on, honey. Don't be pointing that at anyone.'

'You need to listen to me,' Damaris said. The importance of what she was doing hit her and she was aware the gun was wobbling in her grip.

'D, honey, you need to give me that gun. It's loaded and the trigger is off.' He was moving away from her as he spoke. 'Just the slightest pressure...'

She waved it at him, suddenly feeling very powerful and even more frightened at the same time. What if this went off by accident? She didn't want to kill Cammy, just stop him from causing any more harm.

'Give me the gun,' he roared, taking a step towards her, as if his fear of being accidentally shot was overcome by his temper.

'No,' she replied. 'No.' She willed more strength into her arms and held the gun up. This time moving the barrel closer to her head. 'You need to listen, Uncle Cammy. Please.'

'Honey, move that gun away from you,' Amelie said. She was still on her knees by Dave's side. 'I'm sure we can talk about this properly.'

Cammy shot Amelie a look of surprise, but then he echoed her statement. 'Yeah, D, we can talk about this properly. Calmly.' He held a hand out for the gun.

'Dave didn't touch me,' Damaris shouted. 'I fell off my bike. Mum was desperate for cash so she made up the story about him, and before she knew it the lie had grown so big she couldn't stop it.'

'You might believe that.' Cammy narrowed his eyes. He clearly didn't believe her. 'But we all know that's not true. This man molested you. And he's got to pay.'

'That's the thing. He didn't, Uncle Cammy. You've got to believe me.' As Damaris spoke she began to cry. She hated showing that weakness. 'He was lovely. He did nothing but nice things for me and you've been horrible to him. I never want to see you again.'

'Aww, babes,' he said. 'Don't be silly.' He sounded calm, but there was a look in his eyes she was now beginning to understand. She was seeing her much-loved uncle for who he really was; she nearly sagged under the realisation. The gun grew too heavy and her arm dropped.

'Give me the bloody gun,' he shouted.

'No.' She found the energy to lift the gun high and once again pressed it to the side of her head. 'You don't believe me yet. Maybe you will if I kill myself.' She gritted her teeth, knowing she was incapable of carrying out the threat but desperate that he should believe her. 'It won't be the first time I gave that a try.'

'What?' Amelie cried. 'No, baby, no.'

'Whoa,' Cammy said, holding both hands up. 'You've got to stop all this silly talk about killing yourself. I know you were cutting, but this is a whole other story.'

'You were cutting … oh, Damaris,' said Amelie. 'I'm so sorry.' Her concern was like a shot of warm emotion through Damaris's body.

'You should be sorry,' Cammy turned on her. 'You and your sick boyfriend.'

'Oh for God's sake, Cammy,' Damaris shouted. 'Will you bloody listen? This is all on my mother. Your sister.'

'Give me peace,' Cammy replied.

'And my dad,' Damaris added sadly. 'Her idea, but he was just as bad.'

The line of his shoulders drooped a little and Damaris thought she may be actually getting through to him. His eyes darted around the room as if he was unsure where he should look. 'But, he was found guilty.'

'It was a lie, Uncle Cammy. They planted all this stuff in my head. Made me believe it, but it was all a lie.' She aimed this last part at Amelie and Dave. This was her explanation, her partial apology for what they went through. 'I'm so sorry,' she said to Amelie.

Cammy studied her face.

'Give me the gun.'

'No.'

'I won't shoot anyone.'

Damaris caught a look of concern from Amelie.

'If you're not going to shoot anyone then you don't need this gun,' she replied.

'You were never raped? So why were you cutting yourself?' Cammy demanded.

'Guilt,' Damaris replied. She wasn't sure where the word came from but she felt the truth of it as it slipped anchor from her tongue. 'The policewoman and my mum and dad persuaded me I'd been hurt, but I knew, somewhere deep inside I *knew* that the words they were making me say weren't true. That it was all a lie.' She was aware that her face was wet. With a free hand she tried to wipe it dry.

'Honey,' Amelie said. 'None of this is your fault.'

Cammy looked at Amelie as if she was a complete stranger, as if the words she was uttering should come from another's mouth.

'You can sit there and shut up,' he told Amelie, but Damaris could hear there was no conviction in his tone. As if something about Amelie's genuine concern for her had edged the truth onto a more solid footing in his mind.

He turned to Damaris. 'C'mon, honey, we're family.'

'Family?' Damaris spat. 'I'm ashamed of the lot of you. If it wasn't bad enough that they set up Dave as a paedophile, you then stole Amelie's money.'

'It was only a piddling amount,' Cammy replied. 'We could have had more if we'd been really clever.'

At this Damaris noticed Amelie's head go up.

'You helped Claire take a few thousand? Who took the rest?'

'You lost more?' Cammy's eyes brightened as he asked the question. 'How do you like them apples?'

'If it wasn't you, who was it?' Amelie demanded.

'Don't have a clue, doll. If I did I'd be sending them a quick toast.' He held a hand up as if it was holding a pint of beer.

'You and Mum's big cars?' Damaris studied the look of pleasure on Cammy's face and wasn't sure she believed him. 'Matching Range Rovers is a bit clichéd, isn't it? How could she afford one of them?'

'Don't sneer, D.' Cammy took a step forward as he spoke. 'I owed your mother big. Money came through from the States. I paid her back.'

'She did time for you, didn't she?' Amelie asked, as if the thought just entered her head.

Cammy's eyes narrowed, as if he wanted to strike her. Damaris moved a little making sure she and the gun were in his line of sight.

A siren sounded in the distance.

'You didn't phone the police, did you?' Cammy demanded, back on high alert.

'You should go before they get here,' she replied.

'My own niece grassing me up...' Anger sparked in his eyes.

'Hurry.' She felt a momentary sting – she was letting him down. And then she was immediately disappointed at herself for feeling that way.

'Hurry,' she repeated.

'What about...?' He nodded towards the weapon.

Realising he was about to acquiesce Damaris allowed herself to relax a little. 'I'll give it to your sister.' Saying 'Mum' was momentarily beyond her. 'She can get it back to you.' It was a lie. She was going to make sure it went to the police.

'If it gets into police hands...'

Damaris was chilled by that statement. What else had her uncle been up to?

The siren grew louder.

'Before you go,' she said, pulling her phone out of her pocket, placing it on the sideboard next to her and bringing the handle of the gun crashing down on it. 'Don't be following me. I don't want to see you ever again.'

'Damaris...'

'You disgust me.' She was trembling now, and didn't care that he could see it.

'What?' She'd hit home. 'This was all for you, Damaris. For you.'

'That's the story you tell yourself, Uncle Cammy, but this was for *you*. I was your excuse to give in to all that ... anger and ambition. It was horrible what happened to Mindy, but you can't use me as a replacement.'

At the mention of his dead daughter's name Cammy reared back as if she had tried to shoot him.

'This is all about you, Uncle Cammy. Your need for power. You want to be the big man. The new Glasgow gangster. The man that everybody has to fear, and it's just so...' she struggled to find exactly the right word; '...pathetic.'

'D, please...' he began.

'I see you now, Uncle Cammy,' she said. 'Now go before the cops arrive.' As she spoke she felt relief: she was safe from him now and from his twisted version of love.

Throwing one last look of defiance and thwarted fury at Damaris, Cammy ran from the room and towards the back of the house. Moments later a door slammed shut.

Damaris forced a breath and then turned to Dave and Amelie. Dave was motionless, Amelie on her knees beside him, her face turned up to Damaris in a plea for help. Her voice and expression were full of anguish.

'I can't feel a pulse,' she cried. 'I can't feel a pulse.'

Chapter 64

Amelie was back in a hospital. But this time the outcome was going to be a happier one. Dave was mostly doing well. Concussion, and some bumps and bruises, so the medical staff wanted to keep an eye on him.

Eventually, he fell asleep, so Amelie dropped onto the chair at the side of his bed, cadged a blanket from a passing nurse and settled in for a long night.

Fractured scenes played through her mind. The look of pleasure on Cameron's face as he stood over Dave with his gun. His denial about the money. Damaris standing up to her uncle. Feeling almost weak with relief when Cameron ran out of the back door just as the police came in the front.

She didn't think she'd ever be able to thank the young woman enough. There was no doubt she'd saved both her and Dave's lives.

After Damaris had given her statement to the police they let her go with a promise to stay available should they need to speak to her again. She agreed without a quibble, but demanded that she stay with Amelie and Dave until they got to the hospital and she was sure Dave was not going to die.

Eventually, after the paramedics had arrived and performed their checks, confirming Dave would survive, she'd allowed Amelie to arrange for a taxi to take her to her friend, Chrissie's place.

Before she got into the cab Amelie placed a little piece of paper in her hand.

'It's my number. Call me when you get home. Call me tomorrow morning and let me know you're alright. Just … call me, will you? I can't thank you enough.'

'Hey.' Damaris ducked her head, pink with pleasure. 'It was the least I could do.'

They hugged, hard, one more time and then Damaris left.

What an amazing young woman she was turning into, Amelie thought as she reached for Dave's hand and was reassured by the warmth of his skin. She regarded his sleeping profile and wondered about the waste of the last few years.

Her phone rang.

'Bernard,' she said, fighting to rouse herself from her thoughts.

'I just saw you on TV,' he said, his voice high with panic. 'Oh dear lord. Are you safe? Are you well? How's Dave?'

She caught him up with what had happened, and just as she was finishing she was alerted to another call. This time from Lisa.

'We're both fine, Leece. I'm on the other line with Bernard. Can I call you back once we're done?'

'Sure, babes.' Lisa sounded hugely relieved. 'As soon as, yeah?'

'I'm back,' she said to Bernard, sitting back in her chair and settling in for another one of their long, rambling conversations.

'What you've been through is just staggering, Amelie. I'm incredibly impressed by your fortitude, my dear.'

Something snagged in her mind from a previous conversation they'd had.

'It beggars belief. But, silver lining: I'm relieved that the guy in France didn't turn out to be that crazy wedding stalker.' As the words issued from her mouth part of her mind was wondering why she was talking to Bernard about events from that night all those years ago. 'I don't think I could have handled that.'

'Thank the good lord he vanished back to wherever he came from,' Bernard said. 'But hey, no such thing as bad publicity.'

The snag pulled. An all but forgotten conversation and a thread unloosened. 'It's funny, Bernard. I think I only ever told you the bare facts about what happened. I couldn't bear to go through all the details with you.'

'Why do you say that?'

'The last time we spoke about this, you mentioned something

that no one knew. The wedding cake. No one knew about that. No one.'

'Amelie, the shock of all of this...'

'Bernard, how did you know?'

'You must have told me. How else?'

'I didn't. I told no one. Even Dave doesn't know what really happened in that house. And the taxi driver who saved me promised on his children not to tell anyone.'

No such thing as bad publicity.

'Oh my God, Bernard. You set it up. It was you.'

'Amelie, you've gone positively barmy, my dear.'

'Shut up, Bernard. I may have been stupid about certain things over the years, but I'm not an idiot. Before the Hardy movie my career was on its last legs...' Her mind was going into overdrive. What she was saying was the stuff of melodrama, but she was convinced she was right. 'You arranged the whole stunt. I can just see the headline you were working up ... Actress in the biggest movie of the year gets kidnapped by a whacko.'

'Amelie—'

'Except it didn't go to plan, did it? The taxi driver spoiled it all. How on earth did you think I would come through that unscathed?'

'Please, my dear, you're overwrought after all of this stuff with Dave.'

'Who was he? Some unemployed actor? Was the red dress and the big cake your idea, or did he go off script?'

There was a long pause, and then Bernard spoke in a quiet, wavering voice.

'You were never really in any danger, dear.'

'Oh Bernard,' she said as her high energy drained from her. 'Your big plan backfired, didn't it? Your cash cow couldn't handle the glare of publicity after that whole...' She couldn't think of an adequate word. 'I was so scared, Bernard. It was traumatic. I've not been the same since. I spent years terrified of my own shadow.

How could you?' She felt tears build up and pushed them down. She would not allow herself to cry. 'And I walked away. All of that for nothing.' Another thread unspooled. 'Except...' She thought about her missing money.

'There was never any big money scheme that lost a bunch of celebs their money, was there? That was you, you bastard. What happened – did the masked wonder demand a bigger payday once he saw how successful I'd become?'

Bernard said nothing. His breath was loud and fast in her ear. And that set off another thought.

'You didn't even have a heart attack, did you? Did you?' She re-called their telephone conversation when she was sitting in that small garden space in the middle of Bordeaux. When he was breathing like he was now. Bernard must have been pretending to hit an oxygen tank. She was such a fool. 'You were worried I might work out what had happened and got yourself into such a state you had a panic attack.'

'I...'

'When the thing about Dave came out, this guy came back to you, didn't he? He wanted more money. So you thought, there's Amelie all the way over there in France. She won't notice it's missing.' By the time she got to the end of her sentence she was shouting. 'God, I am such an idiot.'

'Miss, please.' A nurse popped her head in the door. 'People are sleeping.'

'Sorry.' Amelie waved an apology.

Then she noticed Dave was looking at her, awake, his eyes full of love. He held a hand out. She took it and held on tight.

'Bernard, go away. I never want to speak to you again.' She ended the call.

The money was nothing, that was a loss she could bear, but the betrayal, and the scale of it, from one of her oldest and most trusted friends would never leave her.

Epilogue

One month later
November 2019

The morning's mist had dissipated under the gentle heat of the late autumn sunshine. A buttered light settled over everything so all Dave could see were tones of warm gold. Even the ranks of vines, stretching across the landscape looked as if they might be gilded.

'It was great to have the company for a few days,' Amelie said to Dave as she approached bearing a tray with a cafétière and a plate of canelés. 'But it's nice to have the place back to ourselves.' She placed the tray on the table and sat. 'It was fun though, wasn't it?'

Minutes ago they had waved off Lisa and Damaris, who were in a taxi to the airport. Now they were having a quick coffee before Amelie's next shift over at the winery.

'Damaris was in good form,' Dave replied. 'She's really coming out of her shell, eh? And Lisa was much less diva-ish than I remember.'

Amelie laughed, then looked around at their beautiful surroundings. 'I think there's something about this place that strips away all our pretensions.'

Dave nodded his agreement, and set his hand on her forearm. He did that a lot, he realised. Casual moments heated through with the silk of casual touches. A solid and constantly needed reminder that she was back in his life, and he in hers.

Amelie put the tray on the table, topped up his coffee and kissed him on the forehead before taking a seat beside him. She sighed as she relaxed into the cushions. 'I don't think I'll ever tire of this view.'

Dave followed her gaze over the vineyards to the tall oaks and firs beyond. To the red-roofed fourteenth-century buildings that housed the workings of one of the world's top wine producers. And from there to the clear, blue, endless skies.

'Do you think the owner will let us buy it?' Dave asked before he took a sip at his coffee. He'd moved over from Glasgow when a gite adjacent to the chateau where Amelie worked became available for rent. It was on a little rise, tucked in to a corner of the estate, and had three bedrooms, a large kitchen and a small courtyard overlooking the Smith Haut Lafitte basin. All that was missing to make it perfect was a tortoiseshell cat called George.

'Once the legal stuff has been sorted you'll certainly have enough cash.'

That was the irony in all of this, thought Dave. He'd ended up ridiculously wealthy following his father's death. Sure, he knew the business was worth something, and the house in Bearsden was in a prime spot, but the full extent of his father's dealings, as revealed by his will, had taken him by surprise.

'It's been a lovely few days,' Amelie said. 'Thanks for putting up with Lisa.' He read concern for him in her eyes, an acknowledgement of his difficulty around other people.

'It was fun actually,' Dave said, and meaning it. He'd always found Lisa better in small doses, and it was a real joy to see what a lovely human being Damaris had grown into, despite everything.

He caught Amelie looking at her watch.

'You know you don't have to work,' he said. 'You won't need to work ever again.'

'I don't *need* to do anything,' she replied mock-sternly. 'I *want* to. This place has gotten under my skin. I love being a part of the tradition. Seeing the grapes grow, and then being carefully transformed into this wonderful drink.'

'Hey,' he laughed. 'You're not talking to a bunch of tourists here.'

'You could come to work on the estate as well. I'm sure Florence and Daniel could find something for you to do.' They were the owners of the entire operation and they'd warmly welcomed Dave as part of the extended family.

Despite this, Dave felt himself retreat a little at the thought of too much human connection. Too soon. This was a conversation they had regularly, and while he knew Amelie only had his best interests at heart he couldn't allow himself to be at risk with anyone ever again.

The thought of being forced to mix with other people was the only taint in this new life. On his own, or with Amelie, and he was fine, but the moment other people intruded he felt the shutters automatically bang down. Even these beautiful views and this wonderful new lifestyle weren't enough for him to become more trusting.

'Does it make it easier for you to let your guard down, now that your name has been cleared?' asked Amelie.

'*L'enfer, c'est les autres,*' he replied. Only half joking. *Hell is other people.*

'Get you with your fancy French,' Amelie laughed. A sound Dave thought he would happily hand over every last penny for. 'And by the way, Sartre was talking about the gaze of other people and how we judge ourselves through their eyes. So maybe we both need to learn to stop doing that?'

Damaris had gone public as soon as Dave was released from hospital, caring little for the risk to herself, determined that Dave and Amelie should get back to some kind of normal life. In response, the media had shifted their attention to Roger and Claire, demanding an enquiry. Damaris hadn't wanted to talk about it, so as far as Dave and Amelie knew, the authorities were currently considering whether charging the Browns with anything was in the public interest.

It wasn't in Dave's. Retribution wasn't something he ached for. Another trial would mean it would all be dragged through the court of public opinion one more time, and he just wanted to forget.

Here. This moment. Coffee with Amelie in the calm of these surroundings. That was where and how he was going to get back to himself.

'It was so lovely to see Damaris,' Amelie said after she'd finished chewing her little pastry.

Another thing Dave loved about her was her new ability to eat whatever she wanted, whenever she wanted. Even in that time when she first retired from public life she was hyper-alert to criticism of her appearance and consequently ate to stay skinny rather than for health. He thought back to her comment on Sartre. If she was able to take her own advice, maybe he could learn to do the same?

'She's keen to come back and work in the vineyard in the summer.'

'Excellent.'

That was another surprise in this new life they'd built. Their connection with the girl at the heart of this.

'You should have seen her,' Amelie had said to Dave, after he got out of the hospital. 'She was so brave, standing up to her uncle like that. She was a warrior. And seeing how she stopped cutting when she realised her abuse wasn't real? It's helped me deal with my own faked trauma.' Amelie had bit her lip. Wiped away a tear. 'What an amazing young woman. Despite everything I feel honoured to know her.'

In the days after Damaris rescued them from her uncle she had gone back to live with her friend Chrissie, only tentatively allowing contact with each of her parents. She'd finally gone to live with her father just a couple of weeks ago.

'He's really, really sorry,' Damaris had explained. 'So's Mum, to be fair, but she's also kinda in denial.' Damaris's view was that

Claire was on her daughter's side but torn by her loyalty to her brother. 'And while she's still defending him she can forget it.'

Of Cameron, they'd seen and heard very little since that night. As far as they knew the police were actively trying to bring him to book – for what he'd put him and Amelie through, and any number of other charges.

Dave considered Amelie's invite to Damaris to come back anytime. And saw her at the funeral service, her wave, the look of contrition and shame on her face. People might think it was strange that the girl who was at the heart of all their problems was now a friend. So what. He could live with that.

Amelie smiled and stood up, the metal feet of her chair squealing a short, high and happy sound against the stone tiles of their little patio. She leaned over, pressed her lips against his and he savoured the heat of her lingering kiss. Towards the end, he pushed his tongue towards hers and she gave a low groan as if experiencing the sweetest ache.

'Oh my,' she said when she stepped away. 'Mr Robbins.' She fanned her face dramatically.

Dave laughed, feeling so much joy in the moment he wondered that he wasn't about to burst out of his skin.

'I *really* must go. You going to be alright?'

He knew she meant in the next few hours while she toured the vineyard with tourists from various parts of the world, but he looked at her clear-eyed and heart-sure, thinking of the rest of his life. And certain that whatever it took, he was going to edge his way back into life and be fully among the living. He patted the little, black velvet box in the pocket of his jeans and felt a surge of hope. Lisa had travelled to Bordeaux via Glasgow and following his instructions to get into the house she'd collected the ring and brought it over with her. Now he was waiting for the right moment.

'I'm going to be fine, my love. Just fine.'

Acknowledgements

As always, to all my fellow authors, booksellers, bloggers, book festival organisers and reviewers, thanks for your support. Book people really are the best people.

Thanks to Karen Sullivan, surely the hardest-working person in publishing, for her steadfast and ceaseless efforts on my behalf.

Thanks also to Karen and editor, West Camel for their clear-eyed attention to detail.

Appreciation also to Alan Yuill, Barry Richardson and staff of the Scottish Prison Service. Also to Helen Fitzgerald. Any errors around the penal and legal system in Scotland are strictly mine. (It's fiction, innit!)

Also huge thanks to Claire, Guillaume, Anna, Tess and Noah – for sharing your beautiful home with me, and for providing a gateway to your stunning city. And Claire, what a wonderful cook you are! It was only when I got home that I realised I hadn't eaten any meat the whole time I spent with you guys. (Apart from that one visit to Le Poulailler D'Augustin.) I'm just sorry I couldn't work out how to mention Marche Des Capucins in the book. A must-see for anyone visiting Bordeaux.

Thanks to Meggy for the afternoon tour and for answering my Bordeaux questions.

To Florence and Daniel Cathiard, Valerie, Alix and all the staff at Chateau Smith Haut Lafitte – my time at the chateau was bliss. Thank you for the space, your kind attention and for putting up with my schoolboy French. I hope I've done justice to your wonderful setting in the book.

And finally to you, dear reader. Without you this would be just a collection of black marks on white paper. It only comes to life when you open the pages and allow those scratches to settle in your mind. Thank you for your continued support – as every competitor on *The X Factor* ever said – it means the world!

Newport Community
Learning & Libraries